Falcon Song

A love story

By

Kristin Cross

Spirit Dance Books

Falcon Song

By Kristin Cross

Copyright © December 2015 Kristin Cross

Published and distributed by Spirit Dance Books. Spiritdancebooks.com

855-648-5559

Cover design by Kaycee Chambers

Printed in USA

First Printing December 2015

Library of Congress cataloguing in publication data 2015958716

ISBN: 1-944588-00-7

ISBN-13 978-1-944588-00-7

Acknowledgements

Thank you to the team at Spirit Dance Books who helped me take this story from idea to paper. It's a gargantuan project to create a book, and I would never have made it without you.

And thanks to my family for always believing that I wasn't wasting my time. I love you.

Dedication

This book is dedicated to my wonderful husband. He's wise, and kind, and patient, on top of being so handsome, which is definitely the deluxe combo! I adore him and am eternally grateful for him in my life.

Chapter One

Holy cats this commencement speech was boring! These chairs were torturous. Kate Birch tried to discretely stretch and tucked her feet from the left side of her chair to the right. If she had known this guy was going to drone on and on and on like this, she'd have snuck in her IPOD. This last week of finals, she'd not gotten nearly enough sleep.

She tried to stifle a yawn and glanced one more time up into the stands to where her parents and Jason's were sitting, and then checked her watch. He was probably almost here, if his plane had landed on time. He'd have had to drive fast, but since he got the new black Corvette, he usually drove pretty fast. He probably shouldn't have gotten it. It lent itself to getting tickets, but dang he looked good in it! And now that his band had a #1 hit on the country charts, he could afford a ticket or two. Kennen would have loved it.

Her stomach growled fiercely and she thought about dinner. Jason was taking her to celebrate her associate's degree and his new contract. It was a restaurant she hadn't been to, but she'd heard it was excellent. Maybe if she got payroll done at her parents' restaurant without any interruptions, and then finished the produce order, they could go early. She should have made time for lunch.

It was going to be heavenly to have Jason home again. Even after three years with the band, she still missed him desperately when he left. And this time he'd been gone nearly a week. It seemed longer.

She felt that strange, tiresome worry set into her belly again at the thought of how popular his band Aerie had gotten. They were incredibly talented. At first, she had handled all the business for the band and she'd worked hard to promote him, although now they were too much to handle and she'd finally hired a manager to help her, who'd hired a publicist. But sometimes the sheer magnitude of the fame frightened the dickens out of her. Jason had loved her for years, and they'd been best friends nearly their whole lives, but lately there were thallions of girls throwing themselves at him. It made her worry that someday he'd decide he liked another flavor better than Kate. It was a horrible thought.

She was looking back up towards her parents when she saw him come through the dark curtain at the portal. His eyes scanned the stage and then he saw her and gave her that heart stopping smile and a thumbs up before sitting down in the row in front of their parents. Man, he looked like a movie star smiling up there. There was something about him that made her tummy nearly turn itself inside out at times like this. It was going to be heaven to be in his arms again.

****

After having driven like a madman from the airport, Jason Falcon strode into the stadium of Oklahoma's East Central University, paused for a moment to assess what was going on and then took a deep breath. He hadn't missed Kate being handed her diploma after all. In fact, his timing was perfect. He'd missed all the boring stuff, but was just in time to see her float across the stage to accept her associate's degree. How could anyone be that pretty and graceful in those baggy gowns?

But then she'd always been that pretty. From the day she was born. He'd only been four, but he could still remember walking across the lawn with his parents to the house next door to see the unbelievably small, sleeping black haired baby the neighbors had just brought home. Even at two days old, she'd been like a tiny, raven haired fairy sent just to entertain him and his baby brother Kennen.

Of course, Kennen hadn't been born then. He didn't show up for another few weeks, so Jason had had her all to himself for a little while. What would he give to have Kennen back to see her cross stage and receive her diploma? Kennen would probably have been receiving one just like hers. She would have kept after him to strive until he'd made it right alongside her. There was something about her that tended to bring out the very best you had in every situation. She was like a brisk wind that blew you to greater heights without you even realizing it was happening. That's how it had always been.

He looked back down at her, unbelievably grateful for that beautiful, happy girl down there who lit up every aspect of his world. She was more than a soul mate. She was the very oxygen that gave him life. He wished things hadn't been so weird between them sometimes lately.

On stage, the final speech ended and a huge cheer went up. As people began to stand up and head for the exits, their parents started to maneuver Kate's father's wheelchair out, but Jason stayed there in the bleachers as planned, rather than try to fight the crowds coming up the stairs to go down and meet her. When she finally made it up to his row and he stepped out onto the landing of the walkway, she looked radiant as she pushed through the last few people to rush into his arms.

For just a second they didn't speak, simply held each other like they hadn't seen each other in weeks rather than days. Man, it had been a long six days without her. She finally looked up, smiling and he leaned in to kiss the tip of her pixy nose. "You did it, Kate! I'm so proud of y'all I could kiss you!"

She grabbed her cap just before it fell off, laughed and brushed the tassel out of her face. "You just did. How was your flight? Are you as tired as you look?"

"More. Y'all look a little hammered yourself. Finals and projects must have kept you up late."

"For several nights in a row. But I'm done! We need to do some serious celebrating!"

"We do. Can I steal you away tonight after dinner for our own personal fire in the sky extravaganza? Well, ours and Cody's. He's bringing some girl he just met on the plane. There's supposed to be the best meteor shower in like a century tonight."

"It was a little over the top to arrange for the very heavens to cater to you, don't you think?"

He turned to look into her eyes before they followed their parents. "Kate, for you, I'd take the stars from the sky and put them into a crystal bowl." He kissed her again. "I love you, Katelyn Birch. And I'm absolutely proud of you and the work you've done to get through these last couple of years. You're amazing and it would be an honor to hand you the very heavens."

She looked back quietly and he wondered if he was seeing worry deep in her eyes before she smiled and turned away saying, "It's no wonder your songs are hits and the meteors obey you when you're that eloquent. I swear you could just talk the stars from the sky, Jason

5

Falcon. Thank you. And I'm proud of you too. I think this contract is just the start of something huge for you all. I can't wait to watch the journey."

He pulled her back around to face him for a minute and then said softly, "Kate, you know you don't have to just watch the journey. You could be on the journey with me. Now that school's out for the summer, come with us. Y'all could travel with the band and we'd have such a rippin' time." He searched her eyes and then whispered, "C'mon baby, how long are you going to insist that I need to spread my wings before we can move on to more commitment? We're supposed to be together forever, Kate. You know that as well as I do. Don't you?"

She nodded her head and he wondered about the worry again as she dropped her eyes. "Yeah, Jason, I've known that since forever. We both know that." She looked back up earnestly. "I just don't want to hold you back. You have so many opportunities and things to experience right now. And the last thing you all need hanging around is a nineteen year old girl who can't even legally get into the clubs you play in. I know it sounds backwards, Jase, but you can grow faster and go farther without a wife in tow. All those millions of women who are buying concert tickets and now CDs are more willing to pay to see a hottie than someone else's husband."

She shook her head and looked back down. "We've been through this before, Jason. Falcons have wings, but Birches have roots. You go and fly and I'll hold down the fort and help take care of your business from home. Just give it some time and let's get through this transition from local band to number one hit band. I'll keep going to school and someday I'll be old enough to actually get in to some of your concerts."

He pulled her face back up and kissed her gently as he watched her eyes. "I won't always be playing in smoky clubs, I promise. But take your time if you need to, Kate. I'll wait forever." She nodded and looked away again as they followed their parents and walked outside.

What she wasn't saying was that all those "millions" of women intimidated the heck out of her and even though she couldn't say it, he knew that deep down she worried that eventually he would choose the fame and money and groupies over the girl next door with the magnificent eyes and wispy, short, dark curls. It would never happen, but how could he convince her of that? He'd been devoted to her for years now.

He thought about all of this as they walked to where their parents were waiting. He was sure about Kate. He never had doubts. Sure, it was easy to push her more to the back of his mind in the thick of things when the crowds were screaming almost as loud as the guitars and drums. It was an incredible high to have girls--lots of girls, throwing themselves at him. In a way, she was right and that was all part of building the business of this band. It sold music. But, at the end of the night, his heart firmly belonged to Kate and he couldn't even imagine it any other way.

He didn't mind playing the game of wild boy musician when it came to the fans and the concerts and the travel. It was kind of fun to laugh a little too loudly sometimes and play the Hollywood game. He could admit it. Heck, he'd been friends with Cody, the ultimate wild boy, since he was a kid, and it was a rush sometimes. Nobody questioned that Cody was a party going somewhere to happen. He was a maniac and they had a great time together. But Jason had always been the designated driver. Right from the start, and he was as committed as Kate was to the solid religious values they both had been raised with. He'd never let her down before. Why wasn't she as sure as he was?

Kate hadn't always worried like she did now. In fact, Jason didn't ever remember seeing that look deep in her eyes until just the last several months. Always before, she'd looked at him with a sort of hero worship.

When she was really little, Jason had been like the big brother who did things for her. Then over the years, that had slowly changed. Eventually, he began to notice that she wasn't just a skinny little kid anymore. He began to notice that she was sweet and smart and funny and was growing into an exquisite young woman.

By the time he was in high school, he felt somewhat silly for being so attracted to the little girl next door, but there was something about her that had him forgetting all the other girls in the county, let alone the high school and he got past his qualms in a hurry.

Neither of their parents had been very happy that Jason and Kate had become an item as young as she was and they'd agreed jointly to insist that they wait to date until she was sixteen. Even then they only let her group date for awhile, and she had to have at least one date with another boy between every date with Jason.

Kate was a woman grown now and though the friendship was still as solid as ever, there weren't any doubts in either of their minds that what they were was in love. They'd known it long ago. In fact, they'd made a promise to each other when she was sixteen and he was twenty that had made more of an impact on his life than nearly any other thing that had ever happened.

They'd dropped Kennen at a dentist appointment and then had driven out to a peaceful spot near a nearby lake. Jason had brought his acoustic guitar and Kate had brought sandwiches and they'd sat and watched the sun go down in a blazing ball of glory across the water. While they watched, a pair of falcons began to soar on the wind currents that sunset brought on and Jason had turned to her, looked into her eyes and then looked away and whispered, "Falcons mate for life, Kate. Did you know that?"

He'd looked back at her and wonder had dawned in her eyes as she realized what he was trying to tell her. He'd never looked away as he said it again, "Falcons mate for life." That was all he'd said, but it was all he'd needed to.

As evening had turned into dusk and then into twilight and night, Jason had played for her and then sung her a new song he'd written for her about forever and a love stronger than this world and a friendship deeper than eternity. It was a ballad of commitment and devotion and hope that made her cry. He'd pulled her into his arms and hugged her, waiting for her to tell him what was wrong.

She never did. All she had done was snuggle closer into his neck and cry quietly as she whispered that she loved him. He'd already known it, just as he'd known how he felt about her, but other than his lyrics, they'd never admitted it out loud before.

They'd talked for hours about forever and God and what they each wanted out of life. In the end, they'd made a wish on the first star of evening and then sealed it with a pinky promise to carefully guard their virtue until she grew up and they could get married. Like the falcons. For life. For forever.

It had felt so right and good then. And never once since then had there been any second thoughts as far as Jason knew. He knew there weren't any for him. He'd meant what he'd said about the falcons.

Kennen had always seemed to understand what Jason and Kate had and although he'd become the third musketeer, it was definitely all for one and one for all.

Right up until the day he'd died. They'd been dirt biking on the gravel road up South Fork wash and Kate had been riding behind Jason. To this day, Jason didn't really know what happened. One minute Kennen was there in front of them on the road and the next, his bike had swerved and gone off the edge into the wash. One minute he'd been there laughing as they rode and the next he was laying under his motorcycle gasping for breath with punctured lungs and broken ribs.

That had been the longest night of Jason's life. Both families had been at the hospital all night, crying together and praying together that God would somehow heal the lungs that were unable to give that vital life-giving oxygen to his organs.

In the end, Kennen lost the fight. Jason and Kate had been standing beside his bed holding his hands and just in that darkest hour before dawn, he'd given the most feather light squeeze and slipped away.

As they visited with their parents in the stadium parking lot before leaving for home, Jason wished once more for Kennen's healing influence in his and Kate's life. Kennen could have gotten to the bottom of whatever it was that was making Kate a touch reserved with him lately.

***

Kate knew Jason had been disappointed that she'd brought her car to the graduation ceremony. He'd wanted to pick her up and start celebrating right then, but she had other things that needed doing before she could relax. It was payday at her parents' restaurant and she needed to get back and process the payroll and place an order with the produce wholesaler before four o'clock. She'd left Jason there in the parking lot of the stadium watching her with a thoughtful look on his face as she drove away to head back to the small town of Wye, Oklahoma where they both lived.

He'd asked her in a round about way again about being more committed and she pulled out of the lot, wondering if she'd lost her mind for not saying yes in an instant. Jason was the love of her life and she absolutely wanted to marry him, so then why was she hesitating? In a way, it made no sense. In another way it made a lot of sense. At any rate, she had to do what she thought was best here. What she thought God intended, and so far, waiting was what she felt she needed to do. She just hoped Jason didn't give up on her in the mean time. She'd never forgive herself if he did.

Her mother must have been thinking the same thing as she walked into the kitchen as Kate sliced fruit onto a plate later that afternoon just before Jason was coming to get her. He mother snagged a bite of melon as she asked, "Isn't Jason taking you out to dinner?"

Kate nodded. "He is. He'll be here in about fifteen minutes. I just haven't had time for lunch today and needed something. What are you going to do tonight?"

Laura Birch smiled at her daughter to soften her sad words. "Oh, the usual. Feed Daddy and get him settled and then maybe a little TV or Sudoku while I wait up to make sure you get home safely. I hope you're appreciating this fun time in your life."

Kate knew her mother had resigned herself to the fact that her husband would never walk again because of being hit by a driver who was high on drugs at the time, but she also missed the socially active life they'd enjoyed before. Jason's parents spent a lot of time at the Birch home, but it wasn't the same.

Kate tried to cheer her up. "I absolutely am. Hey, you could come watch the meteor shower with us once you got Dad settled."

Laura laughed. "Oh, sure. You and Jason, and Cody and his date, and your mother. That might be just a tad awkward. Thank you, but no."

"I don't know." Kate mused almost to herself. "You might be just what I need out there tonight."

Her mother studied her quietly for a couple of moments and then asked, "What's going on, Kate? Why are you not on cloud nine like you usually are when you're going somewhere with Jason?"

Kate paused as she thought about that. "Maybe it's just that I'm so tired from finals. I don't know." She hesitated again and then continued, "Jason hinted about wanting to move on to more commitment again. Part of me wants to laugh and kiss him and go buy a ring. But part of me also feels this incredible need to make sure that I'm what he really wants."

"Kate, you've been what that man wanted since you were tiny. Why do you doubt him?"

"You know, I don't really doubt him. I know Jason better than I know myself. And he is the greatest man I've ever known. I just have this need to make triple sure he's not going to become rich and famous and have regrets about marrying the girl next door." She turned to her mother. "I can't take a chance on being just another wife who gets left behind when the husband starts to move in those bigger and bigger circles. I'm a great fish in this little pond, Mom, but Jason is headed for the big time."

"He is headed for the big time, Kate. I believe you're right, but that doesn't change his character. And I believe you're a fish who can hold her own in any pond on the planet. In looks and brains, and all the rest. You're one of the most dynamic women I've ever known, even if I am your mother."

Kate shook her head and thoughtfully took a bite of fruit. Ignoring the sweet compliments her mother had thrown in at the end, she asked, "So does that mean that all the broken marriages on those magazine covers at the grocery store are just because all of those people had weak characters going into their fame? Or is there something about fame and money that puts some huge amount of pressure on otherwise good people's judgment? I need your wisdom here, mother. I love Jason, but I don't want to be a statistic. If he's going to have regrets, I want to get to them before we have children involved."

Her mother hesitated for a moment and then commented, "I see your reasoning, Kate, but aren't you, in effect, saying that you don't trust Jason to be faithful?"

"No. I don't think so. I don't think he'd ever cheat in a marriage. I just don't want him to ever wish he wasn't stuck with me. I'm just hoping and praying that by giving him some freedom now, that he'll see all the other flavors out there and still decide he prefers Kate. But absolute fidelity isn't really optional. Is it?"

"No, Kate, it isn't. But absolute perfection isn't possible either. If you're going to hand Jason enough rope to hang himself, you have to face the reality that he might and that you facilitated it. You'd probably regret that more than diving in head first now. Wouldn't you?"

"At that point, wouldn't it just prove I was wise to hesitate?"

Her mom came around the counter and put an arm around her. "I don't know, Katie, honey. I hate to admit it, but mothers don't know everything. And this is certainly a decision you have to make for yourself and then be completely at peace with. You're the one God is sending personal inspiration to for your life and you're the one who has to live with all of it. Pray about it. Pray that you'll be wise but still be able to enjoy your young life. This is supposed to be a happy night, remember? And y'all don't look very happy just now."

Kate began to clean up the cutting board and put the fruit away. "You're right. As usual. I'm not sure why I'm uptight tonight. Sometimes lately I just feel a little like I don't really know this new Jason, the country music star. Silly, huh? It's probably just that I'm so tired. I'll be fine tomorrow." She went to the bag she was going to take with them and began packing the car blankets she was taking.

Picking up the other blanket, her mom cautioned, "Use your head out there tonight, Kate. I know you and Jason always try to make good decisions, but he's not a little boy anymore and that figure y'all are sporting would tempt Saint Peter himself. Remember that you're a daughter of God."

Kate smiled and hugged her mother. "I will, Mom. And we won't share a blanket. Don't worry."

"It's a mom's job to worry, Katelyn Birch. Have fun and don't let any meteors fall on you. Okay?"

Lifting the loaded bag, Kate grinned and said, "When a meteor falls on you, Mom, then it's no longer called a meteor, it's a meteorite. And you don't care what it's called because you're squished anyway." She kissed her mother. "Love you, Mom. See ya later."

Kristin Cross

Chapter 2

Actually, Kate would have been good with a meteor falling on them an hour later as she sat in an elegant restaurant with Jason and Cody and some girl named Ryanna with a big chest and a little brain. It wasn't the chest or the little brain that Kate wanted to be crushed by a meteor. It was the bottle of champagne that sat chilling on ice on the table between Jason and Cody that was troubling her just now. Kate was in complete shock that it was even sitting on their table. She and Jason didn't drink. And Cody knew that as well as anyone.

Ryanna obviously didn't as she encouraged the server to fill four beautiful champagne flutes with the sparkling, pale pink liquid. Kate wasn't sure whether to get to the bottom of what was going on, or simply discreetly ignore it and go on with the meal that had suddenly made her decidedly uncomfortable. After trying unsuccessfully to catch Jason's eye, she decided to play dumb and just eat. Her couple of bites of fruit hadn't gone far and she was starving.

Cody and Ryanna were making a big deal of celebrating the band's record contract and Kate made a commitment to swallow her anxiousness and at least be enthusiastic with them. Even tired, this was a good day and needed to be enjoyed.

Her chicken Marsala was marvelous and she was savoring it as she watched Jason pick up his flute of champagne and sip from it. She put her fork down and looked at him in surprise and Cody laughed and said, "Oh, lighten up, Katie Ree. It's just champagne. It's not like he's drinking Jack Daniels. We're celebrating, remember? There's less alcohol in that than there is in your chicken and you know it. Don't give him the look."

Ryanna laughed a veritable cackle of a laugh that wasn't intended to be friendly as she said in mock horror. "Oh, no! We have one of those goody two shoes non-partakers amongst us? Cody, I never expected y'all to hang with such stiff friends. What's up with this?"

Cody backed his date off. "Easy, Ri. Kate is like a sister to me. And the world needs nondrinkers. Somebody has to drive when the rest of us are plastered." He turned to Kate. "I really didn't think you'd mind, Kate. It's only champagne. That's not real alcohol. It's more like fancy apple cider or something. Try it. You might like it once in a blue moon when we have something really big like this to celebrate."

Kate looked over at Jason who picked up the flute again and sipped it. "You don't have to if you don't want to, Kate, but I really don't think it's a big deal. It's a two hundred dollar bottle of sparkling fruit juice is all. It's not like we're having a kegger and getting swaggering drunk."

She dropped her eyes to concentrate on her chicken Marsala, although right now knowing what it was made with made it seem distasteful as well, even as hungry as she was. She struggled with suddenly feeling as if they were all three of them looking down on her for not joining in with their party. She wasn't used to feeling this way with Jason or even with Cody and in a way it stung.

Not only that, but she was young enough that the management could literally come and take her fancy flute away if they realized it. She could only imagine what Ryanna would comment about something like that, and hoped that at least that wouldn't happen.

Typically self assured about her high standards, Kate realized she was unsure of herself and it made her mad as she sat and tried to ignore the others and focus on her hunger. Who were they to question what she knew in her heart was a wiser course of action than they'd chosen? And what was she doing feeling self conscious about it anyway? It was just because for once Jason wasn't choosing the higher road with her. He'd never done that before, but she was strong enough to stand alone.

She raised her chin and glanced over at Jason who smiled at her as he cut a bite of his steak. When he put his knife down and reached for her hand to give it a squeeze, she felt a little more like herself until he released it and reached for the elegant glass with the pink liquid again.

What was up with him tonight? This didn't even seem like the Jason she knew. Troubled more than ever, she tried to brush it off and eat. There wasn't a thing she could do about the whole situation until they left the restaurant and had some privacy anyway. She decided not to let this get to her so much and looked around at the restaurant. She'd never been here before and it was really lovely. Which was a good thing, because the company tonight stunk. Even Jason.

In the parking lot after leaving, Kate didn't even hesitate to ask for Cody's keys. At the very least it would send the message home that there was a reason she chose not to drink. Cody and his date automatically got into the back seat of the Jeep. That was one thing about Cody. When he was drinking, he didn't try to get behind the wheel.

Kate drove them to the point above the river where they'd decided to watch the meteor shower and they built a fire in the old ring of blackened rocks as they waited for the sun to finish going down and darkness to set in. Kate was even more nonplussed when Cody produced another bottle of champagne out of the Jeep and another set of fancy fluted glassware. What was up with him tonight?

She was relieved when Cody and Ryanna disappeared around the bend of the river with a blanket and their drinks and it was just her and Jason for a while. Even drinking champagne, Jason was an entity she could handle. At least she always had been able to.

Jason didn't seem to notice the champagne. Maybe he hadn't even seen Cody unload it because Jason just got out his acoustic guitar and settled on a huge old log that had been dragged up next to the fire and started to play. As his rich voice began to sound across the flames, blending with the clear, hypnotic notes of the guitar, Kate could feel herself start to relax and she brought a little blanket and came over and sat next to his stump seat to lean against him. This was her Jason. The friend she'd leaned on her whole life.

As tired as she was, it didn't take her long to begin to get sleepy and mellow and she leaned her head back against Jason's leg and yawned. She wasn't sure she could stay awake to watch the shooting stars.

Jason put the guitar down and put a hand on her shoulder and yawned himself. "Oh man, Kate. This grueling week is coming back to bite me. How are you doing? Are y'all as tired as me?"

She put a hand up to rest on his on her shoulder. "I'm fine. A little tired, but I'm okay. So tell me more about your week. How was the big city?"

He got up and went over to Cody's Jeep and started digging around in it, talking over his shoulder as he went, "The city was cool. It's busy and crowded and if I had to live there, I'd be crazed, but it was fun. Didn't Cody bring anything other than champagne to drink? Geez, the man is nuts. There's not even a Coke in here. Where'd they go, anyway? Do you know?" He came back over to her with a flute of champagne. "I know you weren't very happy about the champagne, but I don't really think it's that big of a deal. It's not really wine or beer or something. I'm thirsty and I'm going to have some more. Can I get you some or would y'all just rather not? Would you like to try a taste of mine? It really does just taste like extra sparkling fruit juice."

He sat down on the log again and she leaned back against him one more time. "I don't know, Jase. It seems like drinking. I mean, it is alcoholic."

"Yeah, but so is the cooking wine you use all the time in your restaurant. And although I would never crack open a beer; this doesn't bother me too much. I've never celebrated with champagne before, but then I've never had my own recording contract before either." He offered her the flute. "Try a taste. If you hate it, we'll make a run back in to the C-store at the junction."

She absent mindedly took the stemware he was offering her and closed her eyes for a minute to rest them while she thought about it and then stayed resting against him as he began to play again. He sang her the first song he'd ever written for her and even though it had gone on to become a top ten hit on the radio, she never tired of hearing him sing it to her when it was just the two of them and his guitar.

When the song was over, she opened her eyes and took a tentative sip of the champagne. It wasn't too bad. It didn't really taste like fruit juice, but it wasn't nearly as nasty as cooking wine before it cooked off.

She took another sip and leaned back against Jason again. When it was like this, she didn't have the doubts and fears she'd been fighting lately. She wanted Jason to be as successful and popular and famous as he absolutely could. She did. But it was really nice to be back to just them and their friendship, the way it had always been.

Jason started another song and Kate moved her legs around to the other side to work the kinks out and then settled back again and took another sip from the glass. She was thirsty. She hadn't drunk anything with dinner because she hadn't wanted to draw attention to herself by asking the server for a glass of water.

By the time it was fully dark, Kate was feeling incredibly mellow and relaxed and oh so sleepy. Cody and Ryanna still weren't back and Kate finished Jason's drink and then got up to try and wake up some. She went back to the car and brought more blankets to spread out on the nearby grass so they could watch the stars and then folded another one into a pillow. Feeling a bit guilty for drinking all of his champagne, she refilled the flute and set it back beside him.

Lying on her tummy on the blanket next to Jason, she yawned and looked back up at him in the firelight. It was incredibly nice here. She wished it could be like this all the time. She pulled the folded blanket under her chin and reached for the glass she'd set aside. She was a fool to worry like she'd been. Jason was her best friend and he always would be and she loved him dearly.

Jason let the fire die down so it would be darker to see the stars and then he put his guitar aside, refilled the pretty champagne glass, sipped from it, handed it back to her and then sprawled down beside her. Turning on his back, he moved closer to her and put his head on her folded pillow and looked up at the stars above them. He smelled incredibly nice when he was this close. She drained the glass and then set it aside and leaned to kiss him. He tasted warm and slightly fruity just now.

A moment later, she pulled away and rested her forehead on the blanket she was lying on. Stars were definitely not what she was focused on right this second, and a little nap actually sounded more inviting than watching the meteor shower, but she didn't want to admit that to Jason. Not on their first night with him back from Nashville.

Jason reached and refilled the glass again and as he took a sip, she watched the muscles of his throat move, marveling that such an incredibly attractive man loved her when he could have any girl he really wanted, especially now that the band had made a name for itself. He was watching her as he swallowed and he pulled the glass away, slowly licked his lips and offered it back to her, all without looking away. In the moonlight his green eyes looked like a deep pools of liquid as he whispered, "Falcons mate for life, Kate. I love you."

When he told her that, it made something low in her tummy do somersaults, and she blinked, thoroughly enjoying the way being adored by him made her feel. She finished the champagne and then turned over onto her back and snuggled over to him. It was time to concentrate on the stars or she was going to forget them and just kiss Jason.

For several minutes they looked up into the deep blue velvet heaven with its powdered sugar dusting of Milky Way and there were indeed a spectacular number of shooting stars that crossed the sky in vivid, short-lived flashes of white light. The night breeze felt good on her heated skin.

Jason leaned up on an elbow to look at her. He didn't say anything, just looked and she wondered for a second if you could drown in someone's eyes. His felt like eternity just now and her worries of late were as if they'd never been. She'd been silly to worry anyway. After all, Jason was her rock. He always used good judgment. He'd never let her down and she always knew it was safe to lean on him. She really wanted to kiss him again.

Chapter 3

Her phone vibrating against her side woke her from a sound sleep. Crimonies, her head hurt so badly it made her want to swear. And she was not a swearing kind of a girl. She tried to open her eyes but they felt like they had sand in them and she closed them again to feel for her phone instead.

When she touched bare skin on her stomach, her eyes opened wide in shock and this time she did swear silently when she realized she didn't have a shirt on. Not even her cammy. She tried not to groan as she groped for the kill button on her phone. She swore again bitterly. What had she done? What in the world had she done? What had they done? Her head hurt too much to even try to remember clearly.

Jason slept next to her, the car blanket lying loosely across his gorgeous bare chest, and she dreaded finding out how many more clothes they were missing. Oh, man, what had she done?

Her head was pounding with a vengeance and even the minimal light from her phone hurt as she retrieved her new text message. She swore again. It was from her mom. "Hey, are you okay? You've never stayed out this long before. Just checking. Love you, Mom."

Kate groaned and put a hand under the blanket to find that she was missing a lot more than just her shirt. She licked her dry lips and started to cry, trying to be quiet enough not to wake Jason as she rummaged under the blanket to see if she could find her clothing. There was no way she was going to pull that blanket back to look for them. She was such a fool. Such a complete fool. Man, she felt awful.

She suddenly remembered that Cody and his obnoxious woman had been here last night and she almost panicked as she looked around. Thankfully, there was no one in sight and she quickly pulled her shirts on and then shrugged into her pants. She hadn't found all of her lingerie and she gave up looking with an angry sob and slipped on her sandals, thinking only that she wanted to get out of here and never have to face Jason or Cody or that small brained Ryanna again in her life.

As she stood up in the pitch darkness, her head began to pound with an even meaner throb and she struggled to stifle the urge to throw up as she began walking back up the gravel road toward town. She had the worst morning breath she could even imagine.

Once out of hearing of the burnt out fire, she dialed home and struggled to control her tears as her mom picked up on the first ring. "Katie, are you okay?"

Kate groaned and bit back her tears. "No, Mother, I'm a complete idiot."

"What happened? Are you hurt?"

She sighed and couldn't help the tears that overflowed as she said, "I'm fine, just incredibly, amazingly stupid. Would you come and get me please? I'll be walking your way on the gravel road out by the river."

"Where's Jason? Is he okay?"

"He's fine. I think he's fine. I'm not waking him up to find out. I honestly never want to see him or talk to him again in my life. Just please come get me. I'll explain when you get here."

There was a pause and then her mother sighed. "Oh, Kate. I hope you didn't forget who you are. Stay with Jason and don't go walking alone. I'll be right there."

Kate pushed the end button and slid the phone into her pocket. She wasn't even sure what had happened last night, but she suspected she'd more than forgotten who she was. She started to cry all the harder and then went to the side of the road to deal with her uncontrollable urge to vomit. Geez, she was a disgusting mess. Why in the world had she ever agreed to try his champagne? She'd known better even though she'd always trusted Jason's judgment in the past. Yeah, sure it wasn't really alcohol. Who were they trying to kid?

She kicked at a rock in utter self loathing. Her, of course. She was who they were trying to kid. And it had worked beautifully. She'd never really thought she would turn out to be such a sucker. She knew better. She'd known better since she was a little, tiny girl. She was pitiful. She swore again and swiped angrily at the tears on her cheeks. What in the world had they done?

On the one hand she was furious with him for helping to fool her into such a big mistake. On the other hand, he would be just as sad as she was when he woke up to realize what had happened and she wished she could somehow take it all away before he found out. He would never have let this happen if they hadn't been drinking. Neither of them would have. They'd tried so hard to stay morally clean for so many years. They weren't like this. They really, really weren't like this.

As she walked along in the dark, she thought back to that sweet evening by the lake when she and Jason had made their pinky promise to stay virgins. In a fresh bout of sadness, she didn't see a pot hole in the road and tripped and twisted her ankle and the pain made her cry even harder as she whispered, "Oh, Jason, I'm so sorry. I didn't mean to, I swear it."

Not only was she bawling, but she was limping terribly too when her mother pulled up beside her in the gravel. Wordlessly Kate got in and her mother turned around and headed back the way she had come, the only sound in the car Kate's heart wrenching sobbing.

Back at home, she looked her mother in the eye and then dropped her gaze and said simply, "I blew it, Mom. I let them talk me into drinking champagne, because it wasn't really alcohol." As she said this last, she made quote marks in the air with her hands.

She shook her head again and wiped at the tears on her cheeks. "I knew better. In fact, I was furious at first. But I've always been able to trust his judgment and then when it was just Jason and me by the fire I had a sip of his. It must have affected my thinking right from the start. I don't know how much I ended up drinking. I was so tired and it only made me worse. I'm so sorry. It'll never happen again. I promise."

"What'll never happen again, Katie?"

Kate crumbled into sobbing again. "Oh, Mother, I don't even know for sure. I don't even remember. I just know I woke up with a splitting head and not nearly enough clothing." For a second she couldn't even speak. She turned away from her mom and headed for her room as she repeated, "I don't even remember. I don't want to talk about it anymore. Thank you for coming for me. I'm supposed to be at the restaurant at two. If I'm not up by one will you please wake me? Otherwise, let me sleep and not think about what a fool I am. I'm so sorry. I love you. Good night."

She'd made it to her room when she had to turn and rush into the bathroom to throw up again. Wiping her mouth, she reached to brush the compounded sour taste from her mouth. And she'd thought her head hurt when she woke up. It felt like it was going to burst after hurling.

Reaching into her medicine cabinet, she shook out two aspirin and tossed them back and then groaned from the pain of moving her head too fast. She pulled the shower water on to warm up and stripped off the clothing she *had* found and tossed it into the garbage and then threw toilet paper in on top of it to hide it. That had been her favorite shirt, but she didn't want to ever remember it again.

After showering, she pulled on a pair of plain white panties, cut off sweats and an old t-shirt and limped in to literally fall into bed. With any luck, she'd kill over from this headache and not have to wake up and remember what an incredible, blithering fool she'd been. There was no question that she couldn't say her prayers tonight. God was well aware of what had happened, but she couldn't face him. What in the world had she done?

***

When the sun shining in Jason's eyes woke him up to find himself alone and sans clothing, he knew he was in a lot of trouble.

He had no idea where Kate was and the first thing he did was try to call her phone and check and make sure she was okay. It went straight to voice mail and next he tried her parents' house. Her mother answered and while she was polite, and told Jason that yes, Kate had come safely home at three twenty that morning; she was definitely not the pleasant, welcoming mother she usually was.

When he asked to talk to Kate, Laura politely told him Kate had asked not to be woken. He paused wondering what to say to this woman who was nearly as close to him as his own mom and finally just asked, "When she wakes up, will you tell her I called, please?"

After saying goodbye, he lay back down and covered his eyes with a groan. Yeah, he was in *a lot* of trouble.

Lying there, he was chilled and he threw back the small blanket to see where his clothes had gotten to. They lay in a wad under the blanket and he tried to shake out the wrinkles as he thought back to last night.

Kate had been right; the champagne had been a really bad idea. He'd known Kate was drinking a lot, but he'd somehow bought into the story they'd been telling her that it wasn't really alcohol. And even that was a terrible excuse. He'd had some to drink, but he certainly hadn't been wiped out drunk like Kate was. Just weak. Weak and tired, and enchanted to the bone. Between the three of those things, he'd broken the most important promise in his life, and in the process done what he hoped wasn't irreparable damage to their relationship.

He knew Kate. Knew she was the most honorable, Godly, pure woman on the planet. And if any other guy had propositioned her, she'd have insisted that he take her home and not call again. What she'd think of Jason, after much more than a proposition was yet to be revealed, but the fact that she'd left without telling him goodbye and wouldn't take his call this morning didn't bode well.

And he deserved every bit of it.

Standing up, he walked to his car barefoot to dig out some gum. His morning after champagne breath was horrendous. Going back to the scene of the crime, he reached down and picked up one of the blankets and shook the grass off of it, folded it up and then started on a second one. One of his socks fell out and then a lacy, little tangerine colored bra and he bent to pick it up, wishing that he was only feeling guilt and not remembering how incredibly exquisite she'd been last night.

As much as he regretted things this morning, last night had been the culmination of a lot of years' dreams. Now he just hoped he could talk Kate out of telling him to hit the road because of it. It was awful that they'd taken something so precious and turned it into a negative. All these years, he'd dreamed of waking up in Kate's happy arms after their first time being intimate together and he'd messed it all up royally. And yeah, he needed to shoulder the blame for this one. Kate had been kind of out of it, thanks to his encouraging the champagne, but he hadn't. Just weak. Weak and stupid.

He folded the bra and put it in his pocket, wondering what to do with it. It was pretty much a given that Kate would never want to see it again if he knew her very well. He cleaned up the various odds and ends lying around the campsite and resisted the urge to smash the champagne bottle to bits against the fire pit rocks. He should have listened to Kate on this one. He really should have.

When the only thing left to pack away was his guitar, he glanced around the small clearing and wondered where Cody and his obnoxious date had gotten to. He didn't even remember them coming back to camp. It was anybody's guess how they had gotten back into town.

He picked up his guitar, but instead of putting it into its case in the trunk of his car, he sat back down on the stump and started to idly pick a few cords, wishing he could magically conjure up powerful enough notes and lyrics to somehow undo last night so he could start all over again. It had certainly turned into some celebration. He shook his head and sighed.

Bending over the instrument, he closed his eyes and began to hum a soulful, plaintive melody that went along with his somber, regretful mood and then whispered, "Oh, baby, I'm so sorry."

He was so caught in his thoughts of Kate and his music that at first, he didn't even hear Cody and Ryanna laughing as they walked back up the river path. In a way, he envied them their devil may care attitude about what they had been doing, wherever they had been doing it. But not really. Kate was too precious and too rare a treasure to ever cheapen with casual sex. Even if he'd been that kind of a guy. Which he definitely wasn't. Intimacy with her would never be casual for him to the day he died. Granted she ever wanted to see him again. Just now, that was definitely on the down side of iffy.

Ryanna laughed her cackle as she reached into the back seat of his Jeep to take a small hair brush out of her purse and attempt to tame her straggling, brassy hair. Jason looked up and met Cody's eyes and saw him glance around for Kate. When he didn't see her and looked sadly back at Jason, Jason knew that he wasn't unaware of what a mess Jason had made of his and Kate's friendship with that stupid bottle of sparkling wine and his uncontrolled desire. The regret in Cody's eyes, in spite of his forced smile, spoke volumes to Jason and depressed him still further.

He looked away, unwilling to let even his closest friend see how deeply his frail humanness troubled him. He leaned back over his guitar. *Oh, baby, I'm so, so sorry.*

Kate never called and after waiting all morning and into the afternoon, Jason went in search of her. Her car was gone from where she normally parked it in front of her parents' house and he flipped a uie and headed for her parents' restaurant. She usually managed it on Saturdays, but typically not until after three o'clock. Maybe she had gone in early.

Her car was there and he pulled his to the curb and tried to see if he could see her through the big front windows. It would be a good thing if he could get a feel for what she was thinking before he actually approached her. She was nowhere to be seen and he hoped that meant she was in her office in the back where they could have a modicum of privacy.

As he went to reach for the car door handle, he paused and wondered if he dared pray and ask for help in this situation after what he had done to cause it. Deciding at length that this was definitely one of those mistakes God had hoped His children wouldn't make, Jason held to his faith that his Father in Heaven loved him no matter how much he messed up and he humbly bowed his head anyway. Kate was too important not to ask for divine help with if there was any possibility he could get it.

When he walked past the hostess's stand and through the dining room, both waiters he met looked at him hesitantly and it made him wonder how bad of shape Kate was in. He hoped she wasn't horribly hung over on top of being completely disappointed in her boyfriend.

Kate looked up as he approached her office and she stood and walked right out the back door of the office and out into the parking lot behind the building, pulling the sunglasses that sat on top of her head down as she stepped off the small porch. She set off up the sidewalk at a brisk walk that held a definite limp and Jason had to practically run to catch up with her. In her business slacks and heels, she looked like a million bucks, but her sunglasses effectively covered every vestige of what she was really feeling.

Falling into step with her, he walked along beside her for a couple of minutes before she finally stopped and turned to him. Or turned on him, which was the impression he got from her posture. She didn't say anything, just looked at him and he looked back at her in return and at length reached over and gently pulled off her sunglasses. He had to see her eyes to know what she was thinking.

What he saw made him want to wince. As beautiful as she was, her eyes looked like hell. She looked positively ill, as well as appearing to have spent a great deal of the last ten hours crying her heart out. The headache must have been a corker. Her forehead creased and she was nearly squinting from the glare. And she'd been limping. Geez, what had he done to her?

Unsure of what to do, he just stood there until he finally stepped forward and tried to all but swallow her in a close hug. He pulled her tight against his chest and she hid her face and began to cry like her world had unraveled in one, horribly misdirected evening. Oh, how he wished he could take it all back.

She clung to him and sobbed until his shirt was plastered to his chest and a tear overflowed his own eyes and slid down his face. He wiped at it before it dripped into her hair and put his mouth down close to her ear to whisper, "Oh, Kate. Baby, I'm so sorry." He stroked her back and ran his fingers into her hair and pulled her even closer. "So sorry."

When the tears didn't appear to be slowing at all, he slid a hand under the short, fairy curls at the back of her neck and gently squeezed the muscles that were so tense she felt like she was going to break and spoke to her again softly, "Kate, do you think you can ever forgive me? What are you thinking? Please say you're not going to leave me. I know I messed up abysmally. I know I did. But please don't give up on us. Please."

After several more minutes, she finally, finally appeared to be winding down and he pulled back to look at her. "Are you okay?"

She shook her head and swallowed, unable to speak as more tears dampened her face and he pulled her close again to whisper, "We'll get through this, Kate. We will. I know I can't ask you to trust me, but I promise we'll get through it and end up okay."

Her teary, bloodshot eyes looked up into his for several long moments, and while he searched them almost desperately, for the first time in nearly his whole life, he couldn't tell what she was thinking. He tried again to reassure her. "We will, babe. What we have is strong enough to handle even this."

He pulled her back close and almost rocked her for a second and then took her hand and began to lead her away from her restaurant as he asked, "Do they need you desperately in there right now? Or can I have you for a few minutes?"

She put her sunglasses back on and begrudgingly said, "I have a few minutes, but only a few. There is a ton of stuff to do before the dinner rush."

They walked for another couple of minutes before he stopped and tugged her to a nearby bench where he kept her hand in his. Hesitantly, he asked, "Why are you limping?"

She sighed and quietly answered him without looking up, "I twisted my ankle walking last night."

After a pause, he asked, "I didn't do it?"

She shook her head. "No."

"Is it okay?"

Still without looking up, she said tiredly, "My ankle's fine."

He played with her hand, stroking the back of it with his other hand while he thought about what she was implying. Finally, he softly asked, "How is your heart?"

She started to cry again and then when she could, she said haltingly, "Wiser. Wiser than it was yesterday." She stood up. "And sad. Incredibly sad. I need to get back." She dropped his hand and began walking away.

Getting up from the bench, he caught up with her and tried to take her hand once more, but she pulled it away. Frustrated, he said, "Don't Kate. That only makes it worse. We can make it through this."

At that, she stopped and turned on him again and the tears were momentarily gone as she ground out, "Of course we made it through it, Jason. Were here, aren't we? We made it through it. We just did a lot of damage in the process."

"We can fix the damage, Kate."

"Oh, really?"

"Yes. Really."

"Tell me something Jason. What did we do last night? Did I lose my virginity under that meteor shower?"

He stood there looking at her across the sidewalk and finally reached to take her sunglasses off again. He searched her eyes for several seconds and then asked in confusion, "You don't remember?"

She looked away and shook her head and whispered, "Did I?"

He turned and pulled her with him to begin walking again and at length softly admitted, "Yes. We both did." She started to sob again, and he had to slow down as she stumbled.

Almost back to the rear door of her restaurant, they continued walking in silence. When they made it to the porch, she pulled her hand away and turned to him and said with infinite sadness, "Then you tell me how we can fix the damage." With that, she spun and headed back inside the restaurant.

He stood there for several minutes and then finally turned and walked slowly around the building back to his car, his chest caving not only with sadness, but worry as well. It was a bad situation made exponentially worse by pulling away from each other. No, they could never undo what they'd done, but he wished they could at least get through it together. Kate had seemed more alone just now than he could stand and he got into his car and leaned his head back against the head rest feeling utterly defeated. Last night had been heaven, but it certainly hadn't been worth it. He wished he would have realized that in the heat of the moment. The champagne had been a terrible idea.

He was back at the restaurant that night at ten o'clock, waiting in his car in the parking lot out back. She never knew exactly when she'd get off at night. When he saw her coming out the door, he got out and met her as she headed to her car. She paused when she saw him, looking at him without saying anything. Tonight she wasn't wearing her sunglasses and even in the dark, he could see that the only thing that had changed was that now she looked completely exhausted on top of feeling lousy and being heartbroken.

Hesitantly, he asked, "Can I drive you home? I'll take you to church in the morning and we'll pick up your car on the way home after."

She shook her head and looked down. "I can't go to church tomorrow. There's no way. I'll just drive home now."

Turning toward her car, he fell into step beside her. "I knew you'd say that. But Kate, you're wrong. You may not feel like you can go to church tomorrow, but that's exactly what Satan wants and exactly opposite of what the Savior went through the atonement for."

At the driver's side door of her car, she turned to look up at him and he went on, "We fell off the wagon in a huge way last night, Kate. We did. I'm not saying we didn't. But we can't forget everything we've ever learned or completely lose ourselves because of it. Yeah, we made a huge mistake, but we need to deal with it. Just like we deal with all of the other mistakes we make in this life. We need to face that we blew it and then do what we can to fix it. Of course we can't repair all the damage."

He put a gentle hand to her cheek and said tenderly, "And I'm so sorry for that. So sorry." He paused and then continued, "But we can repent and forsake that sin and do our best to get back on the wagon. The worst thing we could do is turn our backs on the Savior and try to go it without Him when we need Him and our Father in Heaven the very most. Yeah, it's going to be awful to face those people at church tomorrow. I know that. But that's what we need to do. Get back on the wagon as fast as possible. Not going will set Christ's sacrifice for us as useless. Don't you see?"

She looked up at him with big, sad eyes, and then finally dropped her head and nodded. She started to cry again as she whispered, "I can't even pray. I know God already knows what happened, but I can't bring myself to face him. And I feel like turning away from you and it feels incredibly lonely."

Looking up, he sighed and then stepped close to her and pulled her to him in a sweet, tight hug. "Oh, Kate." He rubbed a hand over her back and pulled her even closer. "Don't ever turn away from me, Kate. The whole earth would fall off its axis if you did. Just waiting for you to get off work tonight makes me feel like I've been deprived of oxygen." He kissed her hair and rubbed his cheek against it.

He went on, "I made two huge mistakes last night. The champagne was a terrible idea and I should have gotten up and gone home when we first started kissing when we were laying there. It's all my fault and I know it. But please don't turn away from me. I'm in this for eternity, Kate. I can't give you back your virginity. And I'm so sorry. But last night doesn't make me love you any less. Just the opposite is true.

He nodded. "You're more my soul mate than ever. Let's get through this together, babe. Let's get back on the wagon, together and do our very, utmost best to move past this and get back on track spiritually and as a couple. Otherwise, we've switched teams and are doing just what the adversary hopes we'll do."

He stood there and held her as she cried and finally, she sniffed and said, "It wasn't all your fault, Jason. It was every bit as much mine. I knew better. I knew better than to believe it was just fruit juice. And I knew better than to lay beside you, alone in the dark when I was so tired and get carried away. I knew better. I don't know why I ever gave in. It's my fault too. I knew better." She finally looked up at him with tear filled eyes. "It's just that I trusted you, Jason. You've never led me wrong before. Ever. Not in my whole life. I guess I've learned to trust you too much. I'm sorry."

He groaned and closed his eyes, abjectly ashamed to have her say such a damning truth out loud. He had led her wrong. And she was the one apologizing.

She could try to cushion it, but it was his fault. He knew it in his heart. He pulled her close again and held her to him. How could he ever make this up to her? He couldn't in a million years, but he could die trying. He would die trying. He'd spend the next few eternities trying.

They clung to each other for who knows how long and then he finally said, "You're tired, babe. Let me take you home and we'll come get your car on the way home from church tomorrow." He pulled back and looked at her. "Please." He studied her sad, tired face. "Please say yes. Don't pull away from me. Or Jesus, either one. I let you down, but I'm going to do my best never to let you down again. And Jesus will never let you down. Neither will God. You know that, Kate. Don't turn away. In actuality, we need to turn to them right now more than ever."

She pushed her face tight into his chest and he rested his chin on top of her head. She sounded infinitely sad as she said, "I'll bet Kennen is so disappointed in us." He closed his eyes again and winced. Man, she knew how to kick a guy when he was down. He didn't even want to think about what Kennen would say to all of this.

Taking her hand, he turned and led her back to his car and helped her in. On the short drive to her house, she was completely quiet and once there, he led her to her door somberly. On the porch, she stopped him before they got into the pool of light. When she looked up at him, for the first time, he felt hope again as he saw that some measure of peace had replaced her utter anguish.

She stood there in silence for several long moments and then finally she said, "Thank you for tonight, Jason. Thank you for pep talking me out of crawling into a hole tomorrow and making things so much worse. You're always so wise when you counsel me like that and I absolutely appreciate it. I need it so much." She hesitated and then went on, "I need you so much. I do love you, Jason. More than anything in this life, I love you. Please forgive me for what happened. I didn't mean to do that. I promise."

She reached up and kissed him ever so gently for a long, long moment. When she finally pulled her mouth away, he held her so tightly he worried about crushing her in his arms, but she held him just as tightly. They seemed to draw strength from each other and it was strength he needed desperately. He could hardly breathe when they were at odds with each other.

He reached and tenderly brushed a thumb along the hollow under her ear. "Kate, can I ask you something?" She looked up and waited and he swallowed hard and continued, "Kate, in light of what happened last night. Do you think you would want to talk about getting married sometime? I don't mean to pressure you, but getting married feels like the honorable thing to do. Do we have to keep waiting?"

Her tired eyes clouded momentarily and she sighed. She glanced down and then back up as he felt the disappointment drop into his gut as she said, "Jason, maybe getting married does feel like the honorable thing to do. And heaven knows I want that almost desperately. But it would be a mistake right now. I'm sure it would. We need to get married because we love each other and have no doubts about wanting to be together for eternity. Not because we feel guilty."

Pausing, she leaned her forehead on his chest for a second and then looked back up at him. "Jason, can I be really, really gut honest with you?" He nodded somberly. "I'm afraid, Jason." His eyes narrowed as he tried to understand what she was telling him as she went on in a whisper, "I'm so afraid you'll become more and more popular and famous and rich and… And… That you'll meet someone, someday who will make you wish you hadn't married the girl next door. That someday in this whole super star deal you'll find a flavor you like better than Kate. The thought of you regretting me makes me heartsick."

Still with her heart in her eyes, she continued, "And married people have babies, Jason. I need you to be used to the glitz and fame and know I'm still the one. Before we have children involved. I can't stand the thought of being the failed marriage on the covers of the magazines at the grocery store. Especially with a child or two caught in the middle. I'm sorry, Jason, but I have to know. It seems backwards. But I *have* to know."

She stopped and dropped her eyes and he shook his head and said softly, "Kate, how many times do I have to tell you? Baby, I'm not seventeen anymore. I'm twenty four years old. Do you honestly not know to the depth of your soul that I want only you?" He pulled her face up to look at him and asked gently, "Kate, what do I have to do more than I have?"

Tears pooled in her eyes again. "You have to spread your wings and fly, Jason. Fly and then come home to me and we'll have the biggest wedding on the planet. Just make sure first."

He ran a hand through his hair and shook his head in frustrated disgust. "Geez, Kate, I wish you trusted me. And today I can't even ask that."

He swore bitterly and then pulled her tightly against him again as he let out a long sigh. "All right, Kate. We'll wait. And I'll fly and you'll grow deeper roots and someday I'll figure out how to prove myself to you. But, you know what Kate? I bitterly regret last night. I do.

I'd give anything to take it all back. But you know what else? I probably shouldn't even tell you this. It'll make you sad again."

She leaned her head back and looked up at him as he admitted almost fiercely, "I loved making love to you last night, Kate. I can't even put into words what your body does to me. As wrong as that sounds. I do want you, Kate. I want you desperately. Nothing in my life has been as hard as keeping my hands off of you."

He took a ragged breath and assured her, "I'll wait. I'll wait forever. And I'll respect you. I have the greatest respect for you. But I was telling you the truth about Falcons mating for life. I haven't changed. I'm never going to change. I'm in this for the long haul. I want to marry you, Kate. As soon as y'all can possibly get past this fear of all the other flavors. I want to try to start all over with you and take back having made intimacy with you such a hurtful thing. Because I *want* that Kate."

He groaned and buried his face in her hair. "I need that, Kate. I need you." He looked up and into her eyes. "And yeah, I want to talk to you, and laugh with you and work beside you and all of that. But I don't want all of those things anymore than I want to have you in my bed every night for the rest of forever and ever and ever. Actually, it's more than want. We're way into need on the Richter scale here. Honestly, we're probably even past need."

Her eyes got big and he slowed and then said more gently, "I'm sorry, Kate. But you deserve gut honesty too. I'm just trying to tell you that I wish we could get married now. I wish you knew that there's never a question of where my heart is. Even when there are crowds of different flavors. I will *always* come back to you, Kate Birch. Always. And I do want… Need intimacy with you. That's the truth."

He stayed looking into her eyes and after a moment or two she stretched up and kissed him. At first gently, and then with the same passion that had been in his voice when he'd been telling her of his need. Finally, she pulled back and looked up at him and said, "Then fly, Jason. Hurry and fly. Because I need you too."

Kristin Cross

Chapter 4

On their way into church the next day, Jason felt her grip on his hand tighten as they approached the door. Earlier, he'd gotten a less than enthusiastic welcome from her mother as she invited him in the door when Jason came to pick her up and he'd made a mental note to ask Kate just exactly what she'd told her. Now as they prepared to face their friends at church, he was infinitely glad no one here had an inkling about how much he'd messed up.

Even after the spiel he had given Kate the night before about the atonement, it was all he could do to walk inside those church doors himself. Thankfully, just what he'd hoped would happen when he'd encouraged Kate, did happen. Listening to the service and the lessons about the Savior and his pure charitable love for all men made truly coming back into the fold seem honestly doable. He could feel Kate loosen up a little as she sat beside him as well, and slowly but surely, that belly deep sick feeling began to dissipate.

They did feel better for having come to church, but the worry in her eyes that he'd wondered about lately was more apparent than ever and he wasn't surprised when she refused an invitation to Sunday dinner at his parents'. Pleading tiredness, she left him on her front porch and he went over to his parents' alone and lonely.

He asked her out again several times over the next week, but she only went with him three times and even then she seemed far more distant than he'd hoped. Every time he mentioned doing something with Cody that shadow would reappear in her eyes and he had to wonder if she'd ever want to do anything with his best friend and band partner again.

Finally, the night before he had to fly out for a concert in Mobile, she seemed to get back to the Kate he knew. He took her to a quiet dinner at an elegant restaurant and then back to his apartment where he played his guitar for her. She sat with her back against the couch at his feet like she'd done since she was a child and for awhile there it felt like the Jason and Kate from before that fateful night with the champagne. Even when a couple of women at the restaurant were whispering and obviously talking about him, Kate seemed to be herself for that whole evening and he was able to feel half way decent about flying out the next day and leaving her.

She rode with him and Cody to the airport in Oklahoma City like she usually did and Jason was glad she was able to greet Cody in a relatively normal manner as they picked him up, Jason had been worrying about how the two of them were going to deal with things since that awful night. Kate was none too effluent about her greeting, but she still agreed to take them. That was something.

He should have known she'd deal with things fine. She'd been handling the business for the band for a couple of years. In truth, even though she was only nineteen, going on twenty, she was the most competent person he'd ever known and handled the business end and scheduling and travel arrangements more smoothly than a whole team of help did for other bands their size. And she did that on top of being the general manager of her parents' restaurant now and even going to college full time. She was amazing that way.

She'd had to learn to be professional at an early age as a result of her dad being injured so badly right before she turned fifteen. At that time, Kate had been helping at the family restaurant, while her parents managed it and her older sister Kiersten, who was then twenty, had been off to college just outside of Tulsa.

When her dad was hurt, her mother had needed to be with her dad, and Kiersten could only come home on the week ends. Kate had been the temporary stop gap and had pulled off being a very under aged manager with an amazing amount of aplomb for someone who had to ride the bus from school to get to work, have an older employee sign for the liquor shipments and then finish her homework after the place shut down at night. All in all, Kate ended up being a business and managerial whiz and had been invaluable in managing things for their up and coming band.

She had been too young to go to most of their concerts. She still was for some of them. And after going along a few times when they'd just been starting out, she'd been content to stay at home, where she claimed her roots were, and let Jason "fly" without her. Sometimes too content. Jason knew that the popularity and the huge amount of press were intimidating to her and now he knew why.

Still, Kate had an uncanny handle on the fact that a major portion of the band's success hinged on that very glitz and she'd been incredibly effective at arranging PR events to promote them. They now had a part time manager, Scotty, and they both had agents, but Kate still managed the manager so to speak and Jason was incredibly proud of how well she handled everything. She was indeed amazing.

She usually just dropped them at the curb where they'd both pile out and meet the other members of the band and their techs and roadies, and then she'd take Jason's car home so she could come back and pick them up again when they returned, but this time, they dropped Cody and their gear and he stayed with her for a few minutes.

He pulled ahead away from Cody so they had some privacy and then stopped the car and looked over at her; ridiculously loathe to leave her this time. There was the same sadness in her face that he was feeling, but there was also that slightly uncomfortable shadow of worry she'd begun to carry around with her, and he wished he had about an hour to sit and talk to her and hold her and tell her goodbye.

He didn't, and they both knew it and it made telling each other goodbye under the circumstances worse than it had ever been.

After they looked at each with their hearts in their eyes, he reached over and took her hand without saying anything. He knew she was struggling not to cry and it was incredibly troubling. She had cried more in the last ten days than she'd cried in the last year. He hated what that one stupid, mistake filled night had done to her normally perpetual enthusiasm. That next day she'd said she was wiser, but realistically that computed to quieter and less prone to smile and it killed him.

He didn't know what to say to fix this, but he had to catch a plane and finally, he leaned across and pulled her closer until her face was only inches from his. Trying to smile, he said, "I'm going to spread my wings now, Kate. Kiss me and kick me out of this car. Would ya?"

She gave him a halfhearted smile back as she leaned toward him and snuggled against his chest over the console between the seats. Without looking up, she whispered, "I already miss you, Jase."

His voice was husky as he replied, "I already miss you too."

Looking back up at him, she cranked her smile a notch brighter and tried to be cheerful as she said, "Go get 'em Falcon. You're going to have great concerts. I can feel it." She quickly kissed him. "You're gonna be a huge star some day, Jason. Have fun on the journey."

He gave her a genuine smile. "I am gonna be huge, thanks to you. And I will have fun. I love what I do. I just wish I didn't have to leave you to do it."

The smile didn't quite reach her eyes and she swallowed hard. "We'll figure it out. Be safe."

"You too."

He leaned over to kiss her gently and then held her tightly for just a moment. He kissed her one more time, hard but still with restraint and almost groaned as he pulled an inch or two away. She blinked away tears as she whispered, "Hurry back to me, Jason."

He tenderly brushed away the one tear that spilled over. "I *always* come back to you, Kate. I can't help it. Falcons mate for life. Trust me." He kissed her gently. "Trust me. I love you, Kate. See you Monday."

Opening the car door, he got out as she got out of the passenger side. He reached into the back seat to grab his carry on and then held the driver's side door for her as she finished walking around. They came together for one last, almost painful hug and he kissed her, trying to convey all the emotion that was ripping him apart in that one, intense gesture. Geez, it was hard to leave her today.

Cody yelled from down the curb and Jason reluctantly pulled away, raised a hand to caress her cheek and then forced himself to turn away from her deep, worried blue eyes and jog down the walkway to make his plane. Today, he could feel her worries clear to his soul. *Be okay, Kate. Please be okay.*

At the door to the terminal, he turned back to look at her. She wasn't still standing beside his car, but it was still parked there and he began to silently pray as he ducked inside the door. "Please, God, help her. Strengthen her. Watch over her with an extra measure of comfort for me until I get back home to hold her."

Once he and Cody had finally made it to their seats with the other members of the band in the row behind them, Jason leaned back with a sigh and closed his eyes. He loved performing, but leaving her like that was hellacious.

He sat there for several minutes with his eyes closed and then Cody quietly asked, "Is she okay, Jase?"

Jason opened his eyes to look at his best friend and gave a minimal shake of his head. "No, she is definitely not okay."

Cody's brown eyes held unspeakable remorse. "I'm sorry, man."

"Me too, Cody."

After a long pause, Cody said, "You should pray for her, Jason."

Jason turned and gave a tired grin to his wild and loyal to the death friend and shook his head. "I am. Trust me, Rawlings. I am."

Cody gave him a tentative smile back. "Believe it or not, Jason, I am too."

At that, Jason chuckled right out loud and settled more into his seat. They were going to make it through this. With both God and Cody rooting for them, how could they not?

***

Embarrassed to be sitting at the curb bawling her eyes out, Kate struggled to get her emotions under control enough to be able to drive safely before she pulled away.

Why was she feeling like this today? She'd dropped Jason at the airport about a hundred times and it hadn't been this hard before. Crimonies, she had been an emotional wreck lately.

She sat up straighter and tried to swallow her tears. She didn't want to look like she'd been crying again. Her mother was about ready to commit her and half the wait staff was beginning to wonder if she was losing it. There was no reason to cry anyway. Jason was just going to a couple of gigs and then he'd be back. He'd promised. And he'd never let her down before. Well, almost never. Just once. Just one really big once. She started to cry again as she hit the interchange at highway 40. Where were these tears coming from? This was beyond ridiculous.

By the time Jason had been gone three days, Kate was beginning to wonder what in the world was up with her. She'd been emotional a few times in her life but this was insane. She cried at every thing from stubbing her toe to the National Anthem. Sure she'd been upset about what happened between her and Jason, but she'd made a serious commitment to do better at living within her standards and she knew Jason had done the same, and they were going to get through this, just like he'd promised. Still, she had mood swings that were off the charts sometimes. It was making her nuts. She had a life to live for Pete's sake.

A new request had become part of her prayers every day. "Lord, help me to be mentally tougher." Even with school out for the summer, between the restaurant and business for the band, she was spread too thin to take time to be emotionally ballistic.

That Friday, her mother stopped her as she was heading out to the restaurant in the early afternoon. She put a gentle hand on Kate's arm, studied her face for a moment and asked, "Katie, are you keeping up with taking your vitamins? You look like you might be low on iron. I don't remember you ever having dark circles under your eyes like you have right now."

Kate grinned. "My, but y'all have a nice way of saying I look haggard. As a matter of fact, I always take my vitamins. And eat right. And exercise. I even wash behind my ears. But you're right. The eyes are pitiful. I'll double up on the iron."

"Maybe that's the problem. Maybe you're doing too much. Kiersten was mentioning just the other day that with the twins in school full days now, she's bored out of her mind. Why don't you bump up her hours and back yours off. You could actually spend a day at the spa or go to the Lake when Jason gets back. Take some actual down time. It'd be good for a workaholic like you."

She kissed her mother as she dug in her purse for her keys. "I'll take you up on that." She smiled. "I've earned it. I'll have you know April was the most profitable month ever since you and Daddy opened the restaurant in 1981. Even adjusting for inflation. The building and all the equipment are paid off free and clear, business is booming, I've got two competent assistant managers who can just about run the place and y'all and Daddy are set for life as far as retirement savings. Well, unless you decide you need a yacht." She grinned again. "If I didn't already work for us, I'd hire myself! A couple of my business classes have really paid off on the management end."

Her mother's eyes got wide and then began to water. "Are you serious? Paid off? All of it?"

"And retirement accounts. You and Daddy had a marvelous idea for an Italian restaurant in that location. You get the business patrons, locals, and tourists all three. And you bought when land was bottomed out. You had perfect timing and a good plan. All it needed was your work ethic and good management. And then mine. With Maxine and Jerry, and Kiersten, now y'all don't even need me." She reached to give her mother a high five and then had to wait while her mother seemed almost in a daze. "See you, Mom. Have a great evening."

As Kate drove, she made a mental note to buy more iron. And maybe some B complex as well. Her eyes did look bad and her energy level was in the basement for how she usually was. Maybe it would help the perpetual emotional roller coaster as well. Just now, she was sunny as a new spring day. It had been great to surprise her mother with their strong financial status. She made another mental note to pre-register for next semester's classes. There was a marketing class that would probably be great for both the restaurant and the band.

The next morning, she didn't feel so good and rolled over and buried her head in her pillow with a little groan. Maybe that was why her eyes were hammered. She was probably coming down with something. She pushed her foot down to a cooler spot on the sheets and hoped that whatever it was, it was short lived. Jason would be home in less than two days and she couldn't get him sick. Colds put a professional singer out of commission in a hurry.

An hour later, her mom came in to check on her. She put a cool hand to Kate's brow and gave a grimace. "No fever. I hope you're not coming down with the flu. They say it starts with a sick stomach. If you aren't feeling better in a while, you'd better not go into the restaurant this afternoon. It'd be a shame to take a germ there."

Actually, by around noon Kate felt fine. A fever had never materialized and her headache and sick tummy were gone, so she went into work as scheduled and it was a good thing she did. The pastry chef didn't show and one of the computers went on the fluey and it took everything she and the assistant manager had to smooth out the resultant riffles.

She didn't make it home until after midnight and slept in again when the bug hit the second day in a row. At ten o'clock in the morning, she ruefully looked at herself in the mirror as she gagged brushing her teeth. Maybe she shouldn't have gone in last night. It would be a shame to slow up the restaurant's momentum with negative press from some outbreak.

Thankfully, she was feeling fine again by the time she picked Jason and Cody up from the airport on Monday. He greeted her with a searching look and then a long, sweet hug and kiss. It was heaven to be back in his arms. He did *always* come home to her. She hugged him back, feeling almost a bit silly that one person could control her happiness the way he could. Sometimes it seemed like nothing in the world could go wrong when Jason was with her.

They spent the afternoon together before Kate had to go into work and she thoroughly basked in having him back. She had missed him more than she ever remembered missing him.

When things were going smoothly at the restaurant she decided to leave and surprise Jason with some unexpected time in an evening for a change. Being a restaurant manager didn't often facilitate that. After the dinner rush, she left it in the capable hands of her assistant manager, and headed to find him. It had been too long of a separation to waste the first night he was home working. Their time together lately was so limited anyway. It wasn't fair to him to leave him tonight to work if they weren't desperate for her. As she drove, she decided that maybe having well trained assistant managers would turn out to be a really, really good thing.

Jason wasn't at his apartment and she drove by Cody's to see if his car was there. It was and she parked hers, turned off her phone and went to the door, looking forward to seeing him.

She could hear their music from clear outside and assumed they were jamming, which wasn't unusual, but they did usually try to tone down the amplifiers at this time of night. When no one answered the door, she figured they just couldn't hear the bell which wasn't unusual either and let herself in. Cody was so laid back that even if he wasn't completely dressed it wouldn't bother him a bit.

When Kate opened the door, she was taken aback. They weren't jamming. Their music was coming from Cody's humongous flat screen across the room and they were apparently watching a recording of one of their recent concerts. There were what seemed like hundreds of people in Cody's apartment and about two thirds of them appeared to be female. In fact, slightly scantily clad, somewhat tipsy females.

No one had even noticed Kate coming in the door and she shut it quietly, feeling that old familiar knot in the pit of her stomach. She hated parties like this. She knew groupies were just a part of this business, but she wasn't sure she would ever get used to it.

Looking around to see where Jason was, she saw girls of every shape, color, race and figure draped around various pieces of furniture and the guys who were in them. None of the guys appeared too upset about that to speak of. As she looked around, Kate took a canned Mountain Dew from a nearby tub filled with ice and then stepped back into an open spot near a cluster of partiers where she could watch what was going on without being too conspicuous.

She resumed her search for Jason, but couldn't see him anywhere and her attention was caught by the video on the big screen. The guys did put on an awesome show. She found herself tapping her foot to the heady backbeat as she watched the love of her life on that stage, singing his heart out at ten billion decibels with what looked from the camera's perspective like another ten billion fans screaming in the audience in front of them.

The guys looked good there in their seemingly casual, but incredibly sexy jeans and boots and muscle shirts. Jason was by far the most subtle, and the most heart stopping. At least as far as she could see. Of course, she might be just a touch biased, but then again probably not. He was definitely breath taking. She watched him on the big screen for another couple of minutes and then dragged her eyes away. He had to be here somewhere.

She was about to step around the group she was standing by, when the video caught her eye again. Jason was on the very front of the stage and obviously singing and dancing to the girls in the audience right below him. Her breath caught in her throat as she watched and the sick knot in her stomach doubled in size. She focused on inhaling, telling herself it was just the industry and that Jason was simply being what he was. An entertainer. He didn't care for those women; he was simply playing the concert game.

She hadn't half convinced herself when Jason began to make some moves that were suggestive enough that they were pushing the very edge of the acceptable envelope. Holy cats! What was he doing? Jason wasn't like that. Was he? She felt like she couldn't breath, but she couldn't look away either. Something was knocking on her brain and asking if she even knew Jason, really. From what she was seeing on that screen, she certainly didn't.

The song ended and Jason winked and kissed toward the girls below him and as the crowd went nuts, Kate tried to calm her heart rate and looked around for him one more time. There was still no sign of him, but suddenly Kate's sick stomach raised its head again and she knew she needed to make it to Cody's powder room fast. Something about what she'd been watching combined with the Mountain Dew that she didn't particularly care for anyway, and it was a deadly combination that she knew without a doubt was not going to stay down.

After she was sick, she rinsed her mouth several times, wiped her face off and then snooped in Cody's drawers until she found some mouthwash and borrowed it. For a moment or two, she leaned her forehead against the cold tile wall of the edge the shower and took deep breaths. Man, this was a random bug. Sometimes she felt fine, and sometimes she definitely didn't.

Knowing that there were tons of partying people out there who would need to use this room, she dumped her soda down the sink, discarded the can and let herself back out into the hot, loud, over crowded room. Maybe it hadn't been the soda that hadn't agreed with her. The air in here was definitely a little gamey.

She shoved the window behind her open and took several more deep breaths as she once more scanned the rooms for Jason. This time she found him. He was over near the hall sitting on the arm of Cody's couch with a Pepsi in his hand and lazy smile on his face. He didn't seem to mind the heat or the smell.

As she watched, he joked with a guy who was standing next to him and then turned to a leggy strawberry blonde who was seated on the couch on his other side. He laughed at something she said and then reached out to catch a girl with short platinum blond hair who tripped over someone on the floor as she went to walk by him. She'd almost landed in his lap and he smiled as he pushed the woman away and then brushed something she'd spilled on him off of his pant leg.

At his smile, the platinum blonde came closer and wrapped an arm around his shoulders as she laughed. Kate hoped she was apologizing and she willed her to get her hands off of her boyfriend.

To his credit, Jason continued to smile, but then very politely removed the girls arm and once again pushed her away.

Kate took a deep, stabilizing breath and then prepared to foray through the horde to reach him. She'd only raised her foot to step when another blonde girl approached Jason and offered him some little finger food from the small paper plate she had in her hand. Jason accepted with a smile and Kate felt the knot in her stomach turn over as the girl laughingly fed what him ever it was she was offering and then leaned in close to him with a sultry smile to wipe a bit of it off of his mouth.

Just as the blonde touched Jason's mouth, a man who had been standing beside Kate watching the video turned to her and gave her an appraising look up and down that under the circumstances, she hardly even noticed. He asked her something, but with the noise and her focus across the room, she didn't hear him. She absent mindedly tipped her head to him and said, "Excuse me. What was that?"

He was starting to say it again when the girl across the room fed Jason another bite and Kate made a sudden decision to leave. She didn't belong here. And apparently

Jason wasn't having the lonely night Kate had worried about.

To be polite, she tried one more time to tip her head to hear the man beside her and then instinctively smiled as Cody rounded the corner beside her with a roll of paper towel. He gave her a surprised grin. "Hey, Kate! I didn't know y'all were here. Make yourself at home." He waved the paper towel. "I gotta go, -bean dip on my couch."

He waded back into the crowd and Kate gave the man beside her a tight smile and turned for the door. She still hadn't heard what the guy was trying to tell her.

When Cody's door shut behind her, she woodenly walked to her car out on the curb. Even from there she could hear the music. It was Jason, singing her song.

On auto pilot, she climbed into her car and started it up. Country music came on and without thinking, she pressed the button on her steering wheel to turn it off. She pulled away from the curb and had driven who knew how many miles before she gave a thought to where she was going. Giving a tired sigh, she realized she had no idea where she was, not that it made much difference.

With another sigh, she ruefully thought, *not only that, but I have no idea where I'm going either. In my car, or in my life.* For that matter, she didn't even know who her best friend was. The man she'd lived beside for almost twenty years now. Well, not twenty. He'd moved to his own nearby apartment a few years ago. But his parents still lived next door, and he was just a couple blocks away.

A couple blocks and a million miles. She thought back to the way he'd been dancing on that screen tonight. Was it really as bad as it had seemed at the time? It had definitely been suggestive. Just thinking about how good he had looked made her stomach do flip flops again. Yeah, it had been over the top. Sensual as all get out, but definitely over the top.

Her thoughts went from the dancing to the way he was with the other women around him. He hadn't really done anything that bad. And he hadn't been the one making the first moves, but Kate hadn't been able to stand there and watch him literally eat out of another woman's hand. She pulled on to the freeway and flipped on her blinker to merge.

As she drove, for some reason, she began to pray out loud as if God was sitting right there in the seat beside her. She had never felt so out of her depth in her life as she voiced, "Father, I know I've made some pretty gargantuan mistakes in my life lately. And I'm so sorry. Please forgive me and help me to do better. Oh, I'm sorry; I forgot to say thanks first. I'm so grateful for… For everything, Father. I have a great life and I know it. And I've been so blessed with so many gifts. I'm truly, truly grateful. Please don't misunderstand me. But oh, man, I am so lost right now.

"You know about me and Jason. He's been my best friend for so long. Heck, he's been my life for forever. But lately, I'm bothered by so many things. In some ways, I want to run to him like when I was little, and in some ways I want to run away from him and back off from so much confusion.

"He's a good man, Heavenly Father. I know he is. And I know this man. Sometimes I can even tell what he's thinking. Sometimes I even know what he's *going to* think before he thinks it." She paused in thought and then continued, "At least I thought I knew him Heavenly Father. Sometimes lately, I'm not so sure."

Tears began to course down her cheeks as she went on, "He wants to get married, God. And I'm definitely in love with him. And I've always respected and admired him. He's so talented and strong and kind and wise and... Well, you know how he is. You made him. Anyway, he wants to get married, and I really want that too, but I'm having such huge doubts lately about some things. Actually, about nearly everything. I feel like we should wait until he's sure he's not going to regret me. But then what if he does find some flavor he likes better and leaves me? That would kill me, Heavenly Father. I can't imagine life without him."

She stubbornly wiped at the tears as she drove. "And what about the way he was dancing. Maybe I don't know him. Maybe I'm completely mixed up." She thought of the woman who had shared her food and her breath caught. "And how do I deal with... with... with everything, Father? Watching that hurt. It really did. If it's this bad now, how would I feel if that was my husband doing that? Not just my boyfriend. Am I being too picky? Is this as big a deal as it feels like it is? Oh, Father, please help me to know what to think and how to feel. I'm trying to listen. I know I probably don't even deserve you to answer me. But I really need you. Please help me organize my thoughts and know what Thou has in mind for me." She drove for a few moments and then pleaded, "Please. I'll do what I think You want me to. Just please help me figure out what that is. I know Thou knowest everything. Open my mind and give me guidance to know what to do. I want to do Thy will. I just don't know what that is right now."

She closed her prayer and continued to drive, still not even sure what direction she'd driven. It didn't matter anyway. She couldn't go back to work. What would she tell them? And she couldn't face her mom just now. Her mother would wonder why she had been crying and it hurt too much to even think about, let alone admit out loud. And she couldn't go back to Cody's. She had no idea how to act around Jason right now. She wasn't even sure what the heck their relationship was anymore. And she didn't belong there.

She wasn't the kind of girl who went to crowded, loud parties where everyone was drinking and hustling each other like that. She hadn't even gotten in the door when she could feel the Spirit cautioning her. She recognized that now. She should have listened. If she hadn't gone in there, she would still be as happy as she'd been when she'd left work, thinking she was off to see the gorgeous, talented love of her life.

Of course that was foolish and naïve. As much as she kept trying to make excuses, she had to face facts. They were on different pages here. He may have been the love of her life, but tonight he hadn't been acting like Kate was the love of his. Good men who had decent values didn't behave the way he had on that stage when they were committed to someone. They just didn't. Here in the quiet privacy of her car she could face that matter-of-factly. How she saw their relationship and how he did were definitely not in sync. It was awful to face, but it was what it was. Still, she almost wished that she was still naively unknowing. Happy and hopeful didn't hurt as much as this harsh reality.

The anxious knot that now threatened to stick in her stomach on a permanent basis left no doubt that things were very much amiss in her world. This hadn't been her imagination lately.

Her gas light came on and she absent mindedly changed lanes and took the exit to fill up. Somewhere in the back of her brain, it registered that she was just about to the Texas state line. She glanced at the time as she put the nozzle in. It was after eleven. She'd better head on home. If she got home too late, her mother would worry that she was out being a fool like she'd been the last time she was late.

She was trying to be stoic and analytical, and really look at this mess objectively, but in light of it all, the thought of how intimate they'd been that night made her heart want to shrivel up and die. She was so stupid. Stupid, and foolish, and the worlds biggest small town sucker. Here she'd been worried about getting married and having kids and then becoming a statistic. What she should have been worrying about was becoming something on an even lower level than that. A lot lower level. The proverbial cow that had been milked without ever being purchased.

On auto pilot again, she got back in the car and headed back toward Wye. She still had no answers, but life had to go on. She needed some sleep before going in to work tomorrow.

Chapter 5

Jason looked around the crowded room and then next to him to the even more crowded couch and decided he just wanted to go home. He was friendly by nature, and he didn't want to be rude, but he'd tried to back this same skinny blonde off like seven times now, and she had her hand on his thigh again. He looked around, wondering where his music folder had gotten to. That was the reason they'd come here tonight. At least supposedly.

They'd been going to play. But then they'd decided to watch the video of Friday's concert and go over it critically. Something hadn't been right there and they wanted to fix it. No one was even really sure what the problem was, but several of them had come away from the venue that night feeling less than satisfied.

He glanced around the room again. How that idea had snowballed into this rodeo he had no idea. Cody came up beside him, gave him a pointed look and whispered in his ear, "Man, if Kate sees that girl all over you she's gonna be one hot little number. You'd better watch yourself."

Jason turned to stare at him. "Kate? Kate had to work. What are you talking about?"

Cody shook his head and leaned in close. "Kate's here, Jason. At least she was about twenty-five minutes ago. Hasn't she talked to you?"

Jason shook his head, wondering what was up and Cody shrugged his shoulders and moved on into the noise. Jason began to look for Kate, but she was nowhere in the apartment. He even checked the restroom. He finally sighted his music leaning against Cody's microwave and fought his way to it and then pushed his way to the door.

He hadn't seen Kate and he couldn't imagine her being here. She hated parties like this, thank goodness. But Cody wouldn't have been mistaken. Where did she go and why hadn't she talked to him if she was here? He didn't know the answers to those questions, but just asking them made him worried. They were already on such thin ice lately. That's all he'd need would be for Kate to get the wrong impression about some loud party girl. Now he wished he'd left hours ago.

Once outside, he tried Kate's phone but it went straight to voice mail. Next he tried the restaurant, but they said she'd left more than an hour ago.

When her mom didn't know where she'd gone either, he felt the hair on the back of his neck tense. Kate had been here. Cody had seen her. But she'd left without talking to Jason and was missing in action and wouldn't answer her phone. He put his phone in his pocket with a groan, went to his car and drove around Cody's apartment complex looking for her car, and wondering what he'd been doing while she was there. In thinking about it, he couldn't think of anything he'd done that would make Kate upset, but then that's the one thing Cody had said. If Kate sees that girl all over you she'll be mad. To say he hadn't done anything and that in all honesty he hadn't even wanted to be there wasn't going to cut it. He had been there and there had been a lot of very willing females literally everywhere.

The fact that it had been the girls after him and not him after the girls wouldn't necessarily compute with Kate. And she wouldn't get mad. She knew what this life was like now that they had begun to get a big name. She wouldn't get mad. But she'd be hurt. She'd be hurt and get quiet and go off where she wouldn't bother anyone to try to deal with her feelings.

And she was a rock. She'd come back and go to work and do whatever had to be done like nothing in the world was wrong. But a little more of her tenuous trust would have been killed in the process. He blew his breath out with a rush. He didn't have any trust to spare just now. Not after what they'd been through the last couple of weeks. He tried to think about where she would have gone.

Cussing under his breath as he headed for her house, he wondered what she had been doing at Cody's. He'd thought she would be at work until late. She always was.

A couple of months ago if he was trying to figure out where she would be, he probably could have found her either at their favorite spot near the lake or on the bluff above the river. It didn't take a rocket scientist to know she wouldn't go near either one of those places now. Not after the colossal fiasco of the last night near the river. It had neatly ruined some of their favorite memories. He ran another frustrated hand through his hair. *Kate, baby, where are you?*

***

When Kate finally pulled into her parents' driveway at a quarter to two, she was surprised to find Jason sleeping on the porch swing in the dark.

When Kate had called her mom to tell her she'd be late, her mother had mentioned that he'd called earlier. And he'd tried to call her phone, but by the time she turned it back on to call home it had been too late to return his call. Not that she would have anyway.

In all honesty, she had no answers right now. She had no idea what their relationship was at this point. When he'd flown out, she could have sworn that he adored her. Even earlier this afternoon she would have argued that. But after tonight... What was in his head was just about anybody's guess. For that matter, just about anybody would have a better handle on where she stood and what she needed to do as well. She sighed. Who knew? She looked down at him, sleeping there sprawled on the swing. He was really, really gorgeous.

The one thing she did know was that she loved him. Heart and soul. Whether that was wise or whether he loved only her back, either of those points could be debated, but she loved him. Foolish or not, it was a fact. And the years they'd had together had forged an unbelievably strong friendship. Looking down at him, she knew that come what may, even come who may, Jason would always be her dearest friend and she would always be his. Nothing on this earth could change that. It had been forged in the steel of a lifetime and tempered in Kennen's death and they would always have that.

She had to admit that that didn't necessarily mean that they'd live happily ever after. Or even that they'd end up together. She would be his friend, but she had to have her self respect as well. She couldn't be a toy. A toy or an unpurchased cow. She couldn't. But even if they didn't end up together, they would still be friends.

Even as she told herself that, she knew that if indeed they didn't end up together; her world would come apart at the seams. She knew it would, and she was trying to see her way through to a happy ending, but she was so mixed up. Mixed up and just now bone tired.

Sighing, she sat down next to him on the edge of the swing. Going past him to go in and go to bed without talking to him was beyond her. She owed him better than that, even if she didn't have any idea what to say to him. He was too good a man to play head games with.

She put a hand gently on his cheek and then began to run her fingers through his hair and it wasn't but just a few seconds until he opened his sleepy, emerald green eyes. As soon as he did, his face lit up in a tired smile that did her heart good. There could have been no faking it. He was glad to see her.

He reached up to take her hand, where it had stilled in his hair. "Hey, Kate. I've been looking for you. Cody said you were at his house, but I couldn't find you. Where have y'all been?" He blinked and tried to see his watch in the porch light.

She didn't say anything, and he blinked again and looked up at her in surprise. "Kate! It's almost two in the morning! What are you doing out so late?"

She shrugged and looked away, not sure what to tell him. She couldn't admit seeing him at Cody's and feeling so hurt and confused. It was too revealing. Made her feel too vulnerable. She settled for, "I decided to go for a drive and talk to an old friend of mine. What are you doing sleeping on Mom's porch swing?"

He sat up and rubbed his eyes and then looked at her in confusion. "Wait. Start again. You've been where?"

Smiling sadly, she admitted, "To Texas. To talk to God. What are you doing here?"

Still confused, he looked at her warily. "Why did you come to Cody's but not come talk to me."

She shrugged again and sat back so she didn't have to face him. "Aah, it was too loud at Cody's and didn't smell so good, so I left. I'm not really one for that kind of party. You know that." She put a foot down and moved the swing, knowing he was still staring at her.

"Didn't smell so good. I see. So you left without speaking to me. No. I don't see. Kate, it's me, Jason. Talk to me. What's going on?"

"Nothing's going on, Jase. I got off work and went to find you, but you looked like you were already busy and I hate those kind of things. You know that. So I took a drive to clear my head."

He turned to study her. "You're hedging. You can't fool me, Kate." She didn't reply to that and he finally asked, "Did it work?"

It was a strange question and she looked up in confusion and asked, "Did what work?"

"Did it work? Is your head clear?"

She rolled her eyes and said lightly, "Oh, yeah. I'm all clear. Clear as the blue sky. And you?"

He leaned back and pushed a hand through his tousled hair. "I'm worried as hell."

"Hmm." Her tone of voice was light again. "Anything I can do to help?"

"Yeah, Kate. Y'all can tell me what you've done with my best friend and help me figure out why you get more and more distant from me by the day. What's going on, Kate? What's with keeping things from me? That's not us. That's not like you. Clue me in here." He sounded incredibly bitter and discouraged and her heart went out to him.

"I'd tell you if I knew what was going on, Jason. I feel the same way. Sometimes lately I don't even know you."

He turned to look into her face. "What's not to know, Kate? It's just me. The same old Jason as the day you were born. How can you not know me? You know me better than I know myself."

She pushed the swing again and said quietly, "I used to think that." She hesitated, wondering how much she dared say and finally decided to just deal with it. She had nothing to lose. Or everything. She went on in a sad tone of voice, "Honestly, I didn't know who that man dancing on that screen was tonight, Jason. I didn't know who that man was with those people at Cody's house."

Turning to her, he almost demanded, "What did I do that was so bad? So unJason?"

Glancing at him, she decided that maybe she wouldn't just deal with it. She stood up. "You know, Jason. I'm tired. It's been a long day. I'm not going to sit here and argue. That's not us. I never accused you of doing something bad. I'm not your judge. I'm just Kate. All I said was that I didn't know you. Do you think we could finish this discussion tomorrow?"

He stood up as well and reached out and rubbed a thumb across her cheek and said gently, "I'm sorry, Kate. I'm sorry I snapped. I just hate knowing I've disappointed you."

"I never said you disappointed me. I just said I didn't know you."

"You didn't have to say it, Kate. Y'all may not know me, but I know you to the bone. At least sometimes I do. You were disappointed. I'll go home and watch the concert and see if I can figure out what was so bad.

Although I think I already know what the problem was. And I'm sorry I did something to hurt you at Cody's. At his house I don't have any idea what the problem was, but hurting you wasn't intentional, I promise."

"I know Jason. I don't believe you would ever hurt me on purpose. Me or anyone. You are a kind, good man. Maybe it wasn't you." She shrugged one shoulder. "Maybe it was just the smell. Let's don't worry about it tonight, huh?"

He grimaced in confusion. "What about the smell? What's up with you about the smell? I've never noticed Cody's house smells."

"You're missing the point, Jason. I'm just trying to not offend you. Look. What you do at Cody's, or in a concert, or anywhere is your deal, Jason. It's not my place to judge or even comment. I'm sorry I said anything. I shouldn't have. Please forgive me and let's move on. We're both tired."

Shaking his head, he reached and touched her cheek and said quietly, "What you're not addressing Kate, is that of all the people in the world, the only one who I truly want to like my work is you."

She came close and looked up at him. "Then you don't have to worry, Jase. Because I certainly love your work. You're the most gifted man I've ever known. You're inspiring and evocative and sexy and you're a master at taking your audience anywhere you want to go. You're a magician on that stage. You melt me. You always have and always will."

He searched her gaze and whispered, "Then, baby, what was the problem?"

Kate hesitated at that and finally returned his intense look with a soft spoken, "Well, Jason, maybe you just need to be really careful about who you're taking where. One of your gifts is phenomenal sensuality. It's incredibly powerful. But it's also like a scalpel. Life giving in the right time and place, and lethal other wise."

For several long moments he just looked down at her as he considered what she'd said. Finally, his face broke into a grin and he shook his head. "You always say that I'm eloquent. And I may be at times. But nobody in the world can hold a candle to your way with words, Kate." He pulled her tightly into a hug with a low chuckle. "Tonight might just be the highpoint in my entire adult life." He chuckled again. "You just told me my phenomenal sensuality can be lethal. I couldn't top those lyrics in a million years!"

"You knew what I meant, Jason."

"I don't know, Kate. I think I did. I hope I did. I'm coming to get you in the morning. I need to be with you and I'm not taking no for an answer. We have to get a handle on us. We have to. This weird tension lately is killing me. Whatever it takes, I'm going to find it and fix it, because you matter too much to me, Kate. If I have to quit singing completely to take that shadow out of your eyes, then I will. You matter ten million times more to me than a stupid band. Let alone some loud, smelly party." He grinned again. "What time should I come? Eight? Nine? How 'bout nine?"

Kate glanced at her watch and groaned. "Nine is perfect. But Jason. Please don't ever threaten to quit because of me. I would never forgive myself. You were born to perform."

His smile dampened right down and he looked at her intensely. "Do you really believe that, Kate?"

"Of course, Jason Falcon. I absolutely do."

"Kate, do you know I have always trusted your judgment? Even when you were little? You were always so astute about everything."

Her face fell as she attempted to admit to him, "Be careful, Jason. Not that I don't think you're supposed to keep performing, because I absolutely do. But don't trust my judgment about other things right now. I'm so mixed up. Whatever channel I'm usually tuned to to hear God's instructions to me, is completely jammed right now. I think my whole satellite tower came down in an earthquake or something. I'll be the first to admit to not having a clue what He's trying to tell me."

Jason leaned down and gently put his cheek to hers. "He's trying to tell you to hang with a certain brown haired, green eyed country singer, Katie Ree. God knows that we're meant to be together forever. After all, He's the one who made us. Don't let Him down. He's wise and you can trust that He's all knowing and omnipotent."

"It's not his omnipotence I'm worried about Jason. It's my inomnipotence."

At that, he kissed her soundly and then reluctantly stepped back away from her and teased, "That's not a word, Kate. I'm almost positive of it. In most cases, making up words is cheating in eloquence. However, since tonight y'all got the all time highest point earning quip known to man, I'll let you get away with it. Just this once. I have to go now so I can rest up for my date at nine o'clock in the morning. I'm going to brush up on my power sleeping. You'd be wise to do the same. I plan to thoroughly enjoy you in the morning." He paused as if realizing that sounded a bit questionable. "I mean, in a good way, I promise."

Kate smiled tiredly. "I know, Jason. See you in the morning."

Kristin Cross

Chapter 6

Nine o'clock didn't turn out to be the optimal time after all. Kate's flu bug had come back and she felt lousy, but she wanted to see Jason enough that she got up and got ready to go anyway. She gagged brushing her teeth again, but she made it through without worshipping the toilet and then went and dug through her mother's medical box to see if she had anything for nausea.

She didn't find anything, but oh well. The way this bug had been she'd probably feel fine again in half an hour anyway.

When Jason showed up on the crack of nine, he looked good. Really good. Good enough that Kate could have eaten him right up in spite of her roiling tummy. She walked beside him to the car holding his hand thinking that no man on the planet could wear a pair of jeans like he could.

He took her to breakfast at a tiny French pastry shop in Oklahoma City that was so small and private it felt like the chef's home and they ate a leisurely, comfortable meal that left her wondering why they were struggling right now at all. At times like this, when she had the Jason back who she knew inside and out, she couldn't see that any issue would be insurmountable. Jason was still the good, honorable, sweet man he'd always been. They could work through this whole fame thing. Of course they could.

After breakfast, they window shopped hand in hand down the side walk and from time to time went inside to poke around and buy something. Only once did someone notice Jason and say something to them and by the time he loaded her back into his black Corvette to take her home so she could go in to work, her flu was forgotten and he'd worked a miracle on the anxious knot in her stomach. It was all but gone.

That evening, she didn't wonder about where he was for a second, because he spent a good portion of it sitting in the chair across from her desk leafing through car brochures while she worked and came in and out. He went home during the dinner rush but then was back at her mom's house sitting on the porch step when she drove in at a little after ten.

He got up as she climbed out of her car and once again, he looked every bit as good as he had that morning. It was no wonder he was becoming a star. He was smokin' hot and had an incredibly sensuous way of approaching her. He gathered her to him in a sweet, tight hug and his aftershave made her tired body nearly melt as he held her. Yeah, today, he was definitely her old, adorable Jason.

***

Jason knew Kate was aware he had to leave Friday morning for a gig that night in Fort Worth, because she had been the one to make all of the arrangements, but they weren't talking about it. Not at all. Not either one of them.

He'd been with her every spare moment all week and had just about come to the conclusion that if he could just help her to see him the way she always had, even if he did make it big in the music world, she'd be able to deal with all of this a little better.

Scheduling everything else around her had disgusted the other members of the band some because most of them wanted to sleep all morning and hang out all night, but it was his band. His and Cody's, who was definitely on board with keeping Kate happy. And frankly, Jason didn't give a rip about pleasing anyone else but Kate anyway.

He wasn't sure why he felt like it, but for some reason, he knew that things going well between the two of them right now was hyper important. He would have never believed it before, but for the first time in his adult life, he worried about Kate leaving him. When he thought about it, that seemed so ridiculous, but when he didn't think about it… When he just felt about it, it scared him to the soles of his Justin boots. He couldn't even imagine coping with losing Kate. It was unthinkable. Unthinkable, but for some reason lately, a possibility that left him sick just at the thought.

The band had been invited to open for Tim McGraw several times and its popularity had grown astronomically in the last couple of months. Kate had been instrumental in orchestrating all of that, but the resulting "glitz" had her reeling and he knew it, even if she didn't seem to be able to face it openly. He didn't think she was afraid of the money, or the fame, or the crowds, or the travel, or the groupies, or anything alone. But put all of them together and it intimidated the daylights out of her.

It would probably be better if she would agree to travel with them. At some point she'd become hardened to a lot of it just like he and the guys had. But she hardly ever came with them anymore. Almost to the point that it offended him, in fact. Even when the gigs were relatively close and in a venue that she could get into legally, she was hesitant to come lately for some reason. If he didn't know that she loved nothing more than for him to play and sing for her, he would have wondered what to think about her growing aversion to his concerts.

She loved to come and watch them practice. It didn't matter how many times they went over things or worked through certain sections and moves. She loved watching them and made no bones about it. That made her funny worries seem all the more silly. But she felt what she felt and he had to deal with it as well as he could because nothing was more important to him than her happiness.

Cody was the same. Probably for different reasons. Cody wanted Kate happy because Cody wanted Jason happy and they went hand in hand. Not only that, but Cody knew just what Kate had done for the band on the business end of things and he was protecting her as the asset she was and the treasure she was. The others might not have realized it, but a lot of things would come to a screeching halt for them professionally if Kate wasn't working her miracles on the office end.

Kate had actually become a small problem for the band in one way. Ryan the piano player had begun to be irritatingly enamored with her and if he didn't straighten up and quick, Jason was going to fire his butt out of here, whether he was a gifted keyboardist or not. Even now, thinking about it as he waited for her to get off work again on the night before they had to pull out, it ticked him off. Who did the guy think he was, anyway? Jason rolled down his car window on this sultry, Oklahoma night to cool off. The idea of another man hustling Kate made him positively hot under the collar, literally.

At nearly ten she finally emerged from the back door of the restaurant and Jason got out and came around to open her door for her. She ignored the open door and came to him and wrapped her arms around him tightly and he breathed in the scent of her hair as he held her back. Man, she just exactly fit against him. Hugging her like this was his all time best thing. That hug lasted and he knew again that even though she wasn't talking about it, she was thinking about him having to leave in the morning.

When she finally pulled back, she looked up at him there in the dimly lit parking lot and he leaned down to kiss her. He'd just been going to give her a quick kiss, but there was some intensity about her tonight that turned it into several moments of kissing each other almost desperately. At length, he let her mouth free with a low groan and buried his face in her sweet smelling, soft, dark curls. Leaving her tomorrow was going to be awful again.

Friday morning, he stopped by her house to talk to her before going to meet the others. The band was driving this time and he wanted to be able to tell her goodbye without anyone else watching. It was only eight o'clock in the morning and she didn't look so good when she opened the door to him. All week long she'd worried about kissing him and giving him her bug, but after he kept insisting that he'd rather be sick than unkissed she'd finally let it rest and gone back to her old sweet habit of being marvelously affectionate.

He stepped inside and laughed at her, although even looking a little green around the gills and with dark circles, she still looked sexy as all get out, sleepy and tousled as she was. There was something about her when she was like this that made him want to about eat her up. He would have too, if she hadn't felt so lousy.

Ruffling her hair, he laughed once more. "Not feeling so hot again, babe?"

She shook her head with a guilty smile. "Sorry. I'll kick this thing while you're gone. I'm sure of it."

He came close and gently kissed her and teased huskily, "You may not feel so hot, but you look hotter than a pistol. I'm thinking I should stay in town and kiss you until you're all better. Or at least until you forget you don't feel well."

She smiled again and snuggled up to his chest and he led her inside to the couch and pulled her onto his lap. "Lean on me and maybe you'll feel less queasy." As she laid her head against his chest with a sigh, he wished he could stay and hold her until she was a hundred percent. It was heavenly to hold her and it was so not like her not to be energetic and busy.

They sat like that, silently, neither of them willing to talk about him going. Finally, he sighed and she turned her face to him and he kissed her as gently as if she was glass. "I love you, Kate. I'll miss you. Think about me this week end?"

She touched his mouth with a soft fingertip and whispered, "You know I will. Be safe."

"You too."

She nodded and as she moved to sit up, he gently pushed her off and stood up and took her hand as they walked to the door. Standing in front of it, he wrapped her tightly in a hug and kissed her passionately and then reluctantly pulled away. "I have to go."

"I know." She pushed on him and he leaned and kissed her one more time fiercely.

"I'll come back to you, Kate."

She nodded, blinking back bright tears. "Go. Before I cry and depress you." She smiled and pushed on him again.

He stood looking down at her, trying to memorize her face for this long week end. He gave her one more fast kiss and then went out the door. Man, he wished she would come with. It was getting harder and harder to leave her.

When he was gone, Kate pushed the hair off of her forehead and rubbed it with the back of her hand. She wished she hadn't looked so awful this morning, but she honestly hadn't felt up to dolling up. She glanced at her watch and went and climbed back into bed. This morning even her chest was sore.

She turned onto her tummy and then rolled onto her back. Her chest was too sore right now to sleep on. She was so sick of feeling sick. This thing was hanging on forever. It had been almost a week and a half. The stomach flu never lasted that long, did it? She lifted her head and pulled her curls up off of her neck. Just as long as she felt better by the time Jason got home on Sunday night. She wanted to look and feel better by then. He only had two days before he had to leave again and she wanted to make the most of them.

Kristin Cross

Chapter 7

On Sunday morning, when she woke up in the wee hours before it was light out, still horrendously nauseated and without a sign of a period yet, she got up and went to her purse and took our her little day planner. The persistent, frightening thought that had been bothering her for days now could no longer be ignored. Something was dreadfully wrong with her and she had an incredibly sobering suspicion that it wasn't really the flu.

Counting the days since her last period, her heart began to nearly pound itself out of her chest when she confirmed that her period was thirteen days later than usual. She looked down at her breasts that were stretching the lycra of her cammy more than they ever had and gingerly touched the cleavage that was painfully full for some reason. She put a hand on her pretty, flat belly and felt that now familiar rock of anxiousness turn into a full fledged boulder. She couldn't be. Could she? Glancing back to her planner, she calculated what night it was that she and Jason had messed up so badly. It had been exactly

103

four weeks and one day ago. She sank down onto her bed in absolute shock. Oh, what had they done? What on earth had they done?

Two hours later, as she heard her mother beginning to stir, she quietly let herself out the back door and got into her car. She couldn't face her parents. Not yet. And she needed to do an errand anyway.

She drove all the way into the suburbs of Purcell before stopping at a large market for one of those early home pregnancy test kits. Embarrassed to be buying only it, she added some fruit and bread to her basket and then went to the check out, her heart still in her throat because of her suspicions.

Back in her car, she decided she wasn't going to wait until she got home and stopped at a gas station. While she filled her tank, she slipped into the rest room and used the tiny boxed kit that held her very life in its small wand. The few minutes it took felt like an eternity and she waited inside the restroom stall trying to breathe evenly with a million thoughts going through her head.

With the appearance of that one, small word pregnant across the wand she felt the blood drain from her head and wondered if she was going to be sick again. That revelation stopped every thought in its tracks and she sat down on the toilet seat and leaned her head on the metal stall wall beside her, fearing she was going to pass out. She'd suspected this, but the confirmation of her fears was almost too much to wrap her brain around. A baby! Oh, what had they done?

Knowing the tears were coming, she stuffed the box back into her purse and hurried from the restroom. Nearly colliding with a woman in the aisle back to the entrance to the convenience store, she slowed and as she went to walk around her, the woman reached out a hand to Kate and asked, "Are you okay, miss? Y'all don't look so good. You're really pale."

Kate nodded woodenly, said, "I'm fine, thanks," and walked on out.

Once safely in her car she wanted to scream. Fine? She wasn't fine! She was pregnant! Her. Katelyn Marie Birch was expecting a baby. She started the car up and pulled it to a parking space at the edge of the lot and turned it back off. Pregnant.

The tears finally came with a rush and she leaned her head over her steering wheel, so overwhelmed she wondered if she could breathe. Pregnant. Feeling the tears drip onto her pants, she whispered, "Oh, Jason, what have we done?"

While the tears streamed, emotions washed over her and thought after thought raged through her head until she thought it would explode. She was horrified, and then she felt guilty for not being happy for this baby's sake and then she felt wonder that there was a child inside her very body and then guilt again for how it had gotten there. She dreaded having to tell Jason. Actually, she dreaded having to tell anyone and wondered how in the world she'd face anyone she ever knew again.

The endless gamut went on until the tears finally slowed, her heart settled back to its usual pace and she was left with just what she'd started this trip with. A splitting headache, miserable nausea and her old friend, that tense, sickening anxious rock in her stomach.

She got out of the car and took the box with its tiny earth shaking word pregnant and threw it in the garbage in front of the station and got back into the car with a heavy heart. She reached for her key with a sigh. *Oh, Jason. What have we gotten ourselves into this time?*

As she headed back toward Wye she changed her mind and turned south. She knew she still wasn't ready to face her mom, and church was so far out of the question it was almost ludicrous. She picked up her phone and dialed home. Her mom would still know something wasn't right, but at least she wouldn't worry and Kate could have some time to think this through better and finally let it soak in so she could figure out what she needed to do about it. It looked like another trip to Texas and one of those long talks with God.

She was still a basket case at noon when she hit the state line, minimally better at two when she turned back north and at four, even knowing that Jason was home and probably wondering where she was didn't make her feel like she could face anyone yet. Finally, at a little after seven thirty, she turned her phone back on. She needed to talk to Jason.

Jason walked back to his car after talking to Kate's mom in shock. Kate wasn't here. Hadn't been here all day. This was the first time in his life he'd come home from anywhere and Kate wasn't there waiting. He got into his car and sat there, wondering what to do. Kate wasn't here. He couldn't even believe it. Why wouldn't she be here? What had rocked her world to the point that she wasn't here? That had never happened. Never.

When he'd left two days ago, they'd been tight. He really thought they had. What had happened to change that? Something had to have happened or she would never have missed being here. It was too important to both of them. He knew it and she did too.

He drove to his apartment with a heavy, heavy heart. *Baby, where are you this time?*

He pulled in and got his bag out of the passenger seat and dragged into his house. Well, at least he could take a decent nap. He'd finally come down with Kate's bug and he felt awful. Tossing the bag onto the floor beside his bed, he went back into the kitchen and popped two Tylenol. As sick as his stomach was, he didn't think he could keep anything else down.

Between thinking about Kate and having to hurl, he had only just barely gotten to sleep when she called, but he didn't care. When she said she wanted to come see him, he agreed instantly, wondering what kind of mood she'd be in when she got here. She didn't sound mad or even sad on the phone. He didn't know what she sounded. He was just glad she'd called. He'd already thrown up four times this afternoon and felt positively horrible. He had to hand it to Kate. If she'd been feeling this rough, she hadn't whined much.

**

Jason didn't answer his door and she let herself in to find him just about staggering out of the bathroom wearing cut off sweat pants and an ashen face. He looked about the same as she did and for just a second, she wondered if he somehow already knew about the baby. She approached him hesitantly and finally asked, "You okay?"

. He shook his head and groaned as he collapsed onto his couch with a sigh. "No. I finally got your bug and I feel awful. I'm being ten times more whiney than you ever were. Where have you been?"

She came and knelt by the couch beside him, thinking, *yeah, you definitely caught the same bug I have. If you only knew.*

He'd know soon enough. Granted she could figure out a way to break something this shocking to him. Instead, she gave him a sad smile and said, "Texas again. I needed another long talk with God. How long have you been sick?" He looked like he had something more like food poisoning than morning sickness.

He looked positively wary as he asked, "Your head need clearing again?"

"Yeah." She laughed and it felt wonderful. That had to be the understatement of the millennium.

Still wary, he hesitantly asked, "Was it something I did again?"

She laughed again and then wondered if she was losing it, while he watched her with worried eyes. This understatement topped the last one. "Yeah, it was definitely something you did. I'm not mad or sad or whatever it is you're paranoid about Jason. You can relax and just enjoy being ill. I'm not going to bite you."

He watched her for another minute and then closed his eyes. "Oh, good. What did I do? When you weren't here I thought you must have been really upset about something and I thought I was in a lot of trouble."

She started to laugh again and it grew on her and she ended up totally busting up. She was definitely losing it. It was the biggest understatement of all, but it was absolutely not funny. Jason was watching her and she knew she was going to burst into tears and literally bit her lip to keep from totally dissolving right there in front of him. The only thing that saved her was that he had to get up and go throw up again. She felt terrible for him, but had never been so grateful for an interruption.

By the time he was back, she had a thin shell of poise over her emotions and knew her feelings were far too raw to try to talk to Jason about this right now. She'd come here intending to, but there was just no way.

He threw up two more times before finally drifting off on his couch, and she got up, covered him with a light blanket and let herself out. It was better this way. She needed to have whatever she was going to say to him better rehearsed in her mind anyway.

Jason was terribly ill that day and most of the next and although she checked on him and spent several hours with him, she still hadn't said anything to him by the time he and the rest of the band left on Tuesday for a five day road trip. At least he had finally started to feel better that morning before he left.

She'd told him she wasn't going to bite him, but he'd still watched her for those couple days as if wondering when she was going to blow. Even as he was kissing her goodbye, he was still more than a bit wary and Kate felt bad for not being able to put his mind more at ease. Not that telling him he was going to be a father would put his mind at ease, but at least he'd know why she had gone to Texas.

Her mother had been watching her with that same quiet worry on her face and that next morning Kate sat down next to her at the breakfast table and between sips of orange juice, said, "Mom, there's something I need to tell you."

Her mother almost looked relieved and Kate felt terrible. What she was going to tell her was going to be a horrible blow to this good, Christian woman and Kate dreaded even saying it, but it had to be done. "I'm a... I'm... What I'm trying to say is, I'm uh, sort of going to have a baby."

Expecting tears, or even an outburst, Kate was totally taken aback as her mother said evenly, "I know, Kate. I was wondering when you'd figure it out. I assume that was what happened on Sunday."

Kate just stared at her open mouthed. "You knew? What do you mean you knew? How could you have known? I didn't even know."

So blandly it was infuriating, her mother replied, "I know you pretty well, Kate. I worried about it from the very first. Then when you didn't clue in to what was happening to your body, I worried about how you'd react to figuring it out. I'm glad you're dealing with it. What did Jason say?"

Kate looked at her plate. "I haven't told him yet. He was so sick. And honestly, I don't have a clue how to tell him. How do you tell someone something like this?"

Finally tearing up, her mom shook her head. "We just do the best we can, Kate. That's what we do in all of life. That's what you'll do with this baby. You'll just do the best you can. How are you feeling this morning?"

"Fine. Go figure. I can't seem to see a pattern for why sometimes I'm sick as a dog and sometimes I'm perfect. Is there a trick to this?"

"If there is, I never found it when I was expecting you and Kiersten."

Kate looked at her over the rim of her cup. "You were sick like this too?"

Her mother shrugged and gave her a sad smile. "Sometimes. No rhyme or reason. It just came and went."

There were a million things Kate wanted to ask, but in a way, she just wanted to eat breakfast as usual and pretend like nothing had recently turned her world on its end. She opted for the latter until they were through eating and then she picked up her dishes and said with a sigh, "Wish me luck. I have to go tell Daddy. I'd honestly rather be horse whipped, but here goes."

Still mildly, her mother said, "He already knows, Kate. But still go talk to him. He needs you to and it'll be better to get it over with and out in the open."

"Does Kiersten know as well?"

"No. That one you're going to have to tackle on your own."

Kate nodded, not sure whether she was glad Kiersten didn't know or not. She walked back over to her mom and wrapped her arms around her. "Thanks for not freaking out, Mom. I'm sorry I messed up my life like this. You raised me better and I'm so sorry."

Her mother patted her back. "Life happens, Kate. I'm sorry too, but at least you're not fifteen. Let's just try to make the best of what started poorly. And being a mother is the best thing I ever did in my life. Hopefully it'll be the same for you."

Kate met her eyes as tears filled her own. "Thanks, Mom. I guess in the emotional maelstrom of this, I've forgotten that having children with Jason is something I've dreamed of being able to do for years. It's just a shame this isn't the happy occasion I'd hoped it would be someday."

Kristin Cross

"It will be eventually. You'll see. Do you think you'll marry him now?"

That was a question Kate had asked herself a thousand times and hadn't come up with an answer yet. Haltingly she replied, "I suppose. It seems more backwards than ever as far as worrying about Jason having regrets, but now everything hinges on what's best for the innocent baby who didn't choose to have any of this happen to him or her or whatever it will be. And right now, I can't seem to figure out what to wear to work, let alone deep, life altering questions."

Her mom smiled a minimal smile. "It's only been a couple of days, Kate. Give it some time and it'll come."

Chapter 8

It had been eight days by the time Jason and the band arrived back in town on Sunday afternoon and Kate still didn't have a clue about what she was going to do. Even though she usually couldn't wait to see him when he got home, this time she almost dreaded it, knowing she had to rock his world like she would.

When the van pulled into the parking lot of his complex, she was waiting for them, but she was saved from him knowing she was so uptight because he was too. Tensions were high in the Aerie neck of the woods. Jason and Cody and the others got out without even glancing at Kate and as Ryan, their keyboardist began to stalk toward his car, Jason called him back.

He and Jason and Cody had a very quiet, but very tense short discussion that ended with Ryan almost stomping away and then turning to flip Jason and Cody off before continuing on to his car. Kate stood looking from one to the other, wondering what was up with this. Cody looked at her and smiled and shrugged and got back in the van with the last couple of guys and it headed out. Finally, Jason turned to her, still obviously tense and wrapped her in a tight hug. "Hi, Kate. Man, I'm glad to be home. How've you been?"

How to answer that? Thunderstruck? Completely overwrought? Scared as hell? She settled for, "Fine.", hoping he couldn't tell she was being less than honest as upset as he was. "Rough trip?"

He pulled away and shouldered his bag and began to walk toward his door. "No. The trip was fine. Concerts were great. We've just been having some trouble with Ryan. He keeps forgetting that Cody and I own this band. We finally just booted him, but it's been coming for a while. He's done a couple of things that were uh, lets just say inappropriate." With his door unlocked, he pushed it open and then finally turned to her and kissed her and asked, "You okay? You sick again?"

She turned away and went inside as she said, "No, I'm fine. I'm just tired. Have you eaten? Mom invited you to dinner."

He shook his head. "No, we didn't eat, but I'm not up to visiting just now. You go on without me."

Kate felt like she'd been slapped, but he didn't notice. Just walked toward his bedroom, set his bag inside and then went and began digging through his fridge.

Hurt and unsure of how to take him, she obediently walked across his living room to his door. "I guess I'll see you later then."

From inside the refrigerator, he mumbled something and she narrowed her eyes wondering what was up with him as she walked back out of the apartment she'd only walked into two minutes before, her eyes smarting from tears she was trying to force herself not to cry. At least since taking that awful pregnancy test, she knew why she was an emotional lunatic.

Apparently she wasn't going to be telling Jason about the baby tonight anyway.

She was half way home when her phone rang, and she pulled over to answer it. It was Jason and she wondered what he wanted now as she said, "Hey, Jason."

"Kate, why did you leave?"

"Jason, you told me to. Remember?"

She could hear him sigh on the other end of the line. "If I did, I didn't mean to. I thought we were going to do something. Hang out."

Evenly, she said, "We can do whatever you want, Jason. Just decide."

There was a long pause and then he said, "Maybe it's just as well. I'm in a foul mood anyway. Go have dinner with your parents and we'll get together tomorrow sometime."

Now Kate felt like she'd been slapped twice and finally said into the phone, "Okay. Whatever. Get some rest. Maybe you'll feel better tomorrow. Take care."

"Take care? Not love you? What's wrong, Kate? Are you mad at me?"

Kate rolled her eyes. "No, Jason. I'm not mad at you. Just a touch afraid of you. I do love you and can't wait to see you tomorrow. Have you done something I should be mad at you about?"

She finally heard a smile in his voice. "Probably, I'm a terrible person sometimes, but I can't think of anything right off hand. What time do you work tomorrow?"

"I go in at two."

"Good. Can I have you at nine or ten in the morning?"

"Sure. See you then. And Jason?"

"Yeah."

"Straighten up. I hate it when I have to be mad at you."

"Yes ma'am."

"Love you."

"I love you too, Kate."

Kate had been joking with Jason about being mad at him, but that night while she was flipping through the channels, she happened on to one of those celebrity shows. She was only half paying attention while she folded clothes when she heard Jason's name. Looking up in surprise, she was amazed to see a story about Jason and some nearly six foot tall super model. He was holding the door for her as she entered a swanky Chicago hotel.

Kate was so shocked, she almost didn't think to read the credits to find more information on the stories they had been highlighting that night. They listed a website and she got up and went in and booted up her lap top, all the time telling herself to keep an open mind. The story was, in and of itself, minimal, they were in effect trying to surmise if Jason Falcon, "the consummate up and coming bachelor" did have a thing going with the model. But there were more photos of Jason and other women. Lots of them. In lots of different situations. Most of them were the same type as the one of the super model. Him opening a door or standing by someone, but a couple were of Jason seated at a table with a woman or even with his arm around them.

Kate thought back to the other day when she'd seen Jason at that party letting that other woman feed him. Were these all that same sort of deal? Happenstance photo opportunities where he used poor judgment? Or was Jason playing the "consummate bachelor" when he was on the road and away from her? And how was she to know if he was? Was stuff like this the reason he'd been so lackadaisical this afternoon. Her head was spinning again with what she was seeing on the screen in front of her.

After spending several minutes wondering what was going on and feeling as if her heart was being squeezed into pieces, she finally plugged into her printer and hit the print button and then went to get her purse. She was going to see Cody. She knew he was loyal to Jason to the death, but she also knew he'd be as honest with her as he could if she asked him.

She was a bit embarrassed to find Cody shirtless with a girl sitting on his couch when he opened the door, but she pressed on anyway. "Hey, Cody."

"Kate." He looked out the door and all around. "Where's Jase?"

"He uh, he wasn't in the mood to do anything tonight. He's at his house. Could I talk to you for a minute? In private?"

He looked at her and glanced to the papers in her hand and then stepped out the door of his apartment onto the step outside and closed his door. "What's up? What's going on?"

"That's what I need you to tell me, Cody. I was watching TV today as I folded my laundry. This show came on and did a blurb about Jason and some super model. I went to the show's website and found these. Is there something I should know about Jason, Cody? Be honest."

He hesitated and she could practically see him squirm and it killed her. She watched for a second and figured he wasn't going to say anything and honestly, he didn't really need to after all. "Never mind, Cody. I didn't mean to put you on the spot. Sorry to bother you." She turned to go and he caught her arm.

"No. Kate. Don't go. Don't assume things, Kate. Jason loves you dearly."

She looked up into his eyes and he met hers without hesitation. "Then what's going on, Cody?"

"Jason does love you, Kate. And he's faithful to you, I swear. But he can't avoid every girl, especially when y'all don't ever go with us. A couple of times he's had to take someone to dinner or something when it's official band business, but that's all. I swear. He doesn't fool around. Ever." She looked up into his eyes one more time and he continued, "I'm being honest, Kate. About the worst you have to worry about is just how Jason was at that party at my house the other day. He isn't rude to the girls who come onto him, but he's not a player. No way. You know him. He's still the designated driver when we party when we're on the road. He never gets plastered and fools around the way some of us do."

At that, he tried to smile at her. "He's a hundred times more respectable than me. Maybe a thousand. I'm sure that's why he gets so much more press. They see him as the ultimate conquest."

"That's very reassuring, Cody."

"Anything to help. Let me see the pictures." He thumbed through them quickly and handed her back one of Jason seated with a woman. "That one I was there for. She's a newscaster at some TV station in San Francisco. We had lunch with them after doing a segment on their noon news. It wasn't any kind of a date. And I believe this one is cropped from a larger photo of us and another girl band that opened for Kenny Chesney one time. I don't recognize any of the others. Sorry. But, I'm telling you, Kate. Jason is whipped. He practically worships you. Now more than ever. He'd marry you in a minute if you'd do it. You know that. I know he's asked you like a dozen times."

That was true, but it didn't make her any more anxious to be made a fool of when Jason was away from her. She took the photos back. "Thanks, Cody. I'm sorry I bothered you, but sometimes I just need to know. To be reassured."

He squeezed her shoulder. "I absolutely understand. But he's your love slave, I'm telling you. Trust him. He deserves it. He's not perfect, but there isn't a better man on the planet."

"Thanks, Cody."

"You're welcome. And to tell you the truth, I wish you'd hurry and marry him so he could quit worrying about it."

"You are the last person to lecture me about getting married, Cody Rawlings."

"Man, have you got a point there. Take care, Kate."

"See ya."

Kate drove home in a quandary. Cody had tried to reassure her, and in a way he had. He'd said that Jason loved her. But then Kate knew that. What she didn't know was how Jason was dealing with the other women he came in contact with. Cody had said the worst she needed to worry about was the way Jason had been at that party the other night. He'd meant it to make her feel better, but that party had troubled her deeply.

She was almost more mixed up when she got home than when she'd left and she went back into her part of the house to her computer and Googled Jason Falcon and then the band Aerie. She'd been at it for more than an hour when her mom came in. "What are you up to Katie?

We haven't heard a peep out of you since dinner." She came up behind Kate and looked at the screen over her shoulder and after a second said, "Oh my."

Those two syllables were all Kate needed to hear to know the pain in her heart wasn't unfounded. There were literally hundreds of photos of Jason on the web. Most of them were just great pictures of a truly gorgeous singer. But there were some that were awful. Jason dancing like he had been on stage the other day. Or Jason posing with various people, usually lone females. There were several of him with the girls right on his lap and a lot more of him with his arm- or arms, around them. A few even had him kissing girls who were lined up to greet them along the stage or roped off walkways.

After letting her mother see what she'd been finding, she printed a couple of the most incriminating and then got up from the desk and picked up her keys. "I'm going for a drive, Mom. I might be late, don't wait up. I may have to drive all the way to Texas again." She gave her mother a heartbroken smile and let herself out the back door.

***

Cody sent his female friend home early. Ever since Kate had been here, his mind had been elsewhere anyway. He paced and fretted for close to an hour and then went and got into his Jeep and cruised up to Jason's.

Jason met him at the door in surprise. "Cody! Hey, I thought you'd be entertaining someone on this first night back in town."

Cody walked in the door and tossed his keys and headed for Jason's fridge. "I was. I sent her home. Can I eat some of this pizza?"

"Knock yourself out. What'd she do to get sent home?"

Cody turned full to Jason and said, "Kate came over."

Jason was confused as Cody walked over to the microwave. "You lost me. What about Kate? Or was your girl's name Kate? What?"

Cody pushed start on the microwave and turned back to Jason. "My girl's name was Meridith. No, maybe it was Meridee. Something. Anyway, that's not the point. Your girl, Kate, came to my house while Meridith was there."

"Okay... What did she want? Was she ticked at me? I was a little grouchy when I got home this afternoon and she didn't stay long."

"She mentioned that. Have you got a TV Guide?"

"No. Why? Why do you need a TV Guide? Let's get back to Kate. What did she want?"

Cody walked to the door. "I'll be right back. Watch my pizza."

"Cody!" Jason walked out on the porch.

Cody knocked on the door of the girls who lived two doors down from Jason and they welcomed him in as they opened the door. He visited for a minute and then after having obtained the TV Guide he'd gone in search of, he came back to Jason's. Handing it to Jason, he said, "Here, find out what celebrity show would have been playing that had a segment about you on it this afternoon. I've got to eat my pizza."

He could tell lights were starting to come on for Jason about what Kate had needed. Jason asked, "What did she see? Was it bad? It couldn't have been too bad. I haven't done anything. But she's so uptight about other girls right now."

Around a bite, Cody said, "Just find the show. Then we need to get on their web site.

Three minutes later, they were on the site and Cody heard Jason groan. Cody put a hand on Jason's shoulder. "No. It's okay, man. I talked to her about that one. She's fine with it. When she left, I think she was okay. I told her how you were. I even encouraged her to marry you soon. You owe me. This is what's been bothering me. Why I sent Marilyn home." Jason turned to look at him. "Meridee, whatever. Jason, if you were having the day Kate was having, i.e. you snapping at her, finding her boyfriend in a compromising story on TV and then finding stuff like this on the web, what do you suppose would be her next move?"

Jason groaned again as Cody said, "Maybe you'd better Google yourself."

Jason sat at the computer with the mouse and went from groaning to swearing, while Cody stood behind him noisily eating pizza. Finally, Cody went back and dug in Jason's fridge again. He came back with a bottled water, grumbling, "In my next life, I'm going to pick a best friend who isn't so dang healthy. Water! You've got nothing but bottled water in that whole blinkin' fridge. Hell, Jase, you can get water from the sink. If you're gonna pay for something at least make it have carbonation if you can't hold your liquor."

Absent mindedly, Jason said, "I'm a singer, Cody. My lungs are my tools. Get off it. Maybe you could hit your notes from time to time if you tried the bottled water. Geez, I've never Googled myself before. This is awful."

Cody walked to the door with his water. "I gotta go, dude. I'm gonna go home and Google myself and see if I turn out looking so much nastier on-line than I am in real life like y'all do. This could be epic. I might be legendary."

Jason sighed tiredly. "Yeah, good luck with that."

"I want to give your eulogy."

"What?"

"Kate's gonna kill you. She's got actual photos of you kissing other girls. Several of them. She's gonna kill you. I just wanna give your eulogy so I can defend your character after the fact."

Jason looked at him without smiling and shook his head. "No, she won't kill me. Violence isn't her style. She'll just be incredibly hurt and take a drive to Texas to talk to God and then she'll have that haunted look and no smile the next time I see her."

Cody walked back over to Jason and put a hand on his shoulder. "Geez, man. I didn't even know God lived in Texas. No wonder those Texans are such pathetic braggarts. Good luck, dude. I'm gonna live on the edge and pray for y'all again. You'll know if you hear a news story about God having a heart attack in Texas that I shocked Him into it."

"Thanks Cody. Actually, God having a heart attack would be about the only thing insane enough to get Kate not to be heart broken about me tonight. I'm going to need those prayers. Go ahead and live on the edge."

"That is my specialty! See ya, man."

***

Kate found Jason asleep on the porch swing again. Her drive had left her drained, without answers and somewhat resigned. As she looked down at him sleeping, still, the only thing she really knew was that she loved him. Loved him dearly. In spite of everything.

When it came right down to it, that was what made her happy. She wished there was a way to separate this crushing heartache from the sweet peace she felt when she was with him. Who knows, maybe she could get really good at ignoring the parts of his life she didn't understand. She sat down on the edge of the swing and touched his beautiful hair.

His eyes opened slowly and this time there wasn't a smile, but there was a sweet, sincere tenderness as he quietly watched her for a few seconds. She stroked his cheek and then ran a finger over his sensuous bottom lip. Even if he wasn't perfectly trustworthy, he was definitely beautiful. She kissed the tip of her finger and put it back there on his lip and said softly, "Wake up, sleepy head. You're gonna get a million 'squito bites out here."

He sat up and reached out to touch her cheek. "I'll live. How was Texas?"

She sat down beside him. "Still big."

He smiled sadly, "I told Cody you'd driven to Texas to talk to God. He said he didn't even realize God lived there. He's decided that's why Texans are egotistical."

She laughed. "That's exactly what I needed just now. Laughing feels good. I thought I didn't get to see you until tomorrow? What brings you tonight?"

He groaned and made a sound of disgust. "Ah, I Googled myself. It was awful."

She pushed the porch swing with her foot. "I know."

"I'm not really as bad as it looks. I swear."

"I know."

They rocked in silence for a while until, finally, he asked, "So, what are you at me?"

She thought about that at length and then answered, "That, I don't know."

"Why are you not afraid of me?"

She laid her head against his shoulder. "Oh, Jason. You're my knight in shining armor. You always have been, you always will be. Googling you isn't going to change that."

He turned to look into her eyes and she looked right back. Somehow, knowing she was carrying his child put some things into perspective. After her drive tonight, she still knew she couldn't settle for less than knowing he only loved the flavor of Kate. Not in marriage. She could never do that. But they were best friends. And they now had the embryo of a child together. That was enough to circumvent the bitterness her first gut reaction wanted to feel toward him. The time was past for that. He wasn't trying to hurt her. She knew that. He was simply human. That was his flaw.

At length, he asked her one question, "What do you want from me, Kate? Really?"

She smiled sleepily and quietly answered, "I only want it all from you, Jason." She leaned back against his shoulder again. "Incredibly selfish, aren't I?"

After rocking a few more minutes, he asked, "Kate, do you know I'm doing the best I can to make you happy?"

She reached to take his hand. "Yeah."

Turning back to her, he asked, "Is it good enough? My best?"

"It has been so far."

"But I haven't given you it all."

"We're working on that, Jase. And you've given me more than you know."

He leaned back against the swing again and tipped his head back to look up at the stars. "I'm going to do better, Kate."

"Me too."

He wrapped an arm around her and cuddled her against his chest, and she knew she needed to tell him. As much as she hated to shatter this peace, he needed to know. He had to leave town again for Lubbock day after tomorrow.

She basked in his arms for another couple of minutes, dreading having to rock his world with the news that had rocked hers. Finally, she took a deep breath and said, "Jason, I need to tell you something."

He tensed against her and it made her instantly depressed. At first he didn't answer her and then asked, "Is it going to make us sad, Kate? Whatever you have to tell me?" She nodded without saying anything, tears welling into her eyes. After a short pause, he said, "Then don't tell me, Kate. Not tonight. Let's put it off. Sad things can wait."

She nodded again and struggled to swallow her tears so he wouldn't hear them in her voice. "All right."

He pulled her close again and whispered in her ear, "I love you, Kate."

He did love her. She knew that. She never doubted it. But she'd been serious when she said she only wanted it all. She turned her cheek against his chest. "I love you, too, Jason."

Kristin Cross

Chapter 9

Monday morning seemed to come on with a vengeance and it was definitely Monday all day. He'd had to get Kate out of bed when he called her to let her know he was cancelling on their morning for the time being and said he'd call her as soon as he could. And then she'd had to go in to work early and they never even got together at all.

They'd known when they fired, Ryan that they'd have to come up with an incredibly good pianist and fast to make their concert in Lubbock. They'd had Scotty, the manager Kate had hired, go over there on Sunday and start looking, and he'd found a handful of possibles, but now he wanted Jason and Cody to make the final decision.

Jason spent most of the morning and early afternoon on the phone and then he and Cody decided to head on to Lubbock to try to get things ready for their concerts the next day. They were going to be playing there two days in a row and several things needed to be solidified.

On their way out of town, he stopped at the restaurant to tell her their plans and the way her face fell fairly ripped his heart out of his chest. Lubbock was only a six hour drive away, but from the way she looked it could have been the moon. She'd gazed up at him with that shadow so deep in her eyes that it literally changed the color to indigo.

Still, she hadn't complained. Just nodded and asked if he needed any help making arrangements. Sometimes he couldn't even believe how mentally tough such a sweet, soft girl could be.

Kissing her goodbye was the worst. They didn't have much time and even if they had, he wasn't sure he could have healed the worry she tried to keep hidden from him. In the end, he'd just had to kiss her once, hard, promise her he'd come back to her and go.

***

Watching Jason and Cody pull away that day made Kate feel unbelievable guilty. It had been nine days since she'd found out she was pregnant and she still hadn't told Jason. Now it would be at least a couple more and probably several depending on how they decided to finalize their travel arrangements. She was nearly six weeks along and she needed to clue him in to what was going on. Not only did he need to know he was a father, but she could really use some of his rock solid wisdom in knowing how to deal with everything emotionally. She watched until Cody's Jeep turned out of sight and then she went back to her office to see if she could figure out what to do about this new development.

It didn't take her long to decide that she had to go talk to him in Lubbock. After his second concert, but before he left for California the next day. That was what she would do. She mentally went over how to go about this and what she was going to say to him when she got there as she worked on her afternoon's tasks. She wouldn't tell him she was coming. It might throw him off of his game and mess up the concert. It would have to be late after the second concert in case they caught a red eye that night or an early flight the next morning. Just the thought of facing him made her knees weak and the morning sickness choose that moment to appear again.

She didn't go to a lot of their concerts. It was hard to explain why. At first, it had just been that she couldn't get in because she was simply too young, but since then other factors had come into play. Lately, she so struggled with watching such a large number of women be attracted to the man she had long ago come to think of as hers. It sounded silly, but it bugged the wadden out of her.

She hadn't gone that much, but she decided that since she would be there in Lubbock and near the venue anyway, she would go and enjoy it. She even decided to just buy a ticket like any other Joe so she could experience one of their concerts just the way they did it, without any changes they may have made for her. She wanted to be able to sit in that stadium seat and hear him sing her song and be the only one in the whole place who knew who'd he'd written it to.

Her plans made, Tuesday morning she got on-line and bought her ticket, gassed up her car, told her mother of her plans, packed an over night bag and then went and got her hair cut. The idea of talking to Jason still made her nervous and maybe having perfect hair would help.

Wednesday she slept in as long as she could, knowing it might be a record late night for her. She'd been planning to spend an hour or two at work, but then when she got there, Maxine had things well in hand and Kate went almost straight back out to her car. This was it.

She phoned their manager, Scotty, and asked what hotel they'd be in and what Jason's room number was. He didn't ask why she wanted to know and she didn't offer. Then, with a trepidatious deep breath, she got in and headed one more time to Texas, and this time it wasn't to talk to God.

Lubbock was a long drive from Wye, Oklahoma and she stopped several times en route. She'd eaten a late breakfast and stopped in Wichita Falls for a late lunch and to rest her back again. Arriving in the city of Lubbock, she located the venue at Texas Tech, and then grabbed a deli sandwich before walking in to find her seat.

She was more than forty five minutes early and it was actually kind of fun to watch the last minute preparations from a totally unconnected perspective.

As the stadium steadily filled, she began to be frankly somewhat flabbergasted at how many people were here to see her friends make music. She'd been absolutely aware of the numbers they were attracting lately, but seeing it in the flesh was much more impactful. So was the fact that a huge percentage of this crowd was female.

Finally, the lights went down and for just a second the crowded quieted and then as a whole, they went wild. A shock of excitement went up her spine even though she knew there would be a warm up band appear before Jason and the rest of Aerie did.

The warm up band was good. Remarkably so and Kate didn't doubt they'd go big if they had the work ethic and could keep getting along well enough. Still, she wasn't sad to see them leave the stage. It had been several months since she'd been to an actual concert of Jason's and she could feel her pulse rate go up a notch just thinking about him.

She could tell they were coming up the ramp before she could see them because there were people who started to scream and cheer even before the spot lights were there. Cody appeared first. He ran on to the stage with his usual energy and the crowd around her went into a frenzy. The drummer began and as Jason appeared, the crowd let out a scream and then Jason started on his guitar and the others joined in. The sudden onslaught to her senses of sound and lights, energy and Jason had her feeling like she had taken something illegal and she couldn't help but let her body move to the rhythm . They were really good at what they did. She'd forgotten how good.

She'd meant what she'd said to Jason the other day about being a magician out there. That phenomenal sensuality she'd mentioned began to work on her and she watched him as her pulse rate went up even further. He was incredibly attractive out there under those lights with the slight sheen of perspiration delineating every muscle in the sleeveless shirt he wore. She felt herself almost drowning in his music and his spell as they sang song after song. All she had to do was look at him and she completely lost all sense of time and reality.

They must have been nearing the end of the concert when that sense of reality came back in a hurry. This whole time, she had been entertained and thrilled with watching Jason and the others put on a magnificent show. Suddenly, as the tempo slowed right down to a ballad, Jason began to sing and it looked like he was singing right to one woman near his lower stage left. Kate's breath caught and her heart did some pathetic off beat thing that hurt.

A moment later, Jason focused on another woman and then Kate felt slightly better. He was just working the crowd. That was all. Still, the magic had dissipated and been replaced with that familiar anxious weight in the pit of her stomach and she almost felt like leaving right now. She glanced around and realized it would be swimming up stream and decided to wait. The show would be ending in just a few minutes anyway.

The ballad ended and Kate took a deep breath. It was silly to get this upset over a stupid song and the way Jason sang it.

A hot guitar lick rang out and her attention was drawn back to the stage where Jason and Cody were standing together with their guitars snarling in their hands. The crowd recognized the song and there was a huge, scream that threatened to shake the very structure of the stadium. Kate felt even more shaken as Jason moved out to the front of the stage and began to dance as he sang to the crowd below him.

He began the same skanky, suggestive moves Kate had been so disturbed by that night at Cody's party and the anxious feeling in her tummy intensified. Suddenly the air felt close and the crowd felt suffocating. For the first time, she noticed the almost overpowering smell of hundreds of different perfumes and colognes mixed with body odor and she began to feel light headed. She watched Jason for several more minutes as she struggled to take deep breaths and not let what she was watching him do toward tens of thousands of women bother her.

Everyone in the entire stadium was standing and dancing and screaming, but Kate took her seat anyway. The air in here was stifling and she suddenly wished she hadn't come after all. Deciding to take her chances with being caught in the downstream current, she left her seat and began the long trek through the mass of crowded bodies to the aisle and then up the stairs. It took her most of the next two songs to make her way to a landing at the top of the concourse.

She paused for a breath of the slightly cooler, fresher air and Aerie ended a song and got ready to start another. She stopped as she went to walk out of the curtained door way between two security guards and took one last look down at the guys on the stage. Jason and Cody were laughing together as Jason yelled, "One, two, three, four" and the drummer started in. She sighed, Jason was beautiful, that was all there was to it, and amazingly talented. He truly was a master entertainer, but she wasn't cut out for this.

She pushed aside the curtain and stepped into the lighted hall that circled the perimeter of the venue. As she started to head for the doors, Jason began to sing her song.

Stepping into the clear air of the outdoors was unbelievably refreshing, even though it was probably still nearly eighty degrees on this balmy, West Texas night. Kate looked around, trying to get her bearings and figure out where she'd parked her car. It was actually on the other side of the building and she stayed close under the lights as she headed all the way around on the walkway.

She didn't even realize she'd started to cry as she walked until her tears splashed on her hand where she clutched her keys. Some people were coming and she tried to brush away the tears as she had to walk past and then decided it didn't matter who saw anyway. What did anything matter when you've just truly understood you are foundationally at odds with what you want most in life?

Acknowledging she loved Jason was simple. Acknowledging that what they each deemed appropriate behavior for a spouse was not even close to correlating was the hardest thing she'd ever done in her life.

Locating her car, she got in and locked the doors and then gave in to the heartbreak she felt at having finally come to the decision that she couldn't marry Jason right now, even if he had officially deemed her the best flavor. His behavior toward the women here tonight and the way he had danced were too at odds with her own personal value system to ever make this situation work, even if he had proven his undying love. Even if he was only putting on a show, she couldn't marry that and have the rest of the world believe her husband was that much of a hustler, but knowing that for sure hurt more than anything she'd ever experienced.

She sat in the car and cried and the tears rolling didn't feel like they were helping her feel better like they usually did. Tonight, they were simply the result of an incredibly aching heart, and she sobbed until she finally realized the concert must have ended because people were streaming through the parking lot around her. Remembering why she'd come to Lubbock in the first place, she tried to mop up her tears so she wasn't such a mess when she went to tell Jason they'd conceived a baby together. And then the thought of a baby brought into this situation between unmarried parents made her dissolve into sobbing one more time.

At length she realized she'd forgotten to ask Scotty when she got the hotel information when the band was leaving and she reached for the ignition. She had to get a handle on herself and get this over with, in case Jason was heading to the airport any time soon.

Praying for strength, she resolutely dried her eyes, touched up her make up, combed her hair and drove to the downtown Marriot Hotel. She had to do this. She had to do this right now.

The hotel carpeting was some weird pattern that made her almost a little nauseous as she walked down the hallway to room three forty one and in a disconnected way, she registered that she was hungry again and needed to eat something to settle her stomach.

Her heart was pounding and her hands were moist and she felt lightheaded as she saw the number beside the dark brown wood door. She walked up and knocked, not willing to prolong this any longer. It would be such a relief to get it over with.

As she waited for an answer, she realized she could hear music and laughter on the other side of the door and she hoped she hadn't gotten mixed up and gone to the wrong place. It finally opened and a man she'd never seen answered it. Just as she was going to apologize for knocking on the wrong hotel room door at after eleven thirty at night, he let out a low whistling cat call and said, "My, my, what do we have here? I end up with the prettiest one of all." He looked her up and down appreciatively and then went on, "Everyone else here is taken for the night, darlin', so it looks like it's you and me. Come on in and I'll go next door and grab you a brew. How did y'all like the concert?" He advanced into the hall toward her.

A bit confused at the talk of the concert, Kate was just backing away and starting to explain that she had the wrong room when she heard Cody's laugh and then Jason's. At that, she took a step in to the doorway of the room with perfect timing to come face to face with Jason as he came around the edge of the entry hall. He had a beer in his right hand and a tall, red head under his left arm with her arm wrapped around his waist.

For a moment they were both stunned and the door answerer, who didn't appear to notice the sudden explosive tension, put an arm around Kate's shoulders and laughed again as he repeated, "I guess it's you and me."

Kate recovered first and shrugged off the disgusting arm as she spoke amazingly calmly, "I'm sorry. I seem to have gotten the wrong room." With that, she turned on her heel and headed back down the nauseating carpeting.

Several steps down the hall Jason caught her shoulder from behind and said, "Kate, wait. Don't go." She turned toward him, taking in the worried looks of Cody and the rest of the now quiet band who stood in the hallway outside the door with the clueless guy who had answered it and the willowy redhead. The clueless idiot and the redhead both looked confused.

Kate looked up at Jason and then pointedly looked at the beer he still held and back to his face. He glanced at the beer and said, "It's not mine. I was holding it for Chauncy. I swear it Kate. What are you doing here?"

She rolled her eyes and shook her head. "What? Are you going to tell me you were holding her for someone else too? I mistakenly thought I needed to come talk to you Jason. I was wrong. The concert was good. See you around."

Turning again, she began to walk and Jason came down the hall after her. "Look, Kate. I can explain. Give me a chance. Let's talk about this." She kept walking. "Kate. Stop. We can figure this out."

At that, she did stop and turned to him. "You're right, Jason. We can figure this out. I just did." She started walking one more time and this time he took her by the arm and pulled her to a stop in front of the elevator.

"Kate, listen."

Pushing the down button, she shook her head and said calmly, "No, Jason. I'm sorry, but I can't. I love you. I always will. But I can't. And I shouldn't." A bell dinged and the door opened and she stepped in and turned around. He put a hand to the door to keep it propped open and she shook her head one more time. "Let it go, Jason. There's no point. Good luck Friday."

They stood staring at each other for a full five seconds and then Kate pointedly reached over and hit the G button. They stared at each other again and then Jason sighed and let go of the door. Kate turned to look at the button panel. She couldn't bear to look at him as the doors closed in his face.

She made it to her car. She even made it to the freeway before she let her life dissolve into the maelstrom of tears she couldn't contain. She fought to focus on her driving and kept wiping at her eyes so she could see.

She couldn't even bring herself to question how she'd gotten to this place at this time. There was nobody to blame, no actions to second guess, there was only the knowledge that it was over. She was no longer the other half of Jason and Kate. She wasn't even sure how long his half of them had been essentially gone.

And she had his baby inside her.

That was the kicker. That was the thing that was sadder than any other in this whole mess. Their foolish mistakes had caused an innocent, tiny baby to get dropped smack into the middle of a star crossed romance. Singing star crossed.

And now she had consciously decided that not only would this baby be born out of wedlock, it would be born fatherless, because she'd never even told Jason. It had been a snap decision as she'd taken in the situation in that hotel room, but it had been the right one. She was the one ultimately responsible for this child and there was no way she'd force it to be a part of where that hotel room was headed. It would drag the poor baby through a valueless mess of worldliness and make co-parenting miserable. Cody and his lifestyle was no place for a child. And that was apparently the path Jason was on.

It was the right decision, but it still broke her heart.

She cried all the way to Childress and then had to stop and get a room. She was thoroughly exhausted. As the clerk checked her in, she called and left a message on her mom's cell phone about where she was. She walked inside her room, closed and locked the door and then stripped and stepped into the shower, hoping it would wash some of the deep sadness off and help her sleep in spite of the thoughts that kept swirling around and around her exhausted head.

As she toweled off, she looked at her naked body in the mirror. She couldn't see any outward sign of the tiny body growing inside her, although some of her jeans felt marginally tighter, but it wouldn't be long. She put a hand over her neat, flat belly, wondering if it was a boy or a girl. She sighed and pulled a pair of panties and a night shirt out of her bag. She'd so hoped for some of Jason's wisdom after talking to him tonight. He hadn't seemed wise, standing there in that doorway with his girl and his beer. But she knew he truly was usually.

Tonight, she felt incredibly alone. And she was. She'd already decided that tomorrow she was going to move. She not only wanted to spare having to have this child raised in a party world without values, which it would be if Jason found about it—she knew him well enough to know he'd never walk away from a baby he knew he'd fathered. But she also honestly didn't think she could face living where thoughts of Jason and the life he'd shared with her for the last twenty years completely surrounded her.

Back home, he literally permeated her life. And even though after tonight she knew she finally had to walk away, she also knew she was incredibly human when it came to Jason Falcon. He may not have truly mated for life, but she had, and she couldn't live where she had to deal with him and his memory every day. It would kill her.

There was also the fact that she and her parents and even Jason and his parents, had been extremely active in their church. The last thing Kate wanted would be to cast dispersion on such great Christians because one of their fold was having a baby out of wedlock. Yeah, she knew the world didn't think it was that big a deal now days, but in her heart she knew it was, and knew she needed to move away to where the gossip mill wouldn't tear down the kingdom her parents and others had worked so hard to be building.

She towel dried her short, dark curls and then knelt beside the bed to pour out her heart to her Father. She had long ago made her peace with Him about the baby, now she just needed God to help her make peace with herself. He knew about the pregnancy and how much Kate regretted it and would try to make restitution. There was no way she could completely, but in spite of having made one of the world's most devastating mistakes, she was going to do her best to carry on from here on out with honor.

She told him of all that had transpired tonight and how she felt about it and how scared she was to be responsible for one of His small spirits all on her own. She talked of her plans to uproot her life and take if far from Jason and the people of their small community and asked for confirmation that that was the wisest course of action for everyone involved. And she asked for help in handling everything she needed to as she started out on this new life. She asked for that peace, and she asked for Him to bless and watch over Jason, the friend she would probably continue to pray for all of her life.

It was after three AM when she finally climbed stiffly into the big, lonely bed and turned on her side to go to sleep, but as tired as she was, she still couldn't help the thoughts that crept into her head and the tears that crept into her eyes. She rolled into a fetal position and cradled a hand over her tummy and whispered, "Oh, Jason. I wish things had turned out differently.

Kristin Cross

Chapter 10

For the first time in his life, Jason Falcon smashed an expensive guitar. It wasn't some orchestrated stage trick to send the fans over the edge. It was something to keep him from smashing the new keyboard player who had joked about how everyone in the room was already taken for the night and then assumed Kate was just another groupie. First, he had just handed Jason his beer to hold while he answered the door. Then he had falsely accused Jason of sleeping around, and *then* he had actually thought Kate would agree to be with him! Jason cursed and kicked the remains of the guitar as he thought about it.

At the unaccustomed raging temper, the room cleared out remarkably fast, save for Cody and Jason sent the door crashing into the frame behind them. He stalked to the window and rested his hands on the sill as he ground out through gritted teeth, "Send him packing before I strangle him."

Cody hesitated, "Hadn't we better keep him long enough to get through Modesto and Vegas?"

Jason turned around violently. "You want me to share a stage with that... With him after what he just did? Did you see her face?"

Calmly, Cody said, "I want you to be adult enough to honor our commitment to perform. And it wasn't what Chauncy said that did it, and you know it. I tried to tell you, Jason. You have to quit draping yourself around whoever. It may seem like nothing when it's just us being loud and celebrating, but Kate is worth toeing the line for. Think how you'd feel if she acted the same around a bunch of salivating guys."

"Oh, you're a fine one to talk! You sleep with girls who you don't even know their names. I put my arm around her shoulder!"

Cody didn't answer that and after Jason glared at him for another second, he went and kicked the mangled guitar again, making a discordant jangle that reverberated through the tense room. Finally, Cody asked, "What'd she say?"

Jason snarled at him, "What do you think she said? She said sianara! She thought the beer was mine too! She wouldn't even listen for a second!"

"Calm down Jason. You're gonna get us thrown out of this joint if you don't quit yelling. Give her a minute to think about things and then call her cell phone. Find out where she's staying and go talk to her. She's no hot head. She'll hear your end of the story."

Jason thought about that and then swore viciously and stalked over to the window again. Cody hadn't seen her face. He looked up at the sky and let out a huge breath. She was long gone. And it wasn't like she would take a drive to Texas to talk to God this time.

"What'd she want?"

Jason pulled his thoughts back to Cody. "What?"

"What'd she want? She just drove six hours because she wanted to talk to you. What'd she want to talk about? These concerts intimidate the hell out of her. It must have been important."

Jason closed his eyes and felt like he wanted to throw up. Had she finally decided she could marry him in spite of her concerns about all the other flavors? He swore bitterly. He had a sneaking suspicion that whether Kate was a hot head or not, his asinine habit of being too physically friendly had just cost him big. Huge. He didn't even want to think how huge.

He kept his eyes closed long enough to pray like he'd never prayed before and then opened them and said, "Go away Cody. Go find a trashy girl. I just want to be alone."

Cody walked quietly to the door and then turned back and asked, "Y'all want me to boot Chaunc? Or not?"

Jason shook his head and sighed. "No. You're right. We need him for a couple days. Ask Scotty to check with that Quinn and see if he could be up to speed next week. If he can, we'll lose Chauncy then."

Cody paused for another minute and then asked gently, "I don't need to worry about you not showing up to meet our plane in the morning, do I?"

Turning back to the window, Jason said sadly, "I've never let you down before, have I Rawlings?"

Cody smiled. "Well, there was that one time in first grade when I caught you playing with Shelley Larsen's Barbies. That was a real eye opener."

Jason didn't even crack a smile and Cody turned back to the door as he said, "Hey, off the record, I'm going to pray for the two of you again tonight, okay."

Jason nodded. "Thanks. Your secret's safe with me."

Cody went out and let the door close behind him.

***

Even though she was sicker than a dog, the next morning Kate got up, prayed for inspiration and climbed back into her car to finish driving home. As she drove, she listened for the confirmation that her plans were what the Lord thought best for her, and when she knew that walking away from Jason was what she was truly supposed to do; her heart broke all over again.

Once she'd gotten the emotion under control one more time, she began to unravel the logistics of what she needed to be doing in her life. She'd brought the note pad off the hotel room's desk and as she traveled, she made a list of all the things that had to be taken care of before Jason got home.

Knowing it was going to happen sooner or later, she called Maxine and asked her to plan to fill in for her for the rest of the day. Kate had done nothing, but drive and cry, but she was unspeakably tired any way.

When she finally pulled into her parents' driveway, she simply sat in the car for several long minutes. She dreaded going in and talking to her parents, and frankly, she was too beat to get out of the driver's seat.

Her mom knew when she opened the door and walked into the kitchen that something was horribly wrong and she took Kate's bag for her and followed her into her suite of rooms and then just stood there, waiting quietly. Kate looked at her for a few seconds and then turned away to hide the tears that welled again, but her mother followed her into her room and then took a seat in

Kate's big recliner when Kate dropped onto her bed and turned her face to the wall.

A couple of minutes later, Kate got back up and came and climbed right onto her mom's lap and laid her head on her shoulder and as her mom rocked her like she had when she was two years old, she tearfully told her what had happened on her road trip. By the time she was finished, her mother was teary eyed as well.

Finally, Kate told her she intended to move away and what her reasoning was. Her mother's face twisted in sadness as she listened and Kate felt terrible about bailing on them like she was, but she knew it was best. Her mother must have either understood and agreed, or else considered that trying to counsel Kate any different would be hopeless, because the only thing she said was, "Kate, if you really intend to hide this child from Jason, do you realize this means staying away from home for years and years?"

Kate sobbed bitterly as she nodded her head.

They talked for over an hour and then her mom left to go call her sister Kiersten and ask her to come visit Kate at home one last time and Kate fell into an exhausted, troubled sleep. That was Thursday.

At one o'clock on Friday afternoon, Kate pulled into a Holiday Inn Express on the outskirts of Dallas with everything she owned in the back seat of her car and a handful of resumes and letters of recommendation in the front. She called her mother on the new cell phone she'd bought so she could let her old number go and let her know she'd arrived safely. After she checked in, she brought in her purse, lap top, and an over night bag, pulled the blinds and climbed into the slick white sheets of the queen sized bed. Sadness, lack of sleep and morning sickness had completely drained her.

Toward evening, she got up and went to dinner and then went right back and slept until ten the next morning. Even then she didn't want to get up, but she did anyway. As tired as she was, her sleep was hopelessly broken by what had taken place in her life over the previous few days. Then each time, she'd cry herself back to sleep. Why did he have to turn out so undependable when he'd always been her foundation? She really missed Jason.

And it wasn't just that she missed Jason. She missed everything. Telling her own parents and sister goodbye had been bad, but she knew she'd be able to see them again from time to time. Trying to bid farewell to Jason's parents without letting them know that was what she was doing had been one of the hardest things she'd ever done and she'd cried on and off again for nearly a hundred miles.

They'd chosen Dallas because although it was definitely far enough away and large enough that she could lose herself there, it was still close enough that she could be checked on and helped in case of an emergency. The fact that she would be delivering a baby in less than seven months figured into that decision as well. Deciding to lose herself was one thing. Labor by herself was another.

Only her parents and sister knew where she would be and the only other people who even knew she'd gone were the two assistant managers who would be taking over with Kiersten to manage the restaurant. Knowing that Jason would try to find her, and also knowing their relationship had to end, Kate had made her mom and sister promise her they'd never tell anyone where she was without her permission.

If Jason got ugly about finding her, he could do it. He now had the funds to hire whatever help he'd need. But Kate didn't think he'd do that. Her leaving would have given him a clear enough message that things were over that she assumed he'd leave her alone just because she'd asked him to. The fact that they both still loved each other and wanted what was best for each other had certainly come into play here. It was funny, but even though Kate had left Jason, taking his unborn child with her, Jason was still the first person she prayed for several times a day.

She got up and showered and put on a business suit and started right in making applications and placing resumes in a number of the nicest restaurants in the greater Dallas area. Applying to work in a restaurant was one of the few places she could realistically job hunt on a Saturday. She was hoping the glowing recommendations she had from both professors and some of her parents' fellow restaurant owners who were well acquainted with Kate and her abilities, would open some doors so she could find a job relatively quickly.

It wasn't that she was desperate for money. She wasn't. The restaurant at home had been lucrative and her parents had paid her well. It was that she knew that taking a few needed days rest would get old in a hurry and without any local friends or church activities; she'd be left with nothing to do but watch TV and miss Jason and home if she didn't throw herself into something. Not only that, but she was used to going ninety miles an hour between the restaurant, the band's stuff and her church activities. She definitely needed to get some things going here in Dallas quickly.

Her plan was to find out where she'd be working, and then find housing as comfortably close to there as possible, so she intended to live out of the hotel for the time being. With that in mind, when she was through looking for a job Saturday evening, she brought in another supply of clothing and her toiletries and then set herself up an office at the desk in her room.

She changed out of her business clothes, curled up on the bed and for the first time since she had gone to Lubbock, she turned on her old phone. The one loose end that hadn't been tied up was to tell Scotty, the manager she'd hired for Aerie, that she was through and he needed to take over completely. It made her feel like she was slitting her own wrists. It was the last tie to Jason. Well, except that she was having his baby. Quitting working for the band was the last real tie and she needed to cut it. It had to be done. To do that, she needed to use her old phone.

When the familiar uncomfortable anxiousness in the pit of her stomach made an appearance as she was waiting for the phone to come on, she realized for sure that her decision to leave had certainly been the right one. She hadn't even realized until the anxiety had come back that it had disappeared when she'd finally made the split.

It was definitely back; at least while she made this phone call, and she tried to keep herself from holding her breath as she waited. When it finally came all the way on, there were thirteen new messages and eleven of them were from Jason.

Just the sight of his number there made her heart bleed and she quickly changed screens, scrolled down to Scotty's number and pushed send.

He picked up on the third ring. "Hi, Kate. How's things?"

She swallowed and said, "Fine thanks. And you?"

"I'm great. Well, other than dealing with having to find that second new keyboard player, but then I guess you know about that. Hey, you've been missing in action. Where are you?"

"I'm actually out of town. Listen, Scotty. I need you to do me a couple of favors. Could you plan to wholly take over making arrangements for the band for a bit? I'm thinking about going on sabbatical for a little while."

His voice sounded wary on the other end as he replied hesitantly, "Well, yeah, I could help out, but Jason and Cody aren't going to like that. They always insist I run everything past you before I confirm. How long are you thinking?"

She evaded that question. "I'm not exactly sure. I'll call you and let you know when I'll come back on board. For now, just use your own judgment or ask Jason and Cody. Oh, and I left a folder for you with Jason's mom. You'll need to pick it up before Wednesday. It has their plane tickets and itineraries in it. Thanks for filling in for me, Scott."

"No, problem. Hey, Jason's been trying to find you. Have you talked to him?"

"No. I'll see about giving him a call. Thanks, Scotty. Take care."

"I will. Hey, call Jason like right away. Whatever he needs, it must be pretty urgent. See ya."

"Bye now." She pushed end the final time and then swallowed the huge lump in her throat and powered the phone back down with a sad, teary sigh as she whispered, "Goodbye, Jason."

Chapter 11

Jason's plane touched down in Oklahoma City and he was almost the first one off, even though that wasn't very polite, but for once he didn't particularly care. He needed to get home.

He still hadn't been able to reach Kate, and so it was his mom who had come to pick him up.

He came out the doors of the terminal and was glad to see she was pulled right up at the curb directly in front of him. As she popped the trunk, he tossed his bags into it and then came to the driver's side door and opened it. "Thanks for coming, Mom. Do you mind if I drive home?"

"No, honey. Be my guest. But are you sure? You look exhausted."

"I'm fine. I'll drive." She would never drive as fast as he wanted to go. He walked around the car and helped her back in and then jumped back in behind the wheel and dug out for Wye.

He didn't say much and his mom didn't either as they pulled around and through the airport exits. She was looking at him across the car and finally, she said, "Jason, I'm not sure what's going on, but Kate came by a couple days ago to see your dad and me. It was Friday I believe. It was really weird. She didn't need anything. Didn't really even say anything. Just small talked, left a folder full of some papers and then hugged us both and left. Both of us thought it was a little strange. And she didn't smile once. Isn't that unusual?"

Trying to appear nonchalant, he asked, "That she came by or that she didn't smile?"

"Well, either. She's never acted like that before. Is she okay?"

"I don't know, Mom. I haven't seen her for a few days. I'll check on her as soon as we get home. How's Dad?"

"Oh, he's fine. He's golfing today. How was your trip?"

Wondering whether to tell her the truth or just be casual, he said, "Oh, it wasn't too bad. Busy. Hectic. You know how it goes." Disastrous. That's what he should have said.

She went on, small talking about this or that as they drove and he managed to conceal the fact that he'd never been so anxious in his life. The rest of the band wouldn't even be home until tomorrow, but he'd been too uptight to wait one more night and had bought another ticket and come home to find out why Kate wouldn't so much as even turn her phone on to take a call from him. Surely she wouldn't really let a simple beer bottle and display of affection affect the friendship that had lasted a lifetime. He kept telling himself that over and over, but then he'd remember her face in Lubbock. In all honesty, he didn't know what he'd find when he knocked on her door this morning.

Her car wasn't in her parents' driveway when he drove by, even though it was only seven in the morning and he wondered if she had already gone into work for some reason. He drove there next, but the lot was empty and he pulled his car to the curb to figure out where to try next, struggling to squelch the rising panic in his chest.

Even though he looked like he'd been up all night in a series of airports, he drove back to her parents' house and knocked on the door. Laura answered, still in her robe and Jason felt bad for having obviously woken her up. She gave him a tired smile that didn't quite reach her eyes and said, "Jason, I didn't think you'd be back in town yet. Come on in."

He came in the door and looked around hopefully. Maybe Kate's car was just at the shop or something. "I'm sorry to visit so early, but I haven't been able to reach Kate and I'm worried. Is she here? I didn't see her car outside."

Laura's eyes darkened and Jason was appalled to see them fill with tears as she shook her head. "No, Jason." He waited anxiously while she struggled to get control of her emotions. Finally, she said, "I'm sorry, Jason, but Kate has moved."

"Moved! What do you mean?"

Laura shook her head and the tears began to course down her cheeks. "She left, Jason. She's gone."

He came and took her by the shoulders. "Laura, what do you mean? She's the queen of Birches have roots. She never even moved out to go off to college. She's lived in this house since the day she was born."

Nodding, Laura continued to cry softly and she looked up into his eyes with both sadness and pity. "She came home Thursday pretty upset and told me she was leaving." Laura shrugged her shoulders and went on, "She slept most of that day and then packed up her car. Friday morning, she went next door to talk to your parents for a bit and drove away."

Jason closed his eyes and groaned. Opening them, he asked, "Where did she go? Where is she staying?"

Laura shook her head sadly. "I'm so sorry, Jason. She made me promise I wouldn't tell you."

It felt like she'd belted him in the gut, but somehow he'd been half expecting it. He looked at the woman he'd thought of as his mother-in-law for years now and then sighed. Kate had packed up and moved out of her lifelong home. He turned and looked out the window beside the front door. What did he do now? He couldn't even ask her forgiveness. Turning back to Laura, he asked, "How long? Did she say how long she intended to be gone?"

At that, Laura began to cry like her heart was breaking and the tears rolled down her cheeks. "She was so sad, Jason. She said she couldn't live with memories of your life together all around her. I think she's gone for good. I don't think she has any intention of coming back here at all. Not for years and years at least." Laura was crying so hard Jason could hardly understand her and he stepped to her and put his arms around her and began to pat her back. After a few seconds, she took a deep breath and said, "I'm so sorry, Jason. She just loves you too much. She felt like she had to go."

He sighed again. "I know, Laura. Things looked bad that night. I promise, it wasn't what she thought, but it looked bad. I don't blame her. It looked like just what she's worried about all this time." He pulled back from Laura and said, "But I need you to know. I was only holding the beer because that jerk had handed me his to hold, while he answered the door. I don't drink beer with the guys like that. And I've never, *ever* slept with anyone when I'm on the road. I truly do love Kate."

Laura looked up and wiped at her eyes and sniffled. "I know you do, Jason. And I always try to

169

encourage her about you. But there are more ways to be unfaithful than just sleeping with someone. It was more than that anyway. She felt like you were growing away from her and away from God so much that she didn't really even know you now. She felt like you were more like Cody than like her anymore."

He turned and went back to look out the window again while he thought about that. Maybe Kate had been right. Maybe he was even worse than Cody in some ways. Cody had at least realized Jason was not behaving appropriately for someone who was in an exclusive relationship, even when Jason had thought he was just being a normal member of a band and having a good time.

At length, he turned back and said, "I'll go and let you get back to bed. I'll respect your promise to her, but could you at least relay a message that I do love only her and I'm so sorry and would like to apologize and beg her forgiveness?"

"Sure, I could do that."

"Is there anyone else who knows where she is?"

Laura shook her head, but said, "Kiersten, but she promised as well. I'm sorry."

Sadly, Jason said, "I'm sorry too, Laura. For everything." He turned for the door. "Tell Orrin I said hello. How is he doing?"

"He's taking this rough. He's been really down since he found out about the... Well, lately. He loves Katie dearly and her troubles have set him back a great deal."

Jason looked down and said quietly, "I'm sorry, Laura. Go back to bed. I hope you have a better day." He came back over to her and hugged her again. "I love you, Laura. Thanks for always putting up with me. I'll do better. I promise."

She hugged him back and then whispered, "I just hope it's not too late, Jason."

"Me too. Goodbye."

"Goodbye, son."

Jason walked slowly back to his car and then turned around to look at their two childhood homes. He'd known she was incredibly upset. And he'd known that the sad, eerily calm, resigned face he'd seen in that elevator was different than he'd ever seen her look, but he'd never dreamed she'd pull up those lifelong, deep roots she'd spoken of forever. He closed his eyes to try to deaden the pain of seeing those two lonely looking houses with the empty spot where her car usually sat. She was gone. His deeply rooted Kate was gone. He had to find her.

Kristin Cross

Chapter 12

Walking into her room late Friday afternoon, Kate kicked off her heels and began to change into exercise clothes to go down to the hotel gym. She had been in Dallas a full week and still hadn't been offered a job. She'd known the economy was bad, and that she looked incredibly young for a management position, but she'd hoped her record would speak for itself. Apparently not. Tying on a pair of running shoes, she made a decision to take a job waiting tables if she could get it and start working her way up. It might take awhile, but she knew what she was capable of.

Maybe all she needed to do was humble herself a measure before God, because when she got back to her room an hour later, she had a message on her cell phone about a job she was being offered.

It turned out to be part time waiting, and part time night controller for an elegant seafood restaurant in South Dallas and Kate was thrilled. That way she'd be able to use some of the accounting and business she'd studied and still not be stuck in an office a hundred percent of the time. And hopefully, by the time she was big with the baby she could have worked herself up to a less physically demanding job than server.

As she showered, she tried to remember what the manager at that restaurant had been like, but she'd filled out so many applications she wasn't sure she'd even met that manager. It was supposed to start late on Monday morning, so she had two days to kill before she had much to fill her time. She wouldn't rent an apartment until she'd been there awhile and made sure that was where she wanted to stay, but she could at least be looking around that area to see what she might want if she did. Anything helped to keep her from missing Jason so desperately. She hadn't been able to lie down even once without being haunted by memories and regrets.

That night, she got a long newsy e-mail from her mother. Her e-mail address was the one thing she hadn't worried about changing. She simply blocked Jason's messages and tried to stop herself from hopefully scanning her inbox for messages from him the way she had for years now. The fact he was blocked as a sender didn't help all that much tonight because her mother told her he'd finally come home and learned Kate was gone and how he'd reacted. Kate was both angry with her mother and grateful when she mentioned she'd promised to pass along that Jason loved only her and was so sorry and wanted to ask her forgiveness.

What a strange mixture of emotions that message brought. Foremost, instant heartache, but then a warmth of emotion she didn't even know what to call, and then a self deprecating sense of being a sucker when she remembered he'd told her that all along. The last time he'd said good bye on his way to Lubbock, he promised her he'd come back to her. And he would have. That was the sad truth. If Kate hadn't busted him with the girl right in his arms, she'd have taken him back never the wiser. It was so strange to her that the man she'd known her whole life had such a warped sense of different values for when he was away from her.

After reading it through several times and bawling the whole time she did, she finally replied and asked that her mother not pass on any messages from him in the future. It was too hard to try to put this heartache behind her when she did.

Kate spent Saturday checking out apartments and was completely at a loss as to how to respond to one of the apartment managers when he made it very clear he'd have liked to visit with her a lot more than just long enough to discuss amenities. Men flirted with her often enough, but she'd been Jason's girl since literally before she was old enough to date, and having a guy make such open advances to her now that she wasn't with Jason was thoroughly foreign to her. What was her role just now? She was definitely single, but that certainly didn't mean her heart wasn't still foolishly stuck back in Wye, Oklahoma. For once, the town name was frustratingly apropos. She was single, but she was also expecting a baby. Where that put her socially, was a strange question.

Climbing into her car, she realized it didn't matter a bit what her role should have been. The last thing in the world she wanted right now was to start dating. Which was a good thing because for a long time, now, she'd need to be focused on raising a child, not having a social life. That was reality.

Rather than go straight back to the hotel, she decided to do some shopping. She'd need some more serviceable shoes if she was going to be serving. Plus it would keep her mind occupied for just a few minutes longer.

Sunday, she went to two different churches in that area to start checking out where she would start attending when the time came. That evening, lying in her bed, she thought about church. She was an unwed mother. And although she considered herself a committed follower of Christ, she also knew she now presented some questionable ethics as far as regular church attendance was concerned. Trying to meld the fact that she'd repented of her one night of indiscretion, with the fact that she'd be single and pregnant amid a group of churchgoers was uncomfortable for her and would probably be even worse for others in the congregation. Not only that, but the last thing she wanted was to be a bad example.

Was it better to show that you could make mistakes, even huge ones, and repent and come right back into the fold? Or would it be better to lay low for the duration and ease into the fold later after the baby was born and her situation could be assumed as a broken marriage or something? She absolutely dreaded the thought of not going to church for months.

She thought about just getting a ring and then being closed mouth to anyone she met, but she didn't think she could bring herself to do it. Every time she saw her own hand she'd know she had failed with Jason. It was heartbreaking enough just to think of it ten gazillion times everyday already.

Finally, she turned on her side and put a hand protectively over her stomach and decided to go to sleep and not worry about it all right now. Maybe in time she'd come up with some answers. In a perfect world, everything would be fine, but this world was far from perfect.

She slept in Monday, hoping to sleep through as much of the morning sickness as possible and knowing she might have a long day ahead of her. Actually, it was great to be back in a restaurant and with a purpose ahead of her for the day.

She hadn't been inside the restaurant for three minutes before she started to notice things that could be improved upon with better and more knowledgeable management, but of course she couldn't say anything. Just for kicks, she made a mental list when she noticed something. Maybe in time, she'd be in a position where she could implement some improvements.

The morning passed quickly and she was glad to find that the manager, Kerri, a big, tall, brown haired woman was going to let her have a section of tables during that very first lunch. Kate was intuitive enough to realize Kerri was just trying to get a feel for how Kate would manage on a slow Monday noon, but she was happy about it anyway. Back home, she typically had new people start out bussing to get the hang of the place and to go clear back to bussing would have been very troubling.

After the lunch rush, Kerri took her back into the business office and began to show her the ins and outs of the restaurant's accounting system and once again, Kate found several areas that needed improvement. A couple of them were even to the extent of nearly inviting employee graft or worse and at one point, Kate even commented on how some things needed to be changed in order to protect the company's finances. Kerri laughed and waved a hand as if it was nothing, and made some comment about how Kate was just young and inexperienced and that this was life in the food service industry. Then Kerri went right on and it was all Kate could do to not turn and stare at her. What kind of a manager didn't care if there was overt poor stewardship?

As they continued, Kate wondered who owned the place and what kind of profits it made when the management was this lackadaisical and the book work this shoddy. Whoever owned it must have not had much of a handle on its potential.

Kerri spent the bulk of the afternoon with Kate and by the time she left her to see about some other things and get ready for the dinner crowd, Kate felt like she knew her way well enough around the business end of things to keep the day to day books together, as much as they had been certainly, and have things ready to turn over to the CPA at the end of every month.

She worked as a server again that evening from six until eight and then went back to the hotel tired, but grateful for that. Maybe tonight she would be able to fall asleep without the crushing thoughts of Jason and home breaking her down like they had for the last eleven days.

Back at the hotel, she went and worked out again, hoping that every little bit of fatigue would help.

Within just a few days of starting work, Kate had settled in and made friends with the other staff and had just about decided on where she wanted to live nearby when she came across some troubling questions on the night books. Kerri had her coming in at five thirty to serve the dinner rush and then at around nine thirty or so, when things slowed down, Kate would go into the office and begin to process the payables and receivables and do the books. She would typically finish at midnight or there about and walk out with the last of the dishwashers who were finishing cleaning up the place.

From the first, Kate had been surprised at how little profit this restaurant made for how brisk business was. It was a big place and lots and lots of people came through here, both at lunch and at dinner. There were some inefficiencies, but there still appeared to be an inordinate shortage of receivables in correlation to the supplies that were coming in.

Completely inadvertently, Kate hit a wrong button as she was tallying the night's totals and she pulled up a hidden account that hadn't been listed on any of the other ledgers. For several minutes she looked at it, but was unable to decide what it was an account of. It was labeled with only a number and didn't correlate with anything that Kate could see. At length, she closed the window, finished the books and went back to the hotel, but there was something about that account that kept picking at her. In a way, it helped. That night she was able to think about work more and Jason less as she drifted off to sleep.

The schedule she was on worked well for her. She could sleep late and the morning sickness wasn't so awful. Then she'd work out in the early afternoons before work and still be able to get to work on time and feeling well.

As it was, by the time she was through at night, she was tired and her homesickness was easier to not dwell on.

Surprisingly, Kate really liked most of the people she worked with. Most of them were responsible and hard working, which wasn't always the case in restaurants in her experience.

There was a server named Ben who had begun to be friendly enough to her it almost bothered her. He wasn't inappropriate or anything, but just a bit more willing to do things for her than the rest, and always just happening to take a break the same time she took hers. It made her uncomfortable and she wasn't really sure why. As she thought about it, it must have been that she still considered herself taken, and then she was irritated with herself instead of Ben. Yeah, she wasn't interested in dating, but she needed to get past Jason eventually.

A few days after she had found the mystery account, she figured out what it was. That night at dinner, she had been assigned to a private party of forty eight, served inside a banquet room and it had been very elegant and high end. The appetizers had been King Crab legs and the main dish had been rib eye steaks and Swordfish. For dessert, they'd had fresh berry crepes that had to have cost a fortune. They'd also arranged an open bar that was enjoyed to the point that several of the guests were tipsy enough afterward that the maitre d had to arrange for cabs to get them home.

That night, as she was doing the books, there was no tab for the party listed. It was a big enough party that the bill should have totaled well into the thousands, but even looking to see if it had been prepaid somewhere, Kate found nothing. That was strange; Kate had seen Kerri run the ticket through the order register herself as she'd stood by. Wondering how it had gone through the order register without appearing on the night's till, she went back to find the code it had been rung in under. Maybe it had been comped or something, which wouldn't make any sense for a party of that size and expense.

She had to dig through the actual hand written bar receipts to finally find the code it was under. It wasn't under either the normal restaurant sales or any of the listed employee comp codes and, in fact, Kate couldn't even find an account with that number on it. Then she remembered the hidden account number and pulled it back up. She'd been right. The nearly eight thousand dollar tally was listed there under the hidden account. Somehow, Kerri had run it through just like it had been legit but had used a code that would keep that amount from showing up as a receivable for the night.

Kate quickly scanned the hidden account to realize that while tonight's party was by far the largest sum on the list, there were fifteen other tabs on that same list dated within the last calendar month. Then she pulled up the history of the account and found it had been going since January one which was as far back as she had records for. This was the reason the restaurant wasn't profitable. Well, it was profitable but it was Kerri and whoever else was in on this who was pocketing the profits and not the owners.

Absolutely disgusted by this kind of embezzlement that could potentially shut the entire enterprise down, Kate quickly printed the account ledgers and then the regular accounts, and the year to date list of what had been paid to suppliers and folded the print outs and put them into her purse. She wasn't sure what to do with the information, but she knew she was going to do something. If someone had done something like this to her parents it would have bankrupted them.

The next day, she got on-line and dug through the division of corporations at the state and found the name of the principle owner. It was actually a corporation owned by a corporation and it took her more than an hour to actually find a name and an address to where tax information was being sent. She wrote a short note, explaining what she'd found and what she believed was going on, included her cell phone number in case this Mr. John Garland had questions and the print outs she'd gotten the night before, and sent them overnight to the address listed.

She knew she'd lose her new job, but she had to blow the whistle on this. She'd never be able to live with herself if she didn't.

That morning, she was uptight and worked out for longer than usual to try to calm herself. She went in to work and tried to act as normally as possible, but it was hard to treat Kerri like the same, respectable boss she'd thought her yesterday, and Kate kept wondering if Kerri had somehow found that Kate had gotten into her secret information. By the time she got back to the hotel that night, her nerves were shot and she wished she hadn't worked out for such a long time earlier.

When she opened her eyes the next morning, she was still tired and knew from experience that it was stress that had worn her out and not physical activity. The one good thing about worrying about what was going to happen at work was that she hadn't been so lonely and homesick last night.

She had exercised and was headed to the shower so she could go get some lunch when her cell phone rang. Wondering how things were at home, she answered it and was surprised it wasn't her family. A man's voice with a strong touch of South Texas to it she didn't recognize said, "Yes, I'm calling for Kate Birch please."

Thinking it must have been one of the other restaurants she'd applied to, she answered, "This is she."

Without preamble, the confident, business like voice continued, "Kate, this is John Garland. I own the restaurant you work at. I got an express letter from you this morning. Tell me, do you have any time I could meet with you this afternoon?"

Kate swallowed. "Yes, certainly. I need to be to work at five thirty, but anytime before that I'm free. When did you have in mind?"

"Well, I'm in a plane headed your way. How would say one thirty be?"

"One thirty is fine. Just at the restaurant?"

"No, actually. I'd like to get to the bottom of this before going there and I'm hoping to keep the management there from knowing how I found this out if I can. It might save you some grief. Pick a restaurant near where you are and I'll meet you. Nothing too elegant. I'd hate to be recognized at someone else's restaurant."

"How about the Hojo's on Seventh and Cavalcade Street?"

"That'll be fine. One thirty then. I'm mid forties, dark hair and in navy slacks and a white shirt."

"And I'm nineteen, five eight and have short, dark, curly hair."

"That young? Fine then, I'll see you shortly. Thank you for sending this to me, by the way. I appreciate it."

"No problem, sir. Have a good day."

"I plan to. See you in an hour or two."

***

Jason dropped into a booth across from Cody and took his sunglasses off and tossed them on the table beside his keys. He wasn't in a good mood, but he had to smile when Cody commented mildly, "You look like hell, Jase. How's it goin'?"

"It's goin'. Where's Scotty?"

"Taking a phone call in the Jeep. How's it going really?"

"Why do you think I look like hell? Has Scotty heard from her?"

"No. That's why his phone is glued to his ear. He's gonna get brain cancer from that thing. We're going to have to hire him two assistants so he can get half of what Kate got done started. You haven't heard from her either?"

Jason shook his head and looked away to rub his eyes. The waitress came and Cody ordered for him and Scotty and then waited while Jason ordered and she moved off before he asked, "She still not taking any e-mails?"

"No. Let's talk about something else. Who'd we get to open for us in Phoenix?"

With an exaggerated drawl, Cody said, "Y'all gotta talk about it sometime, Jase. And you gotta shave and start eating too or you're gonna dah and we'll be left hah and drah without a lead guitar."

"There's not much to say, Rawlings. She's been gone for sixteen days without a word."

Cody didn't say anything, just looked at him with sadness in his eyes. Finally, he said, "I'm sorry, man." Jason didn't answer.

***

Kate wasn't sure whether to be thoroughly nervous or not as she waited in the corner of the Hojo's across the parking lot from her hotel. She didn't have to wait long to find out. John Garland came in just a minute or two behind her and she decided he wasn't nervousing in the least. He was probably six feet tall, still slim, handsome and wearing expensive, but conservative clothing.

He came in and sat down around the corner of the table from her and opened a briefcase to take a file out. A server brought water and Kate ordered a chef salad and John simply asked for whatever the special was and a diet Coke and turned back to the folder in front of him. Again without preamble, he asked, "Now, how did you come to find the information you sent me, Kate?"

She explained about coming to work there recently and how she both waited and did books because of her schooling and experience. When he seemed skeptical, she told him about her parents' restaurant and how her dad had been injured and she'd had to take over.

Their food came, and over the course of the meal, he asked her questions about both what she knew about the goings on at his restaurant and how things were run at the one back home. Eventually, he asked if she thought there were ways to improve the management other than just eliminating the theft and he truly had been respectful and attentive enough that she came right out and told him that yes, there were improvements that could be made and what some of the most pressing were.

They'd been sitting there talking for more than two and a half hours, their dishes long taken away when he finally asked, "Kate, would you be willing to stay on there, working for me, instead of the restaurant without anyone else knowing, and helping me first to get to the bottom of this and then tuning the place up? I'll pay you well."

She nodded. "Sure. It needs to be done."

"Things might get ugly. From just what you've sent me there's more than fifty thousand dollars missing. Somebody's going to prison and maybe several somebodies. The police will be involved. In fact, I've already contacted them. Are you sure?"

She met his eyes. "Mr. Garland, these people are stealing huge amounts of money. Whether I'm involved or not, it has to end. And I'm already there, in a position to garner information. Why wouldn't I help? Isn't it my duty as a citizen?"

That made him pause and then smile. "Yes. I guess you're right. I guess as citizens we should all be trying to rid the world of corruption. Please, call me John." He put out his hand. "Welcome aboard."

After another forty minutes of discussing what he wanted her to do and exchanging contact numbers, she happily rushed out to go get ready to go to work. She'd been worrying about losing her job by becoming involved, but it looked like things were going to work out okay after all.

Kristin Cross

Chapter 13

At first Jason had been sad, and then penitent, but after three weeks of no contact with her, he finally got ticked off. They had another concert that night. A smaller one in a club in Shreveport and Jason fairly raged through the concert with an unbelievable amount of energy, but not a whole lot of real smiling. Cody kept looking at him like he was wondering what was going on, but frankly, Jason didn't give a damn. After the show, he was still angry and when somebody shoved him outside the restaurant in the lobby of their hotel, Cody caught his arm just in time as Jason went to plow the guy.

That only made Jason angrier and it took Cody hissing in his face, "Can you say lawsuit?" before he finally calmed down and stalked off. He went up to his room, locked himself in and then picked up his guitar and began to play. By two o'clock the next morning, when Cody finally knocked on his door to check on him, he'd written a bitter break up song with a pounding back beat that would probably be an instant hit.

He played it for Cody, who loved it, in spite of the fact he was too full of Jose' Quervo to really know if he loved it, and then Jason kicked Cody out and spent the next hour writing a ballad about how sorry he was. By the time they hit the road the next morning, Cody was hung over and Jason was too tired to even admit how lonely he was.

***

It only took four more days of snooping around at night while she was working to find the previous records of the mystery account, and with a few innocent questions to Ben, and some good deductive logic, Kate and the police investigator were able to find that Kerri and one of the cooks both had bank deposits to match the embezzled funds.

The next day, the police came and arrested the two of them and took a ton of evidence. As that all came down, John and his accountant showed up and once the police were gone, John had a meeting with the other employees. After explaining what had happened, he gave the remaining staff a pep talk and then sent them all home except Kate and closed the restaurant for the night.

With the establishment closed, Kate helped the accountant find several different types of financial records to go over with a fine toothed comb and then she and John went around the whole of the restaurant going over policies and practices and even the location of some things that needed changing. When the restaurant opened up the next morning, Kate was in control and there was a brand new set of registers that were programmed to prevent the kind of graft that had been occurring there.

Part of the changes Kate made was to shuffle a couple of the employees around. She promoted a hostess to assistant manager, let one cook go and changed the policy for how tips were shared to be more rewarding across the board. She also streamlined the walkways in the kitchen and reorganized the produce delivery schedule and then tweaked several smaller things. Over the next two weeks, the profitability of that restaurant increased by forty three percent. The only problem was she'd been too busy to get settled into an apartment.

At that point, she had another lunch meeting with John, whom she had come to have the utmost respect for. He was savvy and intelligent, as well as being polite and respectful to his employees. This time the meeting was at his own restaurant in a private banquet room and with his accountant present.

After giving her a firm hand shake, sincere praise, and a ridiculously large check, he revealed that he had seven more restaurants in Texas and Oklahoma and one in California and asked her if she would consider doing this same type of thing in all of the others. Almost in a stupor, she agreed. After all, she didn't have any roots just at the moment and she had done some honest good here.

She spent another week in Dallas, working out a few more kinks and shipped some of her things home, and then she headed south to Galveston to the next one.

It was a six hour drive across Texas and that was far too much time to think about her life and everyone back home. She tried to listen to the radio, but it seemed like every ten minutes one of Aerie's songs would come on. She would change the channel every time, but she still spent an inordinate amount of time thinking about Jason. Finally, her song came on and she couldn't do it. She couldn't turn it off and she listened to it all the way through and then spent the next hour wiping at her tears and remembering how many good times they had had. By the time she got to Galveston, she had a headache and all the headway she'd made in Dallas as far as trying to get over him was gone with the car exhaust over east Texas.

This time, she moved into a Marriot Courtyard so that at least she could have a bit of a kitchen. That would help when she needed food at odd hours and didn't want to be out at night, alone, in a town she wasn't familiar with.

Later, it felt like the gods had conspired against her as she saw Jason on the cover of two different magazines at the grocery store when she went to buy groceries. It took her a long, long time that night to fall asleep, and then she dreamed of him. Of that good day, out by the lake, when that pinky promise had been the sweetest memory of her life. By morning, her heart hurt every bit as much as it had hurt that first morning after Lubbock. She decided to throw herself into her work here, just as she'd done in Dallas to help her forget.

Because she and John didn't want to have anyone know she was working for him if possible, she put in an application and resume' at this restaurant just like she had at the last one and then waited to hear back from them.

The day after she got there, for the first time, she had to go and buy bigger clothes. She was almost fourteen weeks along from what she could figure and there was now a small, smooth, rounded bulge where her usually pretty, flat tummy had been. After doing some research on-line, she also made an appointment with a local OB/GYN for a prenatal check up. It made everything seem so much more real and she cried herself to sleep again that night, devastated about what could have been.

After waiting for four days to hear back from the restaurant, she worried that their plan wasn't going to work and she wouldn't be hired. She called back to talk to the manager just in case and was relieved when he did, in fact, offer her a job over the phone.

This time, she was only offered a position with the wait staff, and she had to begin working just lunch, but it was enough to get started. This location was better managed than the last one, and she didn't have access to the financials like she'd had so she had to go with what her gut was telling her as she tried to compare what she was seeing at the restaurant with what she was seeing from the numbers John's accountant supplied her. At first glance, she didn't think there was any level of embezzlement going on like there had been in Dallas, but there were a number of things that could be done to improve productivity and cut costs. She also had to wait for almost three weeks to be asked to work the evening shift so she could assess what went on during the dinner rush and after.

Her first prenatal appointment brought mixed emotions. It was incredible to hear her baby's heart beating so strongly, and talking with the physician about a baby was awesome, but seeing the other women who were there with their husbands made her feel incredibly lonely. For years she had dreamed of having children with Jason and had always imagined it would be such a happy time. To have it come to pass and not have Jason there beside her, even when that had been her decision, was completely depressing.

One night at the hotel, as she came in, the night clerk handed her a package that had come for her that day. It was addressed in Kiersten's handwriting and as she went up the elevator, she tried to tear through the tape to open it, but had to wait until she got into her kitchen to get a knife. Inside was a note from Kiersten that read. "Hey, y'all. How's TX? Jason brought me this and asked me to forward it to you. I hope that's okay. Call me and tell me how Galveston is. I've never been there and I'm jealous. Happy birthday. Love you, K"

Her knees were suddenly so weak she had to sit down before she could carefully slide the knife through the tape on the inner box.

There was no note, no jewelry or chocolates, just a tiny glass figurine of a pair of Falcons in flight beside one another. She held it and looked at it almost reverently, until the tears obscured her vision and she pulled the little birds to her heart with a cry of utter anguish. *Oh, Jason, how could you? I've tried so hard to forget you.*

She'd known her birthday was coming, but she'd tried to ignore it so she wouldn't be so homesick. Her mother had e-mailed her to ask if she would like her and Kiersten to come down, but Kate had encouraged them not to. Her mother would worry the whole time and would get Jason's parents to come and check on her dad.

They had settled on sending Kate a care package and honestly, Kate wished she wouldn't even do that. This year she'd just like forget about her birthday. Her mother's package would arrive tomorrow like clockwork. There would be no question about it. And she'd cry but she'd feel loved. Jason's birds made her feel loved, but more than that they made her feel so sad and lonely and full of regret.

At the end of the three and a half weeks, John had her let the manager know what she had been doing and then she and a slightly offended manager spent another week going over her suggestions and making changes. The manager felt somewhat better about her when she explained what had happened to the manager in Dallas and told him she thought he was a great manager after all and had passed that on to John.

By the time the new profit and loss figures came in, she was in San Antonio, but John met with her and gave her another big check. And a report that although it wasn't as huge a margin, the Galveston restaurant had become fourteen percent more profitable.

John's home was between San Antonio and Austin and he had two restaurants in each town. Rather than have long conference calls between her and the accountant, they all just met in John's home office several times while she investigated. She had come to be incredibly comfortable with these two men over the past several weeks and slowly, she was getting to know them and them her.

Mark, the accountant, was married and had three grown children and his wife had MS. He was a Christian and, in fact, when he found out that Kate was wondering where to go to church, he invited her to go with him and his wife to his, which Kate loved. For just that few weeks, she almost felt like part of the congregation.

John wasn't married, but he had been. He didn't come right out and say it, but Kate got the impression it had ended early and long ago and that they were not amicable. He had two grown children he hadn't seen in years and he also didn't say that he wasn't very happy with them, but Kate got that impression too.

It was here in San Antonio, before Mark arrived one morning that John asked her casually where her family was. She calmly told him they were in Wye, Oklahoma and then he casually asked why she'd left. For several seconds she wondered what to tell him and finally decided he had earned complete honesty from her. Still trying to sound calm, she said, "I, uh, I had a romance there that went incredibly south and decided it would be better to leave."

At that, John looked up and met her eyes and then said sadly, "South bound romances can be hell. I learned that the hard way." He went back to what he was doing and then asked, "Why don't you ever go back and visit your family? You haven't been back, have you?"

Kate was mortified when tears filled her eyes, but she still felt like John deserved to know the truth and she turned to him and painfully told her worst secret, "I'm twenty one weeks pregnant, John. I hate to have to admit that I made some really poor decisions, but I did. I also made a decision not to tell the father because I think he's gotten onto a slippery slope in a really bad direction and I don't want my child to have to be dragged through the mess I think he's headed into. That being said, he'd never walk away if he knew he had a child." She shrugged and wiped at a stray tear. "I had to leave. I had to hide the fact that I'm expecting. And I'm going to have to keep hiding it. Otherwise this child will be forced to deal with the world at its worldliest. It may not have been very honest, but I felt like I had to leave."

After a long moment, he said, "Well, Kate. Sometimes it isn't very fun, but we all have to do what we feel is best. Especially if there's a child involved. How are you doing? Are you hanging in there?"

She nodded and gulped back a sob. When she could speak, she said, "When I'm busy. If I get too much time to think, I'm a wreck, but working for you has helped."

"Good. Because I owe you big. If you need something, let me know."

"Thanks."

That's all that was said at the time, but a couple days later, John handed her an insurance application with her name filled into the top and said, "I added health insurance to your employee benefits. You and the baby will be covered. Finish filling that in and give it to Gwen. She'll see it gets processed."

Kate was surprised and didn't know what to say so she simply said, "Thank you, John. I appreciate that."

"Well, you've earned it. And children are precious. They need to be taken good care of." He sat back down at his big desk and muttered, "I failed miserably with my two. The least I can do is insure yours."

To this Kate said, "I'm sure you didn't fail, John. As good a man as you are, I'll bet they turned out fine."

John shook his head and sighed. "You'd lose Kate. A good father can't overcome a bad mother. Not in this world. They've both turned out to be as shallow and selfish and lazy as... Let's just leave it that they were never very well disciplined. I tried. But I did fail. They're not very respectable people."

Kate put a hand on his shoulder. "I'm sorry, John. That had to have been hard to watch."

"It was hell." He tossed his pen and leaned back in his chair. "You know, Kate. I've been pretty successful. In everything but my family. But you know what? I'd give it all up if I could switch that around. It's taken me a lifetime, but I've finally realized that family is the most important thing."

"I'm only twenty, but what I've realized is that all we can do is our best. There are mistakes along the way." She put a hand on her stomach. "Sometimes huge ones. But all we can do is repent and try to do a little better. Sometimes we make colossal failures, but God knows if we're honestly giving it our all."

"You're amazingly wise for a whippersnapper. I thought you said you were nineteen."

"I was. Now, I'm twenty. My birthday was August eighteenth."

John sighed and picked up his pen. "Oh, Kate. I'm sorry. We should have celebrated."

"My mom sent me a care package with homemade chocolate chip cookies. I was fine. When's your birthday?"

"Not 'til March. I'll be forty seven."

Kate smiled. "We'll celebrate then."

Whether it was because John was closer, or some other reason, the two restaurants in San Antonio were well run, in Kate's opinion. She spent two weeks at each , made minimal changes that helped the bottom line, but only marginally, and moved on to Austin, where John had another two restaurants.

As she carried her bags into the Residence Inn there, she noticed for the first time that her burgeoning tummy was awkward and in the way and carrying her heavy bags made something low in her abdomen pull uncomfortably.

She bought bigger clothes again. This time some of them were actual maternity clothing and she had those same mixed emotions about having a baby that she'd been having. She was beginning to truly get excited about having a baby, but there was something so sad about doing it alone.

She made another appointment with a new OB/GYN and this time when she went in, they did an ultrasound and Kate came out of the office with an adorable photo of this tiny, tiny little boy, but nobody to show it off to. She thought about how she and Jason had planned to have a son together and name it after Kennen. Having the son, but not being able to share him with Jason felt so wrong somehow. She looked at the photo in her car in the parking lot and wished she could have sent it to Jason. He would have been so excited. *Oh, Jason, why did you have to change so much? You would have loved him.*

She cried all the way back to her hotel. There, she scanned it in to her computer and e-mailed it to her mother and Kiersten. They'd have mixed emotions as well, but at least they'd be excited for him.

Kate had gotten into the habit of changing the radio stations to classical or rock when Aerie's songs came on and she automatically did it at the restaurant in Austin one day and one of the other waitresses, who happened to be tall and red haired turned and snarled at her, "Stop doing that Kate. I love Aerie's music and y'all turn it off every time. How can you turn off someone as hot as Jason Falcon? Why do you like that instrument only stuff anyway? Y'all always act like you're so much more cultured and refined than the rest of us."

The girl's attack came out of the blue and Kate, who was still masquerading as a twenty year old waitress, looked at her in shock and the girl went on, "Y'all are so high falutin', but I don't see no boyfriend to go with that baby you're packin'. You wouldn't know what to do with a hottie star like Jason Falcon if he took y'all straight to bed, so stop with the holier than thou case against Aerie just because they're country and not some orchestra. It's not like you own this place."

Kate was stunned at the confrontation and wished she could fire the girl's butt right out of there, but she couldn't. At least not yet. Kate tried to blow off her comments after considering the source, but she kept seeing this tall red haired girl with Jason's arm around her and for some reason, it made her feel like she truly wouldn't have been able to attract Jason Falcon anymore. She'd never felt so awkward and ungainly and her slender, willowy figure was indeed gone.

She turned away from the waitress and went into the restroom and put a hand on her belly. She hadn't meant to get pregnant. In fact, she still couldn't remember much of that night, but she was, and it was Jason's. Whether the rest of the world knew or not, she needed to just deal with the fact and move on. That was all there was to it. She wished she was a week or two closer to telling the staff here what she was doing.

That evening, on her way back to the hotel, when she stopped and got gas, Jason's photo was on the cover of another magazine in front of the C-store counter. He was standing in a tux with a curvy blonde woman, although he didn't appear to be too cozy with her. He looked good. Wilder, with longer hair and a gold chain sporting a tiny gold Falcon on it, but good. Really, really good. She wished she could ask her mother how he was doing. She looked down at her steadily growing tummy and sighed and then took the magazine and turned it over before she paid for her gas.

It was only a couple of days later that she got a letter from Kiersten, which was strange because she e-mailed nearly every other day. It had been sent to John's office rather than the hotel and he gave it to her as they sat down with Mark for a meeting. Kate wondered if there was a problem, but didn't open it right then anyway. John and Mark were waiting for her to get started.

At the first Austin location, Kate suspected there was a problem with comped meals again. The numbers were skewed and the electronics there were somewhat obsolete, although she suspected it wasn't an electronics issue, but a not using the electronics issue. The kitchen staff was positively lackadaisical about enforcing that orders were run through the order register before they were prepared.

They finished their meeting and then as John and Mark were talking, Kate opened the envelope to pull out a photograph that made her heart skip a beat. It was simply a photo of her and Jason's lake with the sun setting across it and all the glory of God reflected in the colors of water and sky. She stared at it, and then slowly turned it over. All it said was, "Please come home, Jason"

She must have made a sound, because she looked up to find both John and Mark staring at her. She slipped the photo back into the envelope and put it into her portfolio and began to gather up the rest of the paperwork they'd brought her. Mark went out the door with a wave and John came back to her and asked, "Are you all right, Kate? Was that letter bad news?"

She took the photo out and handed it to him. "That was where we first talked about getting married."

John turned the photo over and read the back and then looked back up at Kate. "You said he wasn't headed in a good direction but you never said you're still in love with each other. Love can overcome a lot of stuff, Kate. Are you sure you can't go home and tell him?"

She thought longingly about that and then she remembered the red head and the beer. She thought back to the magazine cover those couple of days before and how wild Jason had looked and shook her head. "No, John. I love Jason, but I'm the one who's ultimately responsible for my little son's well being. Jason's lifestyle wouldn't be good for a child."

"It's a boy then?"

She nodded. "Yeah."

"Tell me, Kate. How did a nice girl like you get caught up with man with a bad lifestyle? I can't picture you being that irresponsible, even as a teenager."

"Jason wasn't always wild. I've known him since the day I was born. He was the most rock solid person on the planet for years and years and years."

"What happened?"

"He became a country music super star."

John looked at her for a long moment and then nodded. "I 'magine that'll do it. Hang in there."

"I intend to. See you Thursday. Hopefully I'll have some better information by then. You take care too." He narrowed his eyes at that last and then waved to her before reaching up to rub his head between his eyes.

Kristin Cross

Chapter 14

Kate went to another prenatal appointment and then signed up for a childbirth class. She was the only one there alone and it was a miserable experience for her, even though some of the other couples truly seemed to be enjoying it. Sitting there planning to go through labor without Jason was the most desolate feeling she'd ever known.

On the way home, she called her mother and talked about her maybe being able to come and be with Kate then, although Kate didn't know for sure where she'd be in another two or two and a half months. Her mother said that of course she'd come and that she'd get Kiersten to come and stay with her dad. "How's he doing, Mom? Really. He always says he's fine, but that is such a non word. I only say that when I'm definitely not fine."

"Katie, I hate to admit it to you, but your father isn't doing great. I'm not sure what it is, but to me, he seems like he's fading. That's the only way I know how to describe it."

"Is it me, Mom? If I come home, would that fix it? Is he just worrying?"

"Oh, he's worrying, Kate, but he'd still worry if you were living here and everything was fine. You do what you think is best and don't make decisions based on your dad and me."

"If I thought it would help him, I'd come."

"Is that what you want, Kate?"

"Of course it's what I want, Mother."

"But you still feel like you can't?"

"Not yet. Maybe when the baby is older."

"Jason still asks about you every few days, Kate."

"Don't tell me things like that, Mom. It's hard enough as it is."

"I know, Katie, honey. I'm sorry. I just think you need to know he still loves you. You need to forgive him someday."

"I forgave him long ago. I'm not holding a grudge here. Jason is simply human. It's not a grudge. I'm just trying to make the best choices for the baby. Parties and girls won't make for a stable upbringing."

"But is a stable upbringing worth not having a father?"

"I've prayed about this, Mom. You know that."

"You're right and I'm sorry. Let me know where I'll need to come, and around the first week in February, right?"

"Yes, thank you, Mom. Love you."

"I love you, too, Katie honey. Take care."

That night, Kate tried to estimate where she'd be in early February. Each restaurant had taken an average of three and a half weeks so far. And she had one more restaurant in Austin, one in Amarillo, one in California and one in Tulsa still. And about two and a half months until she was due. This was going to be nip and tuck. She needed to get this done so she could take some time off once the baby was here. Then if John was through needing her, she'd have to decide what she really wanted to do. She decided to talk to John about it in the morning.

She phoned John at about ten and told him what she'd been thinking about and she was surprised when instead of discussing it with her, he asked her what she was going to be doing for Thanksgiving.

"I'm going to work a long day so the others with families can have more time. Why? Do you need me to do something that day?"

"Actually, I was going to see if you wanted to come to my house and have dinner with me? It's just going to be me and my Brittany spaniel this year. Since you're alone too, I thought we could celebrate together. I have some ideas I'd like to run by you. Have you already committed to working? You are the boss there now."

"No, I could come. Are we going to cook dinner or go out?"

"Cook in of course. I know this is going to sound disloyal or something, but I personally think going out to eat on Thanksgiving is unAmerican."

"Well tell me what to bring then and I'll go shopping today so I don't have to fight the crowds."

"No, just come. I'll have everything. Unless there's some traditional family favorite that's unusual."

"No, we're pretty traditional kinds of folks out in Wye. What time do you want to eat?"

"Why don't you come by at about eleven and then we'll eat whenever it's ready. We'll see if we can find anyone who knows how to cook."

"Yeah, good luck with that John. See you day after tomorrow."

Kate had assumed from his comments, that John didn't know how to cook and that the restaurants were simply businesses, but when she got there Thanksgiving morning she found out that he was, in fact, a gourmet cook. The two of them tackled a small turkey with all the trimmings and Kate was again amazed at how comfortable she was with this wealthy business man who was nearly the same age as her father.

They were standing side by side chopping celery and onions when John casually said, "Kate, I need to talk to you about a huge favor."

"Okay. Shoot."

"I don't want you to think I'm crazy. But I'm afraid you might."

Kate laughed. "John, of all the people in this world, you are the least crazy I know. What's your favor?"

He stopped chopping and looked at her with an intensity that almost did make her nervous. "Kate, a few weeks ago, I was diagnosed with an inoperable brain tumor. I've been given from a month, to a year or more to live."

Kate was thunderstruck and tears sprang to her eyes. "A brain tumor? You're the sharpest man I've ever known. How can that be?"

John shook his head and went back to his chef's knife. "Who knows any of the difficult questions in this world, Kate? They have no idea what would have caused it. I've never smoked or done any kind of drugs or worked with chemicals. They don't know. They just know they can't operate and that I'll lose it mentally before I go."

"So what kind of favor do you want from me?"

"I want you to help me keep my businesses solvent and prospering until I can get them all sold. I've hired a realty firm, and Mark is helping me put together a scholarship foundation for the University of Texas at San Antonio, but he can't manage the actual restaurants when I'm too far gone, and I'm worried I'm losing this battle faster than I can get everything done."

Kate wiped at the tears that filled her eyes. "Okay, I'll help. But I'll need you to make a concise plan now so I'll always be doing exactly what you had in mind."

"That attitude is exactly why I'm asking you to do this. I've known from that very first letter that you were completely honest. But Kate, there's more. The brain tumor isn't the tricky part."

She turned to him. "There's something worse than an inoperable brain tumor? Is that possible?"

He sighed and dumped his celery into the buttery sauté pan. "Oh, yeah. Money grubbing children."

"What?"

"Kate, I'm a relatively wealthy man. Not filthy stinking rich, but fifteen or twenty million. Only with money comes responsibility. I pay a generous alimony and I supported my children and offered to pay for most of their college, but I think if my kids got hold of it all, it would be spent on exotic race cars and gambling. I have generous life insurance that will go to my ex wife and kids, but there are better things to be done with the rest. What do you think my kids are going to do when they find out I'm brain dead and leaving my wealth to a foundation instead of to them?"

"John, fifteen or twenty million *is* filthy stinking rich. You really think your children are going to try to fight you?"

"They've already started. I have no idea how they even found out I'm liquidating assets. They've never shown the slightest interest in working at one of these places. When they find out I'll eventually be deemed mentally incompetent, they'll come like three vultures."

She nudged his arm with hers. "That's a horrible way to talk about your children. I thought you said you only had two."

"I do. The ex is bound to come running as well."

"Oh, my. So what can I do to head off the vultures, more than manage your restaurants?"

"Uh, would you like to sit down, while I suggest this?"

Kate looked at him and her eyes got big and she went around and sat at his kitchen desk. "Okay. I'm ready."

"Kate, I want you to marry me and have joint power of attorney with Mark and have you be the executor of my trust until the foundation is all locked up and untouchable. You'd also be the person over my living will so they don't pull the plug while I'm still around or leave me plugged in past when I ought to go." He watched her for a second and then put out a hand. "And don't worry, I'm not asking for any kind of a marital relationship except that you see that I'm kept as comfortable as possible. It shouldn't take long at the end. The tumor is destroying the part of my brain that controls my heart and lungs."

If Kate hadn't been sitting down, she would have fainted. She sat there for a minute, her mind racing, trying to figure out exactly what he was asking. Finally, she asked, "Couldn't you simply get an attorney to keep them from you and what's yours until it's irrevocable? Why would a wife be anymore in control than that?"

"Theoretically, an attorney would be untouchable, but I don't want to chance it. Once I am deemed mentally incompetent, I think they'd try to come in as next of kin and rearrange things."

"Why me? You hardly know me and I'm only twenty years old. Surely there are more mature, educated people who could do a better job."

"Two reasons, Kate. One is that yes, I do trust you after working with you these last months. And that working relationship will hold up in court better than if I'd just marry someone I hadn't been around much. Especially after having been diagnosed. They still may fight you, but any lucid judge could meet you for ten minutes and realize you're the real deal. Not some woman looking for a sugar daddy. The fact that the money won't be coming to you will help as well.

"And secondly, your son. He needs a name, and right now, you can never go home without running the risk of losing custody of him until he's eighteen years old. Your parents will be old by then. Your sister and you will have grown clear apart. And he needs grandparents and cousins and the whole bit. If you get married now, for just a short time you can go home and your Jason won't know your son isn't mine. Your husband who passed away. You'll still be able to remarry respectably because you will have been widowed, not divorced. It all works, Kate."

He went on without a pause, "And I know you're still in love with Jason Falcon. That's okay. If you still want to go back to him someday, you can. You can tell him we weren't ever lovers, just good friends who helped each other when things were tough. Business partners."

He'd been waving his knife around while he spoke and he finally put it down and came to stand beside her. "I don't want you to answer me right now, Kate. I want you to go back to the hotel and think about it and pray about it at least over night. If you think it works, fine, we'll get married. If not, we'll still be fine to finish what we've started with overhauling the restaurants, and we'll go to plan B."

"Which is?"

"I'll stick with that attorney you were talking about and try to make an airtight trust my kids can't crack. And I'll die alone."

Kate continued to sit there in his kitchen chair in silence and then got up and went back to the counter and picked up her own chef's knife. After a moment, she said, "Y'all do know how to spice up a holiday. I think I'll take you up on thinking about this over night. Now where is that other sweet Vidalia onion?"

***

Jason slept in on Thanksgiving morning and then got up and got himself a bowl of Cheerios and took it to the coffee table in front of the TV. He prayed over the cold cereal and began to eat and then decided to pray over it again. After all, it was Thanksgiving and in spite of the fact that without Kate, his life didn't have much meaning, he had a lot to be thankful for.

He crunched into another bite, clicked on the remote and flipped through the channels as he ate. There was nothing that looked terribly interesting except maybe the bass fishing tournament and when he finished eating, he clicked the TV back off. His mother wasn't going to have dinner for another four hours, but he decided to go up to their house now anyway. He could use their unconditional support and this time he wouldn't have to find an excuse to visit.

Pulling in, he sat and looked at the empty spot on Kate's parents' driveway where she used to park her car and wondered where she was today. That's probably why he wanted to come up early. He'd been hoping Kate would come home today. Wasn't Thanksgiving supposed to be more of a family gathering holiday than any other? Even than Christmas? But her car wasn't there. At least not yet. Maybe she would still show up. It wasn't even noon yet.

He walked into his mother's kitchen and gave her a long hug. She pulled back after a minute to look at him critically and he grinned at her. "I know, I know. Cody has already told me I look awful. That wasn't his exact wording, but I think that's what he meant." He dug into a drawer and pulled out one of his grandmother's huge, full length, flowered aprons and strapped it on while his mom still watched him. "Ok, I'm ready. Give me a job."

His mother handed him a pair of white surgical gloves. "Here, you'd better have these too. They'll go perfect with the outfit. Would you mind taking everything out of that turkey and rinsing it and then putting the stuffing back in?"

Jason dramatically snapped on the gloves. "Anything for you, Mother."

They talked as they cooked together side by side and though it didn't feel like old times, it was still nice. His mother must have been thinking along the same lines he'd been, because she stared out the window blankly for a minute and said, "Do you remember that Thanksgiving before Kennen died? It was our whole family and Kate's whole family, and we had that humongous turkey? That was a nice day. I wonder where she is today."

Jason looked down at the turkey he was stuffing. He tried to swallow the lump that threatened to strangle him and he didn't answer. Eventually, his mom turned away from the window, glanced over at him and back out the window toward the Birches and said, "I hope she comes home today. This has had to have been lonely for her. She was really a home kind of a girl. Laura told me she got a job traveling and has been living out of a hotel ever since she left."

Still, Jason didn't answer. He couldn't. He didn't know Kate had been traveling. She hated to travel. At least she hated traveling with the band. It broke his heart, but then again, it almost made him mad. Why would Kate take a job traveling? The answer hit him and he pushed more stuffing into the turkey with a sigh. For the same reason she'd left. She felt like she couldn't come home. She'd had to go.

At first, he'd been hurt and then mad and then rebellious, and ticked off and every other frustrating thing he could feel, but then when that all dulled and it was just him and this soul deep emptiness, he finally understood she'd left because she loved him. If that hadn't been true, she could have stayed right here next door to his parents and gone on with her life and never had to pull up those lifelong deep roots. But she couldn't.

She was either afraid she would give in and come back to him, or she couldn't face the memories and chance running in to him all the time. Or both. When he realized that, it at least gave him some measure of comfort. She loved him. He hoped she always would. That someday soon, she'd come back and be with him and they could get on with their lives and live happily ever after. Maybe she'd even come home today.

He'd quit working on the bird and was just thinking about her when his mother broke into his thoughts. "Jason, can I ask you a question?"

"Sure, go for it."

"I've never pried to find out why she left. In fact, I truly don't want to know, but honey, have you fixed whatever it is, yet? Whatever made her give up on you. Is it resolved so she could come back if she wanted too?"

"Mom, she left because she saw me at my hotel after a concert with a beer bottle in my hand and my arm around some girl. She just misunderstood. It wasn't my beer, another guy had handed it to me to hold while he went to the door. And the girl meant nothing. If Kate had been reasonable enough to listen, I could have explained that. She left because she misinterpreted what she saw."

His mother didn't answer right away and when she did, her answer was thought provoking. She went back to the pie she was making as she said, "Hmm, that doesn't sound like Kate. To end a lifelong relationship just because of one isolated incident. Here, put that turkey inside this bag and put it in this roaster, would you?"

"I hate it when you do that."

His mother turned to look at him. "I thought you liked my turkey cooked in the bag."

"No. I love your turkey. I hate it when you subtly and politely make me realize I'm a bone head. All this time, I've been trying to make myself believe she left because she misunderstood. And you gently steal my rationalization. Thanks a lot."

"Well, Jason, if the girl you had your arm around meant nothing, why did you have your arm around her? Is it that physical touch means nothing? Or that honoring Kate and her feelings mean nothing? I'm not sure I understand. Why would you jeopardize forever if it was for nothing? And why is there beer at your hotel at all? If the roles had been reversed Jason, you'd have walked out too. Especially if it had happened a few times before."

"She'd never seen me with my arm around a girl before. There you go again. And you're right. Dang it."

His mother made one of those mothering noises. "Of, course she'd seen you with your arm around another girl. She's not blind. She does have to walk through the check out at the Piggly Wiggly from time to time."

"You make me sound like some womanizer. I'm not that bad, am I?"

"Of course not, Jason. But Kate was far and away above the not that bad category. She's in the best of the best category. And she had a right to expect that of her other half."

Jason turned to her sadly. "You know, Mother, I was half joking about rationalizing. I do understand all of this. It's not like I haven't had a million hours to think about where I messed up. I'd grovel to her in a minute if she'd let me. Is there anyway we could change the subject?"

She came and patted his cheek. "Of course honey. I just miss her so much. I simply wanted to know if she could come home if she needed to. I'm hoping you've quit hugging girls who mean nothing. Do we want a green bean casserole this afternoon?"

"Not unless we're having a lot of company. Who's coming today?"

"No one. It's just you and me and Daddy today. I tried to invite Laura and Orrin and Kiersten and her family, but they worried you'd feel uncomfortable.

He looked out the window again and paused before he said, "Maybe they were right. It would have been awkward to have to be so careful to skirt any mention of Kate. And honestly. I love them dearly. I do. But sometimes I hate them for not telling me where she is. They could have stood up for me when she made them promise. They know how much I love her. But they didn't."

"Jason, you know Kate. She would have just not told them and then she'd have been entirely alone. They had to humor her."

"I know, Mom, but … Oh, let's just let it go. Do you need anymore dried bread?"

By mutual consent, they stayed off the subject of Kate after that. When dinner was over, Jason and his dad helped clean up and put everything away and then the three of them watched a football game before they all three fell asleep after all that turkey.

In the early evening, Jason gave up all hope she'd show up. If she was going to come, she'd have been here by now. Thoroughly depressed, he kissed his mom and shook his dad's hand and headed out. On the way to his car, he stopped in to Kate's parents and wished them a happy Thanksgiving and then regretted it. They were obviously as sad about Kate not being there as he was.

That night, he sat up with his guitar until early in the morning thinking about her. He'd thought she'd come. He knew he'd let her down so badly, but he never dreamed that night in Lubbock she'd just leave and stay gone. If he had, he'd have stayed in the doorway of that elevator forever. He'd have never let her leave without him

Until tonight, he hadn't realized how much he'd been hoping she'd come home today. He was just sure of it. Kate was a home body. Family was everything to her. Well, family and Jason. At least they had been.

For about the millionth time, he considered hiring a private investigator. She had to be somewhere. He had the money. Someone could find her. But then something would always make him decide against it. As much as he was so empty without her, he also didn't want to force her into anything. If he stayed faithful, someday she'd figure it out and come back to him. She had to. He'd die without her.

When he was so tired he couldn't see straight, he put his guitar back on its stand, went in to his bed and knelt to ask God to keep her safe and bring her home soon. They were the only things that kept him sane. God and his guitar.

Chapter 15

She'd known when he talked about plan B and dying alone that she would agree to John's proposal, but felt like praying about it over night had been a wise idea. It was strange how marriage had gone from her greatest dream in life, to something that didn't really matter, either way. Although she'd come to like and respect John, marriage had been boiled down to a business arrangement. She already knew she'd probably never marry someone other than Jason, because it would be wrong when she was in love still. But John's arguments held a lot of water. She could help him and help her son at the same time.

When that feeling hadn't changed in the morning, she drove back to John's house and knocked on the door. He met her with a smile and welcomed her in and they discussed the details and arranged to go to the county courthouse the next day and get it taken care of. With the arrangements made, she got back into her car and went back to the hotel to get ready to go to work.

When an Aerie song came on as she drove, she reached to turn the radio off, wiped the tears from her cheeks with the back of her hand and resolutely sat up straighter as she drove. So it wasn't what she'd always dreamed of. Under the circumstances, she should be grateful she was warm, and safe and watched over. And if John was as ill as he believed himself to be, the only thing in her life that would be different in a short while would be that she'd have a different last name and hopefully enough of a marriage behind her that someday Jason and his parents wouldn't compute that Kate's child was Jason's.

That night, she told her family about her impending marriage. Her mother cried on the phone and her dad was closed mouthed, but Kiersten raised enough of a ruckus for both of them. She was completely outraged and kept reminding Kate that she was in love with Jason and that it would be wrong to marry another man. She was only slightly mollified when she heard the whole story and insisted she do a background check on John as she and Kate were talking.

Kate wasn't sure what she found, but whatever it was seemed to sooth her worries a bit, because she'd mellowed considerably by the time they hung up, although the last thing she said was, "Kate, Jason still asks about you every few days. Please don't mess up your life with this guy. I always hope and pray that someday y'all and Jason can figure things out. You were so good for each other. And were the best friends I've ever seen. Don't give up forever."

Kate got off the phone and lay awake for hours, trying not to think about the things Kiersten had said. Crying herself to sleep always gave her a headache.

She kept trying to remind herself that she hadn't gone because Jason didn't love her. She'd known all along he loved her. It was just that he didn't love only her and had slowly changed so much from the man she'd known who shared her values.

Mark and his wife came by to witness their marriage and then John helped her bring her things from the hotel and put them in one of his guest suites and gave her a set of keys and a garage door opener. Then John had to go back to San Antonio to some meetings and Kate went back to the restaurant in Austin. She was all but finished with this one and put in an application at the other one, to be getting started while she finished up.

That first night at John's house, he met her in the back entry as she came through from the garage and they small talked for a few minutes and then Kate went off to bed and John went back to the basketball game he'd been watching on TV. Her wedding night was as simple as that and for some reason that was incredibly troubling. She fell asleep that night trying not to be emotional about her marriage being so opposite of what she'd always dreamed. She tried to remind herself she should just be glad she was safe and comfortable. A lot of girls in her situation were struggling just for the basics.

The next morning they met in the home office with Mark again and began to plan the details of what Kate's responsibilities would be with the restaurants and John's trust as time went on and then John caught a plane to Tulsa while Kate went in for her last day at the restaurant she had been tuning up. That night, John was still gone and Kate set up a small office of her own in another spare bedroom and went to her weekly prenatal class again.

She was hired within two days at the second Austin restaurant and at that one she was able to get into the business office again to work on the books part of the time, although in the kitchen she was being asked to begin as a busser. It didn't take long to discover there was a problem with the numbers again and Kate wondered why even though the two restaurants were mere blocks from each other, they used different suppliers and one's costs far out weighed the other.

She tried to befriend the manager, but he was having nothing to do with her short of the most meager dealings required to instruct her, which was minimal because she was under another supervisor. This restaurant might prove to be the biggest challenge of all just because of the manager's superior attitude.

John came home and they began to settle in to some semblance of married life. He made her breakfast and left it warming for her and she tossed his exercise clothes into the washing machine with hers and then folded them and took them up to his room. If she wasn't working in the evenings, she sometimes brought a book into the room where he was and would read while he did too or watched TV.

They still had their meetings and responsibilities, the same as before, but John also had her go back to the restaurants she'd worked with earlier from time to time to check on things on days she had off. Often he went one way on a plane and she went the other in her car, but they seemed to have established a working marriage relationship with relatively little conflict.

She still went to her childbirth class alone. In fact, she didn't even mention to John she was taking it, and she knew he was still going to a number of doctor appointments on his own as well. They both seemed comfortable in living and working beside each other and still keeping their private lives somewhat private.

It was three weeks into her new "job" that she was finally able to start to uncover the questionable purchasing at the second Austin restaurant. With some digging, she was able to determine the main wholesale food supply company the manager used was owned by a series of corporations that were ultimately owned by his brother in law. Kate assumed that the company could charge whatever it wanted and the manager was kicked back a portion of the exorbitant profits.

She talked it over with John to determine if there were any charges that could be filed, but he didn't think there were and so they went on to fire the manager and begin the process of tuning up what remained. The day that John revealed to the employees she was working for him, was the first time Kate ever saw him struggling with a headache.

The whole time he was meeting with the staff, he seemed to be less amiable than usual and then when they were done and headed home, he asked Kate if she would mind driving. He got into the passenger seat and tossed back a white tablet with a diet Coke and then reclined his seat and closed his eyes with a grimace.

He was obviously in so much pain by the time they got home that Kate had to help him out of the car and into the house. Once there, he took another pain pill and then took an ice pack and went to his room to try to relax where it was dark and quiet. Kate went back to the kitchen to eat dinner alone and worry about how feeble he had seemed to become in just a few hours this afternoon compared to how robust he'd seemed this morning. He may have been right about losing this battle much faster than he had expected.

Although not life threatening, Kate was beginning to deal with some physical issues of her own. Her tummy had begun to feel humongous and she could no longer lift things and bend and move around like she was used to. Not only that, but she struggled to sleep comfortably and for the first time in her existence, she experienced heartburn. She'd never been so miserable in her life.

John was always careful to keep their relationship casual and comfortable, but he also came home one day with a big, new Mercedes Benz sedan for her so she would have a little more room and better safety than her Dodge Intrepid for her and the baby. They had a bit of a discussion about the luxury car and finally settled on giving it to her for Christmas not quite two weeks away, but John would still own it and she would sell her car for now. She buckled the seatbelt around her huge tummy that day on the way to work and was grateful John was so considerate.

On one of the last days Kate was going to be working at the second Austin restaurant, she was sitting in the manager's office, going over the payroll records and wondering why she was having such a hard time keeping her mind off of Jason this morning. She could swear she could almost smell his after shave today.

She was still sitting there trying to focus when one of the female servers came rushing back into the kitchen in almost heart failure and several of the other staff gathered around her to see what was going on. Kate was just going to go out and see about it and get them all back on task, when she heard why the girl was breathless after all. The waitress almost squealed, "Do you know who is out there? Jason Falcon and some of his band! Right here in our own dining room! I wonder if he would sign the new CD I just bought."

She continued on, but Kate heard none of it. It took everything Kate had to continue to breathe and walk calmly back to the office and shut the door. Oh, how she wanted to go and look out that window. Just once. Just long enough to see how he was doing with her own eyes. But she couldn't. She knew it would be a mistake and a risk he would see her and realize she was pregnant, not to mention make her miserably lonely again. It was already all she could do to make it through the days without him and it had been more than six months. She put a hand on her tummy and looked down at the baby she was carrying and wiped at her tired eyes and went back to her desk as she whispered, "C'mon baby Falcon; we've got work to do so we can get out to Amarillo on Friday."

Entirely unable to focus, as good as her intentions were, Kate glanced up at the window to the parking lot every few minutes and when she finally saw him and a few guys go back out across the way there, she couldn't help herself and turned her chair to watch. He still had that something about him that spoke of confidence and understated power. And even from this distance as he paused once and looked all around, he was still as handsome and striking as ever.

She saw them pile into a couple of cars and drive away and she sighed a long, shaky sigh and picked up her pen. She had a whole new life now. Her days with Jason were over and she knew it. After all, it was her doing. It was just hard to control the memories sometimes.

Nights were the worst. No matter how tired she was when she finally laid down; there was inevitably a period of wondering what he was up to and if he was okay. She still prayed for him several times a day, just like she did for her family and baby and now John, and now that the advancing pregnancy made resting peacefully impossible, she prayed for him during the night as well when she woke up with him on her mind. Sometimes she would dream they were still together and he was still the same Jason she'd grown up with and for just a second when she woke up there would be this happy, easy peace like she'd felt when he used to hug her close. It was heaven and she hated to have to finish waking to reality.

***

Aerie played a concert down in Austin and then had another one in Corpus Christy the next day and they drove from city to city rather than fly for such a short trip. For some reason, Kate had been on his mind more than ever this trip and it was uncanny enough that he almost wondered if there was a reason for it. He hoped everything was all right with her.

They pulled away from their hotel late in the morning and then stopped at a restaurant on the south end of Austin that had come highly recommended for lunch. There, the thoughts of Kate became even more pervasive and he had to almost wonder if she was around somewhere. Throughout the meal he kept looking around and even Cody noticed and asked him what was wrong. Jason just shook his head. If he told Cody he could smell Kate's perfume and that she was haunting him today, Cody would just nod and give him that look of pity he did anymore now that Cody no longer believed Jason would ever get her back.

But he himself had never given up hope. He never would. It didn't matter how long it took. It wasn't like he would ever start over with someone new, no matter how long she was gone. His was a devotion for life. He'd come to realize that more surely than ever. It was too bad Kate hadn't waited, because Jason had done just what she'd always needed him to do. Gotten used to all the glitz and knew without a doubt Kate was indeed his only flavor.

On the way back to the car, he couldn't shake the feeling she was nearby. It was almost as if he could feel her spirit. That she really was haunting him. In a way, it was almost freaking him out a little. He paused and looked around before finally climbing into the rental car with a sigh. *Kate, wherever you are, I still love you forever.*

***

With Austin wrapped up, Kate began to pack for the all day drive to Amarillo. John had started to recommend she take a week or two off for the holidays, but she knew if she had that much time on her hands, she'd climb the walls missing Jason. John must have understood, because he left it up to her to make her decisions.

She went to her last childbirth class by herself and was glad she'd never have to face all those couples again in her life. She'd needed to do it for the baby's sake, but it had been a heart wrenching experience.

For the first time, pulling up stakes was more troubling to her. Going from a real home back to the hotel, was bad enough, but this time she would be alone over Christmas and it was an intimidatingly lonely thought.

Even worse, John was finally looking like he wasn't feeling great a good portion of the time and for the first time, the other day she had watched him struggle to pull something from his memory and ultimately give up. The tumor was finally starting to affect his amazingly sharp mind.

That last morning, he woke up with the beginnings of a headache. She could see it in the small lines between his eyebrows and the shadows deep in his eyes. They hadn't spoken much of truly important things, but the realization was there all of the time now that this good, honorable man was dying. Even though she had only known him a short time, it was one of the most heartbreaking things she'd ever had to watch.

He came into the kitchen, dressed for work, and she turned from the stove and smiled at him. She couldn't fix his troubles, but she could do her best to brighten this inevitable road to death. She put a plate of a scrambled egg skillet on the breakfast table in the alcove by the window and then put a gentle hand to his cheek and looked at him. "Headache already?"

He nodded silently and went to the fridge for orange juice. She wished they were closer friends and that he felt like he could talk to her about what he was thinking and feeling. Bringing hot croissants, she put them on the table in front of him and came to stand behind him and gently rubbed his temples for a moment. "Does that help at all, or make it worse?"

"Both, I think. But I'm fine, Kate. Sit down and eat your breakfast before it gets cold."

She sat across from him. "Should I say the prayer?" He nodded again and she began. She asked for a blessing on the food and then added one for John and then added one for both of them to be watched over and then closed the prayer and he looked up at her.

"You've never been alone at this time of year before, have you?"

She passed him the eggs as she admitted, "No. It's going to be a little weird. Do you usually spend Christmas with someone?"

"Sometimes. For a while, after my divorce, I spent it with my children. Then when they outgrew that, I'd sometimes visit my mother, or my sister's family. Now my mother has passed away and my sister lives in the Bahamas. But there have been several years I've been alone. It's not too bad. It makes for a more quiet, peaceful holiday, but sometimes that's a good thing. Peace and quiet is good for spiritual introspection. This is after all, a celebration of Christ's birth."

Kate nodded. That would be true. It would still be incredibly lonely, but maybe she could simply focus on Christ and get through it okay. He was watching her as he sipped his juice and wondered out loud, "Why don't you get up there, Kate and then see how things go. If you're busy right away, fine, but if not. You're only going to be a few hours from your family. Maybe they could come to you if you feel like there's no way you could go visit them. And then catch a plane back here Christmas Eve. The restaurant will be closed for a couple of days anyway, even if you've gotten hired. Then you can hit it again after. Just put the tickets on your expense account."

"I'll think about it. What are you going to be doing?"

The same as usual. I'll probably go golfing with friends a few times, and I usually go to some Christmas concerts. That type of thing. Christmas morning I go to the homeless mission and help out there. But mostly, I'll just work here." He gave her a sad smile. "Now that I'm dying, I've finally figured out that a great deal of my life is pointless. When I failed with my family, I switched my focus to building an empire. In retrospect, that doesn't mean much. At the very least, I should have tried again. Don't make the same mistake I made, Kate. Go see your family if you can."

She finished her breakfast in a somber, introspective mood, and then got up to clean up and straighten the kitchen. She needed to be making some plans for after the baby was born. It would be too easy to bury her sorrows under a career in business and make the same mistake John had made. Sure, she would have a child, but as a single parent, it would be even more paramount that she try to live life on a more eternal track.

In a way, she was incredibly grateful for John's perspective. He had certainly had to face facts in the big picture and it was enlightening to be reminded that there's a purpose to this earthly existence. She didn't necessarily believe John had failed the test as he seemed to worry, but she knew he had massive regrets. She had a couple as well, but maybe she could do better in the future, especially where her child was concerned.

She came down the hall with her big suitcase and purse, and John automatically picked the suitcase up and carried it to her car and put it in the trunk for her and then stood beside the car looking at her. "Be safe, Kate. Amarillo is a nice town, but be careful. And don't overdo. That baby isn't far off. Get the bellman to bring this for you and order in room service. I don't want you to be miserable just sitting waiting, but maybe this should be the last restaurant you deal with until the baby is a few months old."

She put an arm around his waist and gave him a half hug. "Thank you for your concern, John. I'll think about it. Don't drive if you have to take pain medication. Get Gwen's son to come and take you if you need to."

At that, he gave her a real smile. "Thanks, but I'll wait for this tumor to kill me and not a reckless driver.

Pulling away from his house, she considered what he'd said about traveling when she was this pregnant. That same issue had crossed her mind, but the down time would kill her. She would go crazy with missing Jason. She thought about her new husband, even though the marriage had been for business and felt guilty just for thinking that. But it was true. All work and no play made Kate a dull girl, but the alternative was too painful.

She couldn't believe her heart was still so sore after this many months, but it was what it was and she needed to keep busy. Still, the airlines wouldn't even let her get on if she was too outlandishly big. She needed to wrap up Amarillo and San Francisco as quickly as she could, both because of the baby and because of how fast John was going down hill.

Having the bellman take her bags up was very nice and she followed him onto the elevator with a sigh. That had been a hellaciously long drive, even with stopping and walking around every hour or so. She walked into the room, tipped the bellman, kicked her shoes off and headed for a long, hot shower and then bed. She was definitely going to take John up on his room service idea.

The next morning, she applied to work at the restaurant, but the manager simply shook his head and said, "Look, lady. I'm sure you need this job, or you wouldn't be asking, but there's no way I can have someone as pregnant as you are walking around here working. The patrons would be outraged."

Undaunted, Kate said, "Then let me work in the office. You can see my training and recommendations."

"I'd love to, but I have a wonderful book keeper slash assistant and we're all under control that way. I'd hire you anyway, but it would be a waste of the owner's money and I take his trust pretty seriously. I'm sorry, but you'll have to try elsewhere."

He was so sincere and she felt so good about him she decided to just go with her gut on this one and let him know right up front what she was up too.

She glanced at his name tag. "Well, Glen, in light of that. And the fact you've admitted you take John Garland's trust pretty seriously, I'll tell you right up front that I work for him. I'm a consultant of sorts, I guess you might say. I usually come in and get to work without anyone realizing that at first, but this baby has become a bit of an issue. And rightly so.

"But I still need to work here for a while and give John my honest opinion of how things here are going. It's not that he doesn't trust you. It's just that I've been able to improve some things at his other locations and he decided to send me to all of them. Even the ones that are thriving, like here. And I hope you'll continue to be as good to work with as you were when you thought you were sending me packing, because we need to work together here as amiably as possible."

Glen had been surprisingly willing to work with her as soon as he spoke to John on the phone and confirmed that what she was saying was true. He ended up not telling the rest of the staff she wasn't just another person he'd hired. He had her start as an expeditor. That way, she could get to know everyone and sort of work between the kitchen staff and the wait staff and when they weren't rushed, he let her help in the office as well.

At first glance, this restaurant looked to be thoroughly under control, but Kate knew she needed to spend some time here to make sure of that. She was also only working five or six hour days because of the advanced pregnancy and was grateful Glen had been so willing to accommodate that.

Back in her hotel after a couple of days of settling in, she relaxed for a few hours and then went out to do some shopping. The shorter work days accommodated that and she needed to get things shipped to Wye right away. Christmas Eve was in just four days.

She bought things for all of her family and for Jason's parents and a couple of her friends back home and for Mark and his family. When it came to John, she had no idea what to get and had to let that go for the time being while she continued to think about it. She wished she could send something to Jason, but that was out of the question. Still, she wished.

She was actually on her way to ship the gifts when she decided not to. Wye was only a four or five hour drive from here. She called Glen on her cell phone and arranged to have all of Christmas Eve off and then only work the late morning and early afternoon of the day before. It might not be completely wise, but she was going to sneak home to see her parents on the night of the twenty third. She'd come after dark and be gone again the same night and hopefully, no one else in Wye would ever know that a humongously pregnant Kate Birch-Garland had finally come home.

Once the decision was made, she phoned her parents and Kiersten and then she was so excited she could hardly wait. Both excited and sad. She wondered how hard it would be to be that close to Jason again and know he was entirely out of her reach.

As she approached the Oklahoma City metropolitan area, she became more and more emotional. She hadn't seen these people in more than six months and coming home made her so happy it was painful. Happy and heartbroken. How was she going to bring herself to leave again?

Knowing she wanted this to be a happy reunion, she struggled to get her emotions under control so she could greet them all with only the smiling portion of what she was feeling.

It was full dark when she slowly pulled up their street and into her old parking spot on the drive. Once again, the emotions threatened to overcome her. She couldn't even stand to look at the house next door. This trip would be good for her. Knowing how much it hurt just to sit here in her car next to his parents' house, she'd be hesitant to do this very often. Maybe next time she'd just have to see if her family could come to her, except she knew how hard it was to take her dad places. Then again, maybe she'd just have to suck it up every few months. She got out of the car a complete wash of different emotions.

The reunion was incredibly sweet and incredibly bitter at the same time. It was heaven to have her mom hug her and she broke down and cried in spite of her good intentions. The hug was a bit awkward because of her size and she was somewhat embarrassed about how blatant her mistakes of that fateful night with the champagne were. Kiersten helped that. She put both hands on Kate's tummy and laughed and said, "Kate, you look like a mountain!" That helped to break the tension.

Seeing her dad was by far the hardest part of it all. He was a shell of the man he'd been six months ago, though he'd been bedridden even then. To Kate, he looked like he'd aged twenty years and not six months. He accepted her awkward hug and then looked into her eyes with his filling with tears and then took her left hand to examine the huge diamond ring John had given her when they'd married. He didn't look very happy about any of it and Kate was crushed, both at what terrible shape he was in and how unhappy her life had obviously made him. The thought that she was the one to blame for his downward spiral made her sick.

They all talked and laughed and ate and exchanged gifts until finally, at twenty after eleven, Kiersten got up and said she had to get back to her family. She reached into her pocket and handed Kate another small box and said, "I promised I'd get this to you. I hope that's okay."

Kate took it without knowing what it was and suspecting it was something that would upset her, put in right into her pocket. She'd look at it later when her family wasn't around.

Kate knew she needed to get going too. She was only going to drive part of the way and then stop and get another hotel, but she still needed to be awake enough to get that far.

When Kiersten was gone, Kate went to tell her father goodbye, and it was a long and tearful process. She knew he'd had such hopes for both of their lives. His hopes for his had been stolen by a foolish driver and many of the ones for hers had been lost through a foolish decision. Both had been hard on him and together they had apparently crushed his spirit. Kate walked back down the hall from his room in complete distress. She'd known it was going to be hard to leave, but that was before she had any idea of the shape he was in.

Saying farewell to her mother was too hard to face for a few more minutes and Kate carefully sat back down beside her in the living room with a sigh. Her mom smiled sadly as she said, "I remember those days of feeling like a great blue whale coming in for a landing. You look really good, Kate. How are you feeling?"

"Like more of a cross between a great blue whale and an aircraft carrier. Sometimes it takes a while just to change directions. You look good too, Mother."

"Thanks, Katie, honey. I'm lonely without you, but I've lost a little weight. That's a good thing."

"You look like you're twenty five again!" Kate smiled at her and then tears filled her eyes as she went on sadly, "Daddy doesn't. I had no idea he was so..."

Her mom squeezed her hand. "He's okay, Kate. He's lost a lot of the enthusiasm he always exuded, but he'll make it through. We really aren't twenty five anymore, you know."

"I know, but he's not seventy either." She sighed and changed the subject. "How are Jason's parents?"

Her mother smiled sadly again. "Well. Lonely. They lost Kennen and then you and now they've even lost Jason in a way. He's changed a lot since you left, Kate. Those dazzling smiles are few and far between now. And he doesn't come by as much as he used to. I'm sure part of it is how busy he is now. He tours all over the country and even beyond, but I would guess most of it is that he can't face coming, without you being here."

"Oh, Mother, surely he's over me by now. It's been six months."

"It's been longer than that, Kate. And he is far from over you. I can't believe you don't realize that. Didn't the lyrics of this last several songs make that clear?"

Kate shook her head. "I don't listen to his music anymore, Mom. I can't."

Her mother paused and looked at her in surprise and then nodded. "I'm sorry to bring him up, honey. So tell me more about this John you married? What's he like?"

For another twenty minutes they talked and finally, Kate heaved herself off the couch and tearfully told her mother goodbye. It was insanely hard to do.

Settled into the luxury of the Mercedes, she once more headed to Texas and she'd certainly talk to God as she drove again. She was almost back to highway forty when the car turned almost of its own volition. She had to at least drive past Jason's apartment. Even if he was outside and saw the car he wouldn't ever know it was her, but she had to at least drive by.

His car was there, but there was no sign of him and all of his lights were off except the porch one. Kate pulled to the curb and killed the engine. What would she give to be able to walk up and knock on that door? She thought back to her decision to just leave and not tell him and for the first time, she wondered if it had been a mistake. She'd prayed about it and felt it was right, but tonight had been a clear demonstration of what it had cost her. Cost a lot of people involved. She thought of Jason up in that room and hoped he never did find out the baby was his. He would be so disillusioned with her for keeping such a big deal from him.

She finally reached into her pocket and pulled out the small box. She assumed it was something from Jason, the way Kiersten had been acting. She was right. In the light of the street lamp she pulled a slender diamond and gold bracelet out that had a tiny gold Falcon in flight dangling from it. Kate had never seen anything quite like it and she let it hang and twist as the minimal light caught the sparkling stones. It was beautiful and she'd treasure it forever, even though she knew she'd never be able to wear it. It would be too painful of a reminder of him every time she saw it.

She put it back into the box, wishing she didn't have to cry so much every time she thought of him. She looked back in the box for a note, wondering why he had sent it even after this many months. It simply said, "I'll wait forever. I love you, Jason." She clutched the box to her chest with a sob. She wished he hadn't changed and begun to follow Cody's lifestyle. She would love to let him know there truly was a little Falcon.

After several minutes, she pulled back out and hit the road for the Texas state line as she whispered through her tears, "Goodbye again, Jason. I'll always love you."

Chapter 16

She did fly back to be with John on Christmas Eve. Sadly, it didn't really matter to her where she was if she couldn't be at home, but she didn't want John to be alone.

Finally, in the airport, she found a small painting of Jesus she loved and hoped John would like. It was of Christ reaching a hand down to a child to help him up over a boulder in a stream. Maybe it would help convince John the atonement included him and the mistakes he so regretted and he would allow the Savior to reach down and lift him up at this last time in his life.

He took her to a concert on Christmas Eve at a local church and then Christmas morning she went with him to help feed the homeless a hot breakfast and pass out gifts of socks and underclothing and toiletries the mission had been gathering.

Afterward, as John helped her out of his own Mercedes in the garage and into his opulent house, Kate realized this trip had been good for her. Until this morning, she'd almost come to take the luxury of her present lifestyle for granted.

She and John made another holiday dinner and as they ate, for the first time, he talked to her about death and how he really felt about it and what he hoped to accomplish this last few weeks here on earth. It was both heartbreaking and enlightening, but by the time she flew back out the next day, she felt much closer to him than she had.

Although she was only in Amarillo for not quite two weeks, while she was there, Kiersten forwarded her another package from Jason. It was a post card of Columbus, Ohio and it said, "We played to thirty thousand. It's lonely without you. Come home soon. I love you, Jason." In the same package she found a section of small birch tree branches that had twisted around each other and finally grown so tightly together their bark had actually become one piece. She knew exactly what he was trying to tell her. She still felt the same way about him.

She flew straight from Amarillo to San Francisco and had her car shipped home. It was the first time she'd ever been that far west and honestly, she was a bit intimidated. Northern California was a long, long way from Wye, Oklahoma.

She'd been working in the restaurant for about a week when she got an emergency call from Kiersten telling her her dad had a blood clot in his lungs and they hadn't been able to get it to dissolve so far and would she please come home as fast as possible. Kiersten didn't use the word die, but Kate knew that was exactly what they were worried about as she hurried out of the restaurant and climbed awkwardly into her rental car, praying for all she was worth.

An hour and a half later, her dad was even worse but she'd been able to find a flight, grab her bag, turn in her rental car and she was hurrying for the right concourse in the airport when she had to slow down and try to catch her breath. Being eight months pregnant and upset definitely cut down on your wind. She glanced at her watch and began to try to run again. She was going to miss this plane.

Approximately fourteen miles of endless concourse later, she finally made it to her gate just in time to see the plane she'd been trying to catch pull away from the building and begin to taxi slowly toward the runway. Kate leaned against the window and started to cry as she silently said, "God, you could have held that plane. You know what's going on here."

Rushing like this wasn't good. Her heart felt like it was going to burst and the muscles in her lower abdomen were pulling tightly. She tried to catch her breath and at the same time try to regroup mentally to begin looking for another plane.

One of the women staffing the gate approached her to ask if she was okay and she nodded. "I'm okay; I just needed to make that plane."

Kate must have looked as uncomfortable as she felt because the middle aged woman encouraged her to sit down while she called to find another flight. Kate did and had just picked up her phone to begin making calls when it rang. It was Kiersten again and fear clutched at Kate's heart. She prayed as she pushed send that it wasn't what she dreaded it was.

Kiersten was crying so hard her husband must have finally taken the phone because he came on the line instead to tell her sadly her father had just passed away. Kate stood up again in shock and couldn't help the tears that flooded down her face. It couldn't be true. Her father was barely fifty years old! Fifty year olds didn't die!

Kate wasn't even aware if she ended the call or not. She wasn't aware of anything until the same clerk came back and put an arm around her as she cried. She tried to explain through her tears, but couldn't even make the words come out of her mouth. The clerk was telling her she'd called for someone from airport hospitality to come and help her out with whatever she needed. Kate didn't know how someone from the airport could help. What she needed was her father to be well and whole and alive. That was what she needed.

She struggled to get control of herself and then a moment later when she felt something pull low in her body and then a trickle of warm water flowing down her slacks, she began to sob again uncontrollably. Just when she'd thought she couldn't handle this heartache at this time and place, now she realized she was going to be delivering a baby more than four weeks early and nearly two thousand miles away from anyone on earth she knew. It was almost more than she could stand.

The courtesy shuttle did indeed come for her but instead of helping her find a plane; they delivered her to a waiting taxi where she sat on a plastic garbage bag for a fifteen minute ride to St. Augustine Hospital. Enroute, she phoned Kiersten's husband and tearfully told him of her situation and then she called John to let him know as well. His gentle words of encouragement, and promise to fly out to be with her as soon as he could were the only bright spots in an otherwise terrible day.

Once at the hospital, she helped herself out of the taxi, paid the driver and then, dragging her bag, began the incredibly long trek to the labor and delivery wing while her body commenced going into labor.

The next several hours were a blur of organized chaos, heartache and pain. The only thing worse than the way her body was feeling was the way her heart was feeling. The thought of losing her father and then not even being able to go home and be with her mother was unbelievably painful. That was even without including the fact she was alone, far from home and delivering Jason's baby prematurely without him. She had never in her wildest nightmares pictured this the way having a child with Jason would be.

At first she was so disappointed in God for letting all of this happen, but between contractions, she realized God had indeed been mindful of her when He let her miss that plane. Had her water broken on board, her baby would have been in an even more precarious position than he was here in this state of the art hospital.

She couldn't help the tears that continued to fall almost non-stop as she labored. Even an epidural didn't end them and the best she could do was to cry quietly while the hospital staff hovered with looks of pity. She'd told them of her father's death, but she couldn't bring herself to talk about how sad it made her to be delivering this baby without her life long friend who was the father. Somehow that fact even eclipsed the loss of her dad. As the hours dragged on, the pain and heartbreak of doing this without Jason broke her spirit down completely.

The attending physician had put a fetal monitor on the baby's head and as her labor progressed, they were watching him very closely. There was a chance he'd be fine this early, but there was also a chance he wouldn't be able to breathe on his own and that birth this early would stress him to the point of harming him or worse.

For more than seven hours she was in labor as they looked on and finally, her tears seemed to run dry and though she was still so sad, she was able to just go through the motions. Then at ten o'clock that night, when she thought they were getting close to finally actually delivering him, when the baby's heart rate plummeted, they wheeled her into an operating room and prepared to take him C-section. The nurse who had been helping Kate since she'd come in went off duty just then and a new one came on, and for some reason Kate felt like she was now doing this by herself again.

When they decided to take the baby surgically, they gave her something to stop her labor, but they didn't remember to mention to her it would make her shiver uncontrollably and the way her body was reacting frightened her terribly.

Once in the OR, the anesthesiologist injected a huge syringe of something into the epidural catheter he'd put into her back earlier and there was a sudden whoosh of heat and then she was numb from the chest down and couldn't even help herself move.

Although she was exhausted and half paralyzed, she was awake and watching and listening to the activity that buzzed around her and she had never been so afraid and stressed in her life. As the doctors and nurses spoke back and forth and the machines buzzed and whirred around her, she stared at the screen that monitored the baby's heart rate and tried to get a handle on the tears that had started up uncontrollably again.

The physicians and staff around her didn't seem to be paying any attention to her and more than ever before, she was completely heartsick to be doing this without Jason. Her thoughts went to him and she wished desperately that he'd been here. He would have helped her through this and kept her calm. He'd have kept everything under control and moving smoothly and he'd have been there to make sure the baby was all right when she couldn't.

Even simply the thought of him helped to calm her somewhat. It had always been that way. Right up until that very last night he'd been the rock solid foundation she rested on. *Oh, Jason, I need you now. Why didn't you stay strong so you could have helped me through this? Where are you, Jase? I need you. Kennen and I both need you.*

Her world felt like it was coming apart at the seams and the baby's heart monitor had begun to be increasingly erratic when finally, she heard that first little cry. It changed the tone in that operating room unbelievably and her eyes flew to where that tiny slippery looking purplish red body squirmed and threw its arms and legs. As he began to scream for all he was worth, Kate began to cry even harder. He was perfect and absolutely beautiful.

Once he was somewhat clean, they wrapped him up and brought him close to her so she could touch him as she lay there and it was the most amazing feeling to actually see and touch a child of her own body. The tears that had become uncontrollable disappeared and she forgot everything except that tiny human being with the dark curls, puffy little face, and small blue black eyes.

He was absolutely alert and once they had him wrapped up he quit screaming and began to look all around as if this new world was fascinating. Even at one minute old there was something about him that definitely reminded her of Jason. That was the only thing she desperately wished at this moment; that Jason had been there and she whispered, "Jason, we finally got our little Kennen. He's as beautiful as you."

She wasn't sure when she'd decided she was going to name him Kennen, but somehow it was right and she never questioned it.

As she watched him and held him to her, the doctor was still doing something to her tummy, but she hardly even noticed it as she marveled at her son. They let her have him for several minutes and then whisked him away to the neonatal nursery to be thoroughly checked out and left her with the physicians who were still putting her back together.

Now that the raging rush of adrenaline from those few intense minutes began to ebb, she was unbelievably tired. The shivering had finally begun to subside and the fear she'd been struggling with dissipated and she closed her eyes, just for a second. It was heaven to finally be able to rest.

They finished with what she assumed was stitching her closed and then wheeled her from the room she was in and back into another patient room further down the wing. This one was very nice with a recliner next to the bed and a rocking chair under the window.

A new nurse came in to help her get comfortable and this time she didn't feel abandoned by the others as she had last time. The nurse settled Kate, dimmed the lights and left her alone for a few minutes to rest from the most stressful day of her entire life.

Now that it was quiet, her mind went back to her father's death and then shied away from that and went to thoughts of Jason. Part of her wanted to shy away from him too, but another part of her heart wanted to dwell on him on this night their baby son had been born. Kate closed her eyes. Jason would have really, really loved their son.

Sometime later, the nurse woke her to take her temperature and blood pressure and when Kate opened her eyes, John was sitting in the recliner beside her bed in the dim lights. He stood up when he realized she was awake and stepped over to the side of her bed and reached for her hand. "You've had quite a day, Kate.

Remind me not to let you out of my sight again. How are you feeling?"

She smiled tiredly. "Thrashed. Did you see him?" John nodded. "He's marvelous, isn't he?"

"Yes Kate, he is."

"Have they decided he's all right yet?"

"They told me he's holding his own. But just to be sure, when you aren't feeding him, they'd like to have him back in the nursery to keep an eye on him. It's actually you they're most concerned with. For some reason you're running a mild fever."

"I wondered if I had a fever. I'm cold. They're going to let me have him in here with me?" It sounded silly when she said it, but the thought of taking care of him by herself scared her to death.

John laughed softly. "Of course they will, Kate. You're his mother. Did you think they wouldn't?"

She sighed. "Honestly, John, after the day I've had. I don't think anything. My brain has gone into overdrive and then sprung something. I'm clueless."

"I'm so sorry about your father."

Tears came to her eyes. "Me too." She leaned her head back. "I think his baby daughter getting pregnant and then leaving was very troubling to him. I keep wondering if I somehow caused this."

John shook his head. "Kate, you have enough on your plate to deal with right now without borrowing more grief. Don't beat yourself up. A blood clot is simply a physiological fact. It's nobody's fault. More likely this was the Lord's way of calling him home when He needed him."

She wiped at her tears. "I hope Kennen's birthday doesn't bring bad memories every year."

"It won't Kate, because you won't let it. You'll be a wonderful mother who will make sure you celebrate his birth. Some grief will be inevitable, but in time you'll learn to remember the good times instead of focusing on the loss."

"In some ways, he died long ago. When he was hit, so much of who he was disappeared. He hated being stuck in that bed. He hated it with a passion, but the spinal damage made it almost impossible for him to use a wheel chair."

"Then maybe his passing is a blessing. I've heard when we're resurrected we'll be whole and healthy and in our prime again. Maybe he's already stretching his legs and running around up there."

Smiling tiredly, she said, "That's a nice thought isn't it?"

He let go of her hand and went back to the chair. "You're still tired, Kate. Close your eyes and rest. It won't be long before Kennen is going to want his midnight snack. You'd better sleep while you can."

"I think you're right. And I am tired. Thank you for coming John. You have no idea how nice it is not to be alone right now."

"Actually, I do have a bit of an idea." He smiled sadly. "And I owe you. Not to mention the fact that I've waited patiently to hold this little guy for a long time. I'm almost glad he didn't wait until he was due. It'll be nice to hold him as long as I can."

Kate didn't answer that. She didn't know how and she closed her eyes, wondering how many sad things a person could handle at one time. She prayed silently, "Father, help me to be able to bear up under it all. I'm not sure I'm strong enough, but I will be if You help me. And thanks for helping the baby to get here safely. He's such a miracle. Thanks."

After her prayer, her thoughts went back to the sweet, beautiful baby she'd delivered earlier. She wished so much that Jason could have been a part of it all. He would have been so thrilled to have a son.

The next time she woke up, John was still sitting in the chair, but this time he had a small white bundle with a tiny hat in his arms and he was talking quietly to it. Kate lay there and it made her smile. It's too bad his own children hadn't turned out like him. He was a good man. She closed her eyes again to listen to him as he told Kennen all about the night he'd had. All Kennen said in return was a series of soft slurping noises as he busily sucked at something.

At some distant point in her brain, she realized she was going to have to learn how to feed this baby. She decided not to worry about that right now, she was too tired.

It wasn't long before Kennen decided she needed to start worrying. He'd finally decided he wanted more than John's soft spoken conversation and began to fuss and by the time Kate was half way awake, he began to cry in earnest.

As a nurse came in, John got up and carefully put him back in the bassinet that sat beside the bed and then came to Kate to help her figure out how to raise the head of her bed. For the first time, she felt pain from the large incision that now graced her low belly and she drew in a breath. This might be way more of a feat than she had bargained for. Although, in retrospect, she'd do it again in a heart beat if that's what the baby needed to get oxygen to his little brain.

Between the three of them, they got her sitting up and then John decided to go to the coffee shop for something and the nurse began to help Kate learn how to nurse the baby. It was not as easy as she'd imagined and she was grateful John had given her some privacy.

Kennen didn't eat for long, but it was apparently enough because he ate and then went right to sleep there in her arms. The nurse was still there hovering and Kate knew she wanted to take him back to the nursery, but Kate held onto him for a minute. He was the closest she'd ever felt to heaven and he even smelled that way.

When John came back in, he smiled as he stood next to the bed and watched her with Kennen. Reaching out one finger, he gently touched the soft curls on the baby's head. "He's got your curls, Kate. He's about the cutest baby I've ever seen, I believe."

"He is beautiful, isn't he? But then all babies must be. How could they not?"

"No, you're right, but he's a very handsome baby. Do we need to let them take him back to the nursery?"

At his question the nurse interrupted them to encourage them to send him back just so nurses and doctors who were very familiar with newborns could keep an eye on him and Kate reluctantly handed him over. She noticed the name on the card at the end of his bassinet as they wheeled him out. Baby Garland. In a way, she was so grateful for that last name, but in a way, that was all wrong. That should have read Baby Falcon.

She read on to take her mind from the baby's last name and realized for the first time that he must have weighed five pounds thirteen ounces. That wasn't a bad weight for a baby who was a month early.

She went back to sleep and dreamed disjointed dreams between nurses coming in to take her vitals. Her dad was there with the baby and then Jason was there talking to John and holding her hand. She even had dreams of Kennen fussing and then woke up to realize it was true and the nurse was back with a very hungry baby

John was still in the recliner, but now it was fully reclined and he slept under a blanket one of the nurses had brought him. Kate thought again about how grateful she was that he was here with her. That had been very kind of him to fly all the way across the country to help her with another man's child.

With the nurse's help, she got the baby fed and burped and then held him again for a few more minutes. She held him right up near her face. He smelled incredible. He was the only human on the planet who smelled even better than his father. She touched the soft curls. Kennen was Jason's color with her own natural curl. She nudged a teeny tiny finger. He truly was absolutely perfect.

Despite the antibiotics that were dripping into her IV catheter, her fever began to climb and she went from unbelievably sore at the incision site, to all around feeling miserable. She alternated between burning up under the sheets to freezing under a pile of blankets as the doctors did all kinds of tests to find out where the infection was.

To be safe, they had her stop nursing the baby in case she made him sick, but they still wanted her to produce milk so they brought her an electric breast pump. Even ill, she was sad not to be able to nurse him and insisted she be able to at least be the one to bottle feed him.

As the fever climbed, John hovered and he ended up taking all the phone calls from her mom and sister when they called to check on her or to let her know what was going on with funeral arrangements.

Kate was so sick that the days began to blur together and ultimately, they took her back into surgery to figure out where the infection was. When she woke up, she was sore all over again and told they were going to have to bury her dad before they would let her out of here. She didn't know what she would have done without John there to talk to her as she grieved all over again.

John became even more attentive and he literally helped her to hold the baby so she could continue to be the one to feed him. Now that the baby had been declared healthy and strong enough for sure, John spent a huge amount of his time sitting in the chair beside her just holding him. Kate didn't know if the baby helped the headaches, or if John just didn't notice the pain when he held him. At any rate, Kate's second surgery cemented a rock solid bond between John and Kennen.

The morning of the funeral, she kept Kennen with her the whole time. It was the only way she could keep herself from breaking right down and crying herself to sleep. At least they'd found that the infection was in the muscles and the skin of her abdomen and not her uterus as they'd feared. It was going to be much easier to treat, although she now had a tube that drained out of a hole in her incision. Telling her she'd be able to nurse Kennen again the next day helped as well.

***

Jason sat in the pew of the church in Wye and tried to swallow his shock and disappointment. She hadn't even come to her own father's funeral. He'd never dreamed in a million years she would blow off something as important as this. Her mother had told his that she'd had a problem in an airport somewhere as she was trying to get here and that she was now in the hospital out in California, but there was a part of him that wondered if that could possibly be true. The Kate he knew would have had to be half dead to miss something like her own father's funeral.

He was so disappointed he was sick. He'd just known he was finally going to get to see her. It had been six and a half months since she'd disappeared from his life that night in Lubbock. The whole time he helped to carry the casket to the hearse, and then through the graveside service, he was still sick about it, and had to wonder if the real reason she had stayed away was him. He'd never dreamed she'd miss her own father's funeral.

***

A day and a half after her father's funeral Kate's mother came walking into her hospital room. She no longer looked like a twenty five year old just now and she and Kate hugged and cried and then Laura Birch finally lit up when they brought her her tiny new grandchild. John shook the hand of the woman he had spent so much time with on the telephone the last several days and then generously left to go make phone calls so they could have some privacy as they visited.

The first thing her mother did was comment that it was good of John to put everything aside to come and watch over her to which Kate readily agreed. The second thing her mother said was that Kennen looked so much like Jason it was uncanny, to which Kate also readily agreed. She had no doubt her son would be as gorgeous as his father when he grew up, he looked like a miniature already.

Kennen was a Godsend for both Kate and her mother as they talked about her dad and memories and how much they missed him. Somehow Kennen's sweet baby spirit softened the grief until it was manageable. He was nine days old before Kate got to be pushed down to the lobby of the hospital in a wheel chair with him nestled on her tender lap. John had gone far above and beyond the call of duty in staying in San Francisco with her the whole time.

After leaving the hospital, he checked the four of them into a hotel suite for two days so Kate could continue to recuperate and then they flew to San Antonio together where Kate's mother agreed to stay with them for a little while longer as Kate's body continued to heal.

Chapter 17

Her mother stayed with them almost a week and then flew back home. By that time, Kate had begun to get the hang of this motherhood thing and could let her walk away without being as nervous as she'd thought she'd be. What she was nervous about was John's tumor. He'd been a rock in California, but the truth of the matter was John was losing his cognitive edge fast.

The care he had given her in the hospital with the baby was proving to be a heaven sent catalyst. He had taken such good care of her that now his care became second nature to her.

She'd planned to take a couple of months off with the baby if the memories of Jason didn't prove too painful, but it wasn't long after Kennen was born that John began to retire in earnest. He wasn't up to the travel because of the pain, let alone making business decisions. Because of both him and the baby, and the need for some occasional oversight at his businesses, Kate hired a full time nanny named Amber, thinking she could leave both John and the baby with her when she needed to take quick out of town trips. She was miserable without them, but it worked out okay for the most part.

She never did finish checking the restaurant in San Francisco and never even got started on the Tulsa location, but as they were relatively profitable at both places, she decided to let things go somewhat while Kennen and John needed her so. Kennen would never be a new born again and John needed her with him more than his restaurants did. If they hadn't sold by the time he passed away, she'd worry about them then.

By the time Kennen turned two months old, Kate was back into her prepregnancy clothes and John was on some kind of pain medication almost all of the time. He adored Kennen and Kennen adored him back and for some reason when John held him he seemed to feel better so he tended to hold him a lot. Unless it was during the night, Kennen slept almost exclusively in John's arms.

This was good and bad. Kennen became hopelessly spoiled about going down in his own crib, but Kate couldn't have asked for someone to love her child any better.

With Amber's help, Kate managed to take a couple of days a week to go to different locations to double check on the restaurants and then the three in Dallas, Galveston and California sold right in a row. At that point, the only long trips she needed to make were to Tulsa and Amarillo so she was able to focus more exclusively on John.

It was just after the first of March that John's son and daughter showed up. They must have somehow realized the restaurants had sold or else they'd found out John was losing it mentally. At any rate, they showed up one morning and as Kate carried Kennen to answer the front door to their ring, they took one look at her in her designer jeans, bare feet and wedding ring and seemed to bristle instantly.

Before she had even let them in, his daughter asked in an unmistakably unfriendly voice, "Are you the housekeeper?"

"You might say that. I'm also the wife. You must be Steven and Karen. Come in. We weren't expecting you obviously, but I'm sure your father would like to see you."

John got credit for trying to be polite, which was a lot more than Kate could say about them. They spoke to him briefly and wondered what was going on with him selling the restaurants and frankly, Kate was taken aback by their blatant selfishness. John told them in a rather nebulous way that he was simply downsizing his work load so he could look at retiring. At least they didn't seem to notice he wasn't well.

She didn't think they had, so she was surprised when a couple of weeks later she got a letter from an attorney representing them who demanded that Kate relinquish any and all business assets and responsibilities to them. Apparently they had heard about the brain tumor somewhere.

She sent the letter straight to John's attorney and simply mentioned it to John in passing that afternoon. He sighed and gave her a tired smile. "I told you they'd come. Don't let them intimidate you. They are far more bluff than they seem unless their mother is with them. Now her y'all should watch out for."

He paused for a moment and then went on sadly, "I loved her dearly at one time. I probably still do, truth be told. But she isn't a very nice person. I had to learn that the hard way. I'm sorry you have to deal with things like this, Kate. But I'm incredibly comforted to know my life is in your good hands. You've been such a relief to me. Thank you."

Kate did, in actuality, get the opportunity to meet John's ex, Ms. Terry Garland, just a few days later. Mark was there at the time, meeting with Kate and she was incredibly grateful for that as this woman swept inside as Kate opened the door like she was still the queen of John's kingdom. She looked Kate up and down with almost a sneer and then fairly stomped into the living room demanding to see John.

John was down in bed with a horrible headache at the time and Kate politely said, "I'm sorry, he's not available just now. Is there something I could help you with?"

Terry made a sound of disgust in her throat. "No, thank you. John may not have any qualms about dealing with an adolescent, but I certainly do. When will he be back?"

"He's not gone, he's just not available. I'm sorry; you'll have to come back later if you want to visit with him. It might be a good idea to call first and see if he can see you. He has a rather tight schedule as far as time to visit actually."

Terry literally stomped her expensively clad foot as she demanded, "Stop playing games and take me to him. Tell him it's his wife and he'll find the time to see me."

"I'm sorry, Ms. Garland, but I am his wife, not you, and he's not available just now. You'll have to come back." She reached back and opened the door and looked at it pointedly but Terry ignored her.

At this point Mark came into the front entry hall and Terry turned to him and seemed relieved. "Oh, good, Mark, I'm so glad you're here. Go and tell John I want to see him, would you? I want to get to the bottom of the sale of all of these restaurants."

Mark smiled, but absolutely stood his ground as he said, "I'm sorry, Terry, but John is busy, which doesn't matter anyway if you want to discuss business. John's wife, Kate here, is his manager and I'm sure she could tell you everything you want to know."

"His manager! Since when does John have a teenager managing multi million dollar businesses?"

Mark smiled blandly as Kate struggled to hold her tongue. "Oh, he's had her managing things for a while now. Her managing has added considerably to John's bottom line actually.

She turned back to Kate in anger. "All right then, why is he selling everything he owns? I've already checked and know what he hasn't already sold is listed. Where is the money being invested?"

At that point, Kate shook her head. "I'm sorry, Ms. Garland, but that is really none of your business. What John chooses to invest in has nothing to do with you. Is there something else that does involve you I could help you with?"

Amber peeked around the corner and Kate handed her the baby, glad to have him away from this woman as Terry went off calling Kate several choice names before ending with, "If you think you can keep me in the dark while y'all take my children's and my inheritance and stash it away for your own baby, you've got another think coming. I'll have my attorney involved and you'll be out of here on you and that baby's ear. Don't y'all even try to mess with me, honey. You'll regret it for as long as you live."

"Trust me. I do already. I think you should leave now. If you have questions in the future, why don't you just contact John's attorney directly." The door still stood open, and Kate motioned to it again and repeated, "I said, I think y'all should leave now."

Terry glanced at Mark who nodded and indicated the door himself and then she went toward it. "Fine. I'll leave now, but don't think this is the end of this. I'm the one who spent years struggling while John started his businesses. Don't even begin to think I'm going to let some adolescent bimbo come in and take what is rightfully mine. I'll fight to the nth degree. You'll see."

"I already do. Actually, not that it's any of your affair, but John and I have a solid prenuptial agreement which prohibits me from making any decisions about his assets. Those decisions are all set between John and his attorney. But I'm so glad you are concerned for him. That's very kind of you. Thank you so much for dropping by. It was so nice to finally meet y'all." Kate gave her the biggest smile she could muster and then used all of her will power not to slam the door behind her. She glanced up at Mark and shook her head. "Poor John. He had to wake up next to that. Can you imagine?"

"No. I can't, thank goodness. I hope John's attorney has both a thick skin and a bullet proof plan, because John's going to need it."

Kate had been going to leave the next day to fly to Tulsa, but she changed her mind. She was hesitant to leave John and Amber and the baby alone without someone to protect them from that dragon woman and her spawn. She worried about it for four days and then finally hired a security firm to send a licensed security guard to come and stay with them as well. John's house was huge and he could certainly afford it. For that matter, Kate would pay for the guy herself just to know everyone here would be safe while she was gone.

Once they'd gotten to know the men who would be coming to stay and she felt like she could trust them, she headed on out to Tulsa. It had been several weeks since she'd been there and she needed to check on how things were going.

She stayed in Tulsa for two days, going over the books and double checking the way things were being managed and triple checking the things the board of health would look at. She had just walked out of the manager's office with her brief case to leave for home, when she nearly walked into Cody and a couple of other guys from the band.

Cody stared at her, and she stared at Cody and for a second neither one knew what to say. And then Kate couldn't help herself. She set down her case, walked right over to him and threw her arms around him and said, "Cody Rawlings, I have missed you!" He may have messed up a few things for her and Jason, but they'd been friends since they were children and she knew he'd take a bullet for Jason any day.

Cody hugged her back and then pulled back to look at her, still in shock and Kate was embarrassed when tears filled her eyes as Cody asked, "Where have y'all been, Kate? Jason has looked over the whole planet for you. What are you doing in Tulsa?"

"I'm working. I travel around to different restaurants as a sort of consultant. What are you guys doing here?"

"What do you think, Kate? We've got a gig tonight. Haven't you heard the advertisements all over the radio?"

She hesitated and then shook her head. "I don't listen much to the country stations anymore. I'm more of a rock and roll and classical girl now. A little rhythm and blues, some new wave. Whatever. Country is just a touch hard for me lately."

Cody looked at her hard and then asked softly, "How lately?"

She tried to keep her voice light as she said, "Oh, for the last eight or nine months anyway. So what have you been up to?"

"Touring, two platinum records, trying to help Jason find his smile. It walked out on him about the same time you quit listening to country. What a coincidence. What about you?"

"Just working. I've tried to stay busy with this kind of thing." She waved her hand to indicate the restaurant and Cody grabbed it out of the air and stared at the ring.

"Kate! You didn't! You didn't get married!" He groaned and looked at her in horrified accusation. "Oh, Kate, what have you done? Jason'll die!"

She pulled her hand away and tried to keep the emotion out of her voice as she assured him. "Don't be ridiculous, Cody. Yes, I got married a few months ago, in fact."

Cody groaned again and asked quietly, "Why, Kate? Why when you knew Jason worshipped you?"

At that, she felt her heart quiver within in her chest and she was tempted to tell Cody just what she thought and felt about a comment like that. Jason had loved her, but he'd let other things get in the way. Kate wasn't the one who had caused this whole mess. Not by a long shot. She felt that old familiar pain rip into her just as it did every time she thought about Lubbock. She swallowed the lump that threatened to choke her.

Instead of snapping at Cody about who had worshipped who, she glanced at her watch. She'd just been on her way out to head for the airport. "Look, Cody.

It was great to see y'all. I've got a plane to catch. Tell everyone hello for me."

She picked up her case and turned to go, but Cody rushed after her. "Wait! Kate! Don't go. Can't you stay and visit? Jason will be here in fifteen minutes. He'll be devastated that he missed you. Hang out for a minute."

Shaking her head, she looked down and then back up. "That would be a bad idea, Cody and you know it. Plus I'm already going to have to speed to get my rental car turned in on time. You talk to him for me, okay?"

"Kate." Cody was almost pleading. "You don't understand. Jason has all but quit living. Don't leave without at least just saying hi."

"No, Cody. It would hurt both of us. I have to go. Take care."

"Then can I at least have a phone number? Where are you living? Can we keep in touch? We've been friends our whole lives, Kate."

Tears finally filled her eyes. "I wish we could, Cody, but we can't. I'm sorry. More sorry than you can imagine. Good luck with your concert tonight. I'm sure it will be amazing. See ya around."

***

She walked out the door of the elegant steak and ribs restaurant and didn't look back and Cody began to swear as her heels clicked away on the sidewalk. Jason was going to kill him. And then Jason was going to lose it when he told him she was married. And he'd have to. There was no way he couldn't. They were too good of friends to keep something like that from him.

Cody stepped back to the door and hit his number one speed dial. Jason picked up on the second ring and Cody asked, "Where are you, man?"

"I'm almost there. I'm on highway two-forty-four headed your way. I'll be to the restaurant in like six minutes."

"Jason, without you getting in a wreck, I want you to take the next exit and then get back on and go to the airport. I just ran into Kate and that's where she's headed. She just left and said she had to speed to get her rental car back and make her plane. I'm sorry, I don't know what airline."

For just a second there was dead silence on the other end of the line and then Jason must have pushed end. Cody stood there for another few seconds and then began to pray silently to himself as he turned to go back inside the restaurant. He'd been doing a lot of that the last eight or nine months. What a coincidence.

***

Jason seriously considered driving down through the median to reach the other side of the freeway, but then an exit appeared just up ahead. He drove like a madman and at the airport nearly slid his car sideways as he headed into the rental car return. He drove all the way to the other end without seeing her and then gave up and parked and headed into the terminal at a run.

He stopped at one of the TVs that listed the incoming and outgoing flights and tried to figure out which gate she'd be heading to from the flights leaving in the next while. It had to be Jacksonville, San Antonio or Detroit. Taking a chance, he headed for the terminal with the flight into San Antonio. Texas had usually worked for her in the past. Usually. There was that one time that had been disastrous for them both. He started to run. He had to catch her before she made it past security.

He'd been literally running when he sighted her just placing her small brief case and a carry on on the tray to go through the x-ray machine. He could never catch her in time. He thought about yelling, but then looked at all the armed guards working right there and decided against it. That's all he needed today was to be arrested by Homeland Security in front of Kate.

Still rushing forward, he tried to find her again in the crowd that was making its way through the check point. There! She walked out of the throng and he felt all the blood rush to his heart and whispered, "Kate. Just turn around. Just wonder if Cody called me and if I've rushed here to find you. Just turn around, baby. Give me two minutes. Just two."

As if she'd been listening, she did. She turned and looked back as if someone had called her and he knew exactly when she saw him standing there as close as he could get to the divider. She froze as she looked at him for a long, slow thirty seconds and then even from a distance he could tell she started to cry, and then obviously reluctantly, she slowly turned and walked up the ramp.

With tears starting in his own eyes, he swore bitterly and watched her until she disappeared toward a gate on the right, he couldn't tell which. He turned and began making his way back to his car. At least he'd seen she definitely wasn't indifferent to him. She still hurt enough to cry the second she saw him. He couldn't decide if that was a good thing or a bad thing and prayed as he walked, "God, watch over her, wherever she's headed. And talk her into coming home soon. I need her. You know that. You know how much I need her."

Chapter 18

Kate struggled not to cry during the entire two hour flight back to San Antonio and for the most part it was a rout and she landed with red swollen eyes and a tired heart. She got her car out of long term parking and made her way out of the airport, wondering why seeing him standing there after so many months could still hurt so badly.

She'd known she would never get over him. That she would love him to the day she died, but she'd been so hoping that at least the pain would dull and she could get on with her life without this heartache.

On the way home, she stopped and got groceries and picked up the dry cleaning, hoping the extra time would erase the signs of her deep sadness, and then stopped and got take out Chinese. She really wasn't up to cooking tonight. At least walking into John's house from the garage was a comfort. Even though John was going down hill fast, this home had always been a haven for her.

***

The band was long gone from the restaurant when Jason got there, but he needed to talk to the manager anyway. He needed to find out who Kate was working for and find a way to contact her.

When he was ushered into the manager's office amidst a great deal of whispering, he tried to explain what he wanted and the manager looked at him strangely when he asked, "There was a girl here earlier today. Tall, with short, dark, curly hair. Her name is Kate. Kate Birch. Could you tell me the company she works for? I believe she's a consultant of some sort. I need to get in touch with her. It's very important."

Shaking his head, the manager said, "The only Kate that was here I know of who fits that description is Kate Garland and she's not a consultant. She and her husband own the place. Y'all must be mistaken. I'm sorry. We have a Kathy, but she's short and red. Are you sure you have the right restaurant?"

Jason froze for a moment in shock. Kate married. He couldn't even begin to process it. She would never marry someone else. She couldn't. It just wasn't possible. She knew that no matter what had happened, Jason loved her forever. Didn't she? She would never go back on the pinky promise they'd made that day at the lake. He knew she wouldn't. That promise had been the biggest deal of their lives. It had meant forever. More than forever.

Then he remembered that they'd also promised to stay pure until they were married and then that night with the champagne they'd ruined it all and his heart felt like it imploded.

He didn't even hear the manager ask, "Is there something else I could help you with?" He just walked out the door in a shocked silence. Kate was married. His Kate. The other half of his soul was married to someone else. No wonder she had cried and then turned and walked away. How could she do this to him? He'd thought she'd cared too much to ever marry someone else. Especially after only nine months.

When he got back to the hotel, he went straight to Cody's room instead of to his own. When Cody opened the door, he took one look at Jason and pulled him inside with a sigh. "I guess I shouldn't have even told you. I guess it would have been better to just not have mentioned seeing her. I'm sorry. I wasn't thinking. I just knew you'd been looking so long. I'm sorry man."

Jason sat down in a chair and leaned his head back and closed his eyes. "No. I needed to know." There was silence in the room for several minutes and then Jason asked without sitting up and opening his eyes. "I didn't ever get to see her up close. Is she okay? How did she look?"

Cody thought about that for a moment. "She looked good, Jason. She's a beautiful girl. You know that.

She looked older. Maybe a little more mature. I'm not sure how to describe it."

"Did she look happy, Rawlings? She's married to the guy who owns the restaurant. Apparently she's been that way for a while. Is she happy?"

When Cody didn't answer right away, Jason opened his eyes to look at him and said tiredly. "You can be honest. Just give it to me straight. The time's past for sugar coating it."

Cody shook his head and walked over to look out the window. His voice was tired too as he admitted, "No, Jason. She didn't look the least bit happy. The sparkle she's had since she was born was completely missing. She was sharp. She was poised. She was in control. She wasn't happy." He turned back to Jason. "But it doesn't really matter anymore does it? Married is married." He sighed. "She made her decision, but y'all are both going to have to live with it."

Jason made a sound of disgust. "Do you think I don't know that? Hell, Cody, I'm in love with her but I'm not going to try to break up her marriage. You know me better than that."

"Sorry."

Jason got up and went to the door. As he walked out, he said over his shoulder, "I'm sorry too, Cody. See you in a couple hours."

Still standing beside the window, Cody listened to the door latch click behind him and wondered just how Jason was going to react to this. This could either make him the most driven performer on the planet. Or shut their whole band right down and he swore under his breath and said, "Kate, I just hope you know what you're doing."

Jason was fine through the concert that night. He was a bit in a zone, but Cody was able to compensate for Jason's lack of energy and Jason did their slow, sad stuff better than Cody ever remembered him doing it. It was when they got back home the next day that things began to unravel. For two days Cody didn't see Jason. Not for a minute. And he wasn't answering his door or his phone.

Just when Cody was going to call out the National Guard and literally break down his door if he had to, Jason showed up at Cody's house. He looked like hell and hadn't shaved and Cody wasn't even sure if he'd changed clothes. He certainly hadn't slept much. That was obvious.

He walked in and handed Cody a folder of music and Cody began to look through it and wasn't really paying attention to what Jason was doing until he heard a cupboard door slam. The new songs looked awesome and then he glanced up to see Jason with a fifth of Jack Daniels on the counter and throwing back a tumbler full of it.

Cody cursed and dropped the music. He raced across the room and grabbed the glass away, spilling whiskey all over both of them in the process. "What the hell are you doing, Falcon?" Jason shoved him away and reached for the bottle again and they got into a scuffle with Cody ultimately winning because he punched Jason with absolutely all he had to try to knock some sense into him.

Jason went flying backwards and stumbled over a chair and he and it both went flying. He landed with his back against Cody's wall and put his hand up to his eye in surprise. "You hit me! You actually hit me!"

Cody put the lid back on the whiskey and put it in the cupboard with a resounding slam. "Yes, and I'm going to do it again properly if y'all ever pull something this asinine again! What's gotten in to you?"

"Nothing." Jason stood up and picked up the chair that now sported only three working legs and gingerly touched a spot on his cheekbone. "Nothing's gotten into me. It's getting something out of me that's the problem. Give me something to drink. I've gotta be able to sleep or I'm going to go crazy."

"Then take a Tylenol PM, Falcon, not a fifth of whiskey! Get a grip! Even the end of the world isn't going to look better through a glass of Jack Daniels."

"It might."

"It won't! It'll look like more mistakes piled onto the first ones."

"That's easy for you to say, Mr. use and abuse 'em. You have no idea what I'm dealing with."

"Oh, knock it off! I have more idea than anyone else on the planet and y'all know it! Just because I've never found anyone I could see forever with, doesn't mean I don't understand that what you and Kate had was amazing." He went back over and began to pick up the scattered pages of music and tried to figure out which page went where. "It only means I've been lonely as hell for a lot of years, wishing I could find my own Kate! You're so busy feeling sorry for yourself you don't even realize you've already been blessed by her more than nine tenths of this world put together. So shut up!"

Cody looked back at the papers in his hand and then sniffed his shirt. "Go bring me another shirt and find one for yourself while you're at it. We smell like a Tennessee still. Geez, you're an idiot!"

Jason began to take his shirt off. "Why, because I did once what y'all do every week of your life? Come off it!"

Cody dropped the papers again and turned on him. "You're wrong, Jason! I have *never* done what you just did. Never! You were using alcohol as a drug! A place to bury yourself. And I hate to be the one to burst your bubble, but she'll be just as married when you sober up, but then your head will hurt as bad as your heart and you'll be ashamed of yourself to boot! I'm sure Kate would be thoroughly impressed. It's one thing to be a worthless partier who has nothing better in life to do than drink and play around. I'm shallow and flaky and all the rest of it. But not you! You're going somewhere! The sky's the limit for you, Jason. And I'll be damned if you're going to screw that up in my kitchen! Not on my watch!" He paused and looked at his hand for a moment and then growled, "Go change your shirt."

Jason walked into Cody's bedroom and Cody crossed to the cupboard where he'd just put the whiskey and yanked it back open. When Jason came back in, he was just finishing dumping the last of his entire supply of alcohol down the drain. As Jason came up beside him, he tossed the last glass bottle into the now overflowing garbage can and went to the sink and began to rinse his hands as Jason asked, "What the hell are you doing, Rawlings?"

"What I should have done ten years ago before I started. You just made me waste hundreds of dollars. Thanks a lot. C'mon." He grabbed a jacket off of the back of a chair and walked to the door.

"Where are we going?"

Still furious and shaken by what Jason had started to do, he ground out, "To have this hand X-rayed and if you've broken my guitar finger I'm going to break your neck. Get in the Jeep!"

By the time they made it to the clinic, Jason was sound asleep in the reclined passenger seat and Cody cracked the windows and left him there while he went to have his hand looked at. He was still grumbling under his breath as he walked inside, "Fool idiot! What did he think sixteen ounces of Jack Daniels would fix?"

Cody hoped his outrage and dumping the booze would bring Jason to his senses, but it wasn't to be. By the time he'd gotten the splint off of his little finger three weeks later, Jason had thoroughly gone off the deep end. It didn't take a rocket scientist to realize he didn't give a rip about whether he lived or died anymore.

On stage, he was a machine that drove the crowds wild and practically whipped the ladies in the audience into a frenzy. But off stage, he became morose and sullen and indeed began to drink to try to forget the girl who had left him and married someone else. He drank himself into the ground and then went home by himself to brood and write more number one hit songs that made Cody want to break down and cry when he initially read the lyrics. The friend he'd had since the first grade was trying to kill himself in one long drawn out binge.

The tabloids went crazy. Watching superstar, Jason Falcon self destruct became the number one story across the magazine racks and from the celebrity shows to the talk shows, the favorite pass time was trying to hypothesize as to why the straight arrow Christian boy of the decade had fallen so hard off the wagon. No one questioned whether it was a woman or not. The simple fact that he partied so hard, but wanted nothing to do with the groupies who threw themselves at him spoke volumes.

***

While Kate struggled to keep her and John's lives together, she knew Jason was a mess. She couldn't miss it no matter how complicated her life became. The tabloids and magazines were plastered with stories of him and she could hardly turn on the TV without finding him on one channel or another.

She also knew that it was probably because of her. Or because Jason had discovered she was married. Why else would it have started almost on the very day she'd seen him and Cody?

At least it was just alcohol and not going crazy with girls or other drugs. That was one good thing. It was hard enough to know he'd become a hard core drinker without having to watch the other as well.

In all honesty, she was too busy to let it overcome her like it probably would have. Kennen, who was now six months old, had learned to crawl and get into everything in sight, and Kate was eternally grateful for Amber's help with him while she struggled to put out all the other brush fires she was up against. She became more grateful than ever before for the blessing of prayer. She had begun to know that it and the help it brought were the only things holding her life together right now. Maybe in a way, all the issues were a blessing that kept her mind from lingering on Jason after all these months, but there were still nights that he haunted her after she lay down and before she got to sleep.

John's children and ex wife had begun to fight her at every step of the way over the disposition of John's wealth and several times she had been very grateful she'd hired the security. They'd finally figured out John was dying and that he was leaving everything to the university and things had gotten ugly fast. For some reason, they figured it was all Kate's doing and they were set on removing her from the picture any way they could, including simply showing up and threatening to harm her if she didn't leave John's home immediately. Thank goodness the legal steps John had taken before losing his business acumen had been able to contain their efforts so far.

Both of John's Austin restaurants had been purchased as well as the one in Amarillo and the funds were settled into the foundation trust, which made her job of oversight easier, but John himself was fading unbelievably fast.

Sometimes the only one Kate was sure he knew was Kennen. The two were still fairly inseparable even though John now struggled to manage the wiggly baby. Kate or Amber had to be right beside him whenever he spent time with Kennen in order to insure that both of them stayed safe. John's pain had to be managed constantly with any number of medications, most of which were heavy narcotics. There was nothing else that would touch the kind of pain he was in. But that level of being drugged brought on even more disorientation than just the tumor was causing, which was certainly enough.

Moreover, physically, he was experiencing other struggles than just the pain and loss of faculties. The tumor was beginning to affect his basic needs like breathing and heart function as well. Kate struggled through the days knowing that the man she had come to not only admire, but love dearly as a true friend, was in the last stage of this earthly estate.

John's attorney and accountant now handled all of his affairs except the actual management of the remaining restaurants that Kate continued to monitor, and she had become less and less involved with his businesses and more and more involved in keeping him as comfortable as possible. His doctors had ordered home hospice care now to help her understand what was happening and how she could best help him.

Every once in a while, Kate would wonder what she was going to do after all of this was over, but she didn't have much time to worry about that. She had her hands thoroughly full.

One night, when it was just her and John and Kennen alone in the TV room, Kate sat down next to him on the couch and picked up his now sadly feeble hand. He gave a gentle squeeze without picking up his head from where it rested against the back of the seat and in a moment of rare lucidity said softly, "We're about there, aren't we Kate?"

She stroked the hand she held and nodded. 'I'm afraid so, John. I'm sorry."

"You've been good to me. Thank you. It was a lot to ask someone to help you die, but you didn't shy away. I'm grateful for that."

"You deserved it, John. You didn't shy away from helping me either. Or any number of others. You're a good man, John. I'm sure God has a wonderful place for you. He must have definitely needed you to take you this young."

"I suppose so. I always wonder why me and at this time. I don't understand, but I trust Him."

Tears welled into Kate's eyes and she said, "That's the big key to this life isn't it, John? Knowing He's there and then obeying. Even when we're not sure why."

He sighed tiredly. "I believe it must be." He was quiet for several minutes and then surprised her by saying, "Kate, will you do me a favor?"

"Sure, what do you need?"

"Will you promise me that if you ever feel like God wants you to go back to Jason, you'll do it? No matter how long it's been?"

She hesitated in surprise and then agreed. "Yes, John. I promise. Why do you ask that?"

"Because, Kennen needs him." His answer was simple and sincere and it cut Kate to the heart.

They sat there in silence, each busy with their own thoughts and Kate tried to establish for the ten thousandth time in the last eighteen months if she'd been right to leave and not tell Jason about the baby. Every time she'd questioned this, she'd always come back to yes, she'd truly felt like that was what she'd been supposed to do and she'd been comforted.

Today, on this couch with John by her side and Kennen climbing at her knee, for the first time, that comfort didn't come. For the first time, keeping this child from Jason didn't feel like what God wanted her to do. Had she been wrong? Or had something changed? She didn't know the answers. All she knew was she was doing the best she could do to do what she felt was right. She could do no more. And who was to say why things turned out the way they do? Only God himself.

***

Cody was at a loose end. Jason's crazed energy on stage, not to mention his massive share of the press, however scandalized it was, increased their popularity exponentially. Add to that Jason's insane creativity as he wrote songs when he was so troubled, and it led to an unbelievable burst of new hits that had them touring like mad and raking in the money, but Cody feared it was all going to end in flames when Jason finally hit the bottom in a blazing ball of fire. He couldn't keep this up and everyone knew it. Cody just didn't know how to save him.

He spoke to Jason's parents and asked if he could ever get Jason to admit he needed help if they would support him in checking him into someplace with padded walls and a straight jacket. It hadn't been a very serious way of putting it, but they knew exactly what he meant and agreed to it readily. They knew as well as he did that Jason was killing himself.

The funny thing about all of it was that since that day in his kitchen when he'd punched Jason and broken his finger, Cody hadn't been able to touch the stuff. Not a drop. He was a certified t-totaller and frankly, the friends who had always known him thought he'd gone as off the deep end as Jason. Not only that, but the womanizer he'd been was missing in action as well. Somehow, it wasn't nearly so entertaining to engage in meaningless relationships since seeing what Kate's marriage had done to his best friend.

It was a good thing he was cold sober, because Jason definitely needed a designated driver these days. Now Cody went out to the bars and clubs just to make sure Jason made it home in one piece.

Chapter 19

John died on a rainy Tuesday in December. At the end, his body failed fast and Kate had been surprised both by how quickly he went and how much his passing hurt those around him. Even baby Kennen missed him desperately. He'd been just her boss and friend when she'd accepted this arrangement. He was more special to her than she could put into words by the time he accepted his final one.

She'd never fallen in love with him. Never even close. Theirs hadn't been a romantic relationship, but it had been one full of mutual respect.

With Amber's help, Kate made it through the funeral arrangements John had requested and then began the final process of settling his affairs. All of the restaurants accept the one in Tulsa had sold and the scholarship foundation was up and running and helping smart kids who otherwise wouldn't have been able to attend college to go on to hopefully achieve more of their potential, thanks to John Garland's generosity.

John's ex and children were still fuming, but Kate hardly noticed. She was still too hurt by John's passing to even care what they did anymore.

She and Amber sorted through the stuff in John's house and after setting aside a handful of things she thought his children might honestly treasure some day, she sent them to them and then arranged for an estate auction company to come in and sell the rest and then listed the house. The proceeds from it would go to John's foundation as well.

She saved a couple of small things she knew his kids wouldn't want to give to Kennen. Nothing valuable. Just things she felt demonstrated John's strength of character. His Bible and his journal and some other items. She didn't doubt that someday when he was old enough to understand, Kennen would treasure these glimpses into the life of the man who had loved him so deeply for such a short time.

Mark agreed to take John's dog because Kate wasn't sure where she was going to be, and slowly, as the house was cleared and things packed, the life of John Garland was being carefully boxed up and sold off. If it hadn't been for that marvelous foundation, the whole process would have broken Kate's heart almost as much as his death had.

Finally, the Tulsa location sold and Kate made the final arrangements for the change of ownership and then met one last time with Mark and the attorney to close out John's affairs. It was with a somber air that they began that meeting. John had been a great man and a friend to all of them and Kate's heart was incredibly heavy with the loss.

She was absolutely blindsided when the attorney slid the deed to the Tulsa restaurant across the table to her and followed that with the title to her Mercedes and some paperwork that detailed the trust John had put in place for Kennen to receive when he was twenty-five. He'd paid her well, on top of her living expenses and she'd had no idea he intended to leave them part of his legacy as well. This was the final straw and she broke down and cried like a baby. He hadn't needed to do this. Letting her work alongside him for the duration had been more than enough. He'd been an amazing friend and mentor.

She walked out of that office both sad and amazed. She hadn't really had time to plan what she was going to do next. Apparently John had helped her decide after all.

After a tearful farewell to Amber, Kate put Kennen into his car seat and then took the rest of her things and her sad heart and this time, she headed for the Oklahoma state line, praying as she drove, "Father, help me to make a new start out there, please. I've learned so much from John. Help me to build on that and make a stable home for my son."

***

The solution to Jason's drinking binge, when it finally came, was far more simple than Cody had ever dreamed and he was almost kicking himself that he hadn't realized it several months sooner. One night as he dragged a mean and drunk Jason into his Jeep, he said sadly, half to himself, "Geez, Kate would be so disappointed, Jason. She'd take one look at you and know she'd made the right decision to go. She probably knows she was right to leave, but I'll bet her heart is breaking seeing what you're doing to yourself. She thought you were the strongest charactered man on the planet."

That's all he said. And in truth, he didn't realize for a couple of days that Jason had even understood what he'd said. But when he stopped by to get him to meet the tour bus two days later, Jason opened the door with clear, bright emerald eyes for the first time in months. Cody just looked at him, stunned. And then the two friends who had been friends forever embraced as Cody said, "Welcome back, dude! I've missed you."

Chapter 20

Having the cold sober Jason back was actually a new experience for Cody. They'd never both been designated drivers at the same time and frankly, with neither of them drinking, the bars and clubs held absolutely no allure for either of them. Almost at a loose end for a little while, they begin to try different ways to get high than chemicals that came in liquid form.

They considered sky diving and then decided a less than perfect ending could put a definite kink in the band that was selling more albums than ever and decided to keep thinking. They tried everything from technical rock climbing, to bungee jumping off of some insanely high bridge in South America, to bull riding up in Wyoming at a gig they were doing there.

After attempting to ride the bulls, they moved that idea over into the more guts than brains column and limped back home to Oklahoma to try something more along the lines of extra spicy Mexican food for a while. That was about all they were up to while their bones and backsides healed.

It was actually something relatively innocuous that nearly got them. Nearly got Cody at least. Cody almost drowned and then almost bled to death. Jason just almost died of trying to save him.

They'd decided to learn to kayak on the Cimarron River north of Oklahoma City near a small town named, ironically enough, Stillwater. It wasn't supposed to be dangerous and even their guides had been surprised to come around a bend and find that the sleepy river had risen due to overnight rains until there was quite a rapid up ahead.

Even as they approached the rapid, Jason and Cody hadn't been too concerned. They'd done this a couple of times now and even knew how to right the kayaks if they somehow rolled one. What they didn't know was that usually white water kayakers wore helmets to protect their heads in case they rolled a craft in the rapids.

It all happened so fast Jason wasn't even sure what had occurred, he just knew that Cody's boat had gone over and it wasn't turning back upright and it had been way too long in that swirling black water. Jason had known he was watching his friend die and paddled like a mad man and then bailed out of his own kayak and dove under Cody's.

It had taken everything he had to right that boat and drag it to shore and roughly rip Cody out of the apron. He'd started CPR and although it had only been a few moments until Cody began to breathe, it had felt like a lifetime of praying for all he was worth and literally willing his friend to inhale. The two guides had arrived and they took over while Jason tried stop the bleeding of a gash on the top of Cody's head where he'd apparently hit a rock at just the wrong moment. It was a few minutes that made you stop and think about how you were doing in this thing called life. That was for sure.

By the time they got him life flighted into the hospital in Tulsa, Cody was in bad shape and Jason wasn't far behind him. Cody had low oxygen saturation, a brain concussion and had bled far too much and they both had hypothermia.

As Jason sat beside his friend, swathed in heated blankets in the emergency room and watched as a very pretty young trauma surgeon encouraged Cody to relax as she stitched, he breathed a prayer of gratitude. They were a mess, but at least Cody hadn't died. His complaints were a huge improvement over how lethargic he'd been a short time ago, and how dead he'd seemed while they'd worked to resuscitate him. They had a lot to be thankful for.

Jason went back to the magazine he'd picked up in the waiting room and in disgust showed it to Cody and the pretty doctor. "Geez, where do they come up with this stuff? Look, Cody I'm being forced into a paternity test with... Mary Ellen Fitzpatrick, whom incidentally, I've never met before in my life, but facts aren't necessarily relevant. And you're secretly attracted to guys. That's awful!" Cody merely grunted as the attractive surgeon took another stitch and Jason went on, "I wouldn't care, but I hate to have Kate see this stuff. She already thinks I'm a player."

At that, Cody finally weighed in tiredly, "It could be worse. She could think you're secretly attracted to guys. Ouch! Save me, Jase. This extremely attractive medical professional is trying to kill me!"

Jason shook his head. "That's what you get for having a thing for men. Besides, I've already saved your sorry hide once today. What do y'all think I am? You owe me by the way."

"No way, Falcon. I've hauled your butt out of so many messes these last few months that you'll be in my debt forever. Y'all probably owe me your first born by now."

Jason handed him the magazine. "Well, there you have it then. It seems I have one out in Nevada. Actually, from what I've read, that's like my fifth. An amazing feat for a man who is deeply committed to celibacy. But don't worry. If it's printed, you can trust it."

Cody groaned and Jason grinned. "She a bit rough on the fragile little guitarist?"

"No. I'm groaning at the thought of having to deal with five of your kids."

Jason was more tired than he ever remembered being by the time he got home that night and was able to get a shower and finally warm up. What an awful experience. Somehow he didn't think kayaking would ever be his and Cody's hot button.

Sitting in Cody's hospital room the next day, watching his still-slightly-looped-from-his-concussion friend hassle that same doctor, he had to wonder if Cody hadn't found a different new hot button. He'd never seen Cody act like this. But then he'd never seen Cody interact with a drop dead gorgeous Harvard Medical School trained surgeon either. It was positively enlightening.

**

Kate found a small house on a quiet street on the outskirts of Tulsa, not far from the restaurant John had bequeathed her and began to slowly furnish it as she and Kennen got settled in. John had been right. Being a widow now, instead of an unwed mother, was perfectly respectable and she was able to go to church and not worry about fitting in or being a poor example. That respectability was truly a priceless gift. A nice looking man there had even shown an interest in Kate already. Not that she cared, but at least she knew she wasn't a leper.

The restaurant was well run and profitable and Kate didn't have to do much but look in on it from time to time and sign the checks and she found that being able to focus on being a mom and watching her son grow was another of John's gifts. He'd been so thoughtful to help her be able to not have the regrets he had had.

She was out in the yard putting together a prefab sand box with Kennen when she looked up to see the little girl from next door looking through the chain link fence. She was the same age as Kennen and had white blonde hair in tiny, curly piggy tails with baby blue ribbons in them that matched the trim on her little overalls. Kate took Kennen's hand and walked over to the fence and said, "Hey, there, Gretchen. What are you doing today?" Gretchen replied only by putting a finger in her mouth and looking up at Kate with big, trusting eyes.

Kennen let go of Kate's hand and toddled closer to the fence and reached his little hand through to hold onto Gretchen's. Kate felt something tug at her heart when she remembered how she and the first Kennen had been. They'd been even younger than this when they'd become fast friends.

She left Kennen there and returned to her project. She only had to set the boards in place and tighten the screws and then she could begin dumping in the bags of sand.

***

Cody held the door to his Jeep open for Dr. Jennika Andrus to get out and almost felt a bit silly that he was enjoying her this much. He was going grocery shopping with her and it was the most romantic thing he could ever remember doing. He gave himself a wry smile and wondered if that meant the brain concussion had never healed or if he was just losing it all the way around. Either way, he was just fine with it. Finding her had been well worth nearly dying day before she stitched him back together.

When Jennika reached for his hand as they started to walk in, he decided he must be losing it. There was no other excuse for how happy simply holding a beautiful, intelligent, dynamic, poised, articulate, competent and graceful woman's hand could make him feel. He grinned again. If Jason could see him now, he'd get an upset stomach. He was that pathetic. Jennika turned and gave him a smile and something in his heart did this little hiccup thing. Yup, Jason would wanna hurl.

They'd selected such romantic and alluring things as a gallon of skim milk, pork chops and dish soap, and were just looking for crackers when Cody could suddenly swear he could hear Kate talking. He shook his head and went back to the Wheat Thins, then he heard it again and this time the hair on the back of his neck began to prickle. Not only was it Kate's voice, but she was talking to someone named Kennen. Maybe his brain concussion really had left permanent damage. The only person he'd ever heard named Kennen before in his life was Jason's younger brother who had died when they were teenagers.

All thoughts of snack crackers gone, Cody walked around the corner of the grocery aisle to see who sounded so much like Kate. When he got into the cereal aisle and realized it really was Kate, he couldn't even believe it. She reached up for a box of Cheerio's and then nearly dropped them when he spoke her name, "Kate. Is it really you?"

She whirled around and put a hand to her chest and he apologized for scaring her. She gave him a small, sad smile and moved closer to her cart as she said, "Cody! What are you doing here? Just decided to cruise on up to Tulsa and do a little marketing?"

He gave her a grin that he knew was ridiculously happy and nodded. "Actually, yeah. I have a friend who lives here who keeps me coming back and we thought grocery shopping sounded absolutely romantic. As soon as she finishes deciding which crackers are the healthiest and go with smoked salmon, she'll be right here."

Jennika's silky voice from the next aisle over said, "I heard that."

He laughed and asked, "What are you doing Kate? Y'all here in Tulsa to market as well?"

For just a second she looked guilty and he wondered what was going on and then he heard a little voice and realized she had a baby in her cart and she had stepped in front of it when he'd walked up. He wondered what was going on as Jennika came around the corner.

He introduced them and then as they spoke briefly, Cody nonchalantly walked forward as if he was going to pick out some cereal and stopped in his tracks. There strapped into the front of her cart was a miniature Jason, right down to the raging green eyes and firm lower lip. Under his breath he whispered, "Holy sh..." *Jason had a kid!*

He struggled for composure and then did his best to go back to small talking as he introduced his Jennika to Jason's Kate. Jennika knew exactly who Kate was. She'd heard about her a few times and Kate smiled a huge smile as Cody admitted to having been smitten as Dr. Jennika had tortulated him with surgical instruments. The two women laughed good naturedly at his expense as he struggled to wrap his brain around what he had just seen.

He was still so shocked he almost missed Kate hesitantly admitting to Jennika that her husband had recently passed away. At that, he did a double take and Kate got wary. He saw that old pain in her eyes as she began to edge away and said, "It was so nice to meet you, Dr. Jennika. Whatever y'all did to his head, it worked. I've never seen him like this. Take care, Cody."

With that, she pushed her cart around the corner and Cody finally came unglued. He grabbed Jennika's hand and whispered, "C'mon. We have to go." Jennika looked at him a bit strangely and then willingly followed him to the check out counter where there was another magazine with a story about Jason's untrue escapades. Cody turned it around, paid for Jennika's groceries and hurried out of the store.

***

Someone began to pound on Jason's door and didn't stop until Jason opened it up with a snarl, "All right! All right! Y'all don't have to break it down! Cody, what the... What are you doing?"

Cody came in and shut the door and said almost intensely, "Sit down, Jason. I need to tell you something."

Jason looked at him like he'd lost it and then obediently sat down on his guitar stool. "Ok, I'm sitting."

Cody let out a huge breath and said, "Dude, you've got a kid!"

Jason rolled his eyes and waved a hand. "I don't even know who it is this time, Rawlings, but it's not mine. I swear it. They're lying. I was an idiot with the booze. I admit it, but I've never been with anyone and you know it. Well. Anyone but Kate that one time. It's just another story."

"No! You're not hearing me, man! I'm talking about Kate! She's got a son! I just saw him not two hours ago!"

Pain darkened Jason's eyes and he shook his head. "I'm telling you Cody. He's not mine. I wish he was. If Kate has a baby, it's her husband's. I haven't been anywhere near her since a year ago last May."

Cody grabbed him by the shirt with both hands. "Jason! Listen to me! Listen to what I'm saying! It's yours! It's not a baby. Well, not a tiny one. It's a little boy! Like one or two or something. Named *Kennen*! With flaming green eyes! Do the math. Kate hasn't been married that long! And her husband's dead! She told Jennika, I heard her. Jason, I'm telling you! He's yours! He's like a clone! I swear it! Go see for yourself! You can't miss it. You got a kid, man!"

Jason stood up and looked at him and then his face blanched and he sat right back down shaking his head. "No." He kept shaking his head. "No, there was just that one time. We couldn't have… Kate would never do that to me. I know she was upset, but… No. She would never." Finally, unable to process this, he asked, "Would Kate really do that to me? Have my baby and never even tell me?"

"Cut her some slack, Jase. She was pregnant and scared and came to tell you and found you with the beer and another girl. If you were her and had a kid to think about, you'd have walked away too."

Cody went to the counter and picked up Jason's keys and went to hand them to him and then thought better of it. "No. You shouldn't drive right now. I'll take you. Y'all want a change or anything?"

Jason looked down at his button down hanging open over his jeans and bare feet and then shook his head. "I'll be okay, Cody. Just give me minute to absorb this. Now where is she?"

"In Tulsa. Damn! I forgot to find out where she lives or anything. We'll have to ask her mom. Surely she'll tell you, now that she's got your kid."

Jason shook his head and rolled his eyes. This had rattled Cody almost as much as it had him. "If what you're saying is true, Cody, then she's had my kid since that awful night with the champagne. Her mother probably still won't tell me if Kate hasn't okayed it."

Cody's face fell and then lit right back up. "Then Kiersten! Kiersten will tell you. She's a softy. She's known this was wrong the whole time. Go ask Kiersten!"

"No. Kiersten would have told me a long time ago if she could have. She's been sympathetic to me, but she'd promised. But you think Kate acted like she lived there in Tulsa?"

"Well, yeah, she was grocery shopping with her kid. Your kid. She wouldn't have him with if she was just there on a business trip."

Jason went over to his laptop and Googled Katelyn Birch-Garland. "Maybe after this much time she didn't bother going unlisted. She knew I would quit trying to find her after I knew she was married." After a long, pensive moment, a Tulsa address popped onto the screen.

Jason looked up at Cody and could feel his heart pounding in his throat. *Geez, a kid!* His mind was racing with a million different thoughts. It had been nearly two years since they'd messed up that night. Cody was watching him and finally asked, "You sure y'all don't want me to drive you? Finding out you have a kid must be kind of a shock."

Jason shook his head and finally smiled. "Ya think? I'll drive myself. Just give me a year to calm my heart rate and I'll be fine. I'm more excited than shocked. Do you realize that I know where Kate is and she's no longer married? You just gave me my life back!"

Cody looked horrified. "Whoa, Tex. She's been upset enough with you to hide something this big and not speak to you in I don't even know how long. Don't go barging in there and scare her out of the country again!"

"Give me *some* credit, Rawlings. I know how much is at stake here. Now get out of my house and let me think." Cody turned for the door and Jason added, "And Cody?" He turned and looked back. "Thanks. I owe you. But forget about getting my first born."

"Fine. Some kind of friend you are."

Kristin Cross

Chapter 21

Jason pulled up to the modest frame house with the big tree in the front yard and instantly zeroed in on the two toddlers digging in the sand box near the front step. He got out of the car, came up the drive and stopped near the gate at the porch to watch the two. A little blonde girl and a small boy with his mother's curls and his father's everything else. Cody hadn't been hallucinating. Jason could almost be looking at a double of himself when he was little.

His heart had been pounding for more than two hours now, but he still hadn't really believed Cody had been right until this moment, and he almost felt light headed. He had a son! He was incredible!

He stood there, transfixed with wonder. His own child. He couldn't take his eyes off of him until he heard steps on the porch and looked up to see Kate standing there in slim fitting jeans and a stretch t-shirt that showed off her perfect figure.

She gasped as she realized he was there, and put a hand to her heart then her eyes got huge. For just a second, he thought she was going to panic and run. Several different emotions flitted across her face and then she appeared to have the same heart issues he had and put her other hand there as well. She watched him in such surprise that it almost seemed like fear and then finally, she almost whispered, "You... You scared me. I thought there was a stranger watching them."

As glad as he was to have found her, what she had done to him sliced his heart and he asked sadly, "Why, Kate? Why didn't you tell me?"

She closed her eyes and then turned around and went back into the house without answering and he opened her gate and followed her in and said quietly but firmly, "No, Kate. This is too much. I had a right to know I had a son." She continued on into the kitchen where she started to cry and he went on more gently, "How could you? Sweet, kind, gentle Kate. You're not vindictive. You're not vengeful. Why? We could have been married and happy all this time."

She put her hands over her face and started to cry harder and he softly urged, "Kate, answer me. What would make you hate me so much you'd make your own son go without a father?"

At that, she shook her head and turned even more away still sobbing and after a moment leaned against her counter without looking at him. He followed her and put out a gentle hand to try to get her to look up at him, but she pulled away. In the softest tone of voice possible he asked again, "Why?"

She finally swallowed and struggled for composure as she said, "I came to Lubbock to tell you, Jason."

There was a long, long moment of painful silence and finally, Jason sighed and asked, "Now what?"

Kate sniffed, wiped her eyes, unconsciously squared her shoulders and said quietly, "You're going to get back in your fancy little sports car and go back to being a superstar and leave us alone. You've seen him now."

"Not a chance and you know it."

She faced up to him in spite of her tears. "Look Jason, you have absolutely no say in his life. He's a year old, and John Garland is his father."

Jason folded his arms and laughed bitterly. "What? Are you going to try to tell me he's not mine? He's a clone. And where is this business man husband of yours? I'd like to meet him."

She picked up a dish that was sitting on the counter above her dish washer and turned away to put it in the cupboard. "He's not home right now."

Jason shook his head and wanted to swear, but said almost resignedly instead, "You're not even going to tell me that he passed away, are you? Give it up, Kate. It's been nearly two years of hell without you. Knowing you hated me and were married to someone else... I can't even begin to voice how much that hurt, but I thought it was what you wanted. Seeing you now... You didn't want that. I can see it in your eyes. Only God knows why y'all made the decisions you've made. But that little boy out there changes everything."

She turned to him defiantly. "No, Jason. Two years ago he changed everything. I tried to tell you. Several times I started to tell you. You wouldn't listen and the time's past. It's too late now. You have your life and we have ours. I don't want him raised in a world of booze and fast cars and faster women. Go away." The last two words sounded unbelievably sad.

Jason came to stand directly in front of her and said softly, "Look me in the eye, Kate, and tell me you hate me and never want to see me again and we'll talk."

She looked up momentarily and then dropped her eyes and turned away. "Jason, I worked late last night and I'm too tired to argue." She put another dish away and then looked back and this time when she looked up, her eyes were challenging. "You have no right to even be here, let alone demand anything from me. Listen to yourself. I'm not some groupie you can manipulate."

Letting out a breath, he said, "Thank heavens for that."

Taking a step even closer, he waited until she looked into his eyes and then he said gently, "You're wrong, Kate. I do have the right. Even more than that, I have the responsibility. You were wrong not to tell me at all. And frankly, I've never been more glad to be shocked in my life. He's a dream come true for me. I've wanted to have children with you since I was seventeen years old. You and I both know I can't walk away from this no matter how ticked off you are at me."

He saw the fireworks go off in her blue eyes. "You think this is about being ticked off? Jason Falcon, we're talking about a child's life! A sweet, entirely dependent child who hasn't been schooled by the ugly realities of this world yet! This isn't about being ticked off!"

Right then, both of the children peeked their heads around the corner. The little girl had her finger in her mouth and Kennen looked frightened. Kate went and put her arms around them both and tried to comfort them and then encouraged them to go back outside and play. When they were gone, she turned back on Jason, but he interrupted her when he said huskily, "You're a beautiful mommy. I always knew you would be. And he's awesome. You've done a marvelous job."

Kate turned away with a sigh. "He's just a marvelous kid. He was awesome the second he was born. And John was a huge help with him until he got too sick."

Gently Jason asked, "When did he pass away?"

"A couple of months ago. He had an inoperable brain tumor."

She said it quietly, but with no emotion and Jason couldn't help but ask, "Were you in love with him?"

Kate looked up at him and then turned and began stacking clean dishes on the counter. "Jason, you need to go now. Kennen and I have things to do."

"Answer the question, Kate."

"You lost the right to ask me questions like that a couple of years ago, Jason. It's none of your business."

He paused and then said softly, "I think y'all just can't answer the question because you don't lie, but you don't want me to know the truth."

Looking out the window to check on the kids, she said, "The truth is, it's none of your business, Jason. Now, please go. And don't come back."

"Why?" She didn't answer him right away and he pressed her. "The truth, Kate. You're not still mad. I know you. You're not a grudge holder. So, why can't I come back and get to know my little boy? And don't argue about that, Kate. You know you can't keep him from me anymore. So tell me the truth."

She spun to look at him. "Okay, I'll tell you the truth, Jason. Walking away from you was every kind of hell. I loved you. I missed you desperately. I was scared and worried and sick and alone. I needed you, Jason. Leaving you was like cutting off my right arm, but it had to be done. I had a child to consider. I had to go. That was one of the ugly realities I was talking about. I won't go through that again, Jason. And I certainly won't allow Kennen to be dragged through it.

"And don't you argue with me. I know you too, Jason. You are too kind of a man to do that to a sweet, happy, little boy, whether he has your DNA or not. So, don't try to dabble in our lives. Just go back on tour and try to forget that you ever knew me. Just like I'm trying to do with you."

Standing right in front of each other, he looked her in the eyes for several seconds and then shook his head. "I can't, Kate. Even if we didn't have him I couldn't. Not now I know your husband is dead and that you aren't in love with him anyway. I lost you, and you were right to walk. I was an idiot and I was wrong and I deserved you walking out on me. In fact, I probably needed it to get me to wake up about where I was heading. And I was right to respect your decision and your marriage. But not anymore. I can't. I love you too much. I've thought about you every hour of every day since that stupid night in Lubbock with that stupid beer that really wasn't mine."

She gave him a look and he put up both hands. "I know, I know. I was foolish and I was wrong and I deserved you leaving, and for a while there, after I found out you were married, I did drink. In fact, I tried to drown myself drinking to try to deaden the pain and forget you. And that was wrong too. And with some help from Cody, I admitted it and straightened up. But I can promise you, on my honor, Kate, that I *never* slept with anyone. Even when I tried to surround myself with girls to try and wipe you out of my mind, every single stinking time I'd see your face and think of our pinky promise out on the dock that night, and I'd go on home by myself."

She looked at him openly for several seconds and he saw pain in her eyes as she shook her head. "I'm sorry, Jason. But I don't believe you. And it doesn't matter anyway. The past is gone. What you do morally is between you and God and doesn't concern me anymore."

Still standing in front of her, he shook his own head and gently took her shoulders and looked into her eyes. "No, Kate, you're wrong. It matters. I don't blame you for not believing me. The tabloids have been unreal. But the promise we made to each other that night does matter. It matters more than anything. And other than that one disastrous night that we drank the champagne, I have honored it. Even when I was at my worst I honored it. Because, as much as I tried to get over you, I couldn't.

You're too deep in my heart. In my very soul. Even if you were to refuse to ever see me again, I'd still love only you forever." He paused and then added softly, "Falcons really do mate for life, Kate. They really do."

As he looked into her eyes, they filled up with tears again and when they welled over, he pulled her into a gentle hug and rested his cheek against her short pixy curls. He eased her against him even tighter and let out a sigh at how good it felt to hold her after all these many, many months. It truly felt like coming home.

His sweet sense of rightness was cut short as she shrugged out of his arms and went to the window to look out at the two toddlers playing in the yard beyond. He could tell she was wiping at her eyes and though he was unsure of what to do, he followed her to look out the window as well.

Again the sight of that little dark head made his heart do somersaults and he breathed against her hair, "He's such a miracle." Sadly, he admitted, "I wish I'd known, Kate. I wish I'd have been able to be excited about you having our baby. I wish I could have been there when he was born and have seen him from the very start. I wish I could have helped you through all of it."

Without turning, she whispered, "I wished that too, Jase." He heard her quietly sob. "But you'd changed. I had to go."

He wrapped his arms around her shoulders. "I know. And I'm so sorry. So, so sorry."

They stood like that for several minutes while her tears dripped onto his forearms and finally, he turned her and pulled her back into the close hug they'd shared for all those years before any of this, and nothing had ever felt so right in his life. Why had he ever, ever let this get away? He wanted to stay here like this forever.

At length, the children outside left the sand box and he knew they were probably headed their way and after a couple of minutes, he reluctantly let her go to step away from her as they toddled into the room. As they came to her, Jason knelt down. Kennen looked at him hesitantly and then took a step behind Kate's leg and wrapped his little arm around her knee.

Kate leaned down beside Jason and whispered, "It's okay, buddy." She put her arm around Jason and said, "This is a friend of Mommy's. His name is Jason. He's okay, Kennen. He won't hurt you. Would you like to meet him?"

Kennen ducked his head and looked away, but the little girl stepped out and took her finger out of her mouth and reached out for Jason. He took her in his arms and Kennen watched as Jason smiled at her and gently touched a tiny piggy tail. Jason was just wondering how to get Kennen to come to him, when Kennen slipped out from behind Kate's leg and pulled the little girl's other piggy tail and let it spring back against her head. Then he laughed like that was the funniest thing ever and Jason smiled at the sound of it.

When Kennen finally came forward, Jason picked him up as well and stood up and Kennen began to jabber to the little girl, but Jason couldn't understand a word of it.

Kate came and put her hands out and said, "Gretchen, can I hold you a minute while Jason holds his... While he holds Kennen?" The little girl leaned into Kate's arms as Kate said, "He's a nice man, Kennen. You can hug him if you want to. He'd probably love one of your huggers."

At that, Kennen almost threw his arms around Jason's neck and gave a huge squeeze for a child that size and Jason wrapped his own arms around the tiny body and closed his eyes. This was his son. The child he had dreamed of having for about as long as he could remember. He cuddled him to him and felt feelings well up inside he'd never felt before in his life. This was his and Kate's son. Their Kennen. He was real and in the flesh and this tiny little body felt like a small piece of heaven here in his arms.

When Kennen began to squirm, Jason carefully let him back down and brushed an embarrassed hand across his eyes. Gretchen didn't appear to want to be left out, and she reached for Jason as well and he gladly took her and got one of her huggers too and was nearly overwhelmed again. Even before Kate had walked away, he'd wanted to get married and start a family. He'd wanted it then. He wanted it even more now.

Kate was watching him as she picked Kennen back up and Jason brushed at his eyes again and put a hand against Gretchen's back and then gently reached and touched Kennen's soft, dark curls. He was absolutely perfect. He couldn't even believe it. He had a son.

They heard a sound from the other room and there was a knock and someone said, "Knock, knock, Kate. Where are you?" A pretty, blonde young woman came in carrying a carton of strawberries and stopped short when she saw Jason. "Oh, I'm sorry; I didn't realize y'all had company. I was just going to pick up Gretchen." Her voice trailed off as she looked him and then looked back at Kennen and back at Jason a couple of times as she compared them and her eyes got big. "Excuse me, but aren't you? You're that country music singer, aren't you? Jason Falcon?"

Jason nodded and she looked back and forth between Kate and Jason and Kennen for another moment and looked puzzled as she said, "Kate, I thought you said that your husband was dead."

Jason looked at Kate, wondering if he had just caused a problem, but Kate simply smiled at the puzzled woman and said, "He is, Elise. He died a couple of months ago. This is Jason Falcon and …" She hesitated for a moment and then said, "And as I think you probably just figured out, he's Kennen's father. It's a long story. I'll tell you sometime."

Elise put the carton of strawberries on the counter top, took Gretchen and grinned at the other three. "Yes, I'd like that very much. Thanks for watching her. She loves Kennen and it's great to be able to just run in."

Kate nodded. "I know what you mean. I'll get even with you probably tomorrow. It's amazing how much faster you can go somewhere toddler free." She patted Gretchen on the head. "See you, Gretchen. Thank you for being such a good princess. Come again, okay."

Gretchen took the ever present finger out of her mouth and said, "Weltum. Bye-bye Tennen. Yuv you."

She put the finger back in her mouth and the two of them went out the way her mother had come in and Jason laughed as Kennen yelled after them at the top of his lungs, "Bye, Dwetch."

Jason shook his head and laughed again. "Tennen and Dwetch. Why am I reminded of you and Kennen twenty years ago?"

Kate finally smiled a hint of the old smile he remembered. "Because we were as adorable as these two are." She sighed and then asked, "Have you eaten?" Maybe she was finally going to loosen up after all.

"Are you kidding? I haven't even breathed since Cody showed up. Can I take you out somewhere?"

She shook her head and smiled sadly. "No. I don't think so. I barely got my respectability back and you and Kennen just blew it out of the water again. I don't think Elise will say too much, but I might not be so lucky with someone else. How about chicken parmasiana at the kitchen table? Would that be okay?"

"Heaven. Can I help?"

"Absolutely. Did you ever learn to chop?"

"Mmm, no. Sorry. There's not a whole lot of opportunity to cook in music."

"Then can you handle washing his hands and face and checking his diaper?"

"Yes, I can. I'm sure of it. I think. I'm good with all of it except that last. If I yell, would y'all come save me?"

"Save you, or save him?"

"Well, whoever might be in need of saving. Just come if I call."

"Gotcha." She nodded toward the hall. "First door on the left."

Five minutes later, she poked her head around the corner into the bathroom to find him and Kennen sitting on the floor together playing with the tub toys. "I wondered why it was so quiet. How was his diaper?"

"Diaper's good. Huh, buddy?"

Kennen chugged a toy boat up Jason's arm. "Yup! Dipo dood."

Kate wrinkled her nose. "So then, what's that smell?"

Kennen drove the boat back down and said, "Yucky dipo!"

Unfazed, Jason said, "That's the old one." He indicated the wadded diaper that sat beside them on the floor. "Where does it live?"

Kate rolled her eyes. "In the diaper pail." Kennen jumped up and he and Kate showed Jason how to put the smelly diaper into the garbage bag part of the pail and twist the top so it didn't smell any more. Then she sprayed air freshener over the top of the two of them. "Just in case."

She went back out and Jason heard her mellow laugh as she walked back up the hall. He had no idea that a one year old kid could be this much fun. Or that a mother could be that sexy either one and he said to Kennen, "Hey, let's go help Mommy, shall we?"

"Yup!" Kennen jumped up and ran as fast as his miniature legs would carry him back to the kitchen and slammed himself into her leg as she stood at the sink.

She glanced down, automatically wiped her hands on the towel she had tied around her waist and bent down and picked him up to put him on the kitchen counter. She began to tug his clothes back into place and tuck his under shirt back in. There seemed to be a problem and she finally had Kennen lay down flat and she undid the snaps on his minute overalls. "Okay, here's the problem. We're snapped up backwards." She redid the snaps and set him down and he took off back down the hall. Kate smiled as she turned back to the vegetables she was washing. "Don't worry; it took me weeks to learn to get his diaper on securely."

"Does he always go everywhere that fast?"

"Only when he's excited. There are times when he'll watch an ant for half an hour. Then he'll try to eat it. Do you still like cheese on your broccoli?"

"Yes, I thought you hated broccoli."

"I do." She dumped broccoli into a bowl and put some plastic wrap over it. "Parenthood makes you do strange things. I don't want him to dislike it. It's good for him." She shrugged and Jason grinned at her.

"You're really cute as a mother."

She glanced over at him and said, "You haven't seen me when I'm really tired. I'm not cute at two in the morning when he's throwing up."

Jason leaned back against the counter and folded his arms. "I have seen you when you're tired. You're still cute. And you're cute at two in the morning. And you're not as cute, but there's still something about you when you're throwing up."

Kate rolled her eyes at him. "That's gross, Jason."

"You're the one who brought it up."

"I'm just trying to get the point across that he's not all fun and games, Jase. I know you think you're all the sudden going to be a dad now, but it's harder than it seems."

"I am all the sudden a dad, no matter what I think. C'mon, Kate. Help me out here. I've known I was a parent for all of what? Two and a half hours. I know you're not thrilled that I showed up here, but go with me on this for just a little while. At least consider forgiving me and burying the hatchet. For his sake." His voice lowered as he pleaded softly, "This is a good day for me. Let me enjoy it."

She got quiet and it took him a minute to realize she was crying over the cheese she was slicing and he came over to her and put a hand on her shoulder and looked down into her face. "Don't cry, baby. It's going to be all right. I swear it is."

She shook her head and wiped at her tears with the back of her hand. "Jason, you don't understand."

"So help me understand. And don't wipe your tears with a knife in your hand. Y'all are gonna poke your eye out."

He'd been trying to make her laugh, and she did. And then he pulled her against him in a hug and whispered in a husky voice in her ear, "Kate, babe. It's been a long time, and we've been through hell. But we've learned and grown and gotten stronger and better for it. And when it all comes down to it. We're still just Jason and Kate. I haven't seen you in almost two years and I can still tell what you're thinking. I still know how to make you laugh. I still even know where you're ticklish, so y'all had better straighten up and quit fighting me. Just let me help you. I promise I won't screw up this time. Well, I may screw up, but it won't be in such a colossal manner and it certainly won't involve alcohol or other women. I've learned. I swear I have."

She shook her head against his chest. "You have no idea what I think anymore, Jason Falcon."

Putting a hand into the back of her hair, he tugged on it until she tipped her head back and looked up at him and he met her eyes and said seriously, "Yeah, I do, Kate.

Right now, you're wondering if it would be worth it to sell this house and disappear again, or if I'd come after you this time." She looked up at him, startled and he knew he'd been right. That's just what she'd been thinking. "The answers are no, and yes. Don't run again. At least give me a chance. Just one. That's all I ask. If I blow it, you can walk away and I'll leave y'all both alone. I promise. And if you do decide to go anyway without giving me a chance, I'm coming after you this time. I'll follow you two to the ends of the earth. So please don't." He leaned back into her ear and whispered, "Please don't, Kate. Life is hell without you."

She snuggled into his chest and began to cry again and without raising her head, she said, "I can't do it. I've sacrificed so much so he didn't have to be fought over and have to deal with the parties and the groupies and the paparazzi and trashy standards. I can't do that to him, Jason. He needs to be able to grow up and know that values and morals and fidelity are important and vital. He needs to be taught that good people don't drink and carouse. He needs roots, Jason. Roots to be able to know who he is and what he's capable of and how to reach his potential."

He pulled her closer and basked in the feel of her breath on his neck. "You're right about all those things, Kate. But me being part of your lives doesn't mean he can't have that. I can help you teach him all those things. He does need roots, Kate. And that's one thing he won't have if y'all keep hiding. He's got some grandparents who would love to be able to spend some time with him. He does need roots and I'll help you provide those. But Kate, he needs roots and wings. You both do. You both need to be able to fly when you want to. You're a Falcon too, Kate. You have been since you were sixteen."

Leaning his face against her temple, he breathed in the smell of her skin and fought the urge to kiss that soft spot between her eye brow and her hair and lost. With infinite gentleness, he kissed her tenderly. "Just one chance, Kate. Please. Just give me one chance."

She finally looked up and he began to drown in the indigo blue of her eyes. He wanted to kiss her mouth more than he'd ever wanted anything in his life, but he was afraid she'd freak out on him if he did. Then she glanced down at his mouth and swallowed hard and looked back up and he knew she wanted it as much as he did. He slowly began to lower his head, watching her eyes. If he saw fear there, he'd stop.

He never saw it and finally, after what felt like days, his mouth took hers and he closed his eyes and lost himself in the feel of her mouth under his. Oh, but he'd dreamed of holding her and kissing her again like this. He wanted to melt in the tenderness of her mouth and never even consider coming up for air.

At first, he kissed her so softly he could barely feel her emotion as she softly touched him back, and then slowly, he felt her remember how they used to be and when she finally leaned closer to him, he kissed her with all the pent up hope and need and fear and despair and every other myriad of emotions he'd been feeling for these two years and she met him half way. This was his soul mate. The other half of his life and without her his wings were tied. Broken. With her...

He groaned and wrapped his arms around her like he'd dreamed of so many thousand times. With her, he could fly anywhere. She tasted just like she'd always tasted and it was the flavor of fantasy. The flavor of forever and always, all rolled in to one moment.

He kissed her until his breath was coming in ragged gasps and he wanted to breathe her right into his brain. Until he could feel her breathing match his own and her heartbeat through both of their shirts and he lost all track of time and there was nothing but her mouth under his and her body pressing close with almost a feeling of desperation. It was as if this was all a dream and they were afraid they'd wake up and it would disappear, so they needed to revel in it while they could before it was gone.

Maybe if he kissed her like he wanted to, she'd begin to understand how it still was with him. That he worshipped her and that without her, life held no meaning or color or heat. Maybe if he kissed her with enough feeling she'd realize...

Kennen grabbed his pant leg and pulled himself up and Jason knew he must have had hold of Kate's too because the spell was broken and he could feel her back away emotionally. He groaned again and pulled her even closer as he finally released her mouth. "Kate." His voice was so husky he almost didn't recognize it as he put his face against her sweet smelling hair. She hid hers against him and drew a shuddering breath as he admitted, "I've dreamed of kissing you, Kate. I've dreamed of your taste. All these months and years, you've haunted me."

He still held her tightly and never wanted to let go, but Kennen began to pound on their legs with his little fists to get their attention and finally, Jason leaned down and picked the little boy up and lifted him into the circle of their arms. He sighed one more time. This was the way they were supposed to be. He was sure of it. He put a gentle finger under Kate's chin to get her to look up at him and then he bent to kiss her one more time, more gently, but with out losing any of that same passion that arced between them.

When he finally released her lips, he asked softly, "If I tell you one more time that I love you, Kate, will it freak you out?"

He felt her shake her head and then nod and then she stilled and he looked down at her with a grin. "What did that mean?"

She sighed and hid her face as she admitted, "Oh, Jason, I don't even know. I'm so mixed up right now."

"Then I'm going to risk it." He pulled her face up again. "I love you, Kate. I always have. I always will." He leaned to kiss her and then gently kissed Kennen as well. "I love you both. And I always will." He was just going to kiss her again, when they both sniffed at the same time and then quickly looked back toward the stove where smoke was rolling in clouds off her pan.

As they looked, the pan burst into flames and she inhaled sharply and twisted Kennen away. Jason pushed them both away, turned off the stove, glanced around and then lunged for the fire extinguisher that hung on the wall just inside the door.

Kate stumbled out the back door with the baby while Jason made sure the fire was out and then shoved the room's windows open and headed out to where she was standing anxiously outside the door and he laughed and sprawled onto her back porch swing and then pulled the two of them down on top of him. "Now, there's a first for us, Kate. I knew we were good kissers, but we've never spontaneously combusted!"

She let out a laugh and smacked him as she coughed again. "Oh, I'm so sorry. I completely forgot what I was doing."

"You and me both, babe. " Their eyes met and then she looked away. "I wouldn't have remembered to breathe just now." He reached and touched her mouth and she looked back up and this time he could see the fear and tried to back off and joke. "I'm just glad you're an organized and prepared woman. I'm afraid your kitchen would have been toast, literally, without that fire extinguisher."

She sighed and he glanced down at her and saw that the laughter had died out of her eyes and he encouraged her. "Don't babe. Don't make that sound. At least for tonight let's just smile and have hope." She looked up at him and he saw that old familiar worry and leaned to kiss it away. "Have hope with me, Kate. If y'all can't do it for me, then do it for Kennen. If there's the slightest possibility he could have a stable, two parent home full of love, let's try. We owe that to him. Children deserve to have two parents, who are married and committed to each other." He patted the small dark head that lay on Kate's chest as she lay against his

That made her sigh again. "I'm sorry, Jason, but there is no way I can talk about marriage tonight. I haven't even seen you in almost two years. And there was a reason for that."

He gently brushed across her cheek with the back of his hand. "Yes, but I know something that y'all don't know, Katie Ree."

"And what is that?"

He sat up and looked into her eyes. "That I've had more than enough of the glitz and I only want the flavor of Kate. I was stupid, Kate. I'll be the first to admit that. I had lost my perspective on what was appropriate, but I was never wrong about being sure where you were concerned. Through this whole hellacious mess, that never changed. Even when I knew you were married to another man and I thought I'd lost you forever. I still knew I could never love someone else."

She searched his eyes and then looked away. "It's still crazy to talk about marriage tonight. I'm sorry.

Wrapping one of her curls around his finger, he said almost lazily, "You know what would be crazy, Kate? It would be crazy to finally find you and actually spend time with you without making absolutely sure you know I love you and want to marry you and be with you for the rest of eternity. That's what would be crazy."

"But, Jason, you don't even know me anymore. How can you say that?"

At that, he sighed and leaned his head back against the top of the swing. "You, know, Kate. In some ways, you're right. You've done some things that hit me out of the blue and I still can't believe. I honestly never dreamed in a million years you would leave instead of telling me we were having a baby. I still can't believe you would do that, even when now I know why you did. But I do know you, Kate. I know y'all better than your mother knows you. I know you nearly as well as God and Kennen know you. My brother Kennen. And you know what's really cool?"

He glanced down at her to see that she was looking up at him. "What's really cool is, the more I know you, the more sure I am I adore you. Most people aren't like that. Usually the more you know about someone, the less you like them. That whole familiarity breeds contempt thing. You're not like that. With you it's familiarity breeds undying love."

He glanced down at her and saw the laughter he'd missed so desperately and she teased him. "Those are terrible lyrics."

"Ah, well, you can't always be brilliant. Are you sure I couldn't interest you in dinner? I know a great steak and rib place not far from here. It smells like smoke too, but they do it on purpose. C'mon. I'll treat you at your own joint."

"Oh, no. That's all I need is for the staff to see you and Kennen together. I'd never stop the rumors. Let's go somewhere more private with low lighting so anyone who sees us won't know for sure if you're that famous star or if that widow's baby really looks that much like you."

"Do we know of a place like that nearby?"

"The drive through at Jack in the Box."

Jason groaned. "Something tells me you're going to be hard to date. Come on. We should feed him before he goes down for the night. Are we already too late?" He lifted her off of his lap and set her gently aside, got up and reached down to tenderly lift Kennen and then snuggle him close and kiss him as she shook her head.

"I'll get him a sippy cup of milk for his car seat. That way if we lose him he won't be hungry all night."

Jason looked down at him as he offered Kate his other hand. "I can't get over him. I can't get over the fact that he is so perfect, and… I can't get over just the fact that he is. Do you know what I mean?"

He saw her get thoughtful for a moment and asked, "What?"

She shrugged and turned to go into the house and he caught her hand. "I want to understand, Kate. I know I'll never get to have those experiences, good and bad, but I deeply regret that. Both missing the good and making you shoulder the bad alone. Tell me."

She hesitated and then said, "You just can not even imagine what it's like to realize you're expecting a baby and the dad is… Well, that you aren't married and settled and committed. It brings a whole new meaning to not being able to get over that he is."

He gently cupped her cheek with his hand. "Do you ever think you'll be able to forgive me, Kate?"

"Oh, I forgave you. I forgave both of us. I had to face that he was coming because we both messed up. And I could understand why you were acting the way you were. Forgiving you wasn't a problem. I just had to get through it. Being alone was the kicker. He was born premie in San Francisco the day my dad died. The closest person I knew was like eighteen hundred miles away. I had to have a C-section and it got infected. It was . . . It was... I just had to get through it."

He could hear the tears in her voice and saw them seeping into her eyes as she pulled away to go back into the house. He followed her, wishing there was some way he could go back and fix the terrible struggle he'd caused her to go through. Thinking about what she was describing made him feel horribly guilty and he wished they'd been together through these last months and years more than ever. The only thing he could do now was to try to make it up to her.

With the sippy cup in hand, Kate turned on the exhaust fan to start getting rid of the smoke smell and then grabbed a soft blanket and a jacket for Kennen and headed out to her garage. "Is it okay if we take my car? That way we won't have to move his car seat. It takes days to get it situated correctly."

"Your car's fine. Just tell me what to do."

Once Kennen was safely buckled in, Kate propped his head comfortably with the blanket and then got back out of the back seat of her car and handed Jason her keys. "Would you drive?"

He thought about that as he helped her into the passenger door and then came around, got in, adjusted the seat and buckled up. She was still the ultimate competent woman, but she had always wanted him to drive everything, from a motorcycle to a horse. She was funny that way.

He pushed the garage door opener and backed out into the gathering dusk of the March evening. Soft rock came on and he adjusted the rearview mirror and reached over and took her hand like he'd done every day of their lives before she'd gone. He glanced over to her as they eased off down her street toward their romantic Jack in the Box drive through.

She was still Kate, but she'd grown up so much that it no longer seemed like the older boyfriend and the teenage girlfriend like it had been the whole time they were growing up. There was no question about whether she was a woman grown now. That had been more than obvious from the emotion of those kisses. But it was more than that too. It really felt more like a married couple with their baby heading out to go somewhere. He hoped she was as happy and hopeful as he was, because he'd be fine with being Kennen's daddy and Kate's husband for at least the next twenty or thirty thousand years.

They ate in the car under the street light in the parking lot and neither one of them had much to say. There were so many things he wanted to say to her. Hopes he had. Dreams he wanted to work toward. Even apologies he desperately wanted to make, but he knew he was crowding her and had to back off.

He held her hand on the way back home again and then carried Kennen in and helped her get him changed and dressed for bed. Then he carried him in and gently laid him in the crib in her room and pulled his soft small blanket up to tuck around him. Afterward, he couldn't help himself and stayed there for a few minutes just looking at him in the dim glow of the Winnie the Pooh night light. He still couldn't get over that he was. He looked at his beautiful Kate standing beside him, the precious baby there in the crib and felt an achingly acute sense of loss that he'd missed so much. He wrapped an arm around her waist and whispered sadly, "I wish I could have known about him, Kate."

Back in her living room, with the stereo playing low, he longed for his guitar. The need to play for her was upon him. To bring her sweet music and tell her through his words and voice how much she meant to him and how he felt inside about her and their son. But he hadn't brought it and had to settle for sitting on her couch and having her nestle against his legs like she'd always done when he had been playing.

He dropped a gentle hand to her shoulder and softly squeezed. There was so much to be said and yet the silence that stretched between them was what made the bond they'd always shared the most apparent. The silence was comfortable and yet fraught with the need they were both feeling and neither one could voice.

She leaned her head back against his knee and closed her eyes and he slid a hand into her hair and let the soft, dark curls slide through his fingers and then tenderly rubbed her head. She sighed and he could feel her relax into him. It was incredibly easy and sweet to sit here quietly with her.

When he had all but decided he never wanted to leave, he swallowed a sigh, pushed her carefully away and stood up. "I gotta go, Kate. If I stay here much longer I'm going to melt. Either that or kiss you until I can't think straight and you'll be afraid of me in the morning. Kick me out."

He offered her a hand and as he pulled her up, pulling her all the way into his arms was automatic, as was leaning down to kiss her breathless.

Kissing her until he couldn't think straight actually only took seconds and then he was back to the dizzying need to want to literally breath her in. It was too late to leave before he melted, she made him feel like he'd lost his very bones as he held her to him and rained kisses all over her face and then moved to that warm, soft hollow under her ear.

He gently nuzzled her ear lobe with his teeth and heard her take in a soft, quick breath and decided he needed to go home *now*. The longer he kissed her the more he wanted to.

With all the will power he possessed, he gently pushed her away and tried to make himself swallow the sound of frustration that rose in his throat. Still holding her hand, he headed for her door and when they got there, he turned, gathered her almost roughly into his arms and kissed her one more time almost fiercely and then raised his head and asked, "Kate, can you promise me one thing?"

Her voice was tired silk as she replied, "I don't know, Jason. What do you need?"

"You, Kate. I need you. You're the other half of my soul. Promise me you won't be gone when I come back here tomorrow. Promise me you won't have taken him and run away again."

She searched his eyes for a long moment and he saw the worry there deep in hers, but at length she nodded. "I promise, Jason. I'll be here when you come tomorrow."

He knew she wouldn't lie to him and took a huge breath of relief and put his cheek against her temple.

"Good Kate, 'cause I couldn't face losing you again. Either of you. It would kill me." He gently kissed her one more time and then met her eyes and asked, "Think about me tonight, huh?" She nodded silently and he said one last time, "I love you, Kate. Good night."

She closed her door behind him and he stood for a moment on her porch marveling at how much a person's perspective on life could change in a handful of hours. He looked up at the stars and thought about the exquisite woman who was inside there, probably getting ready for bed. Geez, he had missed her. He couldn't even believe how much. Or how unreal it still felt that he had found her and she had actually been decent to him. Way decent. He stepped off the porch and headed for his car, thinking about how good it had been to kiss her. Nothing in the world was as incredible as kissing her. He didn't even want to go home, he just wanted to go back and keep kissing her.

Pulling away from her house, there was no question about whether he was moving to Tulsa like tomorrow and he began to look for realtor's signs as he cruised up and down the nearest couple of streets. Writing down the first one's number that he came to, he resisted the urge to call right then. Phoning at eleven thirty at night probably wasn't the best idea if he wanted any kind of working relationship. Seven thirty ought to be late enough in the morning though. After thinking about it, he decided he wasn't going to drive home tonight after all. He'd just get a hotel here and save the drive time. He scrolled down to Cody's number. Even this late, he'd be waiting for word.

Chapter 22

Jason's request that she think about him tonight couldn't have been more superfluous. That she would think about him in depth was the understatement of the quarter century. She undressed and got ready for bed, torn between the happiness and peace she'd felt at being with him and the worry that she'd had a huge lapse in judgment the second she'd seen his heart stopping presence in her driveway. After nearly fainting from the shock, she'd all but fallen into his arms within minutes. It had been heaven, but she was probably a fool.

She'd struggled through nearly two years without even her family to keep him from finding out about Kennen and it had all been wasted because of that trip to the grocery store. Who would have thought she'd need worry about grocery shopping? She should be devastated, but the fact that the opposite was true made her wonder if she'd lost all sense of responsibility toward her son. What was going on here? Was this a subconscious dream come true, or a sure way to wreck her son's life and the path to reopening an excruciating heartache?

After double checking Kennen, she knelt to pray and wasn't even sure what to pray for. Finally, she simply asked for a measure of God's wisdom and the inspiration to make the best decisions for Kennen's sake. She added the same prayer she always did, that He would watch over Jason, wherever he was. Not a day had gone by since she'd left that she hadn't asked that. And finally, she asked for help for herself. She didn't mean to be selfish, but Jason had the power to rip her heart from her chest if he decided to. She obviously didn't have the will to resist him alone if she was supposed to. For that, she'd certainly need a higher power.

She finally lay down, but sleep was long in coming. Oh, but he'd looked like Christmas morning standing there today. And being held by him... It was like coming to water after nearly dying of thirst. A vital need that had gone unattended for far too long. Since Lubbock she could count the times she'd been hugged on one hand and that had only been her family. Life wasn't supposed to be that way. Physical touch wasn't really optional. And without it, her spirit had begun to shrivel up and die.

Turning on her tummy and pulling her pillow into her arms, she sighed. So she was right back to square one, wasn't she? The same point she'd been at before conceiving Kennen, wondering if being with Jason was smart or asking for a lifetime of heartache? No, that wasn't true because now she needed to consider Kennen as well. She was in a far more critical place than she'd been back then. She had a sweet little boy depending on her to make wise decisions for him as well.

Jason insisted she wasn't in the same place. That he'd changed. That they'd both changed and gotten wiser and stronger. But from where she was, that was hard to tell. She'd trusted him foolishly before. How did she know for sure if she could honestly trust him now? Especially as vulnerable and weak as she felt after falling right into his arms tonight?

She tossed and turned as she lay there, and her mind tossed and turned as well, and she felt exhausted both physically and emotionally by the time sleep mercifully claimed her.

Kennen's adorable little voice, talking to himself as he sat in his crib, pulled her from sleep in the morning and she smiled at it before her eyes even opened. When they did, she glanced over at him and he gave her that beautiful miniature smile that was so much like his father's. She turned over on her back.

His father! She hadn't dreamed it. Jason really had shown up here last night and told her several, several times that he loved her and wanted to be part of her life again. A sweet heat filled her as she remembered those kisses in the kitchen. She hadn't felt like that in years. It was really, really nice to be so openly desired. For that matter, it was just as nice to feel desire. For a second, she wondered if it would be okay to just follow her heart and enjoy him again. Then Kennen made another sound.

No, there was too much at stake to be foolish about this. It wasn't a decision to be made based on physical desire. What she decided would affect Kennen his whole life and even beyond. She rolled back to look at the beautiful boy across the room again and he pulled himself up to the side of his crib and smiled and reached his tiny, chubby hand toward her.

Yawning, she pushed back the covers and stood to walk across and get him. As she picked him up, he cuddled right into her shoulder and closed his eyes and she brought him back to her bed. "You wanna come back to Mommy's bed and snuggle this morning, Kennen?"

"Yup. Snuggo." Five minutes later, Kennen was back to sleep, but Kate was awake and worrying in earnest. What to do about Jason? She sighed and then got up and got into the shower. The only thing she knew was that she'd promised not to leave at least for today. The thought of picking up and leaving again left her sick to her stomach. She had Kennen now, so it wasn't quite as lonely as it had been, but she dreaded the thought of starting all over again somewhere. And if she did it now that Jason knew about Kennen it would be a whole new ball game.

He'd already said he'd come after her. Getting away from him if he was serious would be incredibly difficult. He had the funds to hire anyone he wished. She had to find a way to figure out if Jason truly had changed enough to trust him not to drag Kennen through a negative lifestyle.

She toweled off and dressed and did her hair and makeup. Then as she was preparing Kennen's things, she realized she'd completely forgotten to buy diapers the day before. She never put them on the list because she bought them virtually every time she shopped, but she'd been a trifle flustered yesterday after seeing Cody and his surgeon. She'd have to go again first thing this morning.

With Kennen dressed and fed, she called Elise and asked if she would let Kennen hang out with Gretchen for a few minutes while she ran. Ten minutes later as she took him next door, she knew Elise was dying to know all about Jason as she mentioned, "I saw the Porsche there until late. So, now how is it that you were married to someone named Garland, but have a child with a country star named Falcon?"

Kate smiled, but it didn't feel very happy and she decided to give Elise the Cliff Notes version. "Uh, well. Jason and I grew up next door to each other. We'd sort of been close for forever. One night we got too close actually." She gave another sad smile. "Hence Kennen. Things didn't work out and I left and met John and married him, but he only lived a year after that. He had a brain tumor."

Elise nodded. "And?"

Kate shrugged. "And not really anything. After John passed away I moved here. End of story."

"That's it? End of story? Oh, Kate! C'mon! Are you telling me that yesterday was nothing but a friendly parental visit?"

Nodding to appease Elise, Kate wondered how you could describe what yesterday was with any accuracy. Who knew? Not her at least, but she couldn't admit that to Elise and simply said, "Just a parental visit. I actually haven't seen him in almost two years." At that, Elise shook her head and Kate felt guilty about not admitting that Jason hadn't known about Kennen. Leaving him, she hurried back to the grocery store and grabbed the diapers.

She was standing in the check out line, when she glimpsed Jason and a very well endowed blonde on the cover of a magazine on the rack there. So was this divine intervention or Satan having fun at her expense? She habitually reached to turn the magazine around and then on an impulse bought it. She wasn't necessarily going to read it, but it might be a really good reminder to keep her head on straight, later.

***

Jason really did call the realtor at seven thirty and by nine thirty he'd bought a change of clothes and a house. When the realtor had pulled up available properties in Kate's area, unbelievably, there was a home for sale kiddy corner from Kate's house through the block behind her. Actually, only the very corner of his yard would touch hers, but with any luck, he could talk Elise into letting him build a gate across the back corner of her yard. He prayed and thanked God as he went back to his hotel. That had to be divine intervention. That's all there was to it.

And he was going to need some divine intervention. Several times, most likely. Last night had gone more smoothly than he'd ever dreamed it would, but he knew Kate. Once he left, she was probably regretting she had promised she'd still be here today. And he didn't underestimate her anymore. The last two years had more than proven to him that she was a woman of serious self discipline. He knew she still loved him. He'd seen it in her eyes and felt it in her arms, but he wasn't going to take any chances. At this point, it wouldn't take much at all to spook her all the way back to Texas.

He wasn't going to take any chances, but he wasn't going to leave anything to chance either. He had a week before he could move in to help Kate get used to the idea without running for cover.

Assuming she still wouldn't want to be seen in public with him, he stopped and got everything for a picnic and then drove back to the house with the climbing tree and sand box, praying silently all the way. It was a good time for some more divine intervention. He was as nervous about how she was going to take him today as he'd been yesterday.

Kennen helped ease his entrance again. As Jason knocked on the storm door, Kennen came running in from the other room and ran straight into the screen with both hands and yelled, "Mommom! Is freh-en!" He reached up as high as he could toward the door knob, but all he could do was touch it with the tips of his fingers. That didn't stop him. He stayed there on his bare tip toes, reaching for all he was worth and Jason had to take pity on him and open the door.

As he did, Kennen tipped over onto his hands and then jumped back up and launched himself into Jason's arms and gave him another one of his enthusiastic huggers. Jason honestly couldn't believe how strong this tiny one year old kid was!

Kennen had him in a death grip around the neck as Kate appeared on the other side of the screen and Jason could see at a glance that the girl who had melted in his arms last night had been replaced with a close relative of the woman who had closed that elevator door in his face in Lubbock. A tired close relative. He wasn't sure where that look of resignation had come from, but he knew his work was cut out for him and was grateful Kennen didn't have her reservations.

He smiled around the tiny arms that held him and said, "Morning, Kate."

"Good morning, Jason." She opened the door for him, but that was the only sign he was welcome.

Still wondering how to take her, he decided directness might be the best policy and he hesitated to step inside as he asked, "Are you angry with me for something?"

She shook her head and looked guilty for a second and said, "No, come in. Actually, yeah." He had begun to step in and paused, looking up at her and she shook her head again. "No. Come in." He grinned at her and she said, "I don't know. Get in here while I try to figure out what I am at you."

Jason and Kennen came inside and as she shut the door, Jason said, "I don't know, Kennen. That's just the way she is sometimes. But we love her anyway, don't we?" He followed Kate back into her kitchen and the first inkling about what was wrong came as he saw a magazine on her kitchen desk with a cover picture of him standing next to a blonde actress with his hand on the small of her back. Not only that, but there was a newspaper stacked next to it that had a front page article about the frequency of infidelity in marriages in America. The second had nothing to do with him, but the coincidence of them together couldn't be good.

He had been going to hand Kate the basket he carried, but decided to put it on top of her negative literature instead. Then he turned back to her and just watched her for a minute, hoping for an epiphany about how to bring back the melting Kate. Kennen began to pat his cheeks and Jason gently rubbed his back as he watched her. His hand slowed as she looked over at him and he recognized that the hardness was just her way of protecting herself from what she perceived as a threat. Him.

Stepping over to be closer to her, he looked down into her eyes and asked softly, "Did you get any sleep?"

He could see her distrust as she hesitated and then said, "Some."

"Was it Kennen?" She gave one shake of her head, and Jason searched her eyes and then said gently, "I'm sorry. I didn't mean to upset you."

She shook her head again and went back toward a TV room off of the kitchen and picked up a bath towel from a laundry basket and sat down on the couch. She began to fold it and set it on the others piled on the coffee table in front of her. He followed her with their little boy and then set him on the floor next to some Matchbox cars and Jason sat down next to him. He played cars for a moment and then idly picked up a towel and began to fold too as Kennen continued to play in front of him.

They folded without speaking for a few minutes with Kennen's vroom vroom filling the silence and finally, Kate asked, "How was the drive?"

Wondering if he dared to admit he'd bought her neighbor's house, he simply said, "Great. I actually got a hotel here in Tulsa so I could take care of some business this morning before I came back. I didn't end up driving much at all. Tulsa's nice, isn't it?"

"I think so. I've only lived here for a month, but it's not been bad."

"Where were you before that?"

"San Antonio, when I wasn't in a hotel."

"Mom told me you traveled a lot. That surprised me. You didn't use to like to travel much."

She snapped a hand towel. "It was a job. It kept me busy."

Watching her, he asked, "Busy helps when you're alone, doesn't it?"

She looked over the hand towel. "How would you know what alone is like?"

"You don't always have to be by yourself to be alone, Kate. Alone in a crowd is just as lonely. You were gone. I was alone a lot."

"What about Cody and the guys?"

He gave her a sad half smile. "Y'all think Cody could make up for you?" He shook his head. "No way. He's fun, but no one could make up for you."

She didn't answer and he picked up a tiny pair of jeans and held them up and couldn't help the smile. "Holy cow that is a tiny pair of Levis. They're kind of cute."

"His stuff is cute, isn't it? You should have seen the newborn size stuff."

That sense of loss came through in his voice as he quietly said, "I wish I could have, Kate."

She looked up and met his eyes and the hardness softened a little more as she told him, "You may not believe this, Jason. But a day hasn't gone by that I didn't wish I could share him with you. But a lot of the time, you haven't really been father material. You have to admit that."

"Kate, do you really believe for one minute that even at my worst, I wouldn't have shaped up for you and him?"

"Jason, there was a time when I wouldn't have believed you could promise me forever on the way out the door and then be drinking and carousing fourteen seconds later. I learned the hard way. If you had a daughter who had been in my shoes, would you have recommended she encourage her party animal boyfriend to step in as the father?"

"If the boyfriend was like me, I would have in a second."

Kate shook her head. "No, you wouldn't have, Jason."

"You don't trust me anymore, Kate, and I don't blame you. I was off base then. But honestly, I am trustworthy. I would love one of our daughters to marry a man like me. I've had my moments, but except for those couple of major screw ups and a lot of poor judgment, I'm still the same guy who grew up next door. The same guy who has always treated you well. The same guy who made you that pinky promise. I bought that piece of the lake by the way. I'm the same guy who was always there for you."

He paused thoughtfully for a moment and then went on, "You know, at first when you insisted I needed to fly before I settled down so I could know I preferred your flavor, honestly, I was hurt. To me that translated as I don't trust you Jason. But you were right and it was wise for you to set me free to see if I came back to you. And yes, at first the glitz was a bit overwhelming and went to my head a little. But only a little, Kate. I had to mature some before flying straight back. But you know, when you set something free to see if it comes back to you, you're supposed to give it a fair shot and be there when it does."

Tears welled in her eyes and it took her a minute to be able to whisper, "Jason, I suddenly didn't have time." She looked away for a few seconds to gain control. "I'm so sorry I got pregnant. You know I didn't mean to. But I was. And I've had to consider his needs when making my decisions. And you have to believe that I didn't intend to keep him from you. I didn't want that. You know I wanted to tell you. But consider what I found that night in Lubbock. Did I even have a choice? In a way, you were the one who made the decision for me to go. Not me. I felt like I had to for our child."

She pulled her bare feet up onto the couch and wrapped her arms around her knees and buried her face in them and he watched her shoulders shake as she began to sob out the hurt of that night and that decision and the ensuing struggle it brought on. He felt tears in his own eyes for her and for all three of them at the heartache he had caused. Not sure what to do, he finally took his cue from Kennen who got up from his tiny cars and came and wrapped his small arms around her legs, put his face against her and cried too. Jason scooted closer to them and reached up and pulled her down onto his lap and then wrapped his own arms around both of them and the three of them cried together for all the things that could have been if he'd just done some things differently.

When she finally began to wind down, Kennen went back to his cars and Jason kissed Kate's hair, pulled her closer to his chest and whispered near her ear, "Babe, do you know what I still dream about?" She shook her head without looking up. "I still dream of someday getting married and having more children. I dream of having that sweet intimacy be such a special thing and then being so excited about you getting pregnant. I dream of watching you, knowing my baby is inside your body. I dream of helping you through those months and then standing beside you while you struggle to bring it into the world. And then babying you while you recuperate from it. I dream of watching you feed it and care for it and nurture it. Someday, Kate I am going to help you fold newborn size clothes again. That's one of the biggest dreams I have. Someday I want to have more little Falcons with you and do it right this time and treat you like the queen you are to me and it'll be the happiest of times instead of being so sad and difficult. That's what I still dream about." She didn't say anything and he just continued to hold her and occasionally rub her back and kiss her hair.

She started to cry again, but after several minutes, she whispered back without raising her head, "Sometimes I still dream of that too."

He wrapped his arms around her more tightly and felt the tears seep in again. When he could finally get the words out, he promised her, "We'll make it come true, Kate."

Twenty minutes later, he realized she'd fallen asleep, but he just kept holding her until Kennen disappeared down the hall and stayed disappeared long enough that Jason figured he'd better go make sure he was all right. He gently eased Kate down onto her thick carpet and slipped a throw pillow under her head and covered her with a baby quilt they'd just folded.

He went down the hall and after searching for a second, found Kennen sound asleep on the floor between Kate's bed and his crib. Jason scooped him up and gently kissed his sleeping curls and then took him back in the family room and laid him on the floor beside Kate. He went back and got Kate's comforter off of her bed and brought it in and covered them with it, pulled the drapes to darken the room and then lay down on the other side of Kennen to nap with them.

He could feel Kennen's breath on his arm and Kate's on his face and it was incredibly satisfying to lay there beside them. They could be a family. They'd made a mess of the beginning of Kennen's life, but they could do something about that. He reached over to touch Kate's hair. He fully intended to do something about that.

As he was coming awake, Jason felt Kennen roll over next to him and Jason turned on his side to curl around his son and pull him close. He was just adjusting the pillow under his head when he realized Kate's eyes were watching him. He returned her gaze and then reached over and took the hand she had resting on Kennen beside him. He knew she was afraid of her feelings, so he didn't say he loved her out loud, but he hoped she understood he was telling her with his eyes.

After a minute or two, she gently moved Kennen's leg and then scooted closer and put her arm over him and over Jason as well and all the blood rushed to Jason's heart as she pulled him toward her slightly. She looked up at him sleepily and then closed her eyes again. Yeah, they could be a family. It was definitely a good thing that Kennen laid between them, because just now, Jason wanted to start working on some of those other dreams that had to wait.

When he woke up again, Kennen was still cuddled tight against him, but Kate was gone and it was ridiculously lonely. He gently disentangled himself from his precious boy and went in search of her. She was standing in the kitchen stirring something at the stove and he came to her, hoping she would still look at him the way she had a while ago.

Indeed, when she looked up and into his eyes, there was still love and trust deep in those blue depths. She put down her wooden spoon and he pulled her into a hug. This was his Kate. She was older. Sadly, wiser and with a much slower smile, but she was all Kate and he worshipped her. He tried to convey that as he kissed her slowly and tenderly. After a second, he raised his head and turned her stove off and then went right back to kissing her. She was a great cook, but nothing could compare to how she kissed.

They spent the afternoon snacking and playing and kissing and then a little of all three again and Jason hated having to leave her after such a heavenly day, but he had to get back. The band was flying out to Omaha in the morning. For some reason, he was hesitant to tell her that. He was afraid it would break the spell and bring the shadows back to her eyes.

Actually, the shadows didn't come back and it gave him more hope that they'd finally be able to kick her worries. He wished he'd brought her something more than just food today. He wanted her to have something tangible with her while he was away to remind her that he loved her constantly, even when he was two states away.

They were standing in front of her door, trying to say goodbye, when he asked, "Did you ever get the bracelet? From Kiersten?"

"Yes."

"Did you throw it away?"

"Of course not."

"Did you ever wear it?"

She looked down and shook her head. "No. I'm sorry, I couldn't."

"What do you mean?"

"It hurt too much, Jason. It would have made me cry every time I saw it."

Gently tipping her face up, he asked huskily, "Is there any way you could wear it now?" She looked into his eyes and he continued, "That's actually what I want. I mean I don't want you to cry, but I want you to think of me every time it slides across your wrist and know that wherever I am, I'm missing you. And I'm being true to you and I'm coming home to you. I want to come home and talk to you about getting married, Kate."

Her eyes flew to his and this time there was worry. "I'll wear the bracelet, Jase. But it's way too soon to talk about getting married. We don't even know each other any more."

"Go get it." He looked at her, but decided not to argue this one. She could feel the unbelievable pull in this room as well as he could. If she couldn't face it yet, that was one thing, but to say they didn't know each other was hogwash.

She came back a moment later with the small velvet box and he got the bracelet out and gently put it on and then tenderly kissed the inside of her wrist. He could feel the goose bumps break out on her arms and switched to kissing the warm, sensitive curve of her neck under her ear. That was one thing about knowing her to her soul. He knew exactly how to turn her inside out. She could talk about them not knowing each other all she wanted. He knew better.

He kissed her neck until she let out a sigh that was almost a moan and then he ever so gently nuzzled her with his teeth and he smiled to himself as she pressed her body tightly to him. She was having a hard time breathing and he reveled in it and nuzzled her more. It would serve her right if he cheerfully said goodbye and walked out with her this wound up just now. She'd see how well he knew her.

He would have toyed with her longer if it hadn't been making him as wound up as it was making her. He finally kissed her one last time and then pulled away and took a ragged breath. "I need to go, Kate. Right now. Sorry, but you're way too tempting and I'm way out of practice at resisting you." He caressed the inside of her wrist again. "When you feel the bracelet, think about me. Would you? And know I'm thinking of you." She nodded wordlessly, still slightly breathless and he wanted to drown in the indigo lightning he saw deep in her eyes. He watched it for another few seconds and then breathed, "I love you, Kate." He leaned and gave her a second last kiss below her ear. "Good night."

Chapter 23

Waking up to know Jason was going to be out of the state for a few days was enough of a downer that Kate felt foolish. They had caught up way too fast. These feelings couldn't be wise. Still, as she rolled onto her tummy and stretched, she felt the diamond bracelet and her thoughts went back to his tender kisses last night and her body completely abandoned her intentions to slow things down. He definitely hadn't forgotten how to get to her. Some things were like the deep friendship they shared. Built on a lifetime of knowing each other to the core.

She fingered the sparkling gift and then put her arm under her cheek where she could feel the texture of the stones and the gold. She loved Jason, but this bracelet could be almost dangerous. She might have to get a little diamond fire extinguisher to go with it.

Kennen made a sound and she moved her eyes to look at him without moving her face off of the cool, slim bracelet. He was sitting up in his crib with a tired, mostly toothless smile, his dark brown curls tousled across his head. Man, he looked like his father. She was never going to be able to go out in public with the two of them.

She got up and dressed and got breakfast. Maybe Jason being gone for a while would be a good thing. In fact, she was sure it was. She needed to get a handle on her common sense again. She needed to remember that Jason wasn't just an incredibly sexy friend. Attraction that bordered on obsession was insane and she needed to put the brakes on it in a hurry.

That was a good theory. Right up until she answered her door to be handed a huge bouquet of white roses with a note that simply read, "I love you, Jason." How was she supposed to be unobsessed when he did stuff like this? She'd even smell them in her sleep.

Ten minutes later, Elise knocked on her door and let herself and Gretchen in. She advanced into the kitchen with a huge smile and set Gretchen down and Kate had to grin back as Elise said, "So… I'm assuming y'all are not going to keep telling me that end of story line. What's going on with your country star?"

"He just sent me roses, Elise. No big deal."

"Yeah, sure. And bought the house in your back yard."

"What?"

"Peggy Reid was just freaking out because she found out the guy who bought her house is Jason Falcon."

"What! She said what?"

"Your no big deal, end of story, just an old boyfriend bought the Reid's house. In case you don't know who that is; they're the neighbors who live across my back fence."

Kate was so shocked she could hardly close her mouth. "Kiddy corner through the block behind me?"

"That's the one."

Kate sat down hard in a chair. Holy cats! How would she keep her head with him in the backyard? Now she'd probably *have* to move. She got up and went to her desk and uncovered the magazine she'd bought and ripped off the cover and put it on the fridge with a magnet. Maybe keeping that in front of her face would help her use some judgment.

Elise looked from the fridge and back and asked, "What was that all about?"

"I'm hoping it will help me remember that he has girls all over the world."

"Girls who like him or girls who he likes back? He seemed pretty comfortable here day before yesterday."

Kate looked at her relatively new friend and asked, "How can you ever really know the answer to that, Elise? If I knew that, I'd know whether to marry the guy or refuse to ever talk to him again."

"He said he wants to marry you? Jason Falcon? My goodness!"

"The question is Elise, how many others has he said that to? I mean, he always seems so sincere. But... I always believe him when he's around and then feel like an idiot for it when he's gone."

"Kate, this is Jason Falcon. Even the National Enquirer admits he's not a womanizer. Isn't that what you've gotten from all the cover stories about him?"

Kate shook her head. "I haven't read even one of the stories in years. Honestly. I only bought that to help me use caution."

Elise raised her eyebrows. "You have a child with him, but don't keep up on him?"

"It's a long and painful story, Elise. You don't want to hear it, trust me."

"Well, I don't know the man, but the press doesn't think he's fast and loose with the women. Usually they're trying to speculate about whatever girl he's photographed with. And they're never very incriminating photographs. Even when he was drinking so hard for a while, he still steered clear of entanglements. A couple of the magazines even hinted that he was gay. I doubt he's got an affianced in every port."

Kate considered that and then grinned. "So how come y'all know so much about Jason Falcon?"

Elise rolled her eyes guiltily and admitted, "Oh, Kate. You have no idea. It wasn't Jason I had a thing for. But that Cody Rawlings... He had me going for like a year. I thought he was the most adorable maniac on the planet. I mean he seemed like such a hellion most of the time, but then sometimes he'd do something like when he brought that kid who had cancer on stage for the Make-A-Wish Foundation and let him do a whole concert."

"You've been to one of their concerts?"

"Or like all of them." She grinned. "I've had to grow up though, ya know. I'm married and have a child. And actually, Mike is ten times more adorable than Cody Rawlings anyway."

Kate nodded. "Mike is pretty gorgeous. And I'm not sure, but I think Cody is finally going to get serious with a girl and settle down. Which is the most amazing thing. He is a maniac."

"Yeah, but Jason isn't."

"No, Jason isn't a maniac. But he's no saint either."

"Are you sure, Kate? Because other than the drinking there for awhile, he seems pretty saintly. And he did buy a house next door. I'm sure he has enough money that that's not that big a deal financially, but he isn't buying it for status. It's not that nice of a house. And you do have a child together. Maybe he's just suddenly decided he's ready to settle down and he wants to get back together. Whatever made you two break up must not still be an argument. Neither one of y'all look too mad at the other."

Kate gave her a hesitant smile. "No, mad is really not the word."

Elise grinned. "What's the word?"

Kate blushed and shook her head and Elise gave her a full blown smile. "Really? Kate!"

"Elise, it's not what you think. I mean I know that sounds suspect when I have his son, but we're really not that way. At least I don't think we are. I know I'm not. Believe it or not, that one night was the only time I've ever been intimate in my life." She sighed. "I was drunk and didn't realize what I was doing. I can't even remember it. It was the only time I've been drunk in my life too, I promise."

"But you were married. There was your husband."

"I only got married because John needed a way to protect his assets. That's another long story, Elise, but

John was really only my business partner. Realistically, my boss. He was terminally ill and his ex and kids were trying to take everything he had. She would have squandered it, so he put it into a scholarship foundation and married me to tie their hands. We never so much as kissed."

"Never even kissed?" Kate shook her head and Elise was obviously too floored to speak for a second and then finally asked, "Does Jason know that?"

Kate rolled her eyes and shook her head. "No. It's not like did you have sex with your husband is much of a question. No one doesn't have sex when they're married. And it's probably not a really pleasant subject anyway."

With still wide eyes, Elise said, "Man, Kate, you're life is quite a soap opera! What other funky stories have you lived through?"

Kate smiled self consciously. "None that I want to divulge this morning. Do you want me to watch Gretchen?"

"No." Elise laughed. "I wanted you to fascinate me with tales of intimacy and intrigue. Y'all should write a memoir. With Jason in it, you could probably make a lot of money!"

"Elise, other than Jason himself, Cody and my mom and sister, you're the only one who knows who Kennen's real dad is. It's pretty private. Please don't say anything to anyone. You didn't tell Peggy about us, did you?"

"Heavens no. That doesn't mean that I didn't gloat to myself though. But I have to admit I told Mike. But I made him promise not to tell. He's good for it. And it's not like it's not a hundred percent obvious when they're together.

Kate shook her head and sighed. "I know. I'm doomed. That was one of the reasons I agreed to marry John so Kennen and I would be more respectable as a widow and son instead of an unwed mother and son. But their alikeness blows that all to heck."

"You worry too much, Kate. There are more important issues to fuss over. You know, world hunger, that kind of thing."

"That's easy for you to say, Elise. Do you have any idea how awkward going to church as an unwed pregnant person was? I mean to the world, it's no big deal, but it should be. It is a big deal. "

"Kate, stop right there. You can't worry about appearances anymore. You made a mistake. You've moved past it as well as you could and you have to let it go. Focus on the future. All you can do is your best. If someone can't deal with that, you can't let that hang you up. So, speaking of the future. What's going on with Jason really? He's talking marriage?"

"He may be. I'm not. That's insane. He didn't even know about Kennen until day before yesterday."

Elise's eyes got huge. "You're kidding! You've got to be kidding!"

Kate shook her head. "No. Cody busted Kennen and me at the grocery store and after he saw Kennen, he told Jason. And no, I can't entertain you with the intimacy and intrigue. It still hurts too badly and I'd just bawl all the way through the painful details."

Knowing she sounded like she was going to cry, and that Elise knew it, Kate tried to lighten up. "Let's take the kids and go to lunch, shall we? My treat. We'll go to my restaurant."

"I am all about ribs! Just don't let me eat more than two. Is Jason not coming today?"

"He's out of town for a few days. And while he's gone, I need to find my brain where he's concerned."

"I'm not sure what you mean by that, Kate. Do y'all want to explain? Where did the kids go?"

Kate ran a frustrated hand through her curls. "I can't just fall into his arms, Elise. That would be the dumbest thing on the planet earth. And he's just a trifle tempting to me."

Elise laughed. "A trifle? Huh? Have you seen him lately?"

"That's exactly what I mean. Crud. Look at those two. They're filthy. Kennen's been eating a marker again. I'll bet the walls are beautiful."

"Personally, I don't see a problem with falling into his arms. He's got great arms. And he likes you. Maybe even loves you if he wants to tie the knot. What's the problem?"

"Of course he loves me. That's not the point."

"It's not? And he does? How come you don't question that, when you question everything else?"

"He's loved me since I was fourteen, Elise. I just have no idea how to know if he doesn't love all the other girls as well. And will he be a stable father? Or will Kennen have to deal with the whole Hollywood lifestyle?"

Elise turned and put her hands on her hips and said in a sassy southern drawl, "Girl, you have got it all backwards and upside down. I'm sure he doesn't talk marriage to every girl he sees. Did you catch him sleeping with someone? Is that what this is all about?"

"No! Of course not."

"Then cut him some ease, Kate! I can promise you he isn't perfect, because none of us humans are. But you're killing yourself. Do you realize you're not allowing yourself to enjoy him because you're afraid something will come up to make things unenjoyable? That's defeating yourself before you've even begun. You have a kid together. It's not like if you dare to take a chance something big could go wrong. A kid is as big as it gets. And apparently it went way wrong. And y'all still love each other. Forget the other women. He's a superstar. They will drool. So what? That doesn't make him unfaithful. Does it?"

"You make a killer argument, Elise, but you don't really know him."

"Honey, as long as he's been in the public eye, if there was any truly good dirt, don't you think someone would have found it?"

"Yeah."

"You know Kate; it'd be easy to find out if he's serious. All he has to do is ask you to marry him and then do it. He won't if he's not. As long as you don't do anything terribly foolish before he proves himself, you've got your answer."

Kate nodded thoughtfully and finally Elise asked, "Here's the real question, Kate. You believe in God right?"

"Yes, of course."

"And that God tries to guide us with personal inspiration for our own issues." Kate nodded. "And you say you've known Jason all your life. So, in your truly knowledgeable opinion, backed up by personal inspiration from God himself, is he trustworthy?"

"God? Or Jason?"

"Jason, you noodle head. Of course God is trustworthy. Is Jason?"

"Yes. I . . . I . . . I think so."

"And what do you want? What does Kate really, truly want?"

Kate closed her eyes as they began to tear. *Oh, that is too hard of a question.* She hesitated for several seconds as she tried to face the real answer to that and then whispered, "I want to be with Jason."

"Good. Remember that." Elise ripped the magazine cover off the fridge, wadded it up and tossed it under the sink into the trash. "Let's go eat."

***

Two days later, when Kate was watching Jason and the band in a video on CMT, she was trying to keep that in mind as Jason sang about unrequited love to a top heavy brunette in a Daisy Mae outfit. Kate knew it was just a music video, but it still made her uncomfortable.

Then, as she took Kennen for a walk to the park in his stroller, the neighbor who lived in the house next door to where Jason was supposedly buying, wanted to talk and she mentioned just what she'd like to do with Jason Falcon if she ever got the chance. Kate wanted to hurl, right on her sidewalk. She kept telling herself Jason couldn't control what others thought or said about him, but it certainly brought the point home that privacy and discretion weren't ever going to be the backbone of a life with him. She toyed with the bracelet on her wrist, willing the worry to go and some of that sweet emotion from the other night to take its place. It was hard to stay off of this roller coaster.

Kristin Cross

Chapter 24

After being on the road for four days, Jason was tired, and hungry, and incredibly ready to see Kate again. He'd missed her so much this trip that he couldn't figure out how he'd survived at all when she had been gone. As the captain came on and announced final approach, Cody woke up beside him and stretched and asked, "So what are your plans?"

"Drive to Tulsa and see Kate and Kennen. What are yours?"

Cody grinned. "Drive to Tulsa and see Jennika and see if I can talk her into a Kennen."

Drily, Jason counseled, "Take my advice and marry her first. What would you say if I said I want to take some time off of touring?"

"I'd say I've been trying to figure out how to broach that subject for several weeks. But the guys are gonna hate it. We're at the top of our game right now."

Jason shrugged. "It's our band. And you and I both know there are more important things than concerts. I bought a house in Tulsa. If you'll come try to remind me to keep my hands to myself where Kate is concerned, I'll rent you half of it."

"When in the... When did you buy a house in Tulsa?"

"The morning after I found Kate. It's in her back yard. She's gonna kill me when she finds out."

"I thought you said things have been going well. Why would she kill you?"

"Because she's still intimidated by all of the hoopla. She loves me, I love her. But that's not enough. Or it's too much. Something. She's still scared to be committed, just like before she took off."

"You're telling me you've been talking about commitment? In the first two days? Geez, y'all are gutty, Falcon. No wonder she's gonna kill you."

Jason shook his head. "I have a son, Cody. And I love his mother. And Kate needs to know there aren't any doubts." He grinned. "It freaks her out a little, but... Hopefully the feelings that are still there can overcome that. So you want to move to Tulsa?"

"I'm gonna have to behave myself in your house, aren't I?"

"Yup."

"Good. Then I'll take you up on that. But you have to agree to remind me about that hands to yourself policy. Jennika would deck me and then dump me."

Jason laughed. "You could just marry her and not worry about keeping to yourself."

Cody rubbed his chin thoughtfully. "You know? I've actually been thinking about that. It scares the hell out of me."

"Does the commitment scare you or are you just afraid Jennika will find out what you're really like?"

"Hey now. Actually, Jennika already knows what I *used* to be like. And I'm not afraid of commitment. But do you know how weird it is to want to be with the same person twenty four seven three sixty five? That's what's freaking me out. That and that she's raving brilliant."

"Oh, like you're not. Enjoy it. Your children will be prodigies."

"Yeah, and give their poor, mindless-wonder dad looks of pity when he's trying to help them with their homework."

"You just love their mother and the homework thing will work itself out."

"I'm gonna hold you to that, Falcon, and if it doesn't work, I'm sending them to your house."

Jason grinned again. "You just worry about getting Jennika to agree to this. Then we'll talk about homework."

***

When her door bell rang, Kate opened it to Jason's weary smile and she glanced at her watch. "Jason, you just drove here in an hour and fifty minutes, this tired? You'll kill yourself. Come on in. Have you eaten?"

"Yes, I did just drive here, I survived, thanks and no I haven't eaten. Can I take you out, or are you still concerned about being seen with me?"

"That can't be how I worded it. Where are you thinking of going? Will we be mobbed by fans?"

"If I'm honest and say we won't be mobbed but someone might talk to us, are you going to tell me no?"

She screwed her lips to the side as if thinking. "I don't know. What do y'all think I should do?"

"Come over here and kiss me."

She laughed. "And how does that help in deciding?"

"I'm not sure, but even though I'm starving, it sounds way better than food."

Unsure of how to deal with him like this, she laughed again and wrapped one arm around his waist and leaned in and kissed him, but then backed away. He shook his head and followed her. "No way, Kate. I've thought about kissing you all the way across three states. Come back. That was far too quick."

She let him pull her close and kissed him, but then looked up into his eyes and said, "Jason, doesn't the fact that we didn't see each other for so long and then started right back up where we left off, trouble you?"

"Nope." He kissed her again and shook his head. "Not seeing you killed me. Kissing doesn't trouble me one iota. Frankly, it fixes my troubles. Your kiss has always been that way for me. But I also don't think we're right where we left off. I think we've both been tempered by time and the hell we've been through. I think we're stronger and wiser and more mature. It doesn't trouble me, Kate. It comforts me."

Looking down, she admitted, "It troubles me, Jason. I feel like we need to be really careful to be wise in our relationship. For Kennen."

"I know, honey, and I'm sorry I'm not more worried. But I love you, and I missed you and I really want to kiss you. And honestly, Kate. I don't have the doubts you have. I know you, and I have the greatest respect for you, and I know me, and I think I'll be a great husband and father. I wish you believed the same."

Kate thought back to the conversation she and Elise had had and admitted softly, "Sometimes I believe the same, Jason. When I really think about it and listen for what God is trying to tell me, I think the same. I want to think the same. I'm just so afraid sometimes. I'm just so worried that I'll make a bad decision and Kennen will have to bear it."

Jason sat down and tugged her down with him. "Where is he? Is he okay?"

"He's with Gretchen. He's fine."

"Okay, then can you tell me one more time, what it is you're afraid of with me? What is it that scares you? And you can be honest."

She hid her face against his chest. "Honest can hurt sometimes."

"Not as much as not being together, together. I'm trying to get on with getting on to eternity with you, Kate, and in that way, we are still back where we left off. Even after completely settling the issue of coming back to you and knowing Kate is the only flavor. You didn't want to talk about getting married then either. Just help me understand why."

"You're wrong, Jason. I so wanted to talk about getting married. It was just that I needed to know you wouldn't regret me."

He tipped her face to look at him and asked gently, "And do you finally know I'll never regret you?"

She looked up into his eyes, and for just a second that awful night in Lubbock when she'd knocked on that door flashed into her mind and she struggled to not let that pain influence her. She searched his eyes, and what she saw there was enough to make her know that yes, she could trust him to be faithful and that the only thing that would make him regret her would be for her to make the huge mistakes this time.

She snuggled back into his chest. "Yes."

"So, then what else is holding you back?"

She sighed, because right now, she had to face the fact that it wasn't Jason at all she was worried about any more. Over the last few days, she had come to believe he really was hers forever if she would accept him. The problem was wondering if she was strong enough to deal with what being married to Jason would mean. And it was an incredibly intimidating question. Did she have the fortitude to take what he came with and not let it steamroll her? In a low voice, she admitted, "I guess, the real question, Jason, is do I have what it takes to handle being married to Jason the country music star?"

He leaned back from her with a huge smile. "Oh, Kate, that's easy! Of course you do! You're the strongest, most competent woman I've ever known. You can handle way worse stuff than just that."

She hid her face against him again. "I don't know. The fame and the girls and the videos and the dancing and the travel and the rumors and the paparazzi and everything else. Can I really do that?"

"You can. We can. All three of us can. I'll be right beside you every step of the way. And you know, Kate, there are some good things about me."

"Oh, Jase, I know that. There are a million things I love about you. I didn't mean to intimate there aren't. It's just that sometimes I feel so mortal beside you. And honestly, before I left at least, I felt like we were going in different directions as far as values."

"The values thing was valid, Kate. Then it was. I was kind of out of touch then. But I honestly think I'm okay now. Come to some concerts and see for yourself. Cody told me you haven't even been listening to our stuff, but try it again and see what you think. Hopefully, it'll make you feel like I'm still just your Jason. And that mortal bit. You're a precious daughter of God, Kate. Just like I'm one of His sons. We're only as mortal as we allow ourselves to be."

"What do you mean?"

"Kate, if y'all were Satan, wouldn't it help your cause if you could make God's children here on earth believe they were weak? That they were…" He made quote signs with his hands. "Mere mortals? That they couldn't handle things or accomplish much and that they certainly would never return to their Father in Heaven in honor and glory? Wouldn't that be a great tool for Satan's cause? Making us feel inadequate?" She nodded thoughtfully. "On the flip side, doesn't God want us to truly believe that we are like him? Made in His image with a measure of His greatness? And if we truly believe that, is there anything we can't accomplish?"

"I wouldn't think so."

"So, do you see that what you said about being a mere mortal plays right into the adversary's plan?" She nodded again. "So, don't do that, Kate. Remember which team you're on." He grinned at her. "Straighten up and fly right, would ya?"

He was trying to make her laugh and she finally did. "Okay, okay. I'll do better."

"Good." He smiled down at her. "Then, can I kiss you now?"

"You've definitely earned kissing me now. I love it when you give me these little mini lectures."

He kissed her long and slowly and then asked, "Mini lectures? That doesn't sound so good."

He kissed her again and then she assured him quietly, "Oh, but it is. Heaven knows I need your wisdom from time to time. Shall we feed you now? I made turkey enchiladas."

"In a minute. I'm still busy kissing."

A short while later, Kate had collected Kennen while Jason set the table and they'd just prayed over their food, when Jason asked, "Can my parents come meet Kennen? Is it okay if I tell them about him?"

"Of course you can tell them." Tears welled into her eyes. "I have missed them so much. So many times I just wished I could go see them."

"They've missed you terribly too. Can I ask you something else?"

She fed Kennen a bite as she nodded.

"Are you going to be okay with me buying a house nearby?"

She looked at him with a small smile as she chewed for a second. "I was going to ask you about that. It seems the neighbor lady is all excited to be selling to *The* Jason Falcon."

At that, he was surprised. "You're kidding! I had that realtor sign a contract for non-disclosure. If she revealed who I was, she doesn't get paid. And she still told? What a fool."

"Oh, that's not the half of it. Then Kathy Newpark, the neighbor on the other side already has plans for exactly where she intends to lure you to be intimate."

Jason rolled his eyes and handed Kennen a tiny piece of tomato. "Just ignore them, Kate. They aren't serious and I'm certainly not in on her plans. How did you hear this, by the way?"

"Oh, Kathy told me herself about the plans to seduce you. Elise told me about Peggy being thrilled with her buyer." She grinned. "It seems that Elise used to have a thing for Cody. She said she used to think he was an adorable maniac."

"That does pretty much describe him. I think he's thinking about getting married too. Is that weird or what? He's going to come be my roommate so he doesn't have to keep commuting to see Jennika."

She looked across the table at him, wondering how to take this Jason who talked so matter-of-factly about getting married. As if he could read her mind, he asked, "What kind of wedding do you want, Kate?"

She swallowed the bite that suddenly felt huge and tried to remind herself that she did indeed want to marry him, so this shouldn't be such a big deal. "Are we talking church or civil, or private or huge media splash?"

"Yes."

She leaned and fed Kennen another bite. "Years ago, when we were young and unfamous and childless, I thought about having a church wedding and big reception like Kiersten had. But now... I think I would be most comfortable with something much more private. I mean, in the church of course, but maybe just a few of us. I don't want the entire world to know we had Kennen unmarried. What do you want?"

"A happy bride and only the one camera that we've hired. Other than that, I'm open. And then some time with you somewhere alone." He cut some turkey into minute pieces and put it on Kennen's tray. "A really long some time. Maybe we'd better take Kennen with us, in fact. He might feel lost without you if we didn't."

"That's not very alone."

"I think we could figure it out, Kate. How would he understand if you just left him? He isn't used to anyone else is he, since John died?"

"I used to have a nanny who he'd be fine with for a day or two. Or Elise, maybe."

Jason grinned. "So does that mean you'll marry me?"

"You haven't asked, but... If I say I need some time to get used to all of this, is that going to make you sad?"

"Of course. What if I asked and you could say yes, and then we'd give you the time you need before the actual wedding?"

Kate's heart began to pound clear up into her head. "Jason Falcon, don't you dare ask me to marry you over turkey enchiladas and one percent milk."

"What's wrong with turkey enchiladas and one percent milk?"

She took a deep breath. "Nothing. I just... I mean... Jason stop it. This isn't funny. You're going to give me heartburn or something."

"Baby, you've been giving me heartburn or something since you were fourteen years old. I owe you. But actually, I want to surprise you anyway so you can settle down. At least for a few minutes."

"I didn't say I'd say yes."

He looked at her calmly across the table for a long second and then softly said, "Your eyes did."

Their gaze finally broke when Kennen dropped his baby spoon over the side of his highchair and Kate changed the subject. "So when are you and Cody moving in?"

"This Monday."

"When will Reids be out?"

"Tomorrow, I think. Why?"

"Does anything need to be done to it before you can move in?"

"You mean do I want all of that horrendous carpet gone before we arrive? Absolutely. Have you seen it? Maybe you could recommend a decorator from here."

She shook her head. "I've never been inside, or hired a decorator. The back yard seems nice."

"I'm going to see if Elise and her husband will let me put a gate across the corner so Kennen can come back and forth."

"I'll bet they'd agree to that. And she'd probably know a decorator. She's from here and her home is beautiful." She got up and began to clear the dishes. "Would you like dessert?"

He lifted Kennen out of his chair and brought him to the sink next to her to wipe his face off. "Only you, Kate."

She took off Kennen's bib. "Hmm, have I ever been dessert before?"

He put his free arm around her and kissed her hard for a second. "I don't know, but it sounds really delicious." He kissed her again, more gently and then when Kennen began to squirm between them, he asked, "Is it okay if I put his jammies on him right now?"

Kate looked at her little son almost asleep already in Jason's arms. "You'd better. Do you remember where they are?"

"I think so."

The dishes were finished and everything put away and Jason hadn't reappeared and she went to find him. He was rocking Kennen in the rocker in her room with him snuggled up on his chest and he was singing softly to him. As sleepy as Kennen looked, he still had his eyes open as he laid there listening, obviously happy and comfortable.

Seeing them pierced Kate to the heart. What had she been thinking to try to keep them apart? Just now it appeared to be a complete no brainer that that had been a wrong decision. Why had she felt so surely then that it had to be done? Had she put all three of them through hell needlessly? Tears slid down her cheeks and she turned away from the doorway completely sick at heart over what she had done to her own son and best friend, thinking she'd had to.

Jason found her on the back porch swing, still awash in tears. "Hey, what's going on? Was it something I did?" He sat down beside her and gathered her into his arms. "What's wrong?"

She shook her head and turned away. "Oh, Jason, I'm so sorry. So, so sorry. I thought I had to. I truly did. I felt so strongly that the direction that hotel room was headed that night in Lubbock would be such a mistake for a child. I prayed all the way home." She began to cry so hard she couldn't even speak and had to take a moment before she continued, "I thought I had to go and not tell you. I made a terrible mistake and I'm so sorry. For all of us. I put us all through hell for two whole years."

Hugging her, he put a hand gently on her head and said, "Shh, shh, Kate, take it easy. It's all right, honey. Don't cry. Listen. I need to tell you something. Listen. You didn't make a mistake, Kate."

Tears were still sliding down her cheeks as she looked up at him in confusion. "What?"

He looked her in the eye and said, "I've had a couple of years to try to figure out why you took off like you did, Kate. And I've had a few days to think about being a parent. Sadly it took finding out about Kennen to understand. And even then, at first, I couldn't believe you'd do something so mean as hiding the fact that we had a child. And I certainly wouldn't have chosen to go through this, but after thinking about it, Kate. Really thinking about it, I wonder if you leaving wasn't necessary after all."

The tears stopped and her eyes got big with surprise as he went on, "For the longest time after that night at the hotel in Lubbock, I kept telling myself you just hadn't understood. It really wasn't my beer and the girl meant nothing. Finally, thanks to my mom and Cody, I realized I was the one who didn't understand. To me, then, letting the girls hug me wasn't that big a deal. I wasn't sleeping with them; I wasn't off somewhere making out. They meant nothing to me. They were just part of being a singer. At least that was my rationalization. In looking back, that was a bunch of fertilizer. I had no business being that friendly with women who meant nothing. It wasn't fair to them and it certainly wasn't being a hundred percent faithful to you. Whether I was a singer or not, that wasn't right. Physical touch is supposed to mean something. Like it does between you and me. But do you understand, Kate, I was entirely off track and didn't even realize it?"

He gave her a sad smile. "It took losing you, and then Cody asking me what I'd have felt like if you did the same thing around a bunch of men." He shook his head. "Just the thought made me livid, but I couldn't just get it for some reason. I guess I had to be forced to see."

He sat back and gently pulled her head against his chest. "I don't know, Kate. Losing you was hell. Finding out you were married was quadruple hell. I'd like to think I didn't really need that much of a wake up call, but then I know you, Kate. You're the most level headed woman on the planet. And the most spiritually in tune person I know. If you felt like you were supposed to, then you probably were. I must just be unbelievably hard headed to need two years of you being gone. All I do know, is I'm eternally grateful Cody went shopping with Jennika that day."

After another minute or two, he went on, "Some good things have come of this, Kate. The question of whether I only love the flavor of Kate is unequivocally answered. And we're stronger now than we were then, tempered by all of it. And who knows, maybe we've learned just how vital we are to each other. Maybe we'll have a greater appreciation for us and our children for having been apart. But God isn't a God of whimsy. Don't second guess promptings when you're sure. Only He knows everything."

He paused and leaned back so he could see her eyes and said softly, "One thing I do know is having you back in my arms is the sweetest thing I've ever known. I've missed you, Kate. Life without you isn't worth living."

She suddenly felt weepy again. "I missed you too, Jason. Kennen missed you too, and he hadn't even met you yet. He looked so happy in there just now."

"He was. We both were. He's a dream come true for me."

Even through her tears, she smiled as she said, "Isn't it wild, how much he looks like you? I tried so hard to forget you and move on, but there was this miniature

Jason, on top of all the other memories. It was impossible."

"Good." He kissed her for a long moment. "Because I need you. Falcons mate for life. Some of them for forever."

Kristin Cross

Chapter 25

The next day, before coming to her house, Jason visited next door and Elise was willing not only to let Jason put in a gate, but to watch Kennen as well and Kate agreed to go carpet shopping with him.

They found the carpet and then went furniture shopping. Jason would bring the things from his and Cody's apartments, but the house was bigger than them both and they needed a few more things.

Shopping for furniture with him was another activity that was so comfortable to her it almost made her a trifle paranoid, which made absolutely no sense, so it fit right in to the rest of this sudden about face in her life. Changing from struggling to avoid Jason at all costs, to spending most of their spare time together had her head spinning and it still scared her to death. If she didn't felt such peace when she was with him, she'd think she'd completely gone out of her mind.

Shopping with him was easier than she expected because he wore a ball cap pulled low and sunglasses and they weren't so bothered by people who knew who he was.

After they'd found a new larger dining table and office furniture and a set of end tables, Jason said he needed a guest bedroom set. Kate shook her head. "I think I'll go the powder room and then meet you in electronics." She wasn't going to say it out loud, but looking at dozens of beds with Jason would be a huge mistake and they both knew it.

They had agreed to meet Cody and Jennika for lunch and Kate had wondered how that would go, being out with both of them, but Cody showed up in another disguising ball cap and although she thought the hostess knew who they were, she was respectful of their privacy and seemed to understand when they asked for an out of the way table.

Seeing Jennika again was a bit awkward at first. Kate wasn't sure how to behave in front of either her or Cody, but Jason had a firm hold of her hand and Cody wrapped an arm around her and gave her a huge hug when he saw her and then pulled back and looked at her hard and asked quietly, "Are you mad that I told him?"

She shook her head. "No, Cody. I'm not mad."

Still being discrete, he asked, "Are you okay?"

"I'm not even sure what I am. This has all happened so fast."

He hugged her again and whispered when he was close, "I hope you're okay, Kate. I can't even describe how much happier he is. It's like having the old Jason back. He's been missing for a couple of years now. He's a good man, Kate. A great one. A really, truly great man."

She nodded and tried to hide the tears he induced as she whispered back, "I know, Cody, and I'm sorry for everything."

"No." He pulled back just far enough to see her eyes. "I'm the one who's sorry, Kate. I'm sorry for so many things. Mostly, for the champagne that night. I was such an idiot for so long, please forgive me. I've tried to start making up for things." He grinned. "I'm a new man. Y'all won't even recognize me. I don't drink a drop anymore and I haven't so much as even glanced at another girl except Jennika in months. I'm following Jason's lead now." He pulled away from Kate and put his arm around Jennika again as they followed the hostess.

Kate looked up at Jason and asked, "Really? No girls and no alcohol?"

Jason laughed at her disbelief. "He's not kidding. If I didn't know better, I'd say he was possessed or something. But that's backwards."

Kate glanced at Jennika walking to their table ahead of them and whispered, "She must be something else to get him to do that."

"I know you're not going to believe this, but he'd gotten that way months before he even met her." Jason sobered as he said, "He quit drinking when I found out you were married and went off the deep end. He said that cold sober, playing around like he had been wasn't nearly so appealing. I don't know if that was really it, but I know I owe him my life. For a while there, I didn't care if I lived or died."

She tugged on his arm to stop him. She had to admit to him about her marriage to John. He'd never so much as asked about it since that very first moment on that first night and she needed to come clean and explain. She should have told him days ago. "Jason, I need to tell you something."

He turned to her and she glanced around at the other people in the dining room looking at them as they stood in the aisle and she pulled him to walk with her again as she whispered, "I, uh need to talk to you some time about John. I need to explain some things."

The hurt in his eyes made her feel horrible and when they finally got past the other diners she pulled him to a stop again and whispered, "Jason, you need to know that I didn't marry John because I was in love with him. I mean, I know you already know that, but it's not what you think. John was just my boss and it was basically a business deal. We weren't... He just needed me to help him get through dying." She dropped her eyes. "We weren't lovers. I never even kissed him."

He didn't answer her and she looked up at him to see confusion mixed in with the hurt in his eyes. "What?"

She shook her head and whispered again, "John, Jason. It's a long story, but we weren't really married. I mean married married. I need to explain it to you. It's not what you think. We weren't lovers."

Jason's eyes narrowed as he looked at her and he pulled her into the nearby hallway to a banquet room and backed her up to a wall and put a hand on both sides of her head. "What? What are you saying, Kate?"

"I'm trying to tell you why I got married. John was dying and believed his ex-wife and kids would squander the fortune he'd amassed on trivial things. He wanted it put into a scholarship foundation, but the tumor was affecting his brain. He was afraid that once he was gone mentally, they'd come in and take it anyway when he was deemed incompetent. His accountant and his attorney and I worked with him at the end to make sure they didn't get it and he didn't die alone."

The most amazing light started in the back of Jason's eyes and she could see he was finally starting to understand what she was saying as she went on, "I had a great deal of respect for John, he was a good person. And I did grow to love him as things progressed, but it was never a romantic thing. John and I were just partners and friends. I never slept with him."

Jason's face slowly mellowed with an emotion she could only describe as joy and he leaned right into her. "You're kidding. Are you kidding me, Kate?"

She shook her head slowly all the time meeting his eyes. "I would never kid about something like this, Jase. I couldn't. I couldn't kid and I couldn't go back on my promise to you." She finally looked down. "At least not again after the night we conceived Kennen."

He laughed softly and then pulled her almost roughly into his arms. "You're really not just telling me this?"

At that, Kate's eyes narrowed. "I would never lie, Jason. Especially not to you."

"Oh, honey, I know, I just..." He shook his head. "You have no idea... Geez, you can't even imagine the nightmares I had about... I tried to drown them because they were killing me. I wasn't even sure I would survive knowing you were married. Aw, Kate, I wish I'd known. I couldn't even believe it when I went back to your restaurant to find out who you were working for and they told me you and your husband owned it. I couldn't conceive that you would just leave me behind like that and move on."

She looked up at him and said, "If I was honest, Jason. I should tell you that I tried desperately to move on. At that time, I thought I would never be able to come home. I did everything I could—short of drinking like you did, to forget you. I'm sorry. Your memory was killing me and I tried so hard. But getting married was simply to help John die as he wished and gain some respectability. John thought it would be easier if I was a widow instead of an unwed mother." She smiled hesitantly at him. "Which would have worked relatively well, if you and Kennen weren't nearly clones. You two ruined my whole plan."

He put his fingers up into her hair. "He has your beautiful curls, babe." He leaned and kissed her for a long moment and then pulled back with a mellow sigh. "Kate, I can't even believe what you just told me. I thought things were perfect to have you back, even though I knew you'd married another man. I mean, it killed me, but I knew you would have done what you felt was best, but..." He searched her eyes for a long several seconds. "Kate, are you telling me that the only time... There's never been anyone but me that night? The night we made him?"

She was too shy to meet his eyes and simply nodded and he pulled her to him again almost reverently. He held her that way and then finally pulled her face up and leaned down to kiss her, slowly and gently, still sighing against her lips.

Somewhere in the back of her brain, she could hear footsteps and she had begun to push him away when there was a gasp and then shattering glass. They looked up to see a very surprised waitress standing in a tangle of broken stemware.

At first her face registered shock and almost anger, but when she saw Jason, she began to beam as she breathed, "Holy Moses, Jason Falcon. What are y'all doin' back here?"

Jason grinned down at Kate and said, "Having my world unwrinkled in one sweet revelation."

Kate blushed and in that moment, three other servers appeared around the corner, followed by Cody. She was grateful for her food service background as she shook off her sudden color and said to the moonstruck girl, "We're so sorry we startled you. We'll pay for the goblets. Could you find me a broom and I'll help you clean up this mess?"

The girl didn't even register that Kate had spoken and was still staring at Jason in a fog and Kate turned to the next young man and made her request again as Jason grabbed a nearby tote and leaned to begin gathering up the largest pieces.

By the time they made it to their table, Kate was beginning to seriously worry about the girl who still hadn't come out of her stupor. Kate had to laugh as she and Jason sat down and Jennika innocently said, "I've heard a good hard slap in a situation like this brings them out of it. Maybe you could help her out, Kate. You could say it was doctor's orders."

Kate decided she was really going to like Cody's heart throb. If anyone could side Cody Rawlings, it was this quick witted vixen. She apparently knew just how Kate felt. Regardless, Kate still wasn't going to try to eat with this mindless waitress standing there staring and she got up and went in search of the manager and requested a more experienced server. A middle aged male would be nice.

Actually, Jason appeared to be in a bit of a zone himself. Every few minutes he would get quiet and introspective and then he'd look at Kate and give her a small smile and lean to kiss her. Eventually, Cody and Jennika started making fun of them and mimicking him and he finally came out of it some.

Back at his Porsche, he waved the others off and then backed Kate against the car once more just as he had inside in the hallway. She looked up at him, wondering why he was doing this instead of simply opening the door as he usually did. He had that mellow joy on his face again and she wasn't quite sure how to take him as he leaned to kiss her, the deep green of his eyes looking liquid this close. His kiss was more insistent than she expected and she pushed at him and then looked around. Jason wasn't usually prone to public displays of affection like this. "Jase, we are like standing in a parking lot in broad daylight. What are you doing?"

"I can't help it, Kate. I'm so happy about you not being uh really married I almost feel guilty. He sounds like a nice guy who tragically died young but . . . I almost wish I could somehow thank him except I'm still a little jealous of him."

"You needn't be jealous. And he really was a nice guy. He made me promise to think about coming back to you someday."

"He's sounding better all the time."

Jason leaned in to kiss her again and she put her hands on his chest and looked up at him one more time. "Jason, let me go and let's get into the car. We're starting to get spectators."

Without backing off a bit, he whispered, "Kate, can I just tell you how grateful I am that you are the kind of girl who honors promises and doesn't take intimacy lightly? Knowing that you didn't... That I'm the only one you'll ever..."

She put a gentle hand up and covered his mouth. "Jason, don't. Don't finish what you're saying. We can't talk about this. Not right now. Not with how volatile the attraction is between you and me. It would be foolish and it would be wrong. We need to be so careful not to play with fire. You know that."

He sighed. "You're right. But..." He looked down at her and she looked up at him and he finally groaned and pushed his fingers up into her hair and pulled her to him to kiss her once, almost desperately. He pulled away and said, "Falcons mate for life, Kate. You *are* my mate. Not talking about it isn't going to change that."

"Jason, I don't want to change it. Just, tell me on our wedding night, not right now. We need to be careful."

"I know." He took her hand and pulled her away from the car so he could open the door and help her in. Once she was in and he'd come around and gotten in as well, he turned to her and gave her a long, long look that was almost searing before starting up the car.

Kate sat down on the edge of her bed and rolled her neck. This had been the longest Tuesday of her life. Okay, probably not really, but it had been a long, long day. It had to have lasted more than twenty four hours.

The carpet layers had taken two full days and then the movers had brought the furniture and other things and the four of them had been moving and rearranging furniture and putting things away for hours and hours with Kennen napping and looking on from his playpen.

At least when she and Jennika had finally left, Jason's new house really felt like a home.

Then she had just wished the gate between the yards had already been installed. She was honestly too tired to want to go out and load into the car and drive around the block to come home. She was really glad she didn't have to get up and go to a job in the morning.

Morning. She didn't really want to think about tomorrow morning. Jason was leaving early for a four day road trip to Arizona and California. She kept having to remind herself that four days wasn't that long because from tonight's perspective, it seemed interminable. She lay back on the bed as she said, "Get a grip, Kate. You lasted two whole years without him. You can handle this." How she had ever managed to survive being apart had become a mystery to her.

The next morning, she and Kennen had only just gotten out of bed when her doorbell rang. Expecting it to be Elise, she was surprised when she opened it to find Jennika on her porch. "Jennika, this is a surprise. Come in. Honestly, I'm still tired and Kennen and I are just finishing getting dressed. Would you join us for breakfast?"

The pretty, petite physician nodded. "I'll take you up on that. As long as you're not having something terribly rich. I have a huge day ahead. I'm working a twelve hour shift."

As they walked into the kitchen, Kate asked, "Do you have to do that very often? That seems brutally long for a trauma surgeon. I'd imagine what you do takes it out of you."

"It does. Even an eight hour day can be grueling. I don't usually work twelves."

"We were thinking of pancakes, sausage and fruit, but if you'd rather have something lighter."

Jennika shook her head. "No, that sounds heavenly."

They'd been eating for several minutes before Jennika brought up what she'd come for. She'd been pushing her food around with little interest and then tentatively asked, "Kate, can I ask you a question? Do you ever have a hard time dealing with the whole member of a famous band thing?"

Kate's gut reaction was to roll her eyes and laugh, or cry, one of the two, but she resisted it. She wanted to down play the negatives as much as possible if it would help Jennika. From all appearances, she was in this for keeps and Kate hoped and prayed it would be easier for Jennika than it had been for her.

In a way, it should be. Cody had already learned to cope with the fame and money and seemed to be handling it. They wouldn't have to wonder if he'd still love the flavor of Jennika when he got huge. He already was.

But in a way, for Jennika it might even be worse. She hadn't had much of a chance to get used to all of this slowly. She hadn't even listened to country music before meeting Cody.

After hesitating a second, Kate nodded to her new found friend and admitted, "At times it was very hard for me, Jennika. Sometimes it still is. I'm sure their fame had a lot to do with me leaving when I did. What is it that you're struggling with?"

"A couple of things, really. I know this is going to sound so paranoid, but sometimes when I hear things or read the magazine covers or occasionally even when I watch the news, I wonder how Cody really is when he's away from me. I know that sounds like I don't trust him, but how do you know? And how do you learn to handle the sheer numbers of girls who are in love with them? It seems like we can't even leave the house without being interrupted by some adoring female fan."

Kate's heart went out to her and she smiled sadly. "I hope it helps to have empathy, because I don't have a miracle fix, Jenn. I'm sorry to have to tell you that. At least the one good thing is that you can know for sure Cody's sure about you. He's never been like this about anyone I've ever seen in the nearly twenty years I've known him."

She smiled sadly and patted Jennika's hand. "I'm not sure how to comfort you, Jennika, because how Jason was when he was away from me was the reason I finally walked, even as good a man as he is. And I'm still struggling with the fame and all it brings."

"So then how can you be as happy as you seem to be with him now?"

"I am happy with him. When I'm with Jason and it's just us or us and you two, it's no different than when we were growing up. He's just my Jason and I'm his Kate. Those times are heaven. And yes, it's different now than before I left and had Kennen. I'm not even sure I can explain, but somehow the time apart has made us realize what we have is precious and we have to treasure it and protect it. I don't wonder any more if Jason is hanging out partying around with a bunch of girls with back stage passes when he's on the road. He wouldn't risk losing Kennen and me again, and he knows now I would go if he did."

She shrugged. "I have to be honest with you and tell you that before, Cody was a partying machine. Who he was with or what he was doing didn't seem to matter much to him. He seems completely different since I've been back with Jason, but I couldn't tell you how he really is on the road."

"So why did you leave Jason in the first place? Do you mind if I ask?"

"They haven't told you?"

Jennika shook her head. "All I know, is Jason did something and Cody carries a truckload of guilt about it. For some reason, he feels like all of your troubles were his fault. I think that's the reason he straightened up in the first place."

"No, Jennika, Jason's and my mistakes are all our own. We weren't four year olds. Cody just wasn't always the best influence. But even after growing up next door to Jason my whole life, I'd been struggling for a while with wondering if I really knew him before I finally left. He'd been doing some things that just didn't seem like him and it had been troubling. Then we messed up way bad after they recorded their first big album. We were supposed to be celebrating it and my associate's degree, but they talked me into some champagne- which I knew better than. It was my own mistake. But we ended up pregnant, which Jason didn't know, and we were on thinner ice than ever as far as our relationship went.

"Finally, I'd put off telling him about the baby and he had to leave unexpectedly for a road trip and I decided I needed to go to Lubbock and tell him. While I was there, I decided to go to their concert without them knowing I was there and honestly, the way Jason behaved on stage was more troubling than ever. Then when I went to his hotel room after, he came to the door with a beer bottle in one hand and a redhead in the other."

Even after this long, the telling of it hurt deeply and she struggled not to let it show before she continued. "He tried to tell me the beer wasn't his, but as awful as seeing him with the beer was, it wasn't nearly as big a problem as that red head. I couldn't deal with it. Not when I had a baby to think of. I left his hotel and prayed all the way home and then I left him. I knew if Jason found out about the baby he'd talk me into getting back together and I knew I couldn't subject an innocent baby to that lifestyle. Plus, I couldn't face seeing him all the time, so I had to leave." She wiped at a stray tear and went on, "I put us all through hell, but I felt like I had to. Jason knows how I felt, and thank goodness, he's forgiven me, but at the time I didn't have a choice. At least it didn't feel like I did."

Jennika looked at her quietly and finally said, "I can't even imagine what you went through, Kate. And I'm so glad you've been able to get back together. At first, I didn't really understand, I just knew that Cody was on pins and needles those first couple of days for wondering if he'd done the right thing. You obviously hadn't wanted Jason to know where you were."

"No, you're wrong, Jennika. I've always been in love with Jason. I wanted to be with him desperately, I just didn't think I should. Being back with Jason and having it work at least to this point, is a dream come true. So far, Jason seems to have come back to center as far as being the man I knew and trusted. And make no mistake, Jennika, trust is imperative. At least I think it is. I couldn't live with the wondering. That's why I couldn't get married before any of this happened. And I know just how you feel. I felt so guilty for not trusting blindly, but in the end, verifying was wise. Who knows where Jason and I would be if I hadn't busted him and left. Even he admits his perspective was skewed then and he had to have a wake up call."

"So then what should I do, Kate? How do I know for sure what he's like on the road short of hiring a PI and trying to set him up and see if he messes up? That's so underhanded and negative. I can't do it."

Kate shrugged. "I'm not sure. Going to a concert under the radar and then showing up at his room was what hung Jason, but then I was able to call their manager and ask where he was staying without sending up a red flag. I'm certainly not in that situation anymore. Are you privy to any of that information, or could you ask their manager without him asking what's going on?"

Jennika considered that and then shook her head. "No, I think they'd figure out I was snooping right off. If I actually went, even without knowing where they were staying, would you be interested in coming at all?"

A ripple rolled across Kate's heart for just a second or two and then quieted and she nodded. She really did trust Jason now, and she'd do whatever she could do to help Jennika find the peace of mind she knew wasn't optional if forever was at stake. "Yeah, I'd come with you. I hope Jason and I are past this, but I understand that you need to know for sure. When are you thinking? I don't even know where they have upcoming concerts right now."

"Tonight they're in Albuquerque, and then Tucson, and Friday Phoenix and then over into California Saturday. San Diego I believe. I was thinking of flying into either Phoenix or San Diego. There are tons of cheap flights and I'm not supposed to be on call. Even if we don't know where their rooms are, which honestly I'm fine with. I'd just as soon they not know we're doing this. Unless we find something ugly, I'd rather keep it all under the radar. Even without knowing where their rooms are, maybe we could try to get close enough to them to get a feel for how he is."

Kate smiled. "You are so much wiser than I was. I was only going to talk to Jason, I didn't realize at the time that I needed to investigate like this. As much as that night has hurt for so long, and even after it all, I'm so glad I found out what I did, when I did. Figure out when you want to go for sure and I'll make arrangements for flights and hotels and for Kennen. This might actually turn out to be a really fun girl's road trip."

With a sigh, Jennika replied, "I hope so, Kate. I've never known anyone like Cody. I really want this to work out."

"There's definitely not anyone like Cody on the planet. Hope for the best. Hope and pray for the best. God has a way of helping everything to work out in the end."

Kristin Cross

Chapter 26

Kate couldn't believe how much nicer it was to fly across the country with a friend. It made a world of difference in both the stress level and her being able to actually enjoy this. And Jennika was fast becoming a good friend. She was the perfect combination of competence and entertainment. She had a hilarious off the cuff sense of humor that left Kate knowing just why Cody enjoyed her.

After thinking about it for a couple of days, Kate wondered if the band still stayed in the same hotels they had preferred a couple of years ago. If they did, she could probably guess which hotel they would use, and maybe even where they would eat at around three o'clock in the afternoon before the night's concert.

At a few minutes before two, she checked Jennika and herself into the Phoenix Marriot and forty minutes later, they were discretely sitting in the hot tub where they had a narrow view of the front lobby through the wall of windows of the pool house. If she was correct and this was the right hotel, the guys would probably be leaving the hotel shortly to go have a late lunch and she and Jennika would be able to see them.

She was beginning to wonder if this had been such a good idea after all because of the way her heart was pounding as they waited there. The tightly wound posture of Jennika made her aware that Jennika was thinking the same thing. Being caught here probably wouldn't be a good thing.

The band must have replaced a couple of their guys, because at first Kate didn't recognize the laughing group of young men who exited an elevator and started across the lobby. When she finally recognized one of the roadies, she immediately looked back at the elevators to see if there was another one coming down behind that one. It could be a completely wrong assumption, but there was a possibility they'd even be able to figure out what floor the band was on if more of them walked off the other elevator just now descending from the sixth floor.

When Jason and Cody and a couple of others did indeed step out, both she and Jennika began to hold their breath. One of the men with them was dressed in swim trunks and had a towel draped around his neck. He peeled off from the rest of the group and reached for the pool house door and almost simultaneously, Kate and Jennika slid further down in the water of the hot tub and Jennika turned her back on the lobby in front of Kate's unmistakable dark curls.

Kate whispered, "Do you know him?"

"No." Jennika shook her head and Kate's mind raced to figure out a way to slip away without this man seeing them closely enough to be able to recognize them later. Without even consulting each other, when he dove into the pool and began to swim across, they both got up and hustled out of the closest door without even picking up their cover ups and towels. They arrived back at their rooms five minutes later, thoroughly chilled from not drying off before rushing through the air conditioned halls in just their dripping suits.

Once inside, Kate leaned against the back of the door and started to giggle, while Jennika went straight for a hot shower with a laugh of her own. Man, they were pathetic. They'd done exactly what they'd set out to do and had almost given themselves a coronary in the process. At least there hadn't been a sign of a lovesick groupie with Cody or Jason on their way to lunch.

While Jennika tried to avoid hypothermia in the shower, Kate had another brainstorm and arranged for another room on the sixth floor, just off of the elevator. Maybe she and Jennika could leave the door of that room cracked tonight and see if anyone accompanied Cody back here after the concert. When Jennika emerged from the shower, they hurried to move their things before any of the band got back and then spent a nervous half hour laughing at themselves for their less than graceful sleuthing.

They put the Do Not Disturb sign on the door handle, but then left the door itself ajar so they could hear better what was going on in the hall and when they finally did hear voices they recognized and Jennika looked out the peep hole, she turned back around to Kate with a smiling shake of her head and whispered, "You're not going to believe this, but I think Jason's room is just across the hall and Cody's is the next one down. At least that's what it looked and sounded like."

Kate felt her eyes get big and she whispered back, "You're kidding! Dang, we're good! Almost too good. We're gonna get so busted if we don't be careful."

A few minutes later when her cell phone rang and it was Jason, she tried to keep the smile out of her voice as she shut the door so if he happened out into the hall, he wouldn't hear her on the other end of the line with him. He mentioned how much he missed her and that they were just returning to their hotels to try and catch a power nap after having gone to lunch.

After telling her he loved her, he rang off and Kate gave Jennika a thumbs up as she heard Jennika telling Cody goodbye on her own cell phone and said softly, "So far so good, girl. Except we're going to have to order room service and not hang out around the stadium tonight after the concert. And I wish I knew what time they are flying out to California tomorrow. Let's ask them when we talk to them so we don't get surprised in the hall before they're gone."

Kate tried to take a power nap as well, knowing it might be a long and even stressful night, but every time she closed her eyes, she struggled not to picture that horrible scene of Jason with the beer and the redhead. She'd open them back up and remind herself that they had survived the aftermath of that night and moved on, but there was still a less than festive mood in the room that afternoon and evening as they both tried to gear up for the night ahead of them.

There wasn't a sound out of Jason's or Cody's rooms until nearly six o'clock when they left with the rest of their band members and both Kate and Jennika breathed a veritable sigh of relief that they hadn't been discovered so far.

It wasn't a whole lot later that the two of them headed out as well. They were going to go to dinner after all and then get to the stadium early to watch just as Kate had the last time. Here again, the memories were sobering although Kate tried not to convey that to Jennika. She tried to be upbeat and positive. If they got some kind of an ugly wake up call, there would be time enough to deal with it then. Unless that truly happened, Kate was going to trust in the guys right up until something happened to change that. At least that was the theory. It was the only way to deal with this situation positively and she knew Jennika needed her calm and trusting example to ever be able to make peace with this life.

For the most part, trusting and thinking positively was working, at least that was what Kate kept telling herself. There had been a few bumps, but that was to be expected. The stadium was filled with thousands and thousands of loud and adoring fans and once again, most of them were female, but she and Jennika did their best to deal with them all.

Fans were the name of the game in this business. The very life blood of this whole industry and after all, she and Jennika did want their men to be successful at what they did. And once they could try to tune out the hubbub, it was exciting to be sitting here waiting for them to come out. Kate decided she should try to attend their concerts more often and see if she could get more used to all of this. Perhaps in time it would become old hat to her.

She was incredibly grateful that Jennika was here with her. She was even grateful that she had to keep a smile plastered on her face; because she'd had no idea when she had agreed to do this it was going to be so reminiscent of the last concert she went to. The memories threatened to consume her and even the smell of the stadium made her a little nauseous, in spite of the fact that she certainly wasn't pregnant this time.

The opening band was good. They helped Kate to loosen up enough that by the time Jason and Cody and the others came on stage with a huge surge from the screaming fans, she was able to look over at Jennika's big eyes and smile and give her arm a squeeze and laugh.

Jennika obviously hadn't been expecting the magnitude of this crowd or that reaction to Cody simply walking up onto the stage.

Between watching Jason weave his spell and watching Jennika try to take it all in, Kate was much more at ease this concert than she had been the last, even with everyone around them standing and dancing and continuing to scream. Kate was a good six inches taller than Jennika and it had to have been as intimidating to the diminutive surgeon as it had been to Kate at first. At least this concert didn't feel as hot and stuffy as she'd felt in Lubbock.

Slowly, Jennika appeared to be relaxing and Kate began to focus on Jason, dancing and singing to the world about how lonely it was to have a love gone bad. She hadn't heard half of these songs, but the lyrics of what must have been hits if the audience's reaction said anything, certainly weren't terribly happy and hopeful. Is this how Jason had reacted to her disappearance from his life? The tone of their music had markedly changed in the last two years.

Still, the music was incredibly evocative and Kate found herself in tears as she watched him, knowing what it would have taken to tame his passion like this. As dynamic as ever, he was a different singer out there than he'd been before. He still sang and danced to the crowd and he was still obviously charming them out of their seats, but there was none of the over the top suggestiveness that had so saddened her that night, which was good, but there was also something missing of his smile. Some deep feeling that wasn't coming through the way it used to. Somehow, whether it was him or her, someone had indeed been tempered into a more mature entertainer and entertained than she and Jason had been then.

The interference of the crowd wasn't so numbing and for the first time in a concert setting, even downcast, it felt like when Jason sang to her when they were alone. It was unbelievably sweet, but she still felt a gentle sadness for the exuberant young man who was gone.

When she glanced over at Jennika to see she'd finally begun to smile and enjoy herself, Kate relaxed completely. She let Jason's mellow sexy voice lull her into loosening up the hold the past had on her, and she simply enjoyed watching Jason unleash his magic and take this crowd with him wherever he wanted to go. He was still absolutely gifted as an entertainer.

In the moment between songs, Jennika looked over at Kate and smiled and knowing that this trip had comforted her gave Kate a lift. She hoped she had been able to help in easing Jennika over some of the hurdles that had so tripped her up with Jason. She breathed a quick prayer that tonight after the concert would go as smoothly as well.

Her attention was drawn back to the front of the stage where Jason was standing as the crowd got quiet, waiting. He looked all around and then said, "This next song is a new one. We've never performed it before for anyone so you all will be the first. I'd like to dedicate this song to a friend of mine. She's not here tonight, but I wish she was. And she's never even heard it yet, but she inspired it. So, here's to Kate, the love of my life."

Kate put a hand to her chest as her heart began to pound and she felt Jennika's gaze as Jason's guitar began a sweet, enchanting melody in the dead quiet of the stadium. After a second, the rest of the band slowly came in and then Jason began to sing. Tears pooled in Kate's eyes as he spun a haunting, evocative tale of a lost bird with a broken wing that had found it's way back to its home in the sky and the mate who was the other half of its soul that healed it. The tears rolled down her cheeks as the music picked up and she could hear the energy and passion and happiness back in his voice.

This was the Jason she knew. This was the man she had come to know and love as a child and still worshipped as a woman grown. The sweet, enchanting melody finished wiping the last of the heartache of the past two lonely and troubled years from the deepest corners of her spirit and she finally felt it fly free with his across the expanse of the huge stadium.

Until this moment, as she felt her heart set free, she hadn't even understood how much heartache she'd been harboring. She'd thought she was fine, but realized now she hadn't been truly. What she'd thought had been that tempering, that maturity, had, in fact, been settling for what she'd believed was reality, and wasn't necessarily like the dreams she'd hoped for. What she was hearing now brought back those dreams of forever in all their shining brightness. Finding they had survived the weathering entirely intact brought almost overwhelming emotion. Singing and playing down there, he had healed her very essence and had no idea what he had done. What's more, she hadn't even known she needed healing.

Jason finished the song and for just a second or two, the stadium was silent and then the crowd went crazy as Kate quietly sat down in her seat and let the tears run down her face. The time away from him had been hell, but it was going to be all right. She finally knew without a doubt that everything was going to be all right. She'd thought she'd been sure a few nights ago, but it wasn't until that last shred of doubt wafted away into the smoky colors of the spotlights up in the rafters that she realized she had still been afraid of trusting. Still been afraid of this life and truly giving her heart with no strings attached. She sat there in the deafening crowd that didn't even realize she was there and cried and let the heartache go. It was all going to be all right.

Finally, Jason hit a chord on his guitar and the crowd screamed again when they recognized it and then started to settle down and Kate's tears distilled into even more emotion as he began her song. The song he had sung for her that night at the lake after that tender pinky promise that had channeled her life since she was sixteen years old. The song that spoke of forever and friendship stronger than this life and a love deeper than eternity.

The energy was in his voice again. The passion that was Jason to the core, and she could hear the emotion ring all the way through the stadium as he sang of his feelings for her. Of commitment and devotion and hope. All of the things she and Jason had spoken of that night when he'd told her the first time that Falcons mate for life.

Then it had been sweet and warm and reassuring. Later, when her world had fallen apart, it had been heart wrenching. Tonight it was life giving and grounding and intimate. He had indeed been set free and had come back to her and was hers. This Falcon truly had become one with her for life. She had no doubt of that now.

The song finally ended, but Kate continued to sit, lost in the crowd and in her own thoughts and feelings as the concert throbbed on around her. The noise and heat and commotion that had been such a distraction the last time almost seemed like insulation tonight. It was like the direct line of communication from his music to her heart was cushioned by the deafening roar and pulse of the masses and she was here cocooned inside her own small world of tender, treasured feeling.

As the next song commenced, she knew Jennika was watching her almost warily and she was embarrassed that she couldn't seem to get a handle on the tears. The delicate almost exquisite emotion was so overwhelming and so close to the surface that she was unable to stop it. It was as if the dam she had so painstakingly constructed over the weeks and months and years against being so vulnerable to her feelings for Jason had given away and the sweetness of his love had rushed to almost drown her in it's depths and her defenses had washed away in the flood.

She leaned her head back and closed her eyes and took several long breaths and tried to focus on the music. Yet another song had begun with a rollicking back beat and she soon recognized that Cody was singing the lead. She sniffed and wiped at her eyes as she tried to focus on the lyrics. Jason hadn't written this one. It had to have been Cody and she glanced up at Jennika to see her transfixed as she watched Cody dancing and cutting up there on stage. Standing to be able to see better, Kate began to understand that in his own way, Cody was singing to Jennika as well. This was a song about being happy. About finally figuring it all out and how it made him smile. About how when it was all said and done, love was the fun part worth going through all the rest for.

Jennika glanced over and gave Kate a hesitant smile and then looked back at the man singing on that stage, and Kate hoped she understood that light hearted admission. Kate truly had never seen Cody this ready to face forever before.

The last three songs were classic Aerie pieces that had rocking back beats and those never to be forgotten melodies and the crowd sang with the band as they brought the concert to its height and then did two encores to a close. As the crowd clapped and screamed and then realized they weren't coming back on stage, the house lights slowly came up and their fans began to get up and start heading up the stairways to the exits and Kate sat back down. There was no sense in fighting this crowd and she'd only feel stupid if she started to tear up again anyway.

Jennika sat back down beside her and took a long, deep breath and then looked over and studied her. Kate smiled and then rolled her eyes as the emotions came on again and Jennika asked softly, "You okay?"

Unable to answer, Kate simply nodded and dug into her purse, hoping for another tissue she was relatively sure she wasn't going to find. Man, she needed to stop with the blubbering, which was a great idea until she thought back to how Jason had told the entire world she was the love of his life. His tone of voice had left nothing to doubt and that felt almost overwhelmingly sweet to Kate.

They sat there in relative silence for being in a stadium of twenty something thousand people and finally, Jennika said, "Kate, I know this is going to sound crazy after how hard we've tried not to get busted here by them, but I need to tell Cody I'm here. After watching them tonight, not telling him feels dishonest. I'd rather he knew why we came and that we were here than that we sneak on back home and not tell them.

Kate nodded wordlessly. She felt the same way. They were past this now. The questions had been answered and fears laid to rest and now there was just the raw emotion and need to see Jason and have him hold her as she struggled to swallow her tears. He'd understand her heart. He always had and he'd laugh at her, but he'd know she was finally over that strangling, stalling fear.

The crowd had begun to thin and as they stood to go, Kate asked, "Can you call Cody? I'm still afraid I'll cry if I call Jason just now and he'll think something is wrong."

They began to climb the stairs as Jennika held the phone to her ear, but after a moment, she shook her head. "I didn't think they'd have their phones on them. Do you think they'll hang out here or leave?"

"They usually meet people backstage who have won passes on the local radio stations and that sort of thing. They'll probably be here for hours. Then depending on what time they fly out in the morning, some of them will probably go clubbing and the rest of them will go back to the hotel and unwind. They kind of have to decompress from the adrenaline and high of performing before they can rest."

Jennika shook her head. "I'd think after putting out that kind of energy for a couple of hours they'd be thoroughly exhausted."

"They will be." Kate smiled. "They just have to come down first. Their concerts are a rush to them and it takes a while. Then they'll be completely drained. See if Scotty answers his phone. He'll help us find them. In the mean time, let's see if we can find some security or someone who will know how to get backstage and we'll get as close as we can until someone let's us through."

It was a good plan, but they could never get anyone to pick up their calls and even after finding security, they were brushed off as just another couple of hopeful locals who pretended to be close friends to make it backstage to meet the hunky stars. After standing in a crowd of pushing and crowding groupies outside a carefully guarded door for twenty-five minutes, Kate sighed and turned away. "Let's go back to the hotel, Jenn. This is stealing all of the magic of their show. Maybe we'll just have to tell them we came and we'll see them when they come back home."

They caught a cab and as they drove through the city lights back to the Marriott, the feelings that were still so close to the surface threatened to overwhelm her again. Jason had been incredible tonight. He always was, but tonight... She didn't even know how to get these tender memories to behave enough not to embarrass herself as she rode the elevator back up to the sixth floor.

They were back in their room and had kicked out of their shoes and were deciding about ordering a pizza when Cody called Jennika's phone. Kate heard her start trying to explain so Kate ordered the pizza and then went into the bathroom and began to take her hair out of its messy up do and wash her face. All the tears had done a terrible number on her eye make up and she was grateful she had dark lashes and brows and wasn't one of those pale pastels who melted at times like this. She still hated it when she cried. Even happy tears made her head ache and her nose run.

There was a knock a couple of minutes later and she gathered up her cosmetics and tossed them into her case so Jennika wouldn't have to wade through them as she got ready for bed. Still emotional, she grabbed a tissue and then opened the door to let Jennika have her turn.

It wasn't Jennika. It was Jason standing on the other side of the door looking like a superstar in his jeans and sleeveless muscle shirt. His face was so full of concern that as soon as she saw him, the tears welled again and she walked into his arms and buried her face against his neck and held on. He didn't say anything, just held her and rubbed her back for the longest time and let her cry.

When she finally began to wind down, he took her hand and led her out and to the small couch and sat down on it and then pulled her down onto his lap, let her lean against his chest and wrapped her back in his arms as he asked quietly, "Can you try to help me understand why you're so upset, Kate? What's wrong?"

She shook her head against him and sniffed at the stupid tears. "Nothing's wrong, Jason." She looked up at him and wondered how she could explain what had happened out there tonight. Unable to put her feelings into words, she shook her head again and snuggled back into his neck. "Nothing's wrong."

Sounding somewhat skeptical, he asked, "You're not upset about the concert?"

Leaning back in his arms to look at him, she swallowed the lump in her throat and said, "I'm upset, but it's good upset. I'm sorry. The concert was... It was..." It was several more seconds before she could whisper, "Really, really good."

She leaned back against his skin and after a second could continue, "I knew I missed seeing you, but I didn't realize how much. I'd forgotten what you can do to me. You were incredible out there tonight, Jason. You have such a gift."

He released a big breath and pulled her tighter into his arms and rested his face on her hair. "I thought you were disgusted again at the concert. That you'd want to leave again. I couldn't figure out what I'd done that would make you so sad."

Kristin Cross

Still snuggled against him, she shook her head. "The concert was marvelous, Jase. The only thing even remotely sad about it was how much some of your music had changed. My happy Jason was missing part of the time."

In a low voice, he admitted, "Your happy Jason was missing the whole time you were gone, Kate. How could I be happy when my life had no meaning? Then when I found out you were married..." He let out a sigh that was half groan. "It felt like it was over." He brushed a hand over her back and then put it down to her chin to get her to look up at him as he said softly, "But the happy part is back now, babe. Couldn't you tell?"

She looked up into his brilliant green eyes, nodded and smiled through the last of her tears. "Why do y'all think I'm such a mess? Geez, look at me. I'm laughing and crying at the same time."

She wiped at her eyes with the tissue in her hand and then reached the other up to caress his cheek. "You blew me away out there tonight. It was so different than I expected. I... I... Oh, Jase, for some reason, even though I knew we were back together and committed, somehow I didn't think it could ever be like it was. I mean we're older and wiser. Tempered. We're parents. I thought that was the reason I wasn't as... As, I don't know, hopeful maybe. I'm not sure how to describe it. Some part of me was so holding back, but I didn't really realize it. Not until tonight."

444

His expression was absolutely sober as he asked, "Were you expecting me to mess up again, Kate? Is that why you came? Do you still not trust me?"

Shaking her head, she said earnestly, "No. No. Jason, I swear it. I came here to help Jennika learn to deal with all of this and to let her see Cody as big as life and how he did. I honestly didn't come here to spy on you. I promise. In my heart of hearts, I believed I was past all the hurt. I was fine with knowing you were committed to me. But don't you see? That's what I'm trying to tell you. I didn't understand my own heart or head or something. What I thought was simply accepting life as an adult was actually believing we could never get past the hurt and distrust. I knew some of the magic was gone, but I thought that was just what happened when life tempered you." She laid her head back onto his chest and went on, "But Jason, I was wrong wasn't I?"

His low words sounded reassuring even through his chest next to her ear. "I think you were, Kate. I know that yes, we are a couple of years older, but honestly, I feel twenty years younger now than I did two weeks ago. And my feelings for you have never changed. You're still the love of my life, Kate. You always will be."

She turned her face up to his and smiled even though her eyes still glistened with tears and reached a hand up to caress his cheek again. "And being the love of your life feels so good, Jason. Please forgive me for not understanding all the way. I'm sorry I didn't." She looked into the depths of his eyes and struggled not to let the emotions overcome her again as she went on, "You're the love of my life, too, Jason. My soul mate for this life and the eternities. I can't even tell you how it feels to have the last of the doubt gone." She dropped her eyes. "I can't even put it into words, but it…" The tears overflowed and he gently wiped them and she whispered, "It makes my feelings way tender. Sorry."

He pulled her so tightly into his arms he was almost hurting her, but that was the depth of the emotion that flowed between them as he said huskily, "Don't apologize, Kate. I've prayed for us to find these tender emotions again for forever. I need you so desperately in my life to feel whole. Don't apologize. Just let me bask in them. Let me drown in them. Let me suffocate in knowing you finally trust me again. That you'll finally fly with me again like you used to before. Before we grew up and you grew wary and away."

This time when she looked up at him, the green fire in his eyes was liquid and the emotion she saw there was tender, but explosive as well. The time apart had more than just tempered and refined them. The male who looked down at her was so mature and masculine and powerful that if she hadn't known that what she was feeling equaled him as a female it would have scared her. The need she read there was molten.

For just a second, he simply searched her eyes and then finally, he lowered his mouth to hers in a kiss that started oh so tender and then built around the pent up need and frustration and heartache until it threatened to consume them in an inferno of core deep passion that flamed from one soul to another.

The knowing that they were indeed mates for this life and beyond kindled the strong friendship that had been through the refiner's fire, turning it into a firestorm of desire that became forged into the commitment of forever. Raw emotion filled the void left by the last of her doubts until by the time he pulled away, their breathing heavy and ragged; her very innermost emotional needs had been finally quenched by the surety of his devotion. He had been right all along- they were Falcons who had mated for forever. Knowing to the very depth of her heart that he was hers and hers alone for eternity was the most empowering feeling she had ever experienced.

***

Jason knew without a shadow of a doubt that she'd finally been able to sweep away the reservations she'd been having since long before she'd even left. But the desire that that surety and those kisses aroused was just at this moment threatening to torch the whole hotel and he pulled away with a groan and struggled to get a handle on the passion that had him wanting far more from her than she could give right here and now.

He needed her desperately. And he knew she needed him just the same, but he also knew that this searing hunger for each other could char their whole future if they let it get out of control like they had that one desperate time before. They would be dealing with the ripples from that disastrous night forever as it was and there was no way he was going to take risks like that again. Not when he could taste eternity in her kiss tonight.

Even without her mouth on his, her exquisite sensuality was making him crazy and after fighting his own body for several moments, he finally forced himself to let go of her completely and get up off the small couch and walk across to the window. He stood there and looked out at the lights of the city and then leaned and turned the air conditioner up to full blast. He needed all the cooling off he could get right now.

He heard her get up and glanced around to see her filling a glass with ice at the little bar. She added water and brought it over to him, her face still flushed from the heat of the moment. With a tentative smile, she handed it to him and asked, "Are you okay?"

Returning her small smile, he took the ice water and quietly admitted, "I was just worrying about spontaneously combusting again. You have no idea what you can do to me, girl." She was silently watching him and what he saw in her eyes made him ask softly, "Or do you?"

He set the water glass on the air conditioner and reached for her again to fold her into a gentle, but very tight hug with a deep satisfied sigh. "This is where we're supposed to be, isn't it, Kate? Close enough that I can feel you breathe and feel your heart beat with mine."

She didn't answer and after a few seconds, he looked down into her blue eyes and knew it was time to get on to forever. "Katelyn Marie, would you marry me?"

There was no doubt in her eyes, none of that worry, no fear, just the faint glisten of tears as she answered without hesitation. "I would love to marry you, Jason. I would be honored." With another happy sigh, he bent to kiss her again. This time so gently that the smallest sensation felt huge as they touched. This was definitely where they were supposed to be.

When they finally pulled away, he said, "I'm sorry. I was going to surprise you and take you to the lake, but I couldn't help myself. Tonight, you just feel like forever here in my arms."

She teared up again and he could tell the tender emotions were back as she shook her head and then had to pause before she could whisper, "No, this was perfect. It does feel like forever. Take me to the lake to give me a ring. But maybe we should do it sooner than later." She gave him a shy smile. "Spontaneous combustion is a very real threat."

He chuckled as he bent to kiss her again. It was probably a good thing the pizza was delivered soon after that.

Chapter 27

Cody actually talked Jennika into flying on to California with them for the next concert, but Kate had to get back home to Kennen. Saying goodbye to Jason at the airport was more poignant than she ever remembered. They both almost missed their planes because they were so hesitant to tell each other goodbye.

It was a good thing Kate hadn't opted to stay, because the next day, Kennen came down with a low grade fever and obviously wasn't feeling well. She was glad she was the one to be able to care for him as well as not exposing Gretchen to a bug.

The fact that Jason would be home the next day filled her thoughts as she worked around the house and cared for Kennen. It was incredible the difference that one concert and night had made in knowing everything was going to be okay with them. Having the last of the doubt gone was like having the sun come out after a year of rain. The only problem was that the day dragged by because she couldn't wait to see him. Every time she thought about those kisses on the hotel couch, she'd feel these amazing butterflies dance in her stomach.

Toward evening, Kennen's fever spiked and he started to cough and the thoughts of Jason were pushed into the background as she struggled to bring the fever down and keep Kennen as comfortable as possible. She still felt those sweet warm feelings when she thought about Jason, but there wasn't a whole lot of time to let her thoughts wander. Kennen had had the usual bouts with a cold all babies had, but he'd never gotten this sick, this fast.

By three-thirty in the morning, she was exhausted and beginning to wonder if maybe this wasn't just a cold as Kennen's fever climbed and he struggled to breathe between coughing. She got on-line and then called her mom and was becoming more worried by the moment. Several times she'd thought about taking him into an after hours clinic, but knew they would be packed with other sick children and she was hesitant to expose him to something worse than just a cold. There were some truly nasty things going around and she didn't want to take a chance on him catching something even worse.

When her cell phone rang a few minutes later and she saw it was Jason calling, she breathed a sigh of relief. He'd help her calm down and be able to get through this. He always helped her settle down and focus. His deep, sexy voice made her feel better as soon as he said her name and what he said next made her feel unbelievably better. "Hey, Kate. I'm on your front porch, but I didn't want to scare you by knocking. I got in a minute ago, but I saw your lights are on. Is everything okay?"

"No. Everything is not okay." She felt a sudden urge to break down and cry as she carried her son to the door to let his dad in. "Kennen's really sick." She opened the door and Jason walked inside looking positively exhausted and completely beautiful. The concern in his face was the most reassuring thing she'd ever seen.

He leaned down to kiss her and then put a gentle hand to Kennen's head and gave a low whistle. "How long has he been like this?"

"He got a fever this afternoon, but it was pretty mild until about seven o'clock. Since then he's been getting worse and worse. I've given him everything I dared. I would have taken him in, but I'm worried about him being exposed to something even nastier."

"Can I hold him? You look all in." He squeezed her shoulder and kissed her temple as he took Kennen from her and went to sit in a recliner to rock him. Even Kennen seemed to be calmed as Jason rubbed him and spoke to him gently as the sick little boy was wracked with a coughing spell. When he was quieted again, Jason asked, "Kate, how do you know he doesn't already have something pretty nasty? This is a bad cough. He's having trouble breathing."

Kate felt the hair on the back of her neck prickle to hear him say the thought out loud she'd been trying to ignore for more than an hour now and she nodded her head as the tears she'd been struggling to fight broke free.

Jason got back up and brought Kennen over to her and wrapped one arm around her. "Don't cry, sweetheart. He's going to be okay. And I'm here now and can shoulder some of this." He kissed her temple again and whispered, "Crying will only make him more stressed, Kate baby. Try to be strong until he goes to sleep and then you can rain all over me. Deal?"

Kate nodded but then said sadly, "We need to take him in, Jason. I hate to even admit it, but he's not getting better even with the cold medicine and Tylenol. I feel like he should be looked at."

Jason pulled back and looked at her quietly and then nodded. "It couldn't hurt as sick as he is. Go get the diaper bag and I'll start buckling him into his car seat."

An hour and a half later, Kate had never been more grateful for Jason in her life as he rocked their son who did indeed have a bad case of RSV. Jason sang to him as Kennen struggled to breathe even with the tiny oxygen mask he wore to supplement him. Kennen hated the mask and kept trying to pull it off, but every time, Jason would gently but firmly tell him no and try to distract him.

Finally, Kennen got the message that Jason wasn't going to let him remove it and he cuddled into Jason's chest to listen to him sing to him and finally fell into an exhausted sleep.

Jason was in a rocking chair beside the crib in the room and with his free hand he pulled the other chair over close to him and beckoned Kate to come sit close enough that she could lean on him too. It felt like heaven to lean on his strong shoulder and finally let herself give into the exhaustion she was feeling. He was probably even more tired because he'd done a concert and then caught a red eye back home, but he felt like a rock sitting here beside her.

As she drifted off, she noticed that hospitals all smelled the same. This was exactly how it had smelled the night Jason's brother Kennen had died.

She thought about the other Kennen a lot over the next forty-eight hours. Somehow, sitting here beside the crib and literally willing her son to be able to breathe was eerily reminiscent of that other night so long ago, when she and Jason had kept a vigil like this. It was a different Kennen and a different hospital and even a different life threatening situation, but the sound and the smells and the oppressive fear were exactly the same.

She knew Jason was feeling the same things. She could see it in his eyes, even though he never said anything even remotely less than hopeful. The exhaustion clouded her brain and she could see the exhaustion take its toll on Jason as well as he stayed strong enough for both her and Kennen to lean on.

In some ways, this time together was precious. Praying beside Jason was a sweet experience they'd never shared like they were now. Prayer helped to strengthen them both when the fear became overwhelming and she knew it was strengthening their friendship as well.

Even though they had both believed their relationship had already been tempered and was absolutely strong the other night in that hotel room when he'd asked her to be his wife, this time of waiting and praying together refined it and solidified it even further. Looking back, Kate had to wonder how in the world she had ever questioned this strong man's character. He was more of a rock than she'd ever, ever understood.

Their parents came and it was somehow so wrong to have Jason's parents just meet Kennen and yet be aware he might not live to get to know him. Once again, Kate had to wonder why she'd felt so sure she was supposed to leave after that night in Lubbock.

Cody had been there several times, but on the fourth day, he brought Jennika in to visit and while Kate appreciated their friendship, the look that passed between them as Jennika took in Kennen's condition, made her more afraid than she'd ever been in her life. She'd known

Kennen was slowly getting worse, but seeing that sober look from a medical professional scared her to death.

Deep in the fifth night, as she and Jason stood together beside the crib looking down at the grievously ill small boy, Jason finally spoke about what neither one of them had been able to voice when he tiredly asked her, "Kate baby, what would you think of getting married like tonight so if we lose him, at least he'll be remembered as Kennen Falcon?" Kate was only able to nod her head as she sobbed into his chest. She desperately wanted to raise this little boy, not just remember him.

Cody made the arrangements and honestly, Kate was so tired and worried that it was all she could do to say "I do.", when the judge who came right to the hospital married them early the next morning. They were far too worried about whether Kennen was going to make it through the day to care that this wasn't the way they'd always planned to marry. And filling out the paperwork to have Jason officially adopt Kennen was little more than a heart wrenching blur.

Again, that night, a honeymoon was the furthest thing from their minds as they continued their constant vigil beside his crib, still praying together for their son to be healed. At this point, it felt like a miracle was what it was going to take to bring him back from death's door.

The attending physicians moved Kennen into the intensive care unit in the middle of the night and tensions stretched still further. Now they weren't even allowed to stay with him all the time and after their time to visit him was up every half hour, they crumbled together onto a couch in the nearby lounge to catch a moment of sleep and wait for the next time they could check on him for a few minutes.

The hours came and went in a tangled mix of prayer, fear and nightmares, and the fact that they were now married didn't really register. Even the physical attraction was missing as the night the first Kennen had died haunted them.

Jason had been scheduled to leave with the band on Friday morning for a concert in Georgia on Saturday, but there wasn't much question of him leaving and the tour bus left with him still existing in a tired, fearful haze in the ICU lounge. Though Kate appreciated him not leaving, and she regretted him being unable to keep a commitment the way he invariably did, she had come to know that walking away while his son had such a tenuous hold on life would be as thoroughly impossible for him as it would be for her. This man worshipped the small boy he'd only recently found out he'd fathered.

Instead of traveling across the south to go and perform, Jason spent that day bearing up under the pressure of worrying about his small son dying and being the rock that Kate leaned on to have faith that their Father in Heaven would intervene here and let them have the chance to raise that son.

That night was the longest night in history. It had to be. There were times Kate literally spoke the word "breathe" out loud to Kennen as they stood there beside his bed for those short minutes the staff allowed them to be in there. When they couldn't be and had gone back out to the lounge, the fear his small body would indeed stop breathing without them there was the most fearful thing she could ever imagine feeling. It would be bad enough to lose him, but to have him die in there without them felt unendurable and the fear became suffocating.

The only way Kate felt they could even survive that night of hell was to deal with the overwhelming struggle together, hand in hand and with a prayer in their hearts every single second. There was no way they'd have made it at all if it hadn't been for that sweet relief of prayer. The privilege of being able to take this burden to God and know He was there and listening and comforting had never been more apparent to her.

As it was, when day finally did break outside the big windows at the end of the hallway, the exhaustion was nearly as oppressing as the fear. They'd made it through the night. Whether their little boy would make it through this day was yet to be seen.

They were both standing next to Kennen's bed in the ICU, wondering if it was their imagination that he seemed to be breathing somewhat easier, when for the first time in what felt like a year, he opened his sweet eyes and looked up at them like he actually knew them. Those raging green eyes that were so like his father's were clear and bright and Kate began to cry as Jason reached into the bed to put a gentle hand on Kennen's head and softly said, "Hey, buddy. Good morning! You look like you're feeling a bit better."

Kennen nodded his little head tiredly and rolled toward them as he reached a tiny little hand out to Jason who tenderly picked him up, being careful of the tubes and wires that appeared to truss every part of him. In her tired haze, Kate hadn't even realized his fever had come down in the last while. Neither of them had. The hope that was born in that moment was indescribable.

Jason cuddled him to his chest and then pulled Kate into their embrace as well and she couldn't help the tears that fell as Kennen struggled to speak through the oxygen mask and his sore throat and then finally asked, "Daee, sing to Tennen?" Her heart had never been as full as Jason snuggled the tiny boy close to them and began to softly sing to him about the Falcon with the broken wing. She felt like she'd been handed back forever with her family again.

In the late afternoon, they moved Kennen back out to his regular room and once he was settled and had gone to sleep, Jason sat down in the recliner and pulled Kate down onto his lap and kissed away the unbelievable fear and worry of the last hellacious week that felt like it had lasted a decade. The physical attraction that had been overwhelmed with the thought of their son dying, was now back with a vengeance and even as tired as they both were, they struggled not to embarrass the nurse who came in a few minutes later and interrupted them.

Once she went back out, Jason gave Kate a tired smile and said, "You know, Kate. I could have sworn I married you sometime this past week, but in all honesty, the exact logistics of the whole thing evade me. As much as I want to just enjoy being married to you, how would y'all feel about renewing those emergency vows in the church in front of our families and a minister?" He bent to kiss her again.

At length he reminded her, "You didn't answer about renewing our vows."

Kate thought about that for a minute and then smiled shyly as she said, "Unless it's a huge deal to you, Jason, I'd just as soon not. We *are* married, and frankly, I want to be intimate with you more than I want wedding photos. If we do it again, isn't that going to take a while? I don't want to put off being together for the sake of a party."

Jason chuckled. "My, but I like the way y'all think. But won't you regret that someday?" He smiled as he teasingly went on, "Once the new wears off my body, I mean? Won't you wish we had wedding photos?"

"I can't imagine the intrigue about your body wearing off before we're eighty, but yeah, wedding photos might be nice. How about if we do this. How about if you go find a plane that can get you to Atlanta before your concert in…" She looked at her watch. "A little over three hours. And I'll round up a photographer and some rings and flowers, and when you come home and Kennen can come home, we'll take those photos, have a family dinner and then take that honeymoon we talked about. We can be together and you and I and Cody and our families and that very discrete judge will be the only ones who will know exactly when we got married. Hopefully, the rest of the world won't wonder when we conceived Kennen when the public finally finds out about us. "

"Kate, the press comes up with so much garbage about us that hopefully the public doesn't believe a tenth of it. We can't let what people know or not bother us."

"You're good at that, Jason, but I'm still learning. Let's don't think about that. Let's focus on moving on with our lives. What kind of rings do we want?"

"Honey, I've had your ring for about four years now. You just worry about a dress."

"Really? You have?" He nodded and she laughed and admitted, "Well, actually, I've had the dress for probably about that same time, so all we need are the flowers. I'll work on that. But what about the concert? You committed. Now that Kennen is apparently out of the woods, you should be there if there's any way possible."

"You're right. Call me if he gets worse again and I'll highjack a jet if I have to. Otherwise, I'll be home sometime in the middle of the night tonight."

"Jason, I'd love to have you home, but you're already exhausted. Rest tonight and come home with the guys, and Kennen and I will be way looking forward to you getting here."

She met his eyes and he kissed her hard again and assured her, "I'm kind of looking forward to that too." He pulled out his cell phone and she went to get off his lap, but he stopped her. "No, stay here as long as you can. Let me call Scotty and see what he can manage and then I'll go." He pushed a number and as the call was taken, he asked for their manager to try to find a flight to Atlanta even if he had to charter something and then before he closed, he asked that Scotty have one of the techs rig up a feed to the band's website so Kate could watch the concert from the hospital on a computer.

When Scotty called back twelve minutes later to tell Jason he had a plane waiting at the airport in Tulsa, Jason ended the call and then gently pushed her off of his lap, stood up and pulled her up beside him.

They embarrassed the nurse again, but not too bad and neither one of them cared.

Finally, he reluctantly pulled away and leaned in to kiss Kennen and then hustled out the door, leaving Kate feeling ridiculously lonely when he was gone. He'd been at her side almost constantly for the last week. As she thought about that, even though they had been best friends for most of their lives, this last week had cemented their friendship more than the whole rest of the time put together. He was going to be a wonderful husband and father.

The tech had indeed gotten the feed set up for the concert and then the same nurse they'd embarrassed helped her get the computer in the room interfaced with the web, and at eight o'clock that evening, the band who was opening for Aerie came on as Kate held Kennen in the rocking chair in his room.

His fever had just gone up some again and he lay asleep in her worried arms, his tiny body still exhausted from this fight for his life with this virus. She prayed for the ten thousandth time this week, wishing Jason's calming presence was still here, but knowing he needed to honor his word. As she gently brushed the dark curls off of Kennen's forehead, she marveled again at how much he looked like his handsome father.

Finally, the opener band left the stage and Kate wondered if Jason had, in fact, made it in time. He'd called her just minutes ago after he'd landed and she knew he was trying to get through the city to the coliseum, but it was going to be close. As she watched, the crowd began to scream and she knew the guys were coming up onto the stage and held her breath, wondering if he'd walk out there.

He didn't. It was just Cody and the other four, but the crowd went wild anyway and the band went into one of the few songs Cody sang lead on as Kate felt silly for how disappointed she was that Jason hadn't come out with them. The band just wasn't the band without him, even as good as the others were.

As their first song ended and the crowd quieted, Cody stepped to the front of the stage and began to speak. He explained that Jason was somewhere trying to get there and Cody told of the last days as Jason and Kate had sat at their baby son's bedside as he fought for his life in the hospital. Then he asked for a moment of silence for all those within the sound of his voice to pray for their child and you could have heard a pin drop in that huge coliseum of tens of thousands. Tears filled Kate's eyes at the thought of all those prayers for her small son. How could he not pull through with that many petitioning the Father on his behalf?

When the moment was over, Cody spoke briefly about what a great friend and mentor Jason had been to him over the years and what a great respect he had for him. The love and respect in his voice was obvious as he spoke of how he felt about his friend and partner.

He was still talking as there came the unmistakable rhythmic pound of a helicopter and Cody laughed and pointed to the roof. "I'll bet there's our friend now! He'd given y'all his word that he'd be here, and Jason Falcon is a man of his word!" He hit a rockin' chord on his guitar and the rest of the band took his cue and joined in as he laughed again and yelled, "Let's get this thing started! I'd like to dedicate this next song to Jason and Kate Falcon. May they ever fly!"

The tears in Kate's eyes overflowed and trailed down her cheeks. There had been times in her life she'd wanted to strangle Cody, but she loved him like a brother and she knew that in some ways, she owed him her life for taking care of Jason for her. Who knew what would have become of Jason without him?

Kennen began to stir in her arms and she looked down at him and smoothed the IV tubing that was taped into his tiny arm and rubbed a gentle finger across his velvety cheek. His sweet green eyes opened and he gave her the most precious tired smile and turned his face against her chest as she kissed his silken curls. He seemed to be more with it and she hoped and prayed that his fever was breaking again.

A roar went up from the crowd at the concert and she turned back to the screen just in time to see Jason come up the ramp onto the stage, still in the process of strapping on his guitar. The fans were already screaming, but they came unglued as Cody came up to him and gave him an exuberant high five. The two friends embraced as they spoke briefly and then they were back into the song, singing and dancing and entertaining as only Jason and Cody could, and Kate knew the magic had begun again.

Kennen pulled on her arm and she helped him to sit up as he looked at the computer screen and then looked back at her with a sleepy smile and said, "Daee sing to Tennen."

Still teary with more tender feelings, Kate began to rock him gently as she said, "Yes, sweetheart. Daddy sings to Kennen. You're his baby Falcon, and you always will be. Falcon's mate for life, buddy. Some of them for forever."

The End

About the Author

Kristin Cross was a mostly obedient child — unless her mom wanted her to put her book down.

She grew up in the Rockies and traveled with her family enough to want to travel more and have adventures in all those exotic looking places on the map that she hasn't been to — yet. Now, as an adult, she also loves relaxing at home in the mountains and coming up with stories about those places.

Motherhood has been her best time yet, and she wishes she'd had more than just four marvelous children. She loves a good storm, a beautiful sunset, the wind in her face, puppies, and fresh mangos with her shrimp.

And her husband, DJ. She truly adores DJ.

Author's note

Growing up, my dad raised really well bred race horses. To that end, we trailered broodmares all over the country to the stallions. Often, the stallions resided in Texas or Oklahoma, where men are still masculine, women are treasured, and you haven't lived until you've been in a horse barn where even the stall bedding glistens and sparkles.

As a small child I was too wimpy for the spicy Tex-Mex food, but I loved the sassy spirit and, of course, the smoky sexy southern accents from those places. Call me a romantic if you must, but to me, those y'alls are still the stuff heroes are made of.

Kristin